BARGAIN WITH THE DEVIL

"Tell me the true reason you came to my cabin tonight," Ruark demanded.

Lowering his head, he slid his lips slowly up the slender column of her neck. "You came because you want me to make love to you," he whispered.

Angeleen closed her eyes, hoping by shutting him out of her vision, she could shut out the excitement of his touch. "No. That's not true. I didn't mean—"

"What did you mean to say, Angeleen? Was it that you would even sleep with me to get your horse back?"

Horrified, Angeleen stepped away from him. *Whatever was she doing? Could what he said be true?*

"Don't look so alarmed, my love. I intend to pay you well for tonight's company." Ruark smiled mockingly. "But how could you think I'd give up a valuable thoroughbred for only one night of your favors?"

He swooped her up into his arms and carried her to the bed.

ANGEL HUNTER

ANA LEIGH

LEISURE BOOKS NEW YORK CITY

A LEISURE BOOK®

December 1992

Published by

Dorchester Publishing Co., Inc.
276 Fifth Avenue
New York, NY 10001

The name "Leisure Books" and the stylized "L" with design are trademarks of Dorchester Publishing Co., Inc.

Printed in the United States of America.

FOR THE LOVE OF MIKE—
dedicated to my youngest son.

ANGEL HUNTER

Chapter One

The young black boy sitting at the water's edge jumped to his feet as a shrill blast rent the air, and the *Belle of the Bayou* chugged around the bend, the brown waters of the Mississippi churning beneath the huge red paddle wheel propelling the vessel.

The youngster raced past the people on the bank and up a hill toward a young woman who stood alone at a tiny cemetery plot. "Steamboat's a comin', Miz Angeleen," he called out.

"Thank you, Obbie."

For a brief moment Angeleen Hunter watched the boy scurry back to the river before returning her gaze to the marker of her mother's grave.

Monique Scott had succumbed to cholera during the war, but her family did not have money to purchase the above-ground burial tomb so necessary in the tidelands of Louisiana. So her remains had been burned along with those of the other victims of the epidemic that struck the small community already ravaged from war. Now, a few words crudely chiseled on the face of a rock marked the dates of the Frenchwoman's birth and passing.

Her young face hardened when she glanced at the grave of her husband. "And good riddance to you, Will Hunter," she murmured through gritted teeth. "Momma always said to never speak evil of the dead, but too many good men died during the war to waste a tear on a bastard like you."

Her disastrous marriage was a bitter memory to Angeleen. Will Hunter had been a drinking and gambling crony of her father's, and the worthless rake had pressed for her hand in marriage. At the outbreak of the war, all the local men went away except Will, who shot himself in the foot to avoid having to go to war.

Bowing to desperation, when she turned eighteen after a year's struggle to run Scotcroft without a man's help, Angeleen had married Will, even though he was twenty years her senior. She told herself at the time that she would grow to love him.

On her wedding night, he took her maidenhead, then beat her and her mother when they tried to stop him from taking their last cent. The cowardly bully had then gone to the bed of his mistress.

In the month that followed, Will never lifted a finger to do an honest day's work. He spent his time drinking and demanding his conjugal rights, until his mistress, in a drunken rage of jealousy, had driven a butcher knife through his heart. He died in the sobbing woman's arms.

Angeleen lifted her head when large raindrops began to splatter the ground, quickly turning the brown earth to mud. She pulled the hood of her cloak over the long black hair that flowed past her shoulders.

"Good-bye, Momma," Angeleen whispered sadly. Rain blended with the tears on her face, and she turned away, her steps leading her down the worn path to the river's edge.

Protected from the rain by the Texas deck overhead, Ruark Stewart stood on the middle deck of the riverboat. He had already become bored with the poker game, and the *Belle* was only two hours out of New Orleans. Ruark pursed firm, sensuous lips around a cheroot and drew deeply of the taste and aroma of the Havana cigar. Then he slowly expelled the smoke in round, undulating gray rings.

Impatient with the delay, he let his dark gaze sweep the river bank. *The first of many*, he thought with irritation and wondered whether he should disembark at Natchez and continue the trip to St. Louis by rail.

His curiosity was piqued when he spied a black stallion on the shore. Moving to the rail, he rested his arms on the wooden structure and leaned his long frame over the support for a closer look. Despite the thread-bare blanket that had been loosely thrown over the horse's flanks, Ruark recognized the animal's lines at once. *A thoroughbred*. His mouth twisted in amazement. He hadn't thought there were any more such animals left in the South.

The *Belle of the Bayou*'s experienced river pilot inched the boat toward the bank until the hull lightly bumped the shore. Crewmen tossed ropes toward two waiting men—a tall Negro and an older white man. A Negro woman with a bright red and purple turban stood beside them.

The two men quickly tied the ropes around tree trunks, and a wooden platform suspended from the bow of the ship thumped to the ground. The stallion's hoofbeats struck a hollow clatter as the black man led the horse up the wooden ramp. Then the man hurried back to shore and joined the others.

Huddled to ward off the rain, the white man picked up two worn carpetbags and turned to await a woman, who walked slowly down the hill, a young boy racing ahead of her.

Ruark saw her stop when she reached the river, hug the man and woman, then bend down to press a kiss on the head of the youngster. The hood slipped off her head and Ruark sharply drew in his breath at the sight of her hair, as black and satiny as a raven's wing.

She began to follow the white man up the gangplank, then midway the woman halted and glanced back toward the hill rising above the river. Pouring rain saturated her hair, plastering the satin sheen against her head in dank strands. With despair slowing her step, the woman continued up the ramp.

Within minutes the platform was raised and the lines cast off. The steam calliope struck a gay tune as the *Belle of the Bayou* pulled away to resume her journey up the mighty Mississippi.

Shivering in the heat, Angeleen stood on the deck of the ship as the gap between the steamboat and the shoreline continued to widen. She raised a hand in a plaintive good-bye. The three rain-drenched people on shore waved back.

After a final drag, Ruark tossed away the expensive cheroot and watched it arc gracefully in the air, then plunge into the swirling waters.

Thoughtfully, he left the deck and returned to the card game.

Angeleen put her hands on her hips and glanced around in dismay at the tiny cabin. A set of bunk beds and a small commode holding a chipped ewer in a basin were the only pieces of furniture. There was not even a window or porthole in the dismal room.

As she lit a lamp, she told herself the cabin would have to do. They could not afford one of the finer cabins above. The passage to St. Louis, in addition to a stall and feed for Bold King, had just about depleted their meager funds.

She removed her sopping cloak and hung it over one of the pegs that lined the wall. A steady stream of water continued to dribble from the garment. Angeleen grabbed the basin from the commode and placed it on the floor to catch the run-off.

Her father, Henry Scott, followed Angeleen into the room and dropped the two bags to the floor. "Well, 'twill do us just fine," he said with his usual cheerfulness. "And 'tis sure to keep us high and dry."

"I hope so," Angeleen sighed, sitting down on the bunk only to discover the mattress was nothing more than a straw pallet.

"I'll be seein' to the stallion," he said and quickly departed. Henry knew that his daughter was heart-broken over having to leave their home, but he didn't have the words or courage to comfort her.

He hurried over to Bold King. Skittish because of the unfamiliar stall and the undulating move-ment of the boat, the stallion snorted and pawed the deck.

Henry patted the horse's neck. "Here, here, lad-die," he soothed with the faint lilt of the Scottish burr that the last forty years had not quite dimin-ished. He entered the stall and started to rub down the horse with straw, each steady stroke of his hand a calming caress. Soon the stallion quieted under his attentions and began to calmly chew on the coarse fodder as Henry continued softly crooning to him.

For several moments after her father's departure, Angeleen sat motionless. The picture of dejection with her legs dangling over the side of the bunk, her eyes brimmed with tears as sad thoughts came to mind. If only her mother and brother hadn't died. Robert lost in Virginia; Momma at home. Both vic-tims of the war.

True, soldiers died in war, she told herself. *Soldiers on both sides—Confederate and Yankee alike.*

Her face curled with bitterness. *But how many Yankee women died because there wasn't food or medicine to save them?*

She closed her eyes to shut out the painful memory, but tears slipped from beneath her closed lids and crept down her cheeks.

When Angeleen felt dampness on her shoulders, she realized that her sodden hair was getting her clothing wet. She rose to her feet and brushed aside her tears. Nothing could be gained by dwelling on something that could not be changed. Perhaps her father was right. Perhaps they could build a new life in Missouri.

She unpacked the bags and hung the scant wardrobe on pegs. Her only remaining gowns were a blue satin ball gown and a day dress of pink and white dimity. Angeleen vowed that when they got a stud fee for Bold King, the first thing she would do would be to buy a new gown.

After drying her hair, she brushed the strands to a sheen, then changed into a plain bodice and skirt. Since there was no chair in the room, Angeleen lay down on the bunk to await her father's return. Within minutes, she fell asleep.

Darkness had descended on the river by the time Henry returned to the cabin. When he lit a lamp, the sleeping girl awoke.

"Poppa, did you let your clothes dry on your back?" Angeleen scolded as she sat up. "You're going to catch a chill."

Henry's blue eyes danced with mischief. "I had meself a wee nip to ward off such danger, lass."

Angeleen shook her head in disgust. What was she going to do with him? She might as well be raising a child. He was too much of a dreamer to accept the seriousness of their situation. They had lost everything—everything—except Bold King.

"Father, you know we don't have money for you to waste on liquor." His lack of responsibility was frustrating.

Henry knew that whenever his daughter called him "Father," he had fallen from grace. The old man winked, reached into a pocket, and extracted two hard-boiled eggs.

"I got more for me money than just the nip in the glass."

Angeleen clapped her hands with pleasure. "Eggs!" A bewitching dimple appeared in each cheek. She hadn't even seen an egg since they ate the last chicken months before.

She eagerly shelled and bit into one of the unexpected delights. "Don't suppose you brought some salt?" she mouthed between bites.

"Can't say I did. But what would me lass say to a sandwich?" Henry dug into the other pocket and pulled out two squashed slices of bread with a thick hunk of cheese between them.

Angeleen was ecstatic. "Oh, Poppa, this is a feast!" Henry smiled with pleasure at the return of the loving appelation. She chomped on the thick slices of bread, not letting a single crumb escape her lips.

Love gleamed in his eyes as he continued to watch her. She was the image of her mother—long dark hair, sapphire eyes, and the same delicate, exquisite face. But Angeleen did not have the frailty of his adored Monique. Henry thought his daughter must have the strength and stamina of at least ten women her size. *Her Celtic lineage*, he decided with pride. Then, remembering his daughter's sharp tongue and disapproval of what she called his "sporting ways,"

Henry added, *and her Scottish grandmother's dour disposition.*

Angeleen stopped eating and extended the remaining half of the sandwich. "Here's your half, Poppa."

Henry shook his head and refused the offering. "I ate me fill upstairs. A mighty fine spread on the bar came free with the nip."

"Are you sure, Poppa?" she asked hesitantly.

"Why would ye be doubtin' me word, lass?"

"Because you want me to have it all for myself."

Henry frowned. "Accusin', accusin'. I ne'er met a woman more accusin' than yourself—besides your sainted Grandmother Scott, that is. Accusin' a man of wrong-doin' and in the next breath, accusin' him of right. 'Tis nae wonder ye canna find a braw mon to wed ye," he censured, ultimately slipping into his native tongue.

"Like your friend Will Hunter, I suppose," she retorted, unable to allow the remark to go unchallenged. Her disastrous marriage had taught her one lesson: marriage wasn't the solution to any problem.

Then to soften the gibe, Angeleen chuckled lightly. Two characteristics often walked in tandem with these two people who loved one another deeply: criticism, then absolution.

"And how can I marry, Poppa, when I have to take care of you? The war's made paupers of all the men I know. Besides, none of them could afford your sporting ways. Guess I'll have to find me a rich Yankee up North."

Henry refused to be drawn into his daughter's

ridiculous threat. So Angeleen got to her feet and kissed his cheek, then began to wrap the rest of the sandwich and remaining egg in a towel. "I'll save this to eat tomorrow."

"Do as ye wish, me lass. Ye always do." Henry removed his coat and hung it on a peg. " 'Tis time to get me some sleep." He climbed up into the upper bunk.

"Did you check on King?" Angeleen asked.

Henry yawned and closed his eyes. "Aye, the stallion's fine, lass."

"Goodnight, Poppa." He was asleep before she could even blow out the lamp.

The heat and the rattling vibration from the ship's eight boilers made any further attempt at sleep an impossibility for her. After an hour of restless tossing, Angeleen acknowledged that she had slept herself out during the day. She put on her shoes and slipped out the door.

The night air felt like a soothing balm on her flushed cheeks. The rain had disappeared and the river was unusually calm, except for the paddlewheel lapping at the water. Moonlight glistened on silvery moss hanging from the limbs of trees along the river, and the strains of a waltz drifted down from the main saloon above, muffling the sound of the engines.

Angeleen closed her eyes and began to sway to the music, imagining herself at a cotillion dancing in the arms of a handsome beau.

Actually, she hadn't danced in four years and wondered if she even remembered how. Surrendering to the fantasy, she held up her arms and began to move in graceful circles to the rhythm of the music.

Suddenly she felt the pressure of a hand on her waist as her raised hand was firmly clasped in a warm grasp. Angeleen opened her eyes to discover a handsome face and pair of dark eyes smiling down at her—the manifestation of her fantasy.

"I believe this is our waltz, my lady." Angeleen heard the rich resonance of the stranger's voice flow into her dream.

Embarrassed at being caught in such a moment of whimsy, she laughed nervously and allowed him to glide her smoothly around the deck.

Soon she was smiling and laughing up at him as they whirled together between the crates and bales. Angeleen closed her eyes again and for a few moments allowed herself to be swept up in the pleasure of dancing in the arms of a handsome partner.

When the waltz ended, she slowly opened her eyes. "Thank you, sir," she said and flashed a dazzling smile.

Reluctantly, he dropped his arms and offered a courtly bow. "I can't remember when I enjoyed a dance as much."

The brief illusion ended abruptly with the inflection of his words; the man's accent was not Southern—he was a damn Yankee.

Flustered and disappointed, she sped away without a further reply.

Ruark Stewart smiled, pleasantly surprised to have discovered the woman's face to be as lovely as the flowing mass of black hair he remembered so well. He realized that for a brief moment he had gazed on perfection. He had to learn more about this fascinating woman.

Angeleen felt hot and flushed again. She knew, in truth, that her condition stemmed from embarrassment. She had made a fool of herself in front of that Yankee. Whoever he was.

To her surprise, her hasty rout led her right to the stall of Bold King. The horse nickered a greeting and Angeleen stopped to pet him.

"Well, how are you, old boy?" she cooed softly and put her arms around the animal's neck. "What do you think about all these strange happenings?"

Bold King thrived on affection as much as he did oats. The stallion responded by nestling his long muzzle against the cheek of his mistress until a voice intruded upon the quiet moment.

"I suppose I should feel guilty—being the only one to share the company of two such beauties."

Angeleen recognized the deep timbre at once. She dropped her arms and turned to him. "You should, indeed, sir, considerin' you weren't invited to share that company."

The appearance of the slurring pitch of a soft drawl was intentional and meant as a reminder to him of the differences that existed between them.

"At least let me introduce myself." He bowed politely. "Ruark Stewart, my lady. Your most obedient servant."

Angeleen suppressed a smile. "That being the case, Mr. Stewart, then you'll concede to my wish and *obediently* take your leave."

Ruark clutched his heart as if in pain. "Leave?

You would have me leave without first knowing the name of this vision I'm gazing upon? Oh, spare me, lovely lady."

"The horse is named Bold King."

His dark eyes gleamed with warmth. "Now, lovely lady, you know I was referring to you."

Angeleen smiled, despite a desire to appear indifferent. The man was a devastating rogue. "Angeleen Hunter, sir."

He picked up her hand and brought it to his lips. "Miss Hunter."

"It's Mrs. Hunter," she corrected, removing her hand from his grasp.

He felt an instant disappointment. "I saw you board. Was that Mr. Hunter?"

"No, that was my father. I'm a widow, sir."

For a moment their gazes locked, then he shifted his glance to the stallion.

"Your companion is very handsome."

She smiled up at Ruark. "I should warn you though, he doesn't like Yankees any more than I do. King's been known to nip at one more often than once."

Ruark's warm chuckle sent a ripple of pleasure the length of her spine. He stepped forward and patted the stallion. "He's a real beauty, isn't he?"

Ruark studied the broad forehead and long, sloping shoulders of the stallion. "Have you ever raced him?"

"Only as a two-year-old. Then the war started and we no longer had time for that kind of frivolity." Condemnation showed in her eyes and voice. "We became too busy burying our dead."

21

Ruark looked askew at her. "Mrs. Hunter, I've already fought that war. I have no intention of starting all over again." His look was firm, the tone adamant.

Ruark turned back to the horse. "You say he hasn't raced since before the war?" He examined the horse's teeth while he spoke.

Angeleen had not survived four years of war without having developed a shrewd insight into people's character. In the brief exchange between them, she recognized a strong will beneath the charming demeanor. Ruark Stewart was calculating and determined. She sensed he would make an unrelenting enemy if provoked.

In a further blow to her vanity, Angeleen realized that her presence was now of secondary importance to the man. Having resumed his examination of the horse, he knelt down and ran his hands up and down the stallion's legs, checking for blemishes.

"Has he ever sired a foal?"

Angeleen nodded. "Only once. There was a war on, you know."

He looked up and grinned, his dark eyes flashing roguishly. "Well, Sherman did say war is hell." He turned his attention back to the horse. "So what happened to his get?"

"The foal was commandeered by the army during the war. I hid King so they wouldn't find him and take him too."

His inspection completed, Ruark stood up and stepped out of the stall. "How much do you want for the stallion?"

Angeleen was flabbergasted. "I have no intention

of selling Bold King. We're taking him North and hope to arrange a stud fee."

Ruark smiled confidently; he never lost a business proposition. "Perhaps we could discuss this over breakfast."

Angeleen resented the man's smugness. Her eyes flashed with anger as she balled her fists at her sides. "I don't think so, Mr. Stewart. I've already told you. Bold King is not for sale."

Angeleen spun on her heel and stormed back to her cabin.

Chapter Two

In the obscure light of morning, Angeleen left her cabin to check on Bold King. The deck was enveloped in a thick, gray river fog that had fused with the heat from the ship's boilers to form a stifling, cloying mist.

When the heavy haze had rolled in during the night, the pilot, not wanting to risk hitting a snag or running aground on a sandbar, had pulled over to shore and docked the *Belle of the Bayou* at Baton Rouge. Now lanterns hanging from the hull of the ship glowed eerily through the haze to alert any other ships that were reckless enough to navigate the river's waters.

Feeling homesick, Angeleen stood at the edge of the lower deck, where a low guard rail kept the cargo from sliding over the side.

The bark of an alligator from a nearby swamp caused her to step back. Despite the heat, she shivered and crossed her arms to ward off the chill the scaly killers elicited from her.

At least she didn't mind leaving those loathsome reptiles behind. She hoped the Yankee carpetbagger who bought Scotcroft would wake up every morning and find a whole swampful of the creatures sitting on the front lawn.

" 'What you sow, you reap,' " she reprimanded herself. *Stop wishing people evil; you only end up choking when you have to swallow your words. Think I'd have learned that lesson by now.*

Angeleen began to stroll the deck for needed exercise. She wasn't used to the inactivity of a river trip. At mid-deck, she stopped at the foot of a wide stairway leading to the finer cabins and saw a sign, hanging from a mahogany balustrade, which read *Boiler Deck*, with an arrow pointing to the deck above.

"Makes no sense to call upstairs the boiler deck when all the noisy boilers are down on this deck," she grumbled.

Angeleen started to move on, then hesitated and glanced about her. There wasn't a crewman in sight. No one would know if she climbed up to peek at the first-class passenger deck.

When she reached the head of the stairway, Angeleen stopped and looked around, awestruck. The ceiling of the deck was supported by ornate columns linked together with lattice-scrolled arches.

She couldn't resist opening the door and stepping

into the main cabin that ran down the center of the entire deck. Enthralled, she gasped in wonderment. Not even the opera house in New Orleans was so opulent.

The rich red-and-gold carpet ran the entire three-hundred-foot length of the cabin. Rows of crystal chandeliers adorned with marquise-shaped pendants reflected the many colors of the brilliant murals painted on the ceiling. Both sides of the spacious cabin were lined with individual staterooms, which for passenger convenience were accessible from the deck side as well this main saloon.

Angeleen wandered through the cabin, running her fingers over the soft texture of the velvet chairs and the cool grain of rich leather. She trailed her palm along the smooth, polished surface of a long black mahogany bar. Smiling, she stopped and drank a refreshing glass of artisian water from a silver cooler set on an intricately carved Duncan Phyfe table at the end of the room.

In the midst of the elegance, Angeleen's attention was drawn to a porcelain figurine that stood on the top of a grand piano. She picked up the delicate piece for a closer inspection.

Suddenly, she heard the drone of voices coming from the opposite end of the cabin. She looked around in panic, fearing she would be discovered. How could she explain her presence? Spying a door leading to the deck, she slipped out and sighed in relief when it appeared she had remained undetected.

Angeleen knew she still wasn't out of troubled waters, so she stole stealthily along the deck until she reached the stairway. Suddenly, the ship lurched and she automatically grabbed for the railing, forgetting the figurine clutched in her hand. The statue fell from her grasp and smashed on the deck.

Horrified, Angeleen sped down the stairway in flight.

Ruark Stewart had spent most of the night thinking about Angeleen Hunter. He couldn't get the beauty out of his thoughts. Every facet of the woman was exciting, a fact his loins were not about to let him forget. But as for purchasing the stallion, Ruark guessed she would be difficult.

After pulling on his trousers, he stepped outside his cabin and walked to the stern of the ship. The fog was beginning to lift, and the huge paddlewheel was inching the boat toward midstream.

Alone in the shadows, he was about to light a cheroot when the very object of his restless musings appeared at the stern entrance of the main cabin. He watched Angeleen's furtive movement along the deck until she reached the stairway. Then Ruark heard a crash and watched Angeleen suddenly hurry down the stairs.

Ruark went over and stooped down to discover the broken pieces of porcelain. Frowning, he rose and for several moments stared reflectively into space.

Why in Hell is she sneaking around the deck with a porcelain doll at this hour of the morning?

Breathless, Angeleen rushed into the cabin and slammed the door. She leaned back against the solid support and drew several deep, steady breaths to calm herself.

Having had several narrow escapes, she'd been scared more times than she cared to remember. Dodging Yankees during the four years her father and brother were off fighting a war had made her a veteran at being scared.

Now that she had time to take a breath and think about the whole incident, Angeleen felt she hadn't done anything so bad—except break an expensive figurine, that is. She knew that if she confessed, the captain of the ship would demand payment for the delicate treasure, and she didn't have any money. Then he'd probably toss her into jail at the next port. Sighing, she realized that she would have to remain silent about her crime.

She wouldn't even tell her father.

As it happened, her decision presented no hardship because when Henry awoke, he immediately disappeared. But to avoid speculation in the event talk had spread around the ship, Angeleen spent the day behind a closed door, leaving her cabin only to feed Bold King and muck out the stall.

When midday came and went with still no sign of her father, Angeleen's nervousness increased, but she dared not venture above to find him. She would just have to leave well enough alone until he showed up.

She washed their soiled clothing and hung it to dry, then busied herself mending the worn garments. When her hunger became too great to ignore, Angeleen ate the egg and the other half of the cheese sandwich. Then she returned to pacing the cabin floor and fretting about her father. Late in the evening, although she had struggled to stay awake, she dozed off.

Past midnight, Henry Scott finally slipped into the cabin and crawled into his bunk.

On the crest of the hill rising high above the river stood the once-stately mansions of Natchez society. But below, along the waterfront, a string of dilapidated frame dives housed the worst scum and low life dredged from the river bottom—malingering boatmen, thieves, derelicts, and cutthroats.

Natchez Under The Hill. The most notorious town on the Mississippi.

The first-class passengers watched from the security of the upper deck as armed crewmen made certain that nobody boarded the ship unless they had bought a ticket or were loading cargo.

Henry and Angeleen waited at the stall of Bold King, determined that the stallion would not "mysteriously" disappear during the confusion of loading and unloading.

Angeleen, surprised to see that Ruark Stewart had moved to the lower deck, watched him leaning nonchalantly against a crate. She hadn't seen any sign of him the previous day and assumed he had given up the idea of buying the horse.

Ruark had no such intention. He had examined the stallion again in Angeleen's absence and was more determined than ever to buy the horse—So much so that he already considered Bold King his property and had come below to make certain no river rat stole the animal.

The horse suddenly threw up his head, his eyes distended with fear and his ears perked upright. With a terror-filled whinny, Bold King began to paw and thrash about in the stall.

"What is it, laddie?" Henry asked and moved to comfort the stallion.

A low, feral growl sounded from the crate being loaded. Angeleen and Henry exchanged looks of disbelief when they saw a cage containing a cougar placed on the deck near the stall. The ferocious wild cat was no more a willing visitor than it was a welcome guest. The struggles of this caged creature from the wilds had reached a fever pitch. The cat began to lunge its slender, tawny body, which ran near to eight feet from the top of the head to the tip of the tail, against the bars that restrained it.

The bloodcurdling snarls of the caged animal chilled the spines of the roustabouts unfortunate enough to be handling the crate. The paw of the tawny cat raked out to try to snag the men when they ventured near the cage. All cast fretful glances as the beast barred large yellow fangs, its green eyes glinting with savagery.

Bold King had picked up the sound and scent of the huge cat and Henry fought to restrain the stallion as his struggles intensified.

Angeleen quickly hurried over to the captain's side. "Why are you bringing that dangerous animal on board?" she asked.

"Cat's being shipped to a circus in St. Louis." He offered a smile of reassurance. "Nothing to worry about. Trapper told us there's no way it can break out of the cage."

"Captain, you'll have to move that cat away from our stallion," she demanded.

"My mate's in charge of the cargo, ma'am," he said politely.

The mate, relieved to see the beast had been loaded without a mishap, had no intention of pressing his luck further by moving the cage again until they reached St. Louis.

"Hard enough loadin' it as it was. Ain't gonna try and move it again."

"You must," Angeleen insisted. "Can't you see what's happening to our horse? He'll die from fright if he's kept tied up so close to the cat."

"Then move the horse," he snickered.

"There's no other stall," she said helplessly.

The mate had little concern for the problems of passengers on the lower deck. "If the cat bothers your horse that much, take it off this boat and catch the next steamer," he said in a surly snarl.

Ruark had listened to all of the exchange he intended to. "I don't think your mate appreciates the young lady's problem, Captain," Ruark said.

Ruark's identity was well-known to the captain. He would be a fool to jeopardize his position by arguing with anyone as influential as Ruark Stewart—especially when rumor had it that the man was one of the owners of the *Belle of the Bayou*.

After a whispered conference with the mate, the captain nodded to Ruark and left the deck before any further confrontation could arise. His mate was angry with him, but the captain apparently felt it better to suffer the wrath of a disgruntled crew member than fall into the disfavor of Ruark

Stewart. The captain retreated to the highest and most remote spot on the ship, the pilot house, which stood like a white enclosed belvedere on the top of the Texas deck.

Irritated, the mate supervised the moving of the cage to the far end of the ship so that the horse was now upwind of the cat.

Tension on board eased when the loading had been completed and the landing platform raised. The high-pitched squeal of the steam whistle rent the air as once again the *Belle of the Bayou* resumed her journey.

As soon as the city of Natchez disappeared from view, Henry hurried back to their cabin and quickly began to groom himself, hoping to finish the task before Angeleen returned. He knew the girl would only press him with questions and before long would worm the truth out of him. He had lost a few dollars of their money gambling, but there would be no convincing the lass 'twas only a wee bit. She had the suspicious mind of her grandmother and would surely accuse him of worse.

Last night, with his run of bad luck, Henry knew he could have lost even more had not the Stewart chap stopped the game to announce he was going to bed.

But Henry was certain that tonight would be different; his luck would improve.

He changed into a white tucked shirt and black tie, then donned a vest and pulled on a much-worn, knee-length frock coat.

Henry plopped a top hat at a rakish angle on his head of bright red hair, now gray at the temples, and stepped back to admire his image in the cracked mirror hanging on the wall.

"You're still a fine figure of a man, Henry Scott, even with your sixty years," he said with an approving wink as he stroked his meticulously groomed beard.

Henry opened the door and peeked out to see if the coast was clear. He was in luck; Angeleen, occupied with Bold King, had her back turned. Having a superstitious Celtic nature, Henry knew that Lady Fortune would stay with him for the rest of the evening.

Henry's blue eyes twinkled with merriment and, grinning like a mischievous leprechaun, the old man walked away.

Bold King still seemed so skittish that Angeleen would not consider leaving her beloved stallion until she knew for certain the horse had completely calmed down.

Occasionally a growl from the cougar carried above the noise of the engines, but at last the horse appeared to have adjusted to the sound.

"I know this trip has been unsettling for you, my love. Just a few more days, old boy, and we'll be in St. Louis. Then we'll be off this boat and away from all these strange sounds," Angeleen promised as she stroked the long, sloping shoulder of the stallion.

Unknown to Angeleen, Ruark Stewart stood a few feet away, hidden from her sight by bales of cotton piled high on the deck. He smiled, relieved to hear that she was going all the way to St. Louis because it meant he still had a few more days to convince her to sell the stallion. But where did the woman go during the day? He could never find her when he looked for her.

From his conversation with her, Ruark knew that one of the men he played cards with last night was the father of this ravishing creature. Ruark decided he would find out the man's identity. Perhaps it would be possible to transact the purchase through him, since his lovely daughter was so set against selling.

But as he walked over to the horse's stall, Ruark's handsome face broke into a foolish grin. Was the attraction really the stallion, or the beautiful Angeleen Hunter?

Angeleen glanced up when Ruark appeared beside her. Their glances held for a moment until he nodded. "Mrs. Hunter."

"Mr. Stewart," she acknowledged.

"I see the horse has finally settled down."

"Thank you for your intervention. You probably saved the life of my stallion."

"Our stallion," he teased.

Her sapphire eyes warred with his dark gaze. "Thank you again for your help, Mr. Stewart." She turned away and left him.

As he watched her walk away, Ruark crossed his arms and leaned a shoulder against one of the crates. Grinning broadly, he wondered if she realized that what was developing between them involved a lot more than just a horse.

Later that night, Henry returned to the cabin and woke his daughter. With a grin as wide as the Mississippi itself, he dropped a pack of paper currency on her lap.

"Look at it all, lass," he exclaimed to the startled girl. "And 'tis not Confederate dollars ye be holdin'."

Still groggy with sleep, Angeleen gathered up the stack of bills. "Poppa, where did you get this money?"

The Yankee's offer to buy the stallion immediately crossed her mind. Frantic, she grabbed his arm. "You didn't sell Bold King, did you?"

Henry looked wounded that she would even harbor such a thought. "Of course not, lass. The stallion's yours."

"Then where did you get all this money?"

"I had a mind for a few hands of cards, so I joined one of the games."

Angeleen jumped to her feet, her eyes wide with condemnation. "You risked our money in a card game?" She couldn't believe her father had been so foolhardy.

"Now, now, daughter, dinna get yourself so all fired up. I won, didn't I?"

"But what if you had lost? What would we have done?" She threw up her hands in despair. "We're on our way to Missouri. We don't know anyone there, and we have no place to go. Don't you ever stop to consider the consequences of gambling?"

Her harangue was the very lecture he had wanted to avoid. Henry hung his hat and coat on a peg and issued his favorite complaint. "Woe is me, lass. Ye be just like your grandmother. She never saw the good side to anyone either, 'cept herself."

He climbed up into his bunk. "A man does what he can, and still 'tis nae good enough for some folks."

Henry closed his eyes and within minutes his grumbling had changed to a steady outpouring of snores. Angeleen shook her head in a gesture of hopelessness and began to count the money.

Chapter Three

The following morning, Angeleen made up her mind she had seen the end of tolerance and self-denial. Yesterday she had gone the whole day without food—*so Poppa could risk our money gambling,* she told herself as she stuffed several of the paper bills into her reticule. Well, no longer was she going to play the fool.

As she tightened the laces of her corset, her empty stomach began to rumble. If Angeleen suffered any qualms about her intention to eat, which she surely did not, these growls of hunger were a battle cry to further rally the impassioned zealot.

The bold warrior donned her armor of crinoline, petticoat, and pink-and-white dimity dress, grabbed her reticule, stormed up the boiler stairway, then sallied forth into the main cabin with all the verve and daring of a J. E. B. Stuart cavalry charge.

Two uniformed waiters immediately rushed to her side, and Angeleen found herself seated at a linen-covered table complete with porcelain china, silver flatware, and the pleasant fragrance of a fresh red rosebud about to bloom in a crystal vase.

One of the waiters poured champagne into a glass of Waterford crystal, while the other laid a white linen serviette across her lap and handed her the bill of fare. Both men then moved a discreet distance away while she decided upon a selection.

"I recommend the chicken liver omelette."

Angeleen looked up to discover Ruark Stewart smiling down at her. "May I join you?"

Ruark sat down before she could reply. He knew by her disgruntled look what the answer would be were she to take the remark literally.

As soon as he had stepped out of his cabin, Ruark had been stopped by Mason Denning, a St. Louis business acquaintance, and invited to join the Denning family for breakfast.

The hen-pecked banker was in the company of his daughter and aggressive wife, who had tried throughout the voyage to foist her daughter on Ruark. The girl seemed pleasant enough in nature, but had the disturbing affliction of talking through her nose. The sound grated on Ruark's nerves.

Ruark couldn't believe his good fortune when he saw Angeleen enter the room. Her presence had given him the excuse to tell Denning he already had made other plans. Then he made a beeline to Angeleen's table.

"Of course, the crepes are delicious, too," Ruark

remarked to Angeleen, ignoring her displeasure. "Pierre, the chef, was imported from France."

Angeleen flashed an exasperated look over the top of the menu. "In the same crate as the champagne, no doubt."

Ruark threw back his head in laughter. The three people at the Denning table all looked over, displeased to hear the pleasure in the sound. Cynthia Denning grimaced when Ruark leaned forward intimately to speak to the young woman.

"You look very lovely this morning, Angeleen."

Angeleen put the menu aside and leveled a stare at him. "Ah don't recall givin' you leave to take such liberty, Mr. Stewart." The Southern slur had made a decided return in her speech.

"My apologies, Mrs. Hunter."

Ruark had begun to piece together a few of the mysteries surrounding the woman: she apparently wasn't a first-class passenger, which explained why he had not seen her in the saloon; she and her father were obviously low on funds, which was why he had seen the old man slipping food into his pockets. At the time he had found it amusing; now Ruark suspected the food had been meant for Angeleen.

The puzzle Ruark had yet to solve was how she happened to have a thoroughbred racer in her possession. But he would find that answer in due time. For the present, he was just going to enjoy the company of the most beautiful woman he had ever seen.

And if all she had eaten in the past days was the food the old man could pilfer, Ruark reasoned she must be half-starved.

And for that problem, he did have an answer.

When the waiter returned, Ruark picked up her menu. "I'll order for both of us."

Angeleen resented his brashness. She was used to making her own decisions and didn't need any man, particularly a Yankee, telling her what she could eat. To her horror, her stomach chose that exact moment to resume grumbling. Ruark glanced up from the menu and grinned, then he quickly made a selection.

Shortly after, the waiters returned with compote dishes containing baked grapefruit. Angeleen couldn't remember the last time she tasted anything as succulent as the fruit sections which had been sweetened with brown sugar and baked in Madeira.

As soon as she finished the last bite, the dishes were removed and replaced by steaming plates of eggs en croustade. Two soft-boiled eggs stood on end in the hollowed-out center of a day-old roll which had been brushed with butter and rebaked. The whole thing was then covered with soubise sauce and garnished with dill.

Angeleen waited hungrily as the waiter ladled mornay sauce over the top. She was sure her mouth would begin to water before the other waiter could finish serving Ruark in the same fashion.

Placing a salver of chicken livers and a plate of croissants on the table, the waiters retired to allow them to enjoy the meal.

"Delicious," Ruark said, after sampling a forkful of the savory egg dish.

Angeleen, in complete accord, did not want to give Ruark the satisfaction of agreeing with him.

"The soubise has too much onion," she remarked.

Ruark looked at Angeleen in surprise. Considering her somewhat dire straits and the fact that the dish was usually served in only the finer restaurants and hotels in America, he hadn't expected her to be familiar with the recipe.

"Are you a gourmet, Mrs. Hunter?"

"No. But my mother was French. She made eggs en croustade often before the war." Her face sobered with the memory of that happier, bygone day.

Ruark saw the sudden shift of emotion. Her previous anger had been replaced with sadness. "Here, try one of these," he said, trying to lighten her mood. He put a chicken liver on her plate.

Angeleen forced aside melancholy thoughts and turned her mind to Ruark Stewart. Why did she always react so hostilely to him? Because he was a Yankee? The war had ended six months ago. She couldn't continue fighting Yankees when she intended to live among them.

Because he was so pompous? Or arrogant? Or so self-assured?

Yes. For all of those reasons, she told herself.

She glanced up and found him studying her with his dark eyes hooded in the intense stare that made her feel so uncomfortable.

Ruark smiled and offered her the plate of croissants, but Angeleen shook her head in refusal. "No, thank you."

"You must try one. Pierre is famous for his croissants." He sliced a roll in half and spread one of the pieces with quince jelly. Leaning over with a beguiling smile, he held it up to her mouth.

Angeleen glanced around uncomfortably and saw the Dennings' critical stares. "Mr. Stewart, people are staring."

"Please, just one bite. As a favor to me," he beseeched her.

To avoid a scene, Angeleen took a small bite of the roll. "Yes, it's very good."

"Didn't I tell you?" Knowing they were still being watched, and to her astonished horror, Angeleen saw Ruark pop the remainder of the piece he held into his mouth. He chewed it slowly, as if to savor each crumb. The intimacy of the gesture did not go unheeded. She blushed, but he wouldn't relinquish his hold on her gaze.

Angeleen cleared her throat and began to ramble nervously. "Actually the croissant was not, as believed, created in France. Its origin is Vienna. Marie Antoinette introduced it to the French court when she married Louis the Sixteenth."

Amused, he arched a brow with interest. "Is that so?"

Angeleen nodded. "All the French did was rename it, make it lighter, and change its size and shape."

"They rather did the same thing to poor Marie, too," he remarked.

Her mouth curved into a smile, but she suppressed her laughter. "That remark was shameful, sir." She speared a piece of chicken liver with her fork and popped in into her mouth.

Ruark grinned. "I stand corrected, my lady. But you must admit the gesture didn't get her *a . . . head.*"

Angeleen erupted into laughter. She covered her

mouth with her napkin to keep from losing the piece of chicken liver.

Ruark handed her the glass of champagne. "Here, drink this."

Both continued to be enveloped in laughter, and other diners looked at them, smiling at the young people's gaiety. Only the Denning table appeared to register disapproval.

Finally, after several swallows of the sparkling liquid, Angeleen regained a semblance of composure and brushed the tears out of her eyes. "That remark is unforgivable, Mr. Stewart."

"Please call me Ruark," he said with an engaging grin.

Angeleen hadn't known such laughter in years. Suddenly, like a censurous slap in the face, she felt riddled with guilt. She had no right to laughter. She had no business being surrounded by such elegance. She was a fraud. An imposter. He must know that. He was laughing at her—not with her.

She jumped to her feet. "I must leave now."

Ruark was stunned by the sudden move. He had thought the barriers between them were beginning to collapse. "But you haven't finished, Angeleen. Wouldn't you like a cup of coffee?"

"No. I don't want any." She fumbled in her reticule and pulled out some bills.

Ruark objected immediately. "I insist you allow me."

"I will pay for my own meal, Mr. Stewart." She laid the money on the table and hastily departed.

Ruark shook his head and picked up the crumpled dollars. "All right, Angeleen. This time I'll let you have your way. But next time, my black-haired angel—next time, things will be different."

Long after her hasty departure Ruark sat deep in thought, smiling to himself as he smoked a cheroot.

To avoid any further contact with Ruark Stewart, Angeleen remained in her cabin the rest of the day. The following morning the *Belle* docked at Memphis.

While the crew took on fuel and cargo, Henry and Angeleen led Bold King off the boat to allow the horse some exercise.

"The stallion needs a good run," Ruark said.

Angeleen had not heard his approach and was startled to discover him beside her.

"My father knows what he's doing," she declared and returned her attention to watching Henry walk the horse.

Leading Bold King by the reins, Henry approached them, shaking his head. "The poor lad's anxious to stretch his legs."

"Why don't you let me run him for a short distance?" Ruark asked.

" 'Twould do the lad good, Mr. Stewart, but I nae hae a saddle."

"I can ride him bareback," Ruark offered.

"Well, sir, I'd be most obliged to you," Henry declared.

When Ruark began to remove his waistcoat, Angeleen cast the man a disgruntled glare. "Father, how do we know he'll return? He could steal Bold King right out from under our noses."

With a roguish smile, Ruark handed her his coat and hat. "I leave you my coat containing my wallet, Mrs. Hunter."

Unable to bear his smugness, she snatched the garment out of his hand. "Take care you don't fall off and break your neck. Bold King's no colt, you know."

"I never met a horse I couldn't ride." He stared into her eyes. "Including frisky fillies."

Angeleen didn't miss the intended innuendo, and once again she found her gaze locked in a warring battle with his.

Ruark removed a gold watch and fob from a pocket of the gray vest that was tailored to the lithe lines of his chest and slim waist. Her grudging perusal could not deny the handsomeness of the man. Bared of a waistcoat, a white shirt stretched tautly across broad shoulders, and pinstriped trousers encased his narrow hips and long legs.

Ruark handed her the watch, and for a moment their hands touched. Angeleen felt a sudden electrifying effect from the brief encounter. She looked up at Ruark and, in a shocked exchange of glances, realized he had felt it too.

He dropped gold cuff links into her hand as she watched him roll up his shirt sleeves to the elbows. Her mouth felt dry at the sight of the dark hair on his forearms.

Stunned, Angeleen realized that the man excited her. Her body reacted to his virile sensuousness, and this startling enlightenment reflected in her eyes. Ruark saw it, and his dark gaze narrowed in response.

He took the reins, grabbed a handful of the horse's mane, and agilely swung his long legs over the stallion's back. Ruark lightly goaded the animal, and Bold King sped away like a youngster out of a schoolhouse door.

Bold King was a thoroughbred, bred to run. After the lengthy inactivity, he wanted to stretch his legs and take wing. Ruark could feel the restrained power and energy beneath him as he held the stallion to a steady gait. After a few miles, he turned back to the ship.

When Ruark rode up and dismounted, Henry was all smiles, happy to see the stallion still spirited and hardly winded after the run.

Ruark grinned and patted the horse approvingly. "He's a lot of animal, Henry."

And so are you, Ruark Stewart, Angeleen thought with a belligerent assessment. Ruark's hair, rumpled from the ride, fell across his forehead. The exercise appeared to have had the same effect on him as it had on Bold King; they both looked robust and exhilarated.

As Henry led the horse away to cool him down before reloading, the ship's whistle issued a warning toot to those ashore. Ruark walked over to Angeleen and grinned at her as he rolled down his shirt sleeves.

He's ridden the horse, and now the arrogant bastard thinks I'm next, she fumed silently.

"What are you smirking at?" she asked crossly and shoved the cuff links into his hand.

"Smirking? Why, I'm smiling at you, Miss Angeleen," Ruark said innocently as he slid his broad shoulders into the waistcoat and adjusted the jacket until it felt comfortable over his shirt sleeves. "Can't you tell the difference between a smile and a smirk?"

"I certainly can, so wipe that salacious smirk off your face."

Ruark doubled over with a grunt when she slapped the hat into his midsection and turned to walk away.

He tapped her on the shoulder. "Ah . . . Mrs. Hunter?"

Exasperated, she spun on her heel. "What is it now, Mr. Stewart?"

"If you don't mind." He looked down pointedly at her hand.

As her glance followed his, Angeleen realized she was still holding his gold watch. "Oh, of course. I'm sorry."

She handed him the watch and continued up the loading ramp. Ruark Stewart followed close at her heels. Shortly after, the *Belle of the Bayou* resumed her upstream journey.

Later that night, shamefaced and disheartened, Henry Scott returned to the cabin and confessed his latest shenanigan—he had just lost all their money.

"Every dollar?" she asked, aghast.

"Aye, lass," Henry said sadly, slumping down on the bunk.

"Who'd you lose it to, Poppa? Maybe he'll give it back."

Henry shook his head. "Same two I won from earlier. But now I lost me own money as well."

47

"Oh, Poppa, how could you?" She well knew how he could. Apart from being very unlike the legendary tight-fisted Scotsman, her father was the worst card player south of the Mason-Dixon line. Why did she not keep a tighter rein on him? He could be wilder than Bold King at times!

Angeleen wanted to weep until there were no more tears left in her. She was so tired of being poor, of struggling to survive. Four years of trying to keep from losing Scotcroft, of keeping food on the table to feed Big Charlie, Cleo, and Obbie. Four years of hiding Bold King so no Yankee or stray Reb would steal off with the stallion. She had even endured the debasement of Will Hunter. And for what?

After all the struggle, Scotcroft still had to be sold.

By the time the debts and past-due taxes had been paid, only a couple of hundred dollars remained. Now, even that was gone.

Brokenhearted, Angeleen ran out of the cabin to shed her tears in private. She slumped down on the darkened deck and leaned back against one of the bales, crying until she was exhausted.

When her tears were fully spent, she was on the verge of returning to the cabin to assure Henry that they would make do somehow when, nearby, she heard the voices of two men.

Unaware of her presence, the men were engrossed in dividing a stack of bills into two piles on the top of a crate.

"Here's your half, Charlie. A good night's take, and no one's the wiser," one said.

"If I was you, Pete, I wouldn't be so cocksure,"

the one called Charlie replied. "That Stewart fellow looks suspicious. Maybe we ought to split. Play in separate games."

"Yeah, but don't sit in the same game with Stewart," Pete said. "I'm thinking the same as you. Might be best to stay clear of him. Anyway, his tail feathers don't look as easy to pluck as the others."

Charlie chortled. "Sure not like that old man Scott. The old fool never suspected a thing. Went for the bait as quick as we tossed out the hook. I'd a thought a man who's been around as long as him wouldn't have fallen for that old trick of letting him win first, so's we could come back and clean him out later."

Angeleen sat up. *They're talking about Poppa!* she thought as her eyes widened with indignation. *A couple of crooked cardsharps fleeced my father, and he didn't even know it!*

When the two men walked away, still chuckling over their win, Angeleen hurried back to the cabin.

"Poppa, listen to me. You were set up by a couple of cardsharps," she exclaimed. "I just heard them talking on deck—bragging about how they fleeced you. Let's go and tell the captain. He'll get us our money back."

Henry shook his head. "Willna do, lass. Ye hae to catch them in the act or 'tis only me word against theirs. And they're traveling in first class, so ye know who the captain will believe."

Her blood felt near to boiling. "I hope you don't think I'm going to let them get away with cheating you."

"Let me put me mind to the matter," he said.

"Maybe there's a way. 'Course, I'll need a stake to get back into the game."

"Get back into the game?" Angeleen cried, aghast. "Don't you ever learn your lesson?"

Nevertheless, Henry's spirits became considerably lighter. He lay down and tucked his hands under his head. "We'll get some sleep for now. Nothing more we can do tonight." His blue eyes gleamed. "Yep, just might be a way to get back into the game."

Angeleen lay with her own thoughts fuming in her head. "I'm going to get our money back, if I have to take it from them at gun-point."

Chapter Four

To the lone girl standing on the deck, the rumble of thunder far in the distance sounded more like the boom of cannon. In the past four years, Angeleen had often listened to that sound, knowing the Yankee artillery was drawing ever nearer to Scotcroft.

She tightened her cloak around her when a chilling wind rifled through the trees, stirring up foaming white caps on the river. The low-hanging gray clouds threatened to burst at any moment, once again releasing their torrent upon the earth below.

The recurrent showers had dodged them throughout the day. A long day—another long day—of desolation and hunger. Sighing, she turned away and returned to the cabin.

"Ah, there ye be, lass," Henry declared as soon as she appeared in the entrance to their cabin. Already dressed in his finest garb, such as it was, he took her arm and pulled her aside as he closed the door. "Now, remember our plan. I want ye to be puttin' on your loveliest gown and do exactly as I told ye."

For the next few minutes Henry went over the details of his plan to win back their lost money.

"But, Poppa, so much could go wrong," she protested. "What if—"

"I'll hae nae of your 'what ifs,'" he declared. "We've nothin' to fear, lass. Just remember—thirty minutes." He beamed a puckish grin at her and hurried out the door before she could voice any further objection.

Woebegone, Angeleen reached for her ball gown. Last night's passion for revenge had been drenched by the dampening day. She now had little heart for the scheme and feared they would find themselves floundering in even deeper water than before. Perhaps it would be wiser to go to the captain with the story.

As his disheartened daughter continued her dressing, Henry was engaged in laying his trap in the saloon above. Charlie and Pete stood at the bar looking around the room for their next victims when Henry approached them.

"Well, me good fellows, will ye be givin' me the chance to regain me losses?" he asked cordially.

The two scoundrels exchanged glances. Although they had not intended to sit at the same table together, the old fool was asking to be fleeced.

"Why not? I'm game if you are," Charlie replied.

Pete nodded in agreement and the three men sat down at the nearest table.

Standing alone at the end of the bar, Ruark Stewart watched the whole exchange with interest. He had suspected the two of being crooked from the time they boarded at Natchez Under-The-Hill and had no doubt the pair were members of the unsavory element which flourished in that community. Ruark couldn't understand why Henry would invite another game after losing so heavily to them already.

Henry began with his usual run of bad luck when his full house lost out to Charlie's four aces. But Henry had made a conservative bet so did not lose much.

The deal passed to him, and as he gathered up the cards he was careful to put Charlie's hand of four aces on the bottom of the pile. Ruark saw the move, but thought nothing amiss since the cards still had to be shuffled and cut.

However, Ruark got an unexpected shock when he saw Henry pick up the deck and palm the five bottom cards. The old man had done it so clumsily that the two men at the table could not have failed to observe the move.

Henry was playing with fire for even trifling with them, Ruark reflected. And if he tried to switch the hand as ineptly as he had palmed the cards, the old man was sure to end up floating in the river with his throat cut.

Then Ruark understood why the two gamblers had not observed Henry's bumbling. Their attention had been drawn to the vision of beauty that had just swept through the door of the saloon and floated up to their table.

When Ruark saw Angeleen, the card game was forgotten, along with every other conscious thought in his mind. She wore a sapphire gown, the exact color as her exquisite eyes; her creamy shoulders and slender neck were bared to his hungry perusal, and her wondrous mass of black hair hung to the middle of her back in a lustrous sheen, more glossy than the satin dress she wore.

There wasn't a man in the room who didn't have his eyes trained on her, and Henry used the moment to slip the palmed cards between his knees.

"Oh, Poppa, I knew I would find you here," Angeleen said. The forlorn huskiness in her voice caused the hair on Ruark's arm to stand on end.

"I'm busy now, lass. Leave me be," Henry said gruffly and began to shuffle the cards.

"Poppa, you promised me you wouldn't lose any more of our money," she pleaded pitifully at his side.

Henry cast her an angry look. "Leave a man to his cards, daughter." The men returned their attention to the game.

Distraught and sobbing, Angeleen backed away— but no farther than Pete's chair. She produced a lacy handkerchief and began to sniffle.

Still observing, Ruark began to smell a rat, perfumed though she might be. For the Angeleen he knew was not a sniffling, weak female, but a feisty scrapper who would go down fighting. So what was she up to?

The game: Draw Poker.

Charlie cut the deck and Henry dealt each player five cards. From her position behind Pete's chair, Angeleen saw that he held a pair of fours. She rendered a long, mournful sob into her hankie and casually moved to the next chair. After a quick peek from beneath her handkerchief, three more weepy sniffles emanated from her throat.

Anyone who didn't know her spirit might easily have been fooled—but not Ruark.

He grimaced in disgust. *Don't tell me, let me guess,* he told himself. *I'll bet my last dollar that the man's holding three of a kind. Why doesn't she just announce it out loud?*

Charlie twisted around to look at her. "Lady, I don't like anyone standing behind me when I'm playing cards."

The remark brought forth another pitiful wail from Angeleen, and every man in the room wanted to thrash the cad for adding to the woes of the desolate woman.

"Daughter, go back to the cabin," Henry ordered. He appeared to be flustered and embarrassed by the scene she was creating.

Pete opened the betting, and Charlie, holding three kings, raised the bet. Henry, in turn, raised again. All three men matched the raise, ending the first round of the betting with sixty dollars in the pot.

After discarding their worthless cards, Pete called for three new ones, but did not better his hand. Charlie took only two cards and caught the fourth king. Henry dealt himself a single card to give the impression he was trying to fill either a straight or a flush.

But the ploy did not faze Charlie because neither a straight nor a flush would beat his four of a kind, and since he had all the kings, Henry could not have a royal flush.

Charlie reached down and flattened his palm on the table, a prearranged signal to Pete that he was holding four of a kind. The gesture appeared innocent enough, but did not go unheeded by Ruark.

He shook his head in disbelief. The two men were so engrossed in trying to fleece Henry that they were unaware that Henry and Angeleen were fleecing them. *Who said there is honor among thieves?* he thought contemptuously.

Pete read his cohort's signal and knew he must fatten the pot to keep Henry betting. He checked his hand, giving Charlie the chance to make the first bet.

Henry appeared in doubt as to whether he should continue. He mopped nervously at his brow. Finally, he raised Charlie's bet.

Although holding a worthless hand, Pete had served his purpose; he had raised Henry. Confident that he held the winning hand, Charlie in turn raised the pot another twenty dollars, knowing that Henry wouldn't drop out at this late stage. Even if he did, the pot would fall to Charlie.

Henry did exactly what Charlie expected; he raised the bet another fifty dollars.

Pete, having done his job, threw in his cards. "Too rich for me," he complained.

"I'll call your bet," Charlie declared and pushed his money to the center of the table.

The moment of truth had arrived. The game was now a showdown between Henry and Charlie, and there was more than four hundred dollars in the pot.

Henry picked up his worthless hand as if he intended to turn it over. However, just at that moment, Angeleen emitted a loud scream. "A rat!" she shrieked and dropped her reticule.

All eyes swung in her direction except Ruark's. He was determined to see what move the old man made next. In the few seconds the men's attention was diverted to Angeleen, Henry put his worthless hand on top of the deck and retrieved the other hand from between his knees.

You're damn right there's a rat, Mrs. Hunter. More than one, Ruark scoffed silently.

"For the last time, woman. Go back to the cabin," Henry ordered.

"Oh, Poppa," Angeleen whined. Burying her face in her hankie, she ran tearfully from the room.

After Angeleen's dramatic departure, everyone's attention returned to the game. "All right, old man, let's see if you can beat my four kings," Charlie boasted.

Smiling broadly, Henry turned over the hand containing the four aces and a six spot.

Dishonesty, for whatever reason, was an abomination to Ruark. He had seen enough and, thoroughly disgusted, he returned to his cabin.

Charlie became incensed when he saw the same five cards of his previous hand, even down to the six spot, and realized they had been duped—and the girl had taken a part in it. He decided to hold his tongue for now; later he'd make sure that both she and the old man ended up as 'gator bait. But first he had to win back his money in front of witnesses. He called for a new deck.

The bartender brought over an unopened package of cards. With the slight of hand essential to his dishonorable profession, Charlie pocketed the fresh deck, replacing it with a marked deck from his pocket.

Henry had anticipated such a move, and although he appeared to be stacking his winnings, the sly old man was aware of this covert act by the crooked gambler.

Charlie broke open the deck, shuffled the cards, and after offering them for a cut, began to deal the hands.

At that point Henry called for the captain and accused the two men of cheating. Many of the others watching had lost money to the pair and waited expectantly for the outcome as the cards were examined and proven to be marked.

A quick search produced the ship's unopened deck stashed in Charlie's pocket—all that was needed to render "river justice."

Within minutes, the two crooked scoundrels were left standing on a sandbar in the middle of the river as the *Belle* steamed away.

Henry's flush of victory was short lived. As soon as he returned to the cabin, Angeleen held out an open palm.

"What?" Henry asked, scowling. He knew full well what she meant.

"The money, Poppa. Give me the money. This time I'll take care of it."

Henry was offended; his blue eyes deepened with indignation. "Are ye sayin' I nae can be trusted?"

Angeleen threw back her head and snorted at his absurd remark. "Yes, Father, that is precisely what I am saying." She started to impatiently tap her foot on the cabin floor.

Grumbling, Henry pulled the wad of bills out of his pocket and slapped the stack into her outstretched palm. "Ye hae a hard heart, daughter. Just like your grandmother. Wouldst that ye hae the sweet temper of your mother."

"Momma didn't have the responsibility of raising you, like I do." Angeleen smiled with satisfaction and sat down to count the money.

Still grumbling to himself, Henry hung his coat on a peg and climbed into his bunk. As he lay down, his face split into a puckish grin. *The lass is nae as smart as she would like to think,* he reflected as he thought of the money tucked away in his shoe.

Long into the night, overwhelmed with anger and frustration, Ruark continued to pace the floor of his cabin. He hated dishonesty and had only contempt for any one who cheated, whether for business or pleasure.

He had liked the old man and Angeleen. He had believed them to be impoverished Southerners, when all the time the two of them were nothing more than cheats and liars.

His hurt pride matched his disappointment. She had fooled him completely. Obviously, she and her father worked the river just like any of the other predators who preyed on riverboat traffic.

A lot more was becoming clear to him as well. He now understood the mystery surrounding the broken figurine; she had stolen it, most likely with the intention of selling the valuable porcelain when she reached St. Louis.

Dammit! All this time she's been nothing but a lying . . . cheating . . . thieving little bitch. He cursed silently through gritted teeth. *I've had an ache in my loins from the first time I looked at her, when all I had to do was name a price.*

Oh, she had been clever. She had played him like a puppet and he had danced on the string.

"I'll pay for my own meal, Mr. Stewart," he mimicked angrily at his own image in the mirror.

He continued to glare at his reflection. "And you're the damn fool who leant the old man the money to get into that game tonight. I wonder how else they planned on setting you up?"

Ruark suddenly stopped his tirade and glanced toward his trunk. He stormed over to it and pulled out the promissory note Henry Scott had signed when he borrowed the money. The old man had put up Bold King as collateral.

"I'm surprised they haven't pilfered this out of my room by now," he grumbled.

For a few moments he stared down at the document. If they cheated others, they certainly intended to cheat him as well.

Ruark's dark eyes glinted coldly. Well, he would see about that. The last hand still remained to be played and he would be the one to deal it.

The next day, the talk at the tables, of course,

centered on the ejection of the cardsharps from the ship. Since Henry had been a prime player in that drama, he was treated like a celebrity, each man eager to hear his story.

Intoxicated by the glow of notoriety and the many free drinks lavished upon him, Henry did not realize that he was losing consistently.

But Ruark was much aware of this fact. Keeping a close tally of Henry's losses, he watched to make certain the old scoundrel didn't pull any more of his crooked tricks.

Calculating when Henry would run out of money, Ruark sat at Henry's table and without hesitation agreed to the old man's request for an additional loan.

Nearing midnight, confused and slightly inebriated, Henry staggered back to his cabin. From the deck above, Ruark watched him weave among the crates and cartons below.

"To the victor falls the spoils, old man," he murmured. Yet a tinge of compunction lay heavily in the boast.

"Good evening, Mr. Stewart." The ship's captain joined him at the rail.

"Captain Redman," Ruark acknowledged. Reaching into his pocket he extracted a gold cigar case. "Cigar, Captain?"

"Don't mind if I do," the captain said with pleasure as he accepted one of the expensive Havana cigars.

Ruark held a match to the tip of the cheroot, then lit his own, drawing on the end until it glowed. "Looks like we're running into some fog."

"Aye," Redman remarked, glancing down at the vapor curling around the sides of the ship. "This time of the year the air is colder than the water. Causes a lot of this river fog. And the river has too many treacherous curves and snags to risk moving without visibility. If it gets any worse, we'll have to pull over for the night."

He shook his head. "Means another delay. We sure won't make St. Louis as planned."

"Well, we're not running any race, Captain, so use good judgment." Ruark tossed away the cigar. "Goodnight, Captain."

"Goodnight, Mr. Stewart." The captain watched Ruark return to his cabin, then he climbed up the narrow ladder leading to the pilot house.

Still fully clothed, Angeleen had fallen asleep waiting for her father to return. Tears glistened in Henry's eyes as he sat down on the bunk and gently shook Angeleen to waken her.

At the sight of his tears, she sat up worriedly and embraced him.

"Poppa, what is it? What is wrong?"

"I've done a dreadful deed, lass," he said mournfully.

She had heard these same words often enough before and knew this wouldn't be the last time. She patted his shoulder and prepared to listen to his confession. "I'm sure it's not as bad as you think."

"Nae, lass. 'Tis a black deed," he said humbly.

"You didn't murder anyone, did you, Poppa?" Angeleen cajoled, as if she were teasing a child.

Henry lifted his head and looked at her, his eyes

two watery pools. Suddenly struck by the truth, the words froze in her throat.

"No," she whimpered, shaking her head. "No . . . not Bold King. You promised, Poppa. Not Bold King."

Henry hung his head, unable to bear the pain he saw in her eyes. "I canna remember the full of it, lass. I'd been drinkin' and before I was the wiser, I signed the horse over to Stewart."

Angeleen's head shot up instantly. "Ruark Stewart? You sold Bold King to Ruark Stewart?"

Still dazed, Henry nodded. "Aye. We were playin' cards and he made me a loan. The only way I could repay was to sign over the stallion to him." As if to ease his own conscience, he added, "Had ye nae taken all me money, there'd a been no cause for it."

"You lost Bold King to Ruark Stewart in a card game?" she shouted incredulously.

A wave of rage washed over Angeleen. She jumped to her feet and rushed out of the cabin.

The Presidential Suite boasted the most luxurious accommodations on the ship. The cabin was so huge that two doors in the main cabin opened into the large stateroom, and whenever possible, even the most sophisticated passenger did not fail to steal a glance into the spacious suite.

Such was Angeleen's destination.

Ruark had just removed his shirt and was still holding it in his hand when Angeleen burst through the door, slamming it behind her.

At the sight of the intruder, Ruark's dark brow arched suggestively, and he tossed the shirt onto the red satin-covered bed, another luxury unlike the bunks of the smaller cabins.

"Do come in, Mrs. Hunter."

Angeleen wanted to claw the smirk off his face. "You bastard!" she cursed. "Is owning Bold King so important to you that you would cheat an old man in a card game?" Tears of indignant rage slid down her cheeks.

"I think there's some confusion here, Angeleen. I'm not the one who cheats at cards."

He walked over to a table and poured a glass of wine. "May I offer you a glass of fine Madeira?"

"I'm not here on a social call, Mr. Stewart."

He slammed down the glass and spun around. Before she guessed his intent, he had grasped her by the shoulders. The fingers biting into her flesh felt like steel claws.

"Just what are you here for, Mrs. Hunter?"

Angeleen cringed beneath the strength of his grip, but stood her ground. "I want my horse back."

Ruark released her and picked up the glass. "Bold King now belongs to me, Angeleen. I won him."

Her eyes darkened with fury. "Won him! How? By cheating my father in a card game?" Her angry glare held as much contempt as her words.

Ruark smiled indulgently. "My dear Angeleen, a child could beat your father in a card game. He is the worst poker player I have ever seen."

Even though she had often said as much herself, she wasn't about to let any damn Yankee say so. "Is that why you had to get him drunk first?" she accused him.

"I assure you, I never offered your father a drink. I'm not in the habit of drinking with cheats."

"How dare you?" she raged.

"I dare, Angeleen, because I witnessed your theatrics last night. A stellar performance, I should add," he voiced with acerbity.

The declaration took her somewhat by surprise, but Angeleen railed back in self-defense. "Those men cheated us. We were only trying to get our money back."

"But of course." He smirked.

"It's the truth. We've never done anything like that before."

Ruark laughed in ridicule. "And if I return the horse to you, you'll swear never to do it again."

Angeleen, in too much emotional turmoil to grasp his sarcasm, answered quickly. "Yes. I swear. I'll do anything you ask. I have the money we won last night. You can have all of it. Just give me back my stallion."

Ruark heard the words he had anticipated. "*Anything* I ask?" He put down the wine and walked over to her. He grasped her shoulders, gently this time, and pulled her against him.

"Then tell me the true reason why you came to my cabin tonight," Ruark demanded.

Lowering his head, he slid his lips slowly up the slender column of her neck. "You came because you want me to make love to you," he whispered.

She closed her eyes, hoping by shutting him out of her vision, she could shut out the excitement of his touch. "No. That's not true. I didn't mean—"

She gasped aloud when his tongue began to toy with her ear, sending erotic shivers down her spine. "You didn't mean what, Angeleen?" he murmured

65

in a husky murmur. His warm, tantalizing breath tormented her senses.

She tried to push him away, but her arms felt limp and unresponsive; yet every fingertip tingled with sensation when her hands slid down his sloping shoulders to the muscular brawn of his chest.

When his hands moved to the buttons of her bodice, she parted her lips to protest, but he cut off her words with a kiss. His firm and demanding lips moved on hers in sensual possession. As the kiss deepened, so did their hunger, both appetites feasting until the last breath was consumed. He released her mouth, only to reclaim it again in a passionate probe.

She felt on fire—an exquisite, engulfing sheet of flame which did not blister, but only tantalized. His tongue slipped into her mouth, fueling the blaze to a greater intensity.

Her legs trembled, her heart pounded, and the pulse at her temple throbbed. Driven by need, she pressed against him and felt the bulge of his arousal.

"What did you mean to say, Angeleen? Was it that you would even sleep with me to get your horse back?"

It took several breathless seconds for the icy chill of the words to cool the heat he had fueled within her. Slowly she opened her eyes. Ruark was staring down at her.

Horrified, Angeleen stepped away from him. *Whatever was she doing? Could what he said be true?*

"Don't look so alarmed, my love. I intend to pay you well for tonight's company." Ruark smiled mockingly. "But how could you think I'd give up a valuable thoroughbred for only one night of your favors?"

He swooped her up into his arms and carried her to the bed.

Chapter Five

Suddenly, as the ship pitched violently, Ruark was slammed against the wall. He lost his grasp on Angeleen and she fell to the floor. Within seconds, the ship lurched again, and pictures and mirrors tumbled from the walls, while Angeleen skidded across the cabin on her back until she managed to clutch and hold on to a table leg. After several more tremors, the ship settled to a stop in the water.

Ignoring the shards of broken glass and the wine decanter that had crashed to the floor, Angeleen crawled on her hands and knees to Ruark, who sat slumped on the floor, dazed and holding his head. Blood trickled from a cut on his forehead.

"Are you all right?" she asked, her eyes wide with fear.

Ruark nodded. "What about you?"

"I'm . . . I'm fine," she answered tenuously.

Dabbing at the cut with his handkerchief, Ruark stood up and helped Angeleen to her feet. "We'd better get out of here."

They picked their way through broken glass and a stream of red wine that resembled a pool of blood on the floor.

Pandemonium reigned on the deck. One of the eight boilers had been punctured and clouds of steam belched across the bottom deck. Fearing the other boilers would explode at any moment, the panic-stricken passengers pushed and shoved to get off the ship.

Bales of cotton and smaller pieces of cargo had skidded overboard and were floating around the sides of the ship like pieces of jetsam. Larger crates had slammed into each other and many had broken open.

Ruark put a protective arm around Angeleen's shoulders and forced his way to the side of the captain, who was trying to be heard above the shouting and screaming. "How bad is the damage, Captain?"

"Not serious. We've been snagged by a tree trunk. Looks like it damaged the wheel and one of the boilers. But the ship's not going to sink." The pilot had already reversed engines and was maneuvering the vessel toward shore.

"What about the danger of fire, Captain?"

"Nothing's burning, Mr. Stewart. The way these people are panicking, I'm more concerned someone will get injured from being trampled, or scalded from the steam. Once that boiler empties, we can check the extent of the damage."

He raised his voice and shouted, "Please, everyone return to your cabins. There's no immediate danger."

The words had little effect on the mob as they continued to scramble to gather their valuables and get off the ship.

As Ruark began to help the captain get the crowd under control, Angeleen heard the frightened whinny of Bold King. She shoved her way down the stairway to get to him.

Just as she started to cross the lower deck, a loud roar sounded above the clamor. The blood-curdling, inhuman shriek momentarily rendered everyone motionless.

Angeleen spun around just in time to see the cougar free itself from a broken cage and leap to the top of a crate. Snarling and growling savagely, the huge cat poised to spring. Escape from the ship forgotten in their attempt to flee from the ferocious beast, the same people who had just fought to get down the stairway now scrambled back up.

In a bizarre reversal of circumstances, Angeleen now found herself alone on the lower deck. Peeking out from behind an upended crate, she gaped in terror at the poised cougar perched mere yards away and covered her mouth to force back the scream that almost burst past her lips. Her heart hammered with fright. Although she wanted to bolt, her legs trembled so much she could not move.

Slowly, Angeleen began to back away from the cat, praying for a diversion to keep the animal's attention. If only the cougar didn't see her, she might be able to reach Bold King at the other end of the deck and get the stallion into her cabin until the wild beast could be restrained.

But the cat spied her and leaped from its perch. Angeleen screamed, turned, and fled amidst the crates with the cat in pursuit.

Escaping steam rose above the deck in a vaporous mist and, like a feral predator creeping through a verdant swamp, the cougar stalked Angeleen through the haze, moving stealthily past the disarray of cartons and crates. She dodged among them, trying to remain hidden.

By the time she reached the horse's stall, Bold King, having caught the cat's scent, had become wild with frenzy. Angeleen tried to quiet the animal so she could lead him away, but the stallion bucked in such terror that she couldn't get near his thrashing forelegs.

"Please, King, please," she pleaded desperately. She had no idea exactly where the stalking cougar crouched in the maze of broken crates and bales. Then she heard a predatory growl, turned, and looked up at the snarling fangs and feral eyes of the cat.

She screamed and the cat leaped.

Petrified to unconsciousness, Angeleen did not even hear the shot that caught the animal in midair. She collapsed and, as the cat fell dead to the deck, the cougar's claw scraped her shoulder.

Ruark, occupied with trying to calm the panicky crowd on deck, had first become aware of the scene unfolding below when confronted by the herd of

71

screaming people clamoring in panic up the stairs.

"Jesus!" he cursed. He looked around desperately for a weapon but saw none. Within seconds, the deck became massed with people, blocking his way to the stairway, so he rushed into his cabin and grabbed his Colt. Henry, standing near the stairway, became aware of his daughter's danger and rushed down the stairs.

Ruark had to bull his way back to the railing through the mesmerized crowd who watched expectantly, like Ancient Romans awaiting the fate of a martyred Christian. When the cougar jumped to the top of a cotton bale immediately behind Angeleen's head, Ruark had drawn a bead on the elusive animal and needed only one shot to fell the deadly predator.

Angeleen lay petrified with her face pressed against the deck, expecting the beast to sink its teeth into her neck. Instead, she felt warm arms curling around her, and she began to sob hysterically.

"There, there, lass," Henry murmured soothingly. He gathered her to him and began to rock her back and forth like a child. "Dinna cry, me pet. Ye be safe and sound," he cooed softly.

Trembling, she clung to her father, and through her flowing tears, she saw the blur of Ruark Stewart among the crowd gathered around them. Then Angeleen spied the smoking pistol still clenched in his hand and realized the cat had been shot. The danger had passed.

"Did you . . . ?" Ruark nodded. "Thank . . . thank you." She could barely get the words past her throat.

The captain pushed his way through the spectators. "Are you all right, ma'am?" Angeleen nodded and allowed her father to help her to her feet.

"Captain Redman, some of your crew are armed. Why didn't they use their weapons?" Ruark demanded.

"Mr. Stewart, the ship is damaged; my crew put aside their weapons to help," he said impatiently.

"Well, Mrs. Hunter could have been killed," Ruark said, still disturbed by Angeleen's brush with death.

"Had she returned to the boiler deck with the other passengers, she would have been out of danger, Mr. Stewart," he replied firmly. Although he respected Ruark's position, a ship, especially at a time of crisis, had room for only one captain. And he was that man.

With the ferocious beast dead, the captain had to return his attention to the floundering vessel. "We must get on with the repair of the ship," he said curtly, tipped his hat, and walked away.

One positive consequence evolved from the cougar incident; the panic that had prevailed subsided, and the people returned obediently to their cabins until the ship could be repaired.

At last the *Belle* scraped the shore, the loading ramp was lowered, and the crew got off to investigate the damage. When Henry turned his attention to calming the stallion, Ruark vented his anxiety on Angeleen.

"Just what in hell did you think you were doing?" he growled when everybody had moved away.

"Trying to save my horse," she answered, bewildered by his question. "I raised Bold King from a colt. I love him and I'd risk my life to save him anytime I had to."

"Angeleen, must I remind you that Bold King now belongs to me? You're no longer responsible for his welfare." Ruark walked away and joined the captain.

Henry had listened shame-faced to the conversation. "I'm sorry, lass," he said mournfully. " 'Tis me own fault." He left her standing alone.

Angeleen hugged Bold King and buried her face against the velvet neck of the stallion. "Bold King's not yours; he's mine, Ruark Stewart. I'll never let you have him."

Suddenly, a daring thought entered her mind. Without further hesitation, Angeleen untied the stallion and climbed on his back.

"We lost part of the paddle wheel, but I can probably push her to St. Louis," the pilot was saying as he assessed the damage. "Just gonna take longer to get there. We gotta shut down that damaged boiler and keep the steam down just in case there's any more leaks, or any—"

The hammer of hoofbeats interrupted the pilot's words. The men gathered on the shore looked up as Bold King clattered down the loading ramp and galloped past them.

Ruark tried to stop her. "Dammit, Angeleen, get back here," he called out, but she had already disappeared over the crest of the hill. Enraged, he kicked the dirt at his feet in frustration.

Angeleen had no idea where she was or which direction to take. She turned north and rode Bold King hard to get far away from the ship as quickly as possible. After several miles, she reined up and slowed the horse's gait.

Now, with time to think, she realized that her race for freedom had been impetuous.

"Well, King, I guess I should have thought this out a little bit better. There's just the two of us, I don't have a cent in my pocket and only the clothes on my back, and we're in Yankee territory, the same as a foreign country as far as I'm concerned." She leaned over and patted his neck. "You got any suggestions, boy?"

After a few moments' thought, she decided that to avoid getting lost, they had best stay on the trail following the river until she could get her bearings.

"We're going to have to keep hidden, King. I'm sure that Yankee carpetbagger, Ruark Stewart, will inform the police the first chance he gets," she mumbled in disgust.

After several hours, Angeleen wearily stopped in a copse of trees to rest Bold King and climbed down from the back of the big stallion. "You best get some sleep, King. I don't know how much farther we have to go." Exhaustion soon prevailed, and she fell asleep.

Angeleen awoke to daylight and saw Bold King grazing docilely nearby on a patch of clover. She had no idea how long she had slept. However, her stomach made her keenly aware that it had been a long time since she had eaten. She was very hungry.

When she started to rise, she drew back in pain. Her shoulder felt stiff and sore. After a few moments, she got up reluctantly and trudged over to Bold King.

"Looks like the cougar left his mark after all, King."

The horse nudged her in sympathy. "Think we'll ever be able to forget him?" She sighed as she patted the horse's neck. Bold King whinnied his answer. Angeleen smiled as if she understood the response.

Since she could do nothing about her injury, she slowly hoisted herself onto Bold King and continued on her way.

The sun blazed high in the sky when she came upon a signpost. "Look at that, King. St. Louis, fifty miles north. Think we can make it?" Her spirits buoyed, she decided to head toward the bustling port and await the arrival of her father.

Upon cresting a red clay bluff that overhung the river, Angeleen reined up. For several moments she forgot her own problems as she sat mesmerized, watching and listening to the awesome panorama of the mighty Mississippi.

The shrill steam whistle of a paddle wheel, the strident horn of a coal barge, the crack of a billowing sail on a raft, the slap of a canoe's oar gliding through the water—the sounds of the river could be heard from afar.

Wheat from a Minnesota farm, cotton from a Tennessee plantation, apples from a Wisconsin orchard, shrimp from a Louisiana bayou, corn, tobacco, machinery, people—the sights of the river stirred her imagination. Coming and going, up river and down—incessant wayfarers on the great highway of water that linked North to South.

* * *

Ruark fumed as he finished dressing. It had taken hours to get the ship navigable and already past dawn when he finally went to bed, only to lie awake tossing over the iniquitous Angeleen Hunter.

After tying his cravat, he sought his watch. It was nowhere to be found. He knew the cabin had been thoroughly cleaned after the collision with the tree trunk; if the watch had fallen to the floor, it would certainly have been discovered.

He thought back to the last time he remembered seeing his cherished timepiece. The previous night as he had started to undress, he had removed the watch and placed it on the table. Then Angeleen had come in—Angeleen! The thieving, card-cheating, horse-stealing little bitch had stolen his watch too!

The snap judgment fueled him to fury. Who knew where she might have gone? "The little whore's probably spreading her legs for the price of a meal," he grumbled. After all, she had been willing enough to do as much for him. "Nothing's beneath her," he confirmed to himself and stormed out of his cabin.

Still too angry to be among people, Ruark stopped at the railing and lit a cheroot. Perhaps a quiet smoke would calm his temper. He did not take kindly to having a thoroughbred racer stolen right from under his nose, nor did he cherish allowing "that thieving, card-cheating, horse-stealing little bitch to make a fool of me," he finished aloud, unable to check his tirade.

He vowed that somehow he would find her and then she'd pay for her crimes. He wondered whether her father was a party to her escape. Ruark slowly rolled the end of the cigar between his teeth. He figured the old man must be part of her scheme; but why would she leave him behind to face the music alone? Could the thieves have had a falling out?

Suddenly his attention became drawn to an overhanging butte on the far side of the river. He saw a woman astride a black stallion. A gust of wind caught her hair, whipping the long strands behind her like a streaming black satin scarf.

Ruark leaned forward to study the distant figure, and then resolutely gripped the rail; nothing could disguise that hair.

"It's her!"

His blood coursed with excitement. "It's her," he repeated triumphantly. Several nearby passengers eyed him curiously.

He decided Angeleen must be following the river. She had no intentions of deserting the old man and obviously planned on meeting him in St. Louis.

Tossing aside his cigar, Ruark grinned; tracking the brazen filly would be easier than he had thought. And he had the bait to attract her.

The rain poured down. Angeleen could find no escape from the relentless deluge. Even in the copse, whenever the wind blew, showers of drops rained from the leaves.

"We'll just have to keep going, King," Angeleen sighed and plodded on her way.

Enduring hunger seemed as much of a challenge as braving the rain, but she dared not stop to ask for food or a chance to dry out in a barn. If anyone saw Bold King, the stallion would be remembered when

Ruark Stewart put the hounds on her heels.

"And you realize as well as I do, King, he'll do just that the first chance he gets."

But for now, she felt Ruark had no way of knowing if she had headed north or south, or continued east for that matter.

As she skirted a cornfield, Angeleen saw no sign of the farmer working the fields; surely, the rain had driven him inside. Now would be her best chance to get something to eat. Unwise though it might later prove to be, she decided to take the risk.

"I know you love apples, King. If we're lucky, we might find a tree there, too."

She had just pulled up several carrots from a garden when a dog started to bark and race toward her. As Angeleen ran back to Bold King, she snatched an overlooked ear of corn still on the husk and galloped away with the dog yapping at the stallion's heels. The bedraggled hound soon gave up the chase, turned, and trotted back to the warmth and comfort of a dry hearth.

The rain continued to pour down on Angeleen as she rode along chewing one of the carrots. When she spied a crevice among the rocks, she headed for the opening at once, hoping to get out of the storm.

Although the cave seemed small, it was large enough to offer both her and Bold King much-needed protection. Angeleen shivered so much that her teeth chattered as she rubbed the horse down as best she could with her bare hands, then gathered up a meager supply of firewood and found a few stones to try to strike a spark.

After almost half an hour of rubbing the stones

together, she became discouraged, about to give up when at last the small pile of kindling finally ignited. Unfortunately, she didn't have much dry timber to use for fuel, but the fire provided enough warmth to give her at least some relief from the dampness.

Angeleen ate another carrot and fed the remaining root to Bold King. "Sorry, old boy. I know you're as hungry as I am. Maybe tomorrow we'll find a nice field of clover for you."

She shucked and then tried to nibble on the ear of corn, but the hard kernels tasted so bitter that she rewrapped the ear in the husk and stuck it on the fire. After a short while she tried the corn again and this time hungrily devoured the warm, softened morsels.

With nothing further to do, she curled up before the fire. Her shoulder ached, and she felt feverish, cold, wet, hungry, and despondent. Still shivering, she lay trying to draw warmth from the small blaze.

"I'm so cold, King," she murmured.

Would she ever get out of her predicament?

While she slept, the rain passed over and Angeleen awoke the following morning to a sunny sky. As she and Bold King plodded onward, despite the welcomed warmth of the sun, Angeleen felt worse than she had the previous day. But she wouldn't allow herself to stop.

A cathedral clock tolled twelve as Angeleen rode into St. Louis, so ill she could barely remain in the saddle.

Angeleen went directly to the wharf. Spying a dock worker revising the ships' docket, she waited in the shadow of a warehouse as he scrawled the latest arrivals and departures of the steamers. As soon as the man disappeared into a dilapidated building, she hurried over to the board and quickly scanned the list. To her relief, the *Belle of the Bayou* was expected to arrive that evening.

Angeleen knew she must remain hidden, so she led Bold King to the concealment of a copse of trees on a nearby hilltop that overlooked the dock. From this vantage point, she would be able to watch for the *Belle*.

Feeling worse by the minute, Angeleen sat down, leaned back against a tree, and put a hand to her brow. Her skin felt hot and dry.

"I'm afraid the rain's taken a toll on me, King," she whispered to the stallion. "Once Poppa arrives, he'll take care of both of us," she added confidently.

Angeleen wanted to lie down and sleep, but dared not for fear someone might stumble on her by chance—or worse, she would sleep through the *Belle*'s arrival.

Each hour's passing seemed like a year to her. "Can't sleep, King. Can't fall asleep," she mumbled continually, shaking her head or pinching herself as she struggled to keep her drooping eyes from closing. Yet, despite her valiant effort, Angeleen lost the battle and finally succumbed to slumber.

Toward dusk the shrill blast of a river boat jolted her awake. Angeleen rose weakly to her feet in time to see the *Belle of the Bayou*, broken but unbowed, steam up to the wharf of LeClede's Landing.

Through vision obscured by fever, she anxiously watched as the loading ramp was lowered to the dock. Laughing and calling gaily to one another, the passengers disembarked, but there was no sign of her father among them.

Within a short time the dock workers finished unloading whatever cargo had not been washed overboard the night of the accident. Still her father did not make an appearance, and she began to pace nervously, wondering what was keeping him.

A horse-drawn police wagon rumbled up the dock and stopped before the ship. Angeleen's heartbeat quickened when two uniformed policemen got out of the conveyance and strode up the ramp.

After several anxious moments, which seemed like hours to Angeleen, she saw her father led off the ship with his wrists shackled.

Angeleen lowered her head and began to sob. She had stolen the horse—why was her father being arrested? How could he be blamed for her conduct?

The tears streaking her face felt like streams of hot water on her fevered cheeks. Angeleen lifted her head and saw Ruark Stewart standing at the rail. She saw him smile with satisfaction when the wagon departed, taking her father to the jailhouse.

His smugness was more than she could tolerate. She loathed Ruark Stewart. The man was the lowest, vilest, horse-thieving Yankee she had ever met. Incarcerating her innocent father was the lecherous cad's way of having his revenge on her for taking the stallion.

"You were mine to begin with," she declared to Bold King. "He's the one who got you dishonestly, then dared to point the finger of guilt at the innocent."

But Ruark Stewart had the law on his side—and she knew it.

With a shuddering sigh, Angeleen realized there was no other course open to her; she would have to give up King.

Salty tears stung her cheeks as she put her arms around the stallion's neck and buried her face against him. "I'll always love you, King. I'll never forget you."

As if sensing her misery, the stallion raised his head and snorted. "But you understand, don't you, boy. I can't let Poppa go to prison for my crime."

Her heart wrenched with anguish as she climbed on his back for what she believed would be the last time.

Having voiced his complaint, Ruark stood on the deck and watched the policemen lead away Henry Scott. His glance swept the watching crowd, certain Angeleen was there, somewhere, watching every move.

Ruark smiled with satisfaction. He had baited the trap; the next move was hers.

Tossing away his cigar, he donned his top hat at a dapper angle and strolled boldly down the ramp.

Chapter Six

Ruark sat behind the large oak desk trying to concentrate on the ledgers before him. From somewhere beyond the closed door of his study, the mellow chimes of a clock tolled the twelfth hour.

Nothing stirred within the house. The last servant had retired hours before, and the dogs had been purposely penned for the night, so now even the patter of their paws failed to break the silence that hung over the stilled mansion.

A light breeze from the open French doors ruffled the papers on the desk. Ruark rose and walked over to stare out into the darkness. The light from the study lamp pierced the night like a beacon and for several moments his tall frame filling the doorway was silhouetted in the amber glow.

He yawned and stretched, tautly drawing the corded muscles beneath his white shirt across an expanse of broad shoulders. Then he returned to his chair.

Ruark propped his elbows on the desk and rested his head in his hands. He would have to formulate a different plan. He had only had her father arrested to lure her into the open, but she hadn't fallen for the bait. In the morning he would go to the jail and get the old man released.

Suddenly, an eerie feeling disturbed his thought. Then a voice broke the silence.

"I've brought the horse back, so you can release my father." The words were heavy with accusation.

Ruark slowly lifted his head, a satisfied smile tugging at the corners of his mouth. He rose and turned to face her.

Angeleen had entered through the opened door and was standing in the shadows.

"Release your father? We hang horse thieves, Mrs. Hunter."

She sucked in her breath in shock. "He didn't steal the horse. I did."

"Fine. Then we'll hang you right alongside him."

Angeleen's temper flared. "You know Poppa had nothing to do with it. I stole the horse."

"I know nothing of the sort, Mrs. Hunter. To the contrary, I suspect you and your father have hoodwinked others in the same fashion. First you dangle a thoroughbred in front of your victim; then you milk him for huge sums of money and pay him off with the horse; then to loll the fool to complacency, you throw in a night in his bed. When the time is right, you ride off with the animal and make it look as if your father had nothing to do with the theft. The poor dolt you duped is too embarrassed to admit a woman made a fool of him, so you get away with it."

He smirked scornfully. "A fairly good scheme, my dear Angeleen, but this time you tried to swindle the wrong man."

"Nothing you said is true." She stepped out of the shadows. "My father is innocent. You've got to believe me," she pleaded.

Smiling with contempt, Ruark walked over to her. "Believe you? Madam, why would I believe a lying, thieving, card-cheating, horse-stealing whore?"

Aghast, Angeleen lost her genteel southern demeanor. "You bastard!" She slapped his face with all her might.

In her weak condition, the effort took every bit of her strength. Her knees buckled, and she collapsed in his arms.

"What is this, Angeleen? Spare me any more of your theatrics," he scoffed. "Lord knows, I've had enough of them." Ruark suddenly stopped and regarded her more closely. She hung limply in his arms. The pose she could fake, but certainly not the glazed look in her eyes. He could feel her intense body heat beneath his touch and placed a hand to her brow.

"My God, Angeleen! You're burning with fever." She winced and cried out with pain when he grasped her shoulders.

"My . . . my shoulder. The . . . cougar," she gasped before she slipped into blackness.

Ruark's hold on Angeleen prevented the unconscious woman from falling to the floor. He picked her up in his arms and laid her on a couch.

Seeing no sign of an injury, he gently turned her over on her stomach and discovered the ragged rips in the left shoulder of her bodice. Without hesitation, he unbuttoned the garment and slipped it off her shoulders.

"Oh, my God!" Ruark murmured when he saw the wound.

Yellowish-white pus seeped from three scratches on her back. The skin ripped by the cougar's paw had become puckered and moribund, the area around the wound red and swollen with inflammation.

He hurried from the room and aroused the servants. Within minutes a rider was dispatched for the doctor.

Ruark lifted Angeleen into his arms and carried her up a wide stairway to a bedroom above.

"Myra, open the bed," he ordered to the hastily summoned servant who accompanied him.

After the woman had quickly pulled down the bedspread and parted the sheets, Ruark laid Angeleen's limp body between them. He then covered her securely.

"You better get some water boiling. I'm sure the doctor will have use for it," he said.

"Yes, Mr. Ruark," Myra answered and sped from the room, still perplexed over the young woman's condition. In his haste to take care of Angeleen, Ruark had neither informed the startled servants of her identity nor explained how and why she had suddenly appeared in the middle of the night.

He lit a bedside lamp and two wall sconces, then hurried to his own room, grabbed the ewer and basin, and returned quickly to Angeleen's side.

After pouring water into the basin, Ruark wet a face cloth and sponged off Angeleen's face before he laid the cool cloth across her heated brow.

Under the circumstances, he could think of nothing further to do for her, and he began to nervously pace the floor awaiting the doctor's arrival.

It seemed to Ruark that the doctor had been with Angeleen for hours before he finally appeared in the study.

"You have a very sick young lady on your hands, Mr. Stewart," the doctor informed Ruark.

"How serious is her condition, Doctor March?"

The doctor accepted the glass of brandy Ruark handed him and began to sip the liquid. "She has a very high fever. I've given her an antipyretic. The infection is extremely advanced—could even be blood poisoning. I just hope we're not too late. Do you have any idea what kind of animal caused the wound?"

Ruark sat down behind his desk. "A cougar, Doctor."

Astounded, Doctor March stared at Ruark. "A cougar! Good Lord, man! How did the woman ever come in contact with a cougar?"

"It's a long story, sir, but to be as brief as possible, Mrs. Hunter was on a riverboat; unfortunately, so was the cougar. The cat got loose and clawed her. That happened several days ago."

"But the wound looks as if it's never been treated," Doctor March declared.

Ruark grimaced. "I'm afraid that too is another

story, Doctor." He took a deep swallow from his glass.

The doctor could see Ruark did not intend to tell him any more. He finished his drink and rose to his feet. "Well, let's pray we've caught the blood poisoning in time. I only hope so. She's so young and lovely, I would hate to lose her."

The two men shook hands. "I'll return in the morning. In the meantime, I've instructed your maid to keep hot poultices on the wound. That will help to draw out the infection."

"Thank you for coming at such a late hour, Doctor March." Ruark accompanied the doctor to his carriage.

The night air felt refreshing after all the hurried activity and anxiety. Ruark stood for a moment drawing several deep breaths. As he was about to re-enter the house, he saw movement in the shadows nearby. He walked over and discovered Bold King tied to a bush. During the excitement, he had completely forgotten about the horse.

Ruark quickly led the stallion to the stable and found him a stall, then tossed in some hay and oats.

"I sure wish you could talk, boy," he said, patting the stallion's head. "I bet you've got a tale to tell."

Bold King ignored him and continued to chew on the best meal he had tasted in days.

When he returned to the house, Ruark sent Myra to bed and took over the task of changing the compresses on Angeleen's shoulder.

Feverish, she now tossed in a frenzied delirium,

thrashing and mumbling incoherently. "Robert, come back. Please come back."

Saddened by her plight, Ruark listened to her pitiful ravings. "I'm sorry, Momma," she sobbed.

He sponged her fevered brow and studied the lovely lines of her face. Even flushed with fever, Angeleen was beautiful. As he worked over her, she murmured, "Oh, Robert, you look so dashing in your uniform."

Ruark wondered if Robert could be the man she loved, and for a moment felt envious. Suddenly, she began to sob again. "No, you can't be dead, Robert. I love you. You can't die. You promised me you'd come back."

She wept so hard in her delirium that tears ran down her cheeks. He sat down on the bed and wiped them away, then held a cool cloth to her brow as she began to thrash wildly. "I'm cold, King. So cold." She was shivering violently, and he tightened the quilt around her.

His grievances toward her were forgotten as he listened to the poor girl's mumbled anguish. Suddenly, she quieted. Ruark relaxed and returned to the bedside chair.

As he watched the suffering girl fighting for her life, he couldn't help but feel a sense of guilt. What if she had been telling him the truth? Was he responsible for driving her to the desperate measure of leaving the ship?

Don't be foolish, Ruark, he told himself. *You know what she is. Don't let your good judgment be swept away by sympathy.*

Her delirious ravings began again. "Damned carpetbagger. You're mine, King, he's not going to get you."

Angeleen's constant tossing made his task difficult, but Ruark continued his vigil throughout the night, changing the hot poultices on her shoulder and the cool cloth on her brow. He repeatedly replaced the blankets over her body, wracked with sporadic attacks of chills, and dabbled water on her lips to keep them from drying and blistering.

And he held her hand, hoping that somehow Angeleen would know she was not alone.

"We must hurry, Obbie, the Yankees are coming. We'll hide in the swamp." Tears began streaking her cheeks again. "No, Robert. you can't be dead, too. I love . . . you. I . . . love . . . you." Her voice trailed off to a sob.

As he struggled to restrain her, she suddenly sat up and grabbed his arms. "Momma, where are you? I'm afraid. I need you, Momma," she cried in a pathetic, little girl's voice.

Gently, he laid her back down and sponged away her tears. Her condition appeared to be worsening instead of improving. The fever was consuming her.

"Keep fighting, Angeleen. You must keep fighting," he whispered.

Ruark thought of her laughter, of her eyes flashing in anger at him. She had been such a vibrant, vital being, too alive to slip away like this in the throes of a feverish delirium.

He sat down, picked up her hand, and clasped it between his own. "Just keep fighting, Angel. Little black-haired angel with broken wings."

Doctor March returned later that morning with additional medication. Angeleen had quieted, but her body was still ravished by fever. After a few words exchanged with the doctor, Ruark closed the door and started to return to his own chamber.

He stopped abruptly at the sight of the figure awaiting him in the hallway. "Nana!"

Sarah Stewart leaned heavily on the sterling silver handle of her cane and eyed her disheveled grandson through a pair of penetrating, clear-blue eyes.

"Good morning, Ruark. Since the whole household has been disrupted all night, isn't it about time you tell me exactly what is going on here?"

Her voice was steady, the words spoken in a pleasant modulation; the dowager's regal bearing always garnered immediate attention.

The old woman raised a cheek, still soft and smooth despite her eighty years, to accept Ruark's quick kiss.

"It's been a long night, Nana dear. After I bathe and shave, I'll join you for breakfast and tell you the whole story."

Her alert eyes sharpened. "That will be most appreciated, young man." Sarah's mouth curved into a fond smile as she watched the tall figure of her beloved grandson stride away.

It was Sarah who greeted Henry Scott after the confused man was escorted into the drawing room later that day. Her keen glance inspected him thoroughly.

"Mr. Scott, I am Sarah Stewart."

Henry doffed his hat politely. "Yes, ma'am." The

name of Stewart was certainly recognizable to Henry, but not pleasantly so.

"My grandson has explained to me he brought you here after having you released from jail—along with the full details of his meeting with you and your daughter."

Henry was an easy-going man to an extent, but being incarcerated for a crime he hadn't committed, and fearing for the welfare of his daughter, had put a serious strain on his good nature. He felt he had nothing to lose by being candid.

"I dinna think he hae explained the full details, ma'am. Your grandson is so bull-headed he wouldna recognize the truth if it jumped up and bit him in the nose."

Few people ever questioned Ruark's astuteness. However, Sarah liked this man's spirit and regretted she had to be the one to break the news about his daughter.

"Well, Mr. Scott, I would indeed enjoy listening to your version of the encounter, but I regret that I have something of an unpleasant nature to tell you." Her clear eyes saddened. "Regarding your daughter."

"Angeleen! You know where she is?" he asked urgently.

"She's upstairs, Mr. Scott, but I'm afraid she's not well."

"Not well! What's wrong with her?" Henry was too stunned by this news even to wonder how Angeleen had got there.

"From what I understand, your daughter—ah, Angeleen—received several scratches from a cougar while on board the steamer."

Henry's eyes widened in surprise. "Cougar scratches?" He shook his head sadly. "And the lass said nary a word about them."

"Well, unfortunately, the scratches are now seriously infected and she is very ill," Sarah said.

"May I see the lass?" Henry asked.

"Of course, sir. But I want you to know how much my grandson and I regret this unfortunate development."

Things had been moving so rapidly that Henry had not grasped the seriousness of Angeleen's condition. Now he became overwhelmed with fear.

"The lass will pull through, won't she?"

"We can only pray, Mr. Scott," Sarah said kindly. She picked up a tiny bell and rang for a servant.

Ruark rose to his feet when Henry entered the bedroom. The old man exchanged a startled glance with him, then moved to the bedside. He saw Angeleen resting quietly, but purple circles lined her eyes, and her face looked pale and wan. Her usually lustrous black hair was plastered to her head and cheeks in dank strands.

Henry picked up her hand and squeezed it. "It's Poppa, lass. Can ye hear me?" he asked tenderly.

Tears misted his eyes as he continued to stare down at the silent figure in the bed. When there was no response, he looked helplessly at Ruark.

Ruark put a reassuring hand on Henry's shoulder. "The doctor said she's responding to the medication, Henry. He's very encouraged."

"Aye, the lass is a fighter, she is." His chin quivered as he forced a weak smile. "Has had to be her whole life."

Ruark nodded in understanding and withdrew to leave Henry alone with his daughter. He paused with his hand on the doorknob and looked back; Henry was sitting on the bed holding his daughter's hand.

Angeleen awoke twelve hours later. She opened her eyes and saw Ruark sitting in a chair beside the bed, his eyes closed. For several moments she lay silently and tried to orient herself. What was he doing here? Where was she? She looked about the strange room. Everything looked so elegant. She told herself she must be dreaming.

When she turned her head back to Ruark Stewart, his eyes were open and he was staring at her. "How are you feeling?"

"I'm not sure," she said weakly. "I'm very thirsty."

Ruark poured a glass of water, then slipped an arm under her back to raise her head and shoulders. She felt helpless and ridiculous as he held the glass to her mouth.

"Just take a few sips for now," he cautioned.

In her weakened state, the idea of Ruark Stewart nursing her was too much for Angeleen to comprehend. She lay back. The simple act of sitting up had exhausted her. Angeleen closed her eyes and slept.

He was there when she awoke again—she hadn't dreamt it. She saw the bright sun streaming through the windows. Sometime during the night, her fever had broken and she was now soaked with perspiration.

"Angeleen, are you hungry?" Ruark asked.

She shook her head, surprised at the conciliatory note in his voice. She couldn't understand this change in his personality. The last thing she remembered, he had threatened to have her hung along with her father. Perhaps she was still feverish and dreaming. Yes, that could be the only explanation.

Then she noticed the woman standing next to Ruark. "Angeleen, Myra is going to bathe you and change the bed linens."

He patted her hand. "I'll be back later." He smiled again, and despite her confusion, she returned his smile.

Angeleen looked considerably more refreshed when Ruark returned several hours later. He, too, had obviously bathed, and he looked impeccably groomed. As he stood beside the bed grinning down at her, he seemed as tall as a tree.

"You're looking much better. Are you feeling up to a visitor?"

Angeleen assumed he must be referring to himself. There was no denying she had a dozen questions to ask him, but at the moment, she didn't have the strength to spar with him. She shook her head. "I'm very exhausted. I would like to rest again if you don't mind."

"Well, he's very anxious to see you. I'll tell him he can only stay for a few minutes."

"Tell whom?" she asked suspiciously. She couldn't believe he would call the sheriff while she was still flat on her back.

Ruark opened the door and Henry Scott stepped into the room. At the sight of her father, Angeleen broke into tears. "Poppa!" She opened her arms to him and Henry rushed over to the bed.

Laughing and crying, the two embraced and kissed. As she hugged her father, Angeleen looked over his shoulder at the tall man watching from the doorway. For an infinite moment her glance locked with his steady, dark gaze.

She felt an unfamiliar fluttering in her breast.

Chapter Seven

The day finally arrived when Doctor March announced that Angeleen would be able to get out of bed for short spells. She couldn't wait to tell Ruark. His solicitousness during her illness had come to mean a lot to her, and although his all-night vigils at her bedside had ended, Ruark still visited her every day and evening, often playing cards, reading, or just chatting.

Ruark had relieved Myra of her household duties so she could devote all her attention to nursing Angeleen, and when he discovered the skill Henry had with horses, Ruark hired him to help handle the many animals in his own stable, Bold King among them.

Despite her resentment at having to give up her beloved stallion, Angeleen was grateful to Ruark for all his kindness. With every moment they spent together, her feelings toward him developed to more than just gratitude.

The morning after the doctor's departure, as Myra brushed her patient's hair, Angeleen's face glowed with anticipation, knowing Ruark would soon arrive. "You look lovely, miss. I swear, no one would even know you were sick," Myra said. The older woman had developed a deep affection for the young girl.

"Do you really think so, Myra? I'm feeling so much better, and I can't wait to get out of this bed." Angeleen sighed deeply. "It will feel wonderful to take a hot bath."

"Just remember, I'm available to wash backs," Ruark said, having overheard her comment as he walked into the room. Angeleen blushed, still unable to parry the teasing that he enjoyed so much.

Myra clucked her disapproval. "Must you always be embarrassing the poor dear?" She started to leave the room when Ruark stopped her, and for several moments the two people spoke together in low tones. Angeleen tried to overhear the conversation but the words were out of her hearing.

After the maid departed, Ruark came over to the bed and sat down beside her. "How's my favorite patient feeling today?"

She glanced up and smiled. "Have you heard the good news? Doctor March said I can get out of bed tomorrow."

Adopting the doctor's serious mein, he sternly advised, "But only for short periods of time, Mrs. Hunter. You must conserve your energy for entertaining your visitors."

Before Angeleen could think of a reply, Myra returned. "The room's all ready, Mr. Ruark."

"Thank you, Myra. That will be all for now." Grinning, he rose to his feet. "Myra has informed me, in no uncertain terms, that it is shameless to expect you to recuperate in this cold room. So we're moving you to a warmer one with a fireplace."

Ruark leaned over and picked her up in his arms. Angeleen was too startled to say anything as his dark eyes gazed into hers.

An exciting blend of bay and shaving soap began to tease her senses. Their faces were only inches apart, and her glance shifted to the temptation of his sensual mouth, so close to her own.

She felt flushed, her lips dry. His arms holding her grew taut as he watched her tongue moisten her lips, then he shifted his dark eyes and captured her sapphire gaze.

She didn't realize she had been holding her breath until she began to feel suffocated; the breath burst from her lungs in an explosive gasp, the only sound she could make—no protest, no admonishment.

"You're cold," he whispered in a husky murmur when she began to tremble.

He carried her down the hallway into another room and placed her in the bed. Ruark sat down and tenderly stroked her cheek, tucking a few errant strands of hair behind her ear.

Then he lowered his head and his mouth closed over hers.

His mouth was firm, warm—and exciting. He had intended to give her a gentle, swift kiss, but once their lips joined, the kiss deepened and her lips parted beneath the insistent pressure.

For a brief moment, her conscious thoughts marveled at her unequivocal response. She slid her arms around his neck and let him press her deeper against the soft down of the mattress.

His mouth trailed a moist path to her ear, and she clung to him dizzily, reveling in the burning sensation surging rampantly through her.

"I guess the wisest move is to get the hell out of here at once," he said hoarsely.

She didn't want him to leave. She didn't understand her own passion, but knew she now wanted him with the same intensity she had once lavished on hating him. Weaving her fingers through his thick hair, she drew his head down to hers. This time the kiss was deeper, she the aggressor.

He forced himself to pull away, but stared down at her as his eyes mirrored the battle waging with himself. They were both shocked by the passion of the brief encounter.

He cupped her cheeks in his hands. "Dammit, Angel, I've got to leave on business for a few days. But when I get back, we have to talk about us."

Why had she responded so passionately to his touch? Perplexed as much as he at the intensity of her response, Angeleen belatedly questioned the wisdom of her actions. Her instinct warned her she could only be hurt.

"What is there to talk about, Ruark? I'm grateful for all you've done for me, but you know as well as I that I don't belong here. As soon as I'm well enough, I intend to leave."

He shook his head. "I know nothing of the sort, Angel. What just happened between us proves otherwise."

"What just happened between us was a mistake, Ruark. If you don't intend to fight it, I do." She turned her face away to avoid the temptation of his dark eyes.

Ruark hooked his thumb under her chin and forced her gaze back to his. "You can't fight fate, Angel," he said solemnly. He kissed her again, draining her final strength, then swiftly departed.

The next day Angeleen awoke to discover an unexpected caller sitting at her bedside; the grande dame of the manor had come to pay her a visit.

"So you are Henry's daughter," Sarah Stewart said as Myra put several goose-down pillows behind Angeleen to help her sit up in bed. "Myra, bring us some tea so I can chat with this child without your prying ears listening to our words."

The maid shook her head. "You've no call to make your disparaging remarks, ma'am. If you want me to leave the room, just say as much."

The old woman's eyes twinkled with mirth. "I thought I just did. And remember to bring lemon. You always forget the lemon and you know I like it."

"I'm thinking your tongue is tart enough without adding more sour to it, that's why," Myra declared. She fluffed up another pillow. "Here, let me put this behind your back or you'll be complaining of an ache and expecting me to knead it out of you."

At first Angeleen was shocked by the conversation, but she quickly realized, by the expression in their eyes, that these two women loved each other very much.

Sarah sat with her hands resting on her cane, looking as imperial as she did intimidating. "I'm Sarah Stewart," she said when the maid had left the room. "Ruark's grandmother."

The awestruck girl nodded. "How do you do, Mrs. Stewart."

"And how are you feeling, child?"

"Much better, Mrs. Stewart. Thank you. And . . . I . . ." Angeleen hesitated shyly in the presence of the gracious, yet formidable lady. "I don't know how to thank you, Mrs. Stewart."

"Indeed? For what, dear child?"

"I would have died without your hospitality."

Sarah frowned. "Died! Nonsense, child. If the good Lord intended for you to die, you'd be six feet under by now."

Two fetching dimples appeared in Angeleen's cheeks. "I suppose you're right, Mrs. Stewart." And then she added thoughtfully, "After all, I did manage to survive four years of war."

Angeleen couldn't help wondering about the purpose of the woman's visit. Regarding her visitor closely, Angeleen noted with admiration the bright blue eyes and perfectly coifed silver hair of this frail lady, who was wearing a gown of blue brocade fastened at the neck by a jeweled brooch.

Angeleen thought the elegant woman looked as serene as a portrait of royalty, needing only a gleaming tiara nestled on her proud head to complete the picture of majesty.

"Did I understand you to say that you know my

father?" she asked, somewhat tentatively.

Merriment danced in the blue eyes. "Indeed. Ah, my dear, what an incorrigible rogue he is."

Oh no, what did you do now, Poppa? Angeleen moaned to herself.

"That grandson of mine says your father has a gifted hand with horses."

"Well, Poppa always said as much," Angeleen agreed with a smile.

Despite the lightness in her tone, she was proud of her father; his knowledge of horses and his ability to appraise and train them had long been a source of admiration to all who knew Henry Scott.

For the next quarter of an hour, Angeleen extolled the virtues of Henry's expertise in handling horses. When Sarah saw the young girl begin to tire, she rose to her feet. "I will leave you to rest, my dear. If my grandson is not properly seeing to your needs, tell Myra to inform me."

"There's no cause to do that," Myra scolded as she entered the room. "I'd be sure to tell the young master myself."

"I'm sure you would," Sarah complained as she tottered carefully to the doorway. "And where is my tea?"

"In your sitting room, where it belongs. I thought it best we let the young miss get her rest."

She took the old woman's arm, but Sarah shook off her hand. "I can get around myself, if you please."

"Well, I'm coming along just the same," Myra carped and followed her out the door.

Later, Myra returned carrying several large boxes tied with fetching bows. "Land o' Goshen, will you look at these. And they're all for you."

"For me!" Angeleen exclaimed. "Are you sure?" Her eyes glowed with excitement. She hadn't received a present in four years.

"Mr. Ruark sent them. I'd say they're a bit early for Christmas."

Angeleen trembled like a child as she lifted the top off one of the boxes. "Oh, I've never seen anything so elegant!" she exclaimed at the sight of a blue velvet robe. The long sleeves of the garment were gathered at the wrists with white ermine cuffs.

Another box contained three nightgowns. Two were conventional white cambric shifts daintily trimmed with satin and lace. But on seeing the third gown, her eyes rounded with shock and the red blush that colored her came not from fever. In the matching hue of the robe, the pleated silk muslin gown was transparent, so sheer it could only cover, not conceal.

Myra grimaced and shook her head. "Leave it to Mr. Ruark. The man's a devil." The censure sounded like the tolerant prattle of an indulgent mother rather than the assessment of a critic.

"Why, it's—improper," Angeleen stammered after a further examination of the scanty nightdress.

She quickly shoved it back into the box and opened the final package. "Oh, Myra, look at this!" Angeleen exclaimed.

She held up a high-collared, full-sleeved red blouse trimmed with black braid and epaulets. The fashionable garment had been designed after the uniform of the "Red Shirts" led by the popular Italian military leader, Giuseppe Garibaldi. A braided bolero and black skirt, trimmed with a red band around the hem, completed the ensemble.

"Lord of Mercy!" Myra exclaimed as Angeleen donned the outfit and rushed to the mirror. "Sure does appear as if Mr. Ruark has in mind to get somebody regimented," Myra chuckled as she stood with arms akimbo.

Absorbed with admiring her reflection, Angeleen did not perceive the humorous nuance of suspicion and subtle warning in Myra's remark.

Returning to the bed, Angeleen read the card Ruark had penned and enclosed in the package. *"I thought you would prefer to be properly 'uniformed' for our next meeting."*

She tried to suppress her smile at the challenge, but despite the attempt, two dimples appeared. Knowing how helpless she had been to resist his touch, Angeleen grimaced in despair. Somehow, she would *have* to resist him. The code of war decreed that the victor could claim the spoils. Well, she hadn't been subjugated by any Yankee during the late war, and she wasn't going to be now.

At least—she hoped she wasn't.

The following morning she awoke to bright sunlight streaming through the window. Angeleen could barely wait to get outside to enjoy the fresh air and sunshine. Dressed in her new apparel and accompanied by Myra, Angeleen took her first outdoor stroll since her illness.

They walked down to the stable and found Henry preparing Bold King for a workout. Now, properly fed and groomed, the stallion looked every inch a thoroughbred as Henry led him to a small track nearby. Angeleen and Myra followed behind.

At the sight of Ruark Stewart, standing with a booted foot propped on the fence, Angeleen felt an unexpected surge of pleasure. She had not realized he had returned home. Seeing the two women, he walked over and joined them.

The wind ruffled his dark hair as he grinned down at her. "Well, I see our patient has regained her footing." And he added, as he took a step back to eye her head to toe, "Looks like she's even ready to pass muster."

Angeleen returned his smile and raised a hand to restrain her long locks blowing about her face. "Yes, indeed," Angeleen responded with an emphasis akin to Ruark's grandmother. "My first outing and I'm enjoying it very much," she added demurely. "And I thank you kindly, Mr. Stewart, for my new uniform."

As she twirled around to give him a full view, Myra abruptly changed the subject so that Angeleen need not mention the nightgowns at this time—if ever. "I'll be returning to the house if you can make do without me," Myra said.

"Go right ahead, Myra. She'll be fine with me. I'll bring her back," Ruark said.

"Well, don't let her tire," Myra cautioned in a final note of warning before departing.

"She looks after me like a mother hen with a chick," Angeleen remarked. She had grown as fond of her nursemaid as Myra had of her patient.

Ruark brushed a strand of hair off her cheek. "Myra thrives on having someone to cluck over. My mother died when I was only three. I don't know how I would have grown up without Myra's hand."

"I'm sorry, Ruark," Angeleen said, regretting she had even brought up the subject.

He tucked her hand in his arm and they strolled back to the fence. "Well, I had Nana and Myra, so I was very fortunate."

His hands encircled her waist as he lifted Angeleen up and set her on the top rung of the fence. "You're just in time to see Bold King's morning workout."

The jockey mounted on the stallion guided the horse over to them for Ruark's final instructions. "Don't burn him out in the first half mile. Rate him until the final quarter, then open him up," Ruark ordered. "We'll clock him the last quarter mile."

"Yes, sir," the jockey said and led Bold King away. Angeleen felt like a helpless parent watching her child being fed to the wolves. She had raised him, protected him, and now had become an outsider.

Seeing the look on her face, Ruark said softly, "Are you still mad about losing the stallion, Angel?"

"I don't know," she said. "I've been too sick to think about it very much. My thoughts are so confused. I'm grateful for all you've done for me, Ruark, but I don't know if gratitude could ever compensate for losing something I love."

Unable to meet his gaze for fear she would reveal more of her inner, deeper, and certainly more confusing thoughts, Angeleen looked away from him toward the track.

Henry was standing near them clutching a stopwatch in his hand. Ruark drew a similar watch out of his pocket to time the horse as well. Their conversation ended when Bold King neared the final quarter pole, and they watched the stallion thunder down the track.

When Bold King crossed the finish line, Ruark let out a long, low whistle. "Twenty-eight seconds! 'Tis good time for a first workout," Henry exclaimed.

Ruark nodded his agreement. "Tomorrow we'll see how he does against President."

Henry patted the horse. "Ah, the lad won't disappoint you, I'm sure. But I best be taking him back to the paddock now."

As Henry led the snorting stallion away, Bold King pranced proudly behind him, as if he knew there was a glorious destiny in store for him.

For a short while after Henry's departure, Angeleen and Ruark silently watched the young colts frisking about the fenced meadow, racing across the field of grass like children at play.

Sighing contentedly, Angeleen finally spoke. "They're beautiful, aren't they?" Ruark nodded. "It's as if they know they were bred to run."

"These colts are all two-year-olds. We'll start to race them this summer," he told her.

"I never suspected you owned a racing stable. Now I understand why you wanted Bold King so badly."

A sudden gust of wind caused Angeleen to shiver. "I think it's getting too chilly for you." Ruark lifted her down from the fence, removed his jacket and slipped it around her shoulders. Angeleen could feel the comforting warmth of his body heat still trapped in the folds of the jacket.

"Actually, I'm not going to race him. I'm going to

use Bold King for stud," Ruark said as they slowly walked back to the house.

She glanced at him, surprised. "You aren't going to race him?"

"No. He hasn't raced in over four years. That's too long. But the stallion has good bloodlines. Henry said Bold King was sired by Caliph out of Wellington Princess. I'm familiar with both of those horses. They're good stock."

"I would hope so. Father used all our money to buy the colt. I remember how upset my mother was at the time. Then shortly after, the war broke out and we lost everything anyway."

By the time they reached the house, her legs were trembling with fatigue. Angeleen slipped his jacket off her shoulders. "Thank you," she said, handing it to him. Their hands touched and he clasped her hand in the warmth of his. "I'd better rest. I'm exhausted. But this has been enjoyable, Ruark," she said with a delightful smile.

Angeleen had no idea how dazzling she appeared; her eyes sparkled with exuberance, her face glowed with a rosy blush, and her long, dark hair billowed in the wind.

He returned her smile as he tucked her streaming hair behind her ears. "The pleasure is all mine, Angel." His steady gaze followed as she entered the house.

From a bedroom window above, Sarah Stewart watched the young couple. Her blue eyes danced with cunning.

Chapter Eight

The weather had taken a turn for the worse and St. Louis had been hit by a freeze, unexpected for so early in the fall. By morning the frost would be melted, but for now, the ground and limbs of trees were covered with a delicate coating of white.

After finishing a hot bath, Angeleen slipped into the velvet robe Ruark had bought for her and snuggled down before the fire to brush her hair.

Earlier, she and her father had dined with Ruark and his grandmother. Angeleen had to admit to herself how much she enjoyed their company. After every moment spent with Ruark, her feeling for him deepened until there was no fooling herself—she had fallen in love with him. But Ruark had wealth and position while she had nothing.

Over and over in her mind she wrestled with the dilemma of emotion versus reality until, at last, the battle became resolved by the sheer instinct for survival; she must get as far away as possible from Ruark before she made a fool of herself.

But how would she ever convince her father to leave? He seemed settled in his new position and was certain to give her an argument.

Absorbed in her troubling thoughts, Angeleen did not hear the door open.

Ruark stepped into the room.

Quietly, he stood for a moment observing Angeleen, mesmerized by her profile, which was etched in the carmine glow from the fire, and the glossy sheen of her dark hair.

"You're very beautiful, Angel."

The sound of his voice jolted Angeleen out of her reverie and she swung her gaze to the door. Her sapphire eyes widened in surprise to see the very subject of her musing stand before her.

"Ruark." The word slipped past her lips in a startled gasp.

Dressed only in a white shirt and dark trousers, he looked virile and handsome—a provoking reminder to Angeleen of that day in Memphis when he had climbed on Bold King's back.

"I hoped you would still be awake." He crossed the room to the fireplace and stood above her.

She tried to steady her quickened heartbeat. "I realize this is your house, Ruark, but I would appreciate a knock on the door before you enter my room."

When she started to rise, he reached out and

grasped her hands in his. "Let me help you."

Ruark pulled her to her feet but did not release his grip as his hungry gaze swept her from head to toe. "Lord, Angel, you look beautiful in that robe. But I knew you would," he said in a husky murmur.

Her heart pounded wildly in her breast as she withdrew her hands from his. "I never thanked you for the robe . . . or the other clothes," she said, trying to avoid looking into his dark, hypnotic eyes. She glanced down and stroked the soft fur cuffs on the sleeves. "I can't remember ever owning anything so elegant."

"I want to give you more, Angel. So much more." He moved closer and slowly drew her into his arms. "This is only the beginning. You belong in silks and velvets, ermine and satin. I can give them to you."

Transfixed, she watched his mouth descend and closed her eyes in a languorous gesture of surrender.

His lips were tender and warm as they covered hers in a seductive assault. She parted her lips in response to his demand, her body trembling with a passion she felt only in his arms. His mouth freed hers, to slide to the hollow of her throat.

"I want to show you London, Paris—the world, Angel. Say 'yes,' say you'll come with me."

Slipping his hands into her robe, he continued the ravishment of her senses. As one hand cupped the round mound of her breast, the other played havoc with the tingling nerve ends of her spine, sweeping her back and pressing her tighter against his hard body.

Through the clinging fabric of her nightgown, the

warmth of his hand teased the buds of her breasts to hardened peaks. Moaning with pleasure, she threw back her head and allowed his lips to trail down the column of her neck to the valley between her breasts. Her arms dropped limply to her sides and she offered no resistance as he pushed the robe off her shoulders. The velvet garment fell in a discarded heap to the floor.

His warm, moist mouth closed around her breast and began to suckle. The wet material of her night-gown rubbed against the turgid peaks of her breasts, sending erotic tremors down her spine. The sensation was too seductive to resist and all the pent-up desire she had repressed since their first kiss erupted in the intensity of their mutual passion.

"Say, 'yes,' Angel. Say that you'll stay with me. Tell me you'll be mine alone."

"Yes, oh yes," she cried raggedly, arching against him, pressing deeper into his arousal. "Yours, Ruark. Always," she sobbed.

He swept her up into his arms and carried her to the bed. Laying her gently on the downy soft-ness, he lowered himself to the bed. "Angel, are you sure you're well enough for this?" His breathing was labored by desire.

"Please, Ruark," she whispered and her lips part-ed in a breathless offering as she began to slowly trace the firm outline of his mouth with a trembling finger.

The restraint he had struggled to maintain was crumbling under the demands of passion, but he needed further assurance. "We should discuss this calmly. I don't want any regrets, Angel."

He stopped with a shuddering breath, grabbing her hand away from his mouth. "God! I can't think clearly when you do that."

He ceased any further attempt at words. His mouth crushed down on hers, the weight and warmth of his long, hard body pressing against her soft curves. He rained passionate, quick kisses on her lips, her face, her eyes, the throbbing pulse of her temple, the hollow of her throat—always returning to taste the moist sweetness of her mouth.

Their kisses deepened, their tongues dueled, and their combined passions escalated. Then, with dark spiky lashes hooding his lust-filled eyes, he stopped, raised his head, and stared down, studying her intently, offering her a moment to make the final decision. When he read her desire in the sapphire depths of her eyes, he rose to his feet, satisfied.

Transfixed, she watched him unbutton his shirt. Her heart pounded wildly when he tossed it aside and she beheld his muscular brawn and broad shoulders. She became hypnotized by his smoldering gaze as he divested himself of his remaining clothing. Her eyes followed the trail of dark hair down the long, naked length of him to his enlarged organ. She felt an instant surge of response within herself and began to tremble with excitement.

The sensation was foreign to Angeleen. Her husband's clumsy brutality had never aroused the passion she felt now. On the contrary, Will Hunter's touch and nearness had repulsed her when the insensitive brute took his own pleasure, leaving her only fear and disgust. Ruark's lovemaking awakened within her a new feeling, an exquisite surprise.

Returning to the bed, his weight covered her, and she parted her lips beneath his as all vestiges of resistance slipped away.

He made no attempt to hurry, but let his mouth and tongue toy with hers before he trailed a path to the hollow of her ear. As he slipped her nightgown off her shoulders, her sudden breathless gasp was the assurance he needed to continue, and he slid his mouth down to claim one of the rosy peaks of her upthrust breast.

Her body felt as smooth as satin beneath his mouth and hands, and he continued to lave and suckle in a sensual probe that left her writhing beneath the leisurely exploration.

Raised to the pinnacle of all feeling, she abandoned herself to him, her love and need exploding in an uninhibited reciprocation that brought him near eruption.

When he entered her, she felt an initial pain. Despite her desire, her body was near virginal; several years had passed since her marriage, and even then, her sexual experiences had been limited. He cupped her buttocks in his hands, pressing her upward as he gently rotated her to his rhythm.

The overpowering sensation, an intermingling of pain and rapture, built toward climax. Her pain diminished until only rapture remained as she encased him and tightened around him. He groaned with pleasure. It felt good—it had never felt so good.

She clung to him, crying out his name as he spilled into her and they became one body, one heart—and for an exquisite, shared moment, one soul.

The room was swathed in a mantle of warmth, lit only by the fire crackling on the hearth. Darkened shadows closed in around them, sequestering the two figures on the bed.

Angeleen lay with her eyes closed, basking in the afterglow of their loving, sensitized to everything around her—the flames roaring in the fireplace, Ruark's ragged breathing pounding in her ears, the aromatic fragrance of the pine log, the masculine scent of him tantalizing her nostrils.

Her fingertips tingled from the feel of the soft, silken texture of his hair; her body throbbed with the hard pressure of the strength of him pressed to her.

She licked lips that felt parched and tasted the savory saltiness of him still lingering on her tongue. Slowing raising her eyelids, she met the glory of his dark eyes smiling down at her.

With a shuddering sigh, she reached for him.

Angeleen awoke to discover that the fire had died in the hearth, and for a moment she gazed dreamily at the first light of dawn streaking through the window. She turned on her side, rested her head on her propped elbow, and lay watching Ruark sleep. He looked beautiful and peaceful in slumber, and she loved him beyond reasoning. Unable to resist the temptation, she leaned over and pressed a light kiss to his lips.

Ruark opened his eyes and looked up into her loving gaze.

Then the corners of his dark eyes crinkled with the warmth of his smile.

"I think I'll enjoy your waking me each morning."

She dipped her head and kissed him deeply, passionately. "Now I'm *certain* I'll enjoy your waking me each morning." Grasping her shoulders, he drew her down to him and she nestled her head on his chest.

"I don't know when I've ever been so happy," she sighed, lying contentedly as she listened to the steady beat of his heart beneath her ear.

"We'll have a wonderful time in New York, Angel. I plan to leave on Friday."

"Friday? Oh, Ruark, that's impossible. How can we leave so soon? We have to get married. And I can't sail to England with just the clothes on my back." She lifted her head to look at him. "Beside, there's still Father—"

The words died in her throat at the shocked look on his face. "What is it, Ruark? Is something wrong?"

"Angel, I didn't say anything about our getting married," he said softly, choosing each word carefully.

Not comprehending his meaning, she repeated his very words. "You said you wanted me to stay with you . . . *to be only yours*."

"And I meant every word. But I was not talking about marriage, Angel. I'm sorry, I thought you understood what I meant."

At her questioning look, Ruark thoughtfully attempted to explain. "When I get married, Angel, I intend to have children and—well, I don't want the mother of my children to be a . . ." He floundered helplessly, realizing he had said too much. He knew the cruel words would only hurt her.

"A cheat and a whore." Angeleen finished the sentence for him.

When he made no denial, no response at all, full understanding descended upon her like a debilitating sickness. She felt withered and dead.

Stunned, Angeleen rose from the bed. Oblivious to the cold, she wandered over and stared sightlessly out of the window. Her heart ached so, she thought it would burst. How could she have been such a naive fool as to believe Ruark Stewart would ever consider marrying her? Their lives were worlds apart.

"Oh, God, Angel, I never wanted to hurt you." Ruark slipped the robe around her shivering shoulders and pulled her back against him. She was too numb to offer resistance. The pain in her heart pierced as though a knife had been thrust through her chest.

Tentatively, he trailed his lips down the slim column of her neck. "We're good together, Angel. I can make you happy. Happier than you've ever been. Come with me. I promise to take good care of you."

Ruark turned her in the circle of his arms, his anguished gaze probing the very depth of her soul as he grasped her shoulders.

"I adore you, sweetheart." His face softened with a smile as he gently tucked her hair behind her ears. Cupping her cheeks in his hands, he gazed into her tormented eyes. "My beautiful black-haired angel. I'll give you anything you want, my love, anything you ask for."

Anything except your name . . . anything except respectability, she thought bitterly.

Ruark hugged her to him and within seconds the warmth of his body began to calm her cold, quivering flesh. "Say that you'll come with me," he pleaded. He raised her icy hand to his mouth and kissed each fingertip.

Then he lowered his head and covered her mouth with the warm pressure of his lips, rekindling the fire of desire he had ignited within her. As her traitorous body stirred beneath his touch, her beleaguered mind waged a hopeless battle.

The virtues of honor and respectability were weak weapons against the assault of his mouth and hands. The need for his kiss and touch proved greater than any argument her thoughts could summon. He made her feel alive; he excited her; she wanted him.

Pride and self-respect were cold substitutes indeed for the heat of his touch, the fire of his kiss.

Up to this moment, her whole life had been a struggle for survival, and she knew instinctively that survival for her now lay only in his arms. And she was tired of the fight. Tired of self-denial. She wanted this man and the pleasure he brought her.

She loved Ruark Stewart. Pride and self-respect be damned!

Yet tears streaked her cheeks as Angeleen slipped her arms around his neck and parted her lips to meet his kiss.

After Ruark returned to his own room, Angeleen cried herself to sleep. Myra's cool hand on her brow awoke her several hours later.

"I'm sorry to have woken you, dear, but you've slept long into the morning and I was afraid you'd suffered a relapse."

Myra looked long into Angeleen's face, observing the young woman's swollen eyes and saddened features. "You've no fever, miss, but you don't look too good this morning. You just stay in bed and I'll get you a cup of hot tea. That'll help you to feel better, I'm sure."

"I'm fine, Myra, really I am," Angeleen declared and hastily scampered out of bed.

When Myra's eyes remained fixed on the bed, Angeleen looked back and saw what had caught the woman's attention. The sheet was stained from the previous night's lovemaking.

Angeleen started to stammer an explanation but, too mortified to continue, slumped down on the bed. Unable to contain her tears, she buried her face in her hands and began to sob.

Myra sat down on the bed beside her and drew the crying girl into her arms. "Mr. Ruark?"

Angeleen nodded.

"Forgive me, child, it's not my place to pry."

When Angeleen managed to control her sobs, Myra drew up the hem of her apron and dabbed at the young woman's tears. "Now, now, dearie. It's not as bad as all that. You're not the first woman who tried out the honeymoon before the wedding. My mother always said, 'If virtue was easier to practice than sin, why were there more chastity belts than chaste maidens?'

Angeleen smiled weakly, and Myra continued with words of encouragement. "You've no cause for concern. Mr. Ruark's a handsome and persuasive rogue, but he's a good man, dear. He'll make an honest woman of you."

"No, Myra. He doesn't want to marry me. He's asked me to be his mistress. I'm going to New York with him."

"He did, did he?" Myra exclaimed angrily. "The lad's a rogue, and I should turn him over my knee and spank him, just the way I did when he misbehaved as a youngster."

"Ruark believes that I'm a . . . loose woman. That I've known many other men." She glanced up with desperation. "It's not true, Myra. I've never known any other man but my husband."

Myra's eyes widened in surprise. "Lord, child, anyone can tell you're no fallen woman. The man's a fool and should be told as much."

"Promise me you won't tell him anything I've just told you," Angeleen pleaded.

"I couldn't, even if I tried. It's not a fit subject to be discussing with a man. So, I give you my promise, Miss. I'll not say a word to the rogue. Besides, Mr. Ruark will do right by you, I'm sure."

Angeleen knew Ruark would never offer her marriage. He had made his intentions quite clear. Whatever happened next, both of them would have to bear the responsibility.

"I want to go away with him, Myra." Angeleen forced a false smile and hugged the maid. "Thank you, Myra, I'll always be grateful for your keeping my confidence."

For several moments after Angeleen rose and began to gather her clothing, Myra sat on the edge of the bed, stricken with misgiving at her role in the conspiracy. Then she shook her head in bewilderment, rose to her feet, and began to change the soiled sheets on the bed.

Chapter Nine

As she stepped out of the house, Angeleen tightened her cloak around her and strode resolutely down the path. The threadbare garment showed the ravages of many years of wear and did little to ward off the coming winter chill. Although she tried to maintain a determined stride, the nearer she got to the stable the more her courage faltered. However, resolved to get the unpleasant task over with as quickly as possible, she would not be deterred.

When Angeleen entered the stable, Henry was just leading Bold King to the breeding stall. The preparations had been put in motion to have the stallion produce his first progeny.

The mare in heat had been moved to the large breeding stall and was waiting docilely, rigged in the restraining breeding harness that kept her immobile.

Henry stopped for Angeleen to pat her beloved horse. "How's my love this morning?" she cooed in Bold King's ear.

The stallion's ears perked up when the mare's neigh sounded from the nearby stall. Making a sudden move which startled Angeleen, Bold King shied away from her and tried to bolt toward the stall.

"Let the lad go, lass. He has man's work to attend to," Henry said.

Man's work indeed, she thought bitterly. Bold King's eagerness to mount the restrained mare served as a grim reminder of last night when in Ruark's arms she had been as defenseless as the mare and, even more humiliating—*just as willing!*

Absorbed in thought, Angeleen said nothing as Henry removed the bridle from Bold King. "Can't you see I'm busy, lass?" Henry's voice brought her back from her musing, and, for a second, she almost forgot what she wanted to tell him.

"Poppa, I must talk to you."

Henry shook his head. "Canna listen now. Besides, ye should be gone from here," Henry preached as he continued to work. " 'Tis no proper sight for a lady to be viewin'."

"Good heavens, Poppa, I've seen animals breed before." Angeleen opened the door of the stall and Bold King trotted over to the mare. "Who do you think kept Scotcroft going while you were away? I didn't spend the war doing needlepoint in the sitting room," she reminded him sharply.

"No, lass, ye didna. And I'm fearin' ye spent more time in the stable than the drawing room. 'Tis high time ye put those memories aside and return to being a lady, the way your mother intended ye to be."

Angeleen thought his remark the perfect opening to tell him her plans. She turned away and leaned back against the stall. "That's what I came to talk to you about. You're right, Poppa. I mean . . . it *is* time for me to think of the future." Not knowing how else to prepare him, she simply said, "Ruark Stewart has asked me to go to New York with him."

She fully expected a tirade from an angry father. But, preoccupied with his duties, Henry continued to concentrate on the actions of the horses and missed the relevancy of Angeleen's statement.

"Aye, he's a fine gentlemen, but whatever reason would ye be havin' for goin' East with him, lass?" His voice raised in enthusiasm. "Aye, that's a good lad. I knew ye'd nae disappoint us."

Startled, Angeleen glanced up at him and discovered her father's attention still riveted on the horses. She might as well have saved her breath for all his concern, she thought resentfully.

"We can talk about this later," she murmured, disappointed her effort had been for naught.

Discouraged, she started to leave, but Henry stopped her. "Now wait, lass. Dinna run away. The deed here is finished. Now what is it ye be wantin' to tell me?"

Before she could answer, he opened the stall and began to bridle Bold King. "Tomorrow we'll be givin' the other mare her due. If all goes well, next year at this time we'll hae a couple of King's foals prancin' 'round here."

Angeleen glanced hopelessly at her father. What was the use? First Ruark, now her father. In a short span of time she had been made painfully aware of her insignificance in the lives of the two men she loved.

Spurred by injured feelings, and now convinced her father as well as Ruark had betrayed her love, she lashed out blindly.

"I've become Ruark's mistress. And that's why I'm going to New York with him."

This time her effort got results; Henry immediately felt the sting of her message. Shocked by the announcement, the old man stopped his fussing with the stallion and stared numbly at her, uncertain he'd heard her correctly. "What are ye sayin', daughter?"

"I've become Ruark's mistress. I'm going to New York with him," she repeated.

Like most humans, Henry Scott had his faults and weaknesses. But by nature, he was a gentle man and a gentleman for whom a woman's virtue must remain beyond reproach—particularly that of his own daughter, and especially the daughter who was the image of her mother and the joy of his heart.

Not only had the girl thrown away her virtue, the father's pride had been cast asunder. Whatever his failures, Angeleen's strength of character through good times and bad had made up for the foibles and weaknesses that trailed him through life.

However, the heartache of her shocking announcement reached far deeper than just the loss of self-esteem. Angeleen was the last of all whom he had held dearly. The wife he cherished and the son he idolized had been snatched from him—now the daughter he revered had been destroyed, too.

And by her own hand.

Not only had she betrayed a father's trust, she had betrayed her mother's example of purity and devoutness; she had betrayed the honor and love of a brother who had adored her.

The gentle Henry exploded with righteous indignation.

"Nae, daughter. I forbid ye. Hae ye no shame?"

"I'm sorry, Father. I love Ruark and I want to be with him. But he has no intention of marrying me. He told me so."

"And ye still be considerin' goin' wi' him?" he accused her.

"I love him, Poppa. Can't you understand that?" she cried out, desperate for his understanding.

"No decent Southern woman would consider such—such an *abomination*!" Henry shouted. "Thank God yer blessed mother dinna live to see this day."

Her father's words of condemnation lacerated her tender feelings; tears welled up in Angeleen's eyes. He had put the whole burden of guilt on her shoulders. No censure for Ruark—only for her.

"And when he casts ye aside, girl, what then?" he snarled.

"I don't know." She swallowed hard, determined not to concede. "I'll have to face that when the time comes," she finished bravely.

Crestfallen, Henry turned away. His shoulders

slumped in despair as he led Bold King back to his stall. "I suppose ye be thinkin' I should be sharin' some of the blame for the plight ye be in?" Henry challenged querulously.

"I never said that, Father. It's no one's fault but my own. I wouldn't be going with Ruark if I didn't want to."

His eyes gleamed with desperation as he grasped her shoulders. " 'Tis nae too late to change ye mind, child." His softened tone pleaded. "We'll go away. We'll leave this place."

Sadly, she shook her head. "The time for leaving has passed, Poppa. Maybe yesterday I could have left Ruark, but not now. Now it's too late." Her eyes sought for a sign of understanding from him. She had always been able to forgive his shortcomings and misdeeds; now she needed his tolerance.

But all she could see in his eyes were disillusionment and anger.

Henry's features shifted into harshness and his hands slipped from her shoulders. "Then 'tis ye who'll hae to bear the shame ye bring to the name of Scott."

"I know that," Angeleen said sadly. "I'm sorry, Poppa," she whispered as she kissed his cheek. Then Angeleen left her father standing alone and embittered.

Bold King's nicker offered a plaintive farewell to the grief-stricken girl.

Deepening shadows darkened the bedroom when Ruark returned later that day and found Angeleen dejectedly sitting by herself before a cold hearth.

Casting aside the several boxes he carried, Ruark hurried over to the fireplace and knelt down before her.

"What is it, Angel? Aren't you feeling well?"

For several seconds Angeleen stared blankly into his eyes before she finally shook her head and managed a feeble denial. "I'm fine, Ruark."

His relief vanished when he picked up her hand to bring it to his lips. "Good Lord, Angel! Your hand feels like ice."

He took her other hand and pressed them together between his palms. "Why isn't there a fire in here? And where in hell is Myra?"

"Myra?" Her mind groped for the answer.

From the time she had spoken to her father, Angeleen had slipped into an abyss of shame and misery. Ruark's presence drew her slowly back to the present.

"Myra will be gone for a few days. She received a message that her sister is ailing, and she went to help her."

"Well, why didn't you call one of the other servants to build you a fire? Honey, it's freezing in here."

Ruark jumped to his feet and hurried over to the bed. Rummaging haphazardly through the boxes, he extracted a mink tippet. Mink tails dangled from the bottom of the expensive fur cape he wrapped snugly around her shoulders.

He set to building a fire. As he piled up the wood, Ruark cast several worried glances at Angeleen, who remained sitting silently as if he weren't there.

After he had succeeded in starting a steady blaze in the hearth, he returned to Angeleen and knelt before her. His dark eyes gazed worriedly into her wooden stare.

"Sweetheart, tell me what's bothering you. I can't help if you don't tell me." He gathered her into his arms and held her, the warmth of him shrouding the listless girl like a mantle.

Angeleen hadn't realized how cold she was until his warmth drew her back to the awareness of him—and him alone. She relaxed in his arms.

Smiling tenderly, Ruark cupped her face in his hands. For several seconds he gazed into her eyes, trying to read in their depths what her lips refused to reveal. But he was unable to resist the temptation of her nearness and lowered his head.

As soon as Ruark's lips covered her own, the numbness melted, replaced with a heated desire. Whatever her condition, his touch always had the same effect on her.

In the final moments before surrendering her body to him, she realized a truth she had never recognized until this moment—a sense of security when his arms enfolded her, a feeling more powerful than the burning desire she felt for him.

A feeling of love.

Highly attuned to the essence of her, Ruark sensed the instant of her surrender. He shrugged the fur wrap off her shoulders and, laying her back on the rug, stretched out beside her, resting his head on his propped-up arm.

His fingers toyed with a lock of her long hair as he gazed down lovingly at her. "Now tell Daddy all about it," he teased lightly.

"That's the problem. I did tell Poppa all about it," she sighed.

Ruark grinned and she felt her insides knot in response. "Oh, I think I understand now." He leaned down and kissed the tip of her nose. "Henry wasn't happy about your leaving with me."

"To say the least," she replied, trying to draw a breath as he began to unbutton her bodice.

"And just what did you tell him?" Ruark asked, opening the blouse. Her breasts were exposed to his hungry gaze.

"I told him that I—" She caught herself before admitting that she loved him. Knowing what he thought of her, Angeleen guessed her confession of love would only amuse Ruark. She had already suffered enough ridicule for one day.

Hiding her true feelings behind an indifferent smile, she reached up and slipped her arms around his neck. "I told him I was going because I wanted to."

He lowered his head and his tongue began to toy with the sensitive peaks of her breasts. Angeleen closed her eyes as the first tremors shook her body. *And I told him how much I love you*, she cried silently, pressing his head to her breast.

When Henry declined the dinner invitation that evening, Sarah Stewart was the first to question his absence.

"I regret that your father couldn't join us tonight, Angeleen. Is he not feeling well?"

"It isn't that, Mrs. Stewart," Angeleen began hesitantly. She lifted her gaze and met Ruark's. "He . . . ah, doesn't—"

"What Angeleen is trying to say, Nana, is that her father doesn't approve of our relationship."

Sarah Stewart lowered her soup spoon and placed it carefully aside. "Our relationship? Why should he disapprove of a relationship between a grandmother and her grandson? I'm not certain I understand what you mean, Ruark."

Ruark's eyes gleamed with amusement. "Nana, dear, there isn't anything that happens between here and the Mississippi that you aren't informed about through your various sources. So you know as well as I why Henry is upset. He disapproves of his daughter becoming my mistress."

Angeleen felt the burn of mortification sweep her body. She wished she could sink through the floor or run out of the room, anything to get away from that table and avoid having to look into Sarah Stewart's clear blue eyes.

Ruark's suspicions appeared to be well-founded because Sarah showed neither shock nor distress at his remark. She picked up her spoon and gracefully resumed sipping the soup from the bowl before her.

"I would venture to say that the man has a valid argument. One *would* have reason to question the motive behind your treating this child so ignobly, Ruark."

"Nana, I love you devotedly. I would willingly lay down my life for you. But what I won't do is let you interfere in how I live it. Now, shall we continue enjoying this excellent meal that Mary has worked so hard preparing?"

Angeleen had sat through the conversation barely taking a breath. Her hand holding the spoon remained suspended in midair. Ruark winked at her and grinned. "Honey, if you hold up that spoon much longer, your arm's going to fall off."

Had Ruark looked at his grandmother, he would have seen that, whether he liked it or not, Sarah Stewart was determined to have the final word in the matter. Inside her regal, 80-year-old, silver-topped head, a mind as cunning as that of a field general had already begun to plan a stratagem.

As usual, a night in Ruark's arms succeeded in diminishing the reservations that Angeleen or anyone else could raise.

The moment Angeleen opened her eyes the following morning, her mouth curved into a smile at the sight of Ruark's sleeping form beside her.

Her gaze rested lovingly on his face. Relaxed in slumber, he looked like an innocent boy. She tingled with the desire to reach out and run her finger along his full, sensuous lower lip.

Yet she felt too shy, too insecure in their relationship to take such a bold measure. Instead, she slipped out of bed and padded barefoot down the hallway to her own room.

Last night, when Ruark had carried her to his bed, he declared he would have her belongings moved to his room. Angeleen preferred to keep the existing arrangement. She had to have someplace she could call her own, even if it was a room in his house.

After her morning toilette, she donned a black delaine riding habit that Ruark had purchased for her in town. The fitted jacket bodice had a high collar and buttoned down the front to hug her waist.

She took a last critical look in the mirror before pulling on a pair of shiny black boots. Choosing to ignore the silk hat and veil that completed the ensemble, Angeleen had just pulled on white doeskin gloves when a light tap sounded on the door. Barefoot and wearing a maroon robe that reached his calves, Ruark stepped into the room.

"Good morning. I wondered what happened to you."

He took her into his arms and kissed her deeply. Grinning, he stepped back to admire her.

"Look at you, all dressed up for a morning ride. You look ravishing this morning, Mrs. Hunter. Let's have a closer look."

Laughing, Angeleen spun around for his further inspection. "A perfect fit." He smiled approvingly.

"How did you know my size?" she asked. "Even the boots fit."

His dark eyes danced with merriment. "Well, I admit those first things I bought you involved some conjecture on my part, but now . . ." His hands traced a path down her breasts to her waist. " . . . Now I can visualize every inch of that lush body of yours," he whispered huskily and drew her into his arms.

His kiss left her breathless and trembling. She molded herself against the sinewy litheness of him and the feel of his arousal increased her own passion.

In an attempt to put space between her and the temptation, Angeleen drew away. "Ruark, I just got dressed."

Her gaze was drawn to the deviltry glowing in his

135

dark eyes as he pulled her back into his arms, his breath a tantalizing warmth at her ear.

"Then it appears we have two options, Angel. I can get dressed and come with you, or you can get undressed and come with me."

"I will meet you at the stable," she declared firmly. "While you're dressing, I want to talk to my father. We can go for a morning ride and then have breakfast together."

"Sweetheart, I have the same plan in mind, only in a different order. We can go for a morning ride right here, have breakfast together, then while I get dressed, you can go and talk to your father."

Shoving away his hands, which had begun to sweep her boldly, she shook her head. "Ruark, will you please be serious. I have to resolve this problem with my father. It preys on my mind."

Realizing he'd lost the battle, Ruark growled, "Why?"

"I'm his only daughter, Ruark. Can't you understand why he feels the way he does?"

"No, I don't understand. Your father. My grandmother. To hell with their opinions."

He pulled her back into his arms. "Angel, we're good together. So good. You know that. What is so wrong with the life I'm offering you? You won't want for anything. Isn't that better than a life fleecing fools on a riverboat or working a con game?"

"What is so wrong?" she lashed out angrily. "You really don't know, do you? No matter how many times I deny your accusations, you continue to close your eyes and ears to the truth. How can you say we're good together and in the next breath accuse me of being a liar and a whore?"

Ruark stepped back, dumbfounded by her attitude. "What has one thing got to do with the other? I'm not a saint, Angel, and I don't profess to be. I like you. I enjoy your company. And I derive a great deal of"—his brow arched expressively—"secular pleasure from that luscious body of yours. So—as for your soul, that's between you and your maker."

In her hurt and frustration, Angeleen fought the urge to claw the derisive smirk off his face. Her eyes blazed with contempt—a contempt for herself as much as for him.

"You're a hedonistic bastard, Ruark. But I'm sure you've been told that before."

She shoved him away and slammed the door on her way out.

Chapter Ten

Exuberant over Bold King's successful performance with the other mare in heat, Henry had just returned the stallion to his stall when Angeleen entered the stable. His smile faded at the sight of his daughter.

"Poppa, I must talk to you," she pleaded.

"I've work to do, daughter." He turned his back on her and busied himself with the horse.

"Please, Poppa, don't make me beg," she implored.

"Unless ye hae come to tell me ye changed yer sinnin' ways, I hae naught to say." Henry walked away, leaving her standing alone at Bold King's stall.

Brushing aside her tears, Angeleen forced a smile. "Well, King, I guess I'm just not too welcome here these days."

The stallion snorted and nuzzled her cheek in response. She slipped her arms around his neck. "At least *you're* appreciated, boy. Even your offspring will be welcomed."

She stepped back and patted his neck. "Not like mine, King. I've been informed that a 'lying, thieving whore,' would be an unfit mother—at least for any offspring of Mr. Ruark Stewart."

Angeleen halted her discourse when a groom entered the stable and nodded politely in her direction. "Morning, ma'am."

"Good morning. Would you mind saddling Bold King for me?" she said. "And Mr. Stewart's favorite mount as well."

"Yes, ma'am. Right away," he said affably. Angeleen left the stable to wait in the yard. Within minutes the groom brought the saddled stallion out to her.

When the groom returned leading Ruark's chestnut gelding, he looked around in surprise. He saw no sign of Angeleen or Bold King.

To his relief, he saw Ruark Stewart approaching hurriedly. "Your mount, sir. Mrs. Hunter has already left on Bold King."

"Already left?" Ruark exclaimed. "Which trail did she take?"

Discovering her gone, Ruark felt a moment of alarm. He knew Angeleen was upset with him. Then he chided himself for being suspicious. She wouldn't just ride away again. He had to start trusting her.

The groom shrugged his shoulders. "I don't know, sir. I went into the stable to saddle your mount. When I returned, Mrs. Hunter had disappeared." The groom's answer did not help to ease Ruark's

139

anxiety; his apprehension increased and he climbed on the gelding.

Just then Henry approached them, shaking his head. "Darn fool girl's gonna break her neck," he grumbled.

"Are you talking about Angeleen?" Ruark asked.

"Aye." Henry nodded and pointed in the direction of a nearby trail. "She rode past me at a full gallop."

When Ruark took off in pursuit, Henry yelled after him, "Tell that fool girl to mind what she's doin', before she kills herself!" Unwittingly, Henry's previous tone of disgruntlement had been replaced by one of fatherly concern. His face creased in a frown as he watched until Ruark vanished.

Overhead, towering wooded spires intermingled in a wondrous fusion of orange, red, and gold. Humbled by the autumn cathedral, Angeleen reined up Bold King on a hilltop and dismounted. She leaned back against a tree to enjoy the view and reflect on her dismal situation.

In the midst of God's creation, her earthly woes seemed as insignificant as one of the fallen leaves at her feet. However, Angeleen knew that once she rode out of the wooded stand, her problems would loom as tall as the maple she now leaned against.

The sound of thundering hooves broke the tranquil moment. Angeleen sat down and didn't even turn around. She knew the rider would be Ruark.

She cast a cursory glance at him when he dismounted and came over, standing tall above her. He wore fawn-colored trousers, knee-high boots and a black knitted sweater. His dark hair was rumpled from the hard ride. He looked roguish, virile, and irresistible.

Ruark didn't speak, but sat down beside her. Finally, after several moments of silence heavily laden with tension, Ruark reached for her hand.

"Are you still angry with me?"

Angeleen drew a deep sigh and turned to face him. He was like a chameleon; the rugged, virile male now looked like a mischievous boy fretful of being chastised.

"I can't say I'm pleased to see you, Ruark. I would prefer being left alone. I have a great deal to think over."

"Regarding us?" he asked, succinctly.

She nodded and turned her head away from him. Angeleen thought that if she concentrated on the view, perhaps she could ignore the temptation to reach out and brush back the errant strand of rumpled hair on his forehead.

"Get it out, Angel. No sense in trying to hold in what's bothering you."

It took her a breathless moment to reply. "I don't know if I can go through with this, Ruark."

His mouth changed to a line of dismay, which Angeleen did not see, and he said simply, "Oh, I see."

He released her hand and, smiling in mock indignation, began to toy with a leaf. "Your second thoughts have something to do with your father? Or just the smell of my shaving lotion?"

"You're enjoying all this, aren't you, Ruark? It's not quite so amusing to me." She stood up and walked over to stand on the crest of the hill overlooking the Missouri countryside stretched out below.

Suddenly she spun around to face him, her sapphire eyes filled with torment. "Why me, Ruark? You're wealthy, handsome. You could have any woman you wanted. Why me?"

Why indeed!

Ruark Stewart was a paradox; an astute businessman with a Midas touch, he had more than doubled the fortune left to him, but his mastery did not spill over into his dealings with women.

Several earlier, ill-advised romances, coupled with a busy life that required long absences from home, had left Ruark leery of serious romantic entanglements. He avoided attachments with ladies from proper homes, preferring the autonomy of affairs with women of questionable background.

Ruark acknowledged that he needed a woman in his life—*but he did not need a wife.*

He rose to his feet and walked over to her. "I wanted you from the first moment I saw you."

He grasped her shoulders and for an instant she thought he was going to shake her. In a voice faintly laced with anger, he declared, "I'm not forcing you to stay, Angel. You're free to leave anytime you wish."

"I've given up my honor and self-respect. If I'm that weak, where will I find the strength to leave you?"

She tried to turn away, but he tilted up her chin to meet the full impact of his dark eyes. "Make the decision, once and for all. This is the last time I'll discuss it. I don't want any regrets, Angel. If you stay, you stay because you want to."

Ruark released her and strode back to his horse. After swinging himself into the saddle, he glanced back at her. For an instant their gazes locked. In the quick exchange between them, Angeleen recognized the same inflexible look she had seen on his face the night he decided he wanted Bold King: a look of grim, unrelenting determination.

She felt a sinking feeling in her breast. He had won that battle, too.

Ruark prodded the gelding to a gallop.

Long after his departure, Angeleen sat under the tree reflecting on his words. She knew he was right about one thing; she had to make up her mind. Furthermore, if she intended to remain with him, she must make that commitment to herself as well as to him and stop wallowing in guilt and self-pity. Yes, self-pity, Angeleen thought, disgusted with her mood and her station in life. After all, Ruark was offering her only a brief relationship—a fleeting chance at happiness.

And isn't all happiness fleeting? she reflected. No one knows what tomorrow will bring. War and pestilence aren't the only catastrophes in life. *Besides, just because he doesn't love me, doesn't make my love for him less honest. And just because I'm not his wife doesn't make my love for him less pure.*

She got to her feet and walked over to Bold King. "You got an opinion, King? You might as well tell me, everyone else has."

The stallion nuzzled her cheek. Laughing, Angeleen stepped away and patted the horse's neck.

"Well, you can't complain about the way *you've* been treated. Ruark Stewart has been good to you."

Her words unveiled a kernel of truth, and she stopped the petting to stare in muddled thought. "He's been good to *all* of us, King. You, me, Poppa. He nursed me through my sickness, and he's hired Poppa to be your trainer. He didn't have to do all that. He could have had us arrested as he threatened to do."

Bold King nickered and shoved his muzzle into her hand. She resumed stroking him. "But his being good to us isn't my only reason for wanting to stay, King." She hesitated in order to formulate the words she needed to say aloud. "I love him. He's gentle; he's kind; and he can be very sensitive when he wants to be. And he makes me smile, King."

Her voice dropped to almost a whisper. "He makes my heart smile."

Grimacing, she shook aside her romanticizing. "That is, when he doesn't make it ache. But I never said he was perfect, King. He's a horrible judge of character—at least where I'm concerned. And once he gets an idea in his head, there's just no convincing him to the contrary."

Lovingly, she stroked the long neck of the animal. "And even if he doesn't love me, he makes me feel loved."

She grasped the horse's bridle and looked into the stallion's round eyes. "You know what that means to a woman, King? To feel loved by a man?"

A snort and a haughty toss of his head drew her light laughter. "No, I guess you wouldn't know. You men are all alike."

The words echoed in her head and the smile left her lips. "Come to think of it, you men aren't all alike. My horrible, cowardly husband, for instance. Ruark is everything Will Hunter wasn't."

The comparison triggered affirmation; she was not going to give up Ruark.

No more doubts. No more soul-searching. No more guilt.

She climbed into the saddle. Her mind was made up. Ruark was more important to her than appeasing the conventions of a hypocritical society or placating the dictates of a stubborn old man who preached the credo, "do as I say, not as I do."

"And I'm going to tell Poppa that, too!" she declared.

Henry knew he was in for a battle the moment Angeleen strode into the stable. He had seen the set of that chin and those shoulders often enough to know when she was about to unleash one of her wrathful tongue lashings.

Just like her grandmother, he thought sullenly. Henry grabbed the tack he was mending and headed for the door.

"Oh, no you don't, Poppa." Her voice cut the air like the crack of a bullwhip.

"Dinna use that sharp tongue on me, woman. I've nae a mind for it," he volleyed.

"You're not leaving until I say what I came here to say."

Henry crossed his arms, his eyes sparked with irritation. "Well, then say it and be done with it."

Seeing he had finally capitulated enough to listen to her, Angeleen softened her tone. "I've been doing a lot of thinking in the past few days, Poppa."

"But naught to any good, I'm thinkin'," he scoffed.

"Poppa, I'm sorry I've disappointed you, and I'm sorry you think I've dishonored your name. You believe, just because Ruark won't marry me, that I didn't use my head when I decided to stay with him. Well, maybe I didn't, but I used my heart, Poppa, and there's no dishonor in that. If I *didn't* love Ruark and remained with him, then what you said, and those names you called me, would all be true.

"If you don't understand what I'm telling you, then you don't love me, have never loved me. You don't know what love is all about."

"Nay, lass, ye canna say that," Henry denied, somewhat subdued and amazed by her words. How could she believe he didn't love her?

"Well, when you love someone, Poppa, there's no way of loving just the part of them that's good."

She took his hand and Henry did not try to withdraw it. "Poppa, you were always my hero. No matter what you did, it never affected my love for you.

"Momma and Robert didn't stop loving you when you gambled away all our money, including what Momma had saved to send Robert to college up North."

Henry hung his head, but offered a denial. "I just dinna want my son goin' to any Yankee college."

The outrageous alibi brought a gentle smile to her lips. "Poppa, that was years before we fought the Yankees."

"But I knew that someday we would," Henry parried.

"Oh, Poppa!" Angeleen said tolerantly. "What about your mortgaging Scotcroft to buy an expensive racing colt you fancied?"

This time Henry had a stronger defense and wasted no time giving it. "And nary a soul loves that horse more than ye do."

"But, Poppa, we couldn't afford him. We never recovered from it. Things only got worse after that. Even when King was finally old enough to race, you gambled away the winnings. But Momma didn't love you any less, did she?"

"So ye be sayin' we lost Scotcroft because of me sportin' ways. Next, I'm thinkin', ye'll be blamin' me for the war."

Angeleen took a deep breath. She was about to tell him the most important thing she had come to say. "No, Poppa. I'm trying to say you don't stop loving someone because they have weaknesses."

A trace of his former impishness slipped into his smile. "So ye be sayin' the Good Lord loves his black sheep, too."

"And if He's forgiving, can't you be too, Poppa?"

Henry conceded defeat.

However, Angeleen did not yet recognize that further argument was unnecessary. She marshaled her thoughts for the final plea. "Momma's gone. Robert's gone. All we have is each other, Poppa. I'll love you until the day I die, and if I've destroyed your love, I'm sorry. But that's not going to keep me from staying with Ruark. And if I get hurt—well, I'm the one who'll have to bear that hurt."

She had gone too far. Henry was shocked, indignant, and outraged. "Ye dinna know anything about lovin'. Are ye thinkin' a man doesna hurt when his child is hurtin'?" His eyes glistened with tears. "If ye be hurtin', lass, dinna ye think I'd be hurtin' with ye?"

"Oh, Poppa." Henry opened his arms. Sobbing, she rushed into them.

As Henry held her, he patted her head. "I dinna want to see ye life ruined, like I ruined ye mother's."

Angeleen smiled at him through her tears. "Poppa, Momma loved you and she knew that you loved her. She didn't have any regrets."

Henry's arms tightened around her. "Forgive me, lass, for I'm nae but a foolish old man. I only want ye to be happy."

"Then I can go East with your blessing?"

Henry stepped back, his eyes glowing with the warmth of his love. "I dinna say that, lass. I canna gie ye my blessin' knowin' the day will come when ye'll be hurt by Ruark Stewart. But I'll gie ye my love, lass. 'Twill go with ye always."

As she left the stable, Angeleen hastened to tell Ruark. Seeing no sign of him in his study, she hurried up the stairway. She found his bedroom empty too.

Disappointed to have missed him, she returned to her own room. Brooding in silence until midday, Angeleen responded politely when the serving maid tapped on the door to inform her that lunch was ready. Angeleen hoped Ruark had returned, but instead, she and Sarah Stewart shared a quiet meal.

"Aren't you feeling well, my dear?" Sarah asked. "You've been so quiet."

"Oh, I'm sorry, Mrs. Stewart. I guess my mind's elsewhere. I apologize."

"Indeed, I do understand, my dear. It must be difficult to contain your excitement knowing you'll be leaving tomorrow."

Angeleen realized that she had been so preoccupied with other problems, she had not given the details of the trip serious thought.

"Have you finished packing?" Sarah asked.

"I'm afraid I haven't even started. I haven't much to pack, so it won't be a problem."

"I'm going to miss the two of you, but Ruark has promised to return for the Christmas holidays." Sarah's eyes twinkled with warmth. "Besides, a month in New York is more time than enough."

Angeleen giggled with pleasure. The old woman was delightful. "Then you've been there before, Mrs. Stewart?"

"Lord, child, 'Mrs. Stewart,' sounds so formal. Why don't you call me, 'Nana Sarah.'"

"Have you been to New York before, Mrs.—Nana Sarah?"

"Oh, yes. My husband was a sea captain. I often accompanied him on his voyages."

"A sea captain! How exciting," Angeleen exclaimed.

"You wouldn't say so if you knew the whole story. The darn fool let himself get killed. Went down with his ship during a storm off Cape Hatteras."

Angeleen felt as if she had just committed a *faux pas*. However, Sarah appeared not to mind.

149

"Oh, what a man he was, my dear. I can still see him standing tall and straight at the helm of his vessel." Her face creased with a poignant smile. "And that rogue, Ruark, is the very image of his grandfather."

Sarah's mind slipped back again to a bygone day. Angeleen smiled fondly as she watched the shifting emotions on the woman's face and began to imagine how incredibly interesting Sarah Stewart's life must have been.

After a lengthy pause, Sarah wiped a tear from her eye. "Forgive an old lady, my dear." She smiled impishly. "You see how it is; we old ladies tend to spend most of our time sleeping or boring people by relating our past."

"I'm not bored, Nana Sarah," Angeleen said kindly as she patted the fragile, blue-veined hand lying on the table. "It's easy to tell, just by the way you say his name, that you loved your husband very much."

"That I did, girl." Sarah gazed deeply at Angeleen. The blue-eyed stare seemed to probe the soul of the younger woman. "I adored my Charles. I cherish the memory of every moment I spent with him. I loved him dearly—the way you love Ruark."

Angeleen felt the hot blush. "I never said . . . I mean, I didn't think . . . ." Flustered, her faltering denial revealed her true feelings. "How did you guess?"

Sarah smiled and clasp Angeleen's hand. "These old eyes have seen a great deal of life, child. My grandson may be a fool—but I'm not."

This shared intimacy with Ruark's grandmother and the woman's understanding helped to relax

Angeleen. She returned to her room with a lighter step, eager for Ruark's return.

Later that day, Ruark sent a message that he had been detained on business and would not be home for dinner. The continued delay only added to Angeleen's disappointment.

After the evening meal, Sarah and Henry sat before the fireplace while Angeleen dallied at the piano.

"Oh, how I used to love to play," Sarah told Henry. "But, alas, my fingers are no longer as limber as they once were. My Charles would sit for hours, just listening."

"Aye, the lass's mother played beautifully, too," Henry offered nostalgically. "It warmed me heart to hear her golden melodies."

Lost in thoughts of Ruark, Angeleen played on, wishing he would return soon. She had so much to tell him.

After several more selections, Angeleen turned around to discover both her father and Sarah dozing in their chairs.

Angeleen tiptoed out of the room without disturbing the sleeping pair. She knew the maid would soon come to assist Sarah to bed and that Henry would return to the room he preferred above the stable. She went back to her own room to wait for Ruark.

Everyone had retired for the night when Angeleen heard Ruark arrive home. She followed the sound of his footsteps as he walked down the hallway and entered his room. Waiting expectantly, she heard him come back and pause at her darkened door. Surprised—and disappointed—she heard him return to his room.

Angeleen got out of bed and began to pace the floor. Was he angry with her? Dammit! Here she had done all that soul-searching today; she was ready to tell him her decision, but he didn't appear to be interested enough to hear her out.

She stopped pacing as a mischievous gleam appeared in her eyes. Well, she would find out just how uninterested he was.

Angeleen quickly shed her nightgown and slipped on the blue gown Ruark had bought her. Her eyes widened with shock and her mouth gaped open when she saw herself in the mirror. She might as well be naked! Her breasts and the dark patch of hair at her legs were clearly outlined through the transparent gown.

"Myra was right, Ruark Stewart. You are a shameful rogue," she murmured.

She brushed her hair until it hung past her shoulders in a long, satiny sheen, then stepped back for another inspection.

"I can't do this," she said as her modesty warred with her courage.

She turned away to pull off the gown, then stopped and looked at herself again. No, she would do it. After all, she loved him. What was the shame in . . . seducing him?

She gave her hair another quick pass with the brush, saw her mirror image smile in approval, and bravely murmured, "He loves my hair."

The thought served to bolster her courage, and she reached for the tiny crystal phial of perfume Ruark had given her. After putting a dab behind each ear, she ran the stopple of the phial across the cleavage of her breasts and stepped back for a final inspection.

"Well, what do you think?" she asked her image.

She didn't wait for the answer.

Angeleen stepped into Ruark's room and softly closed the door, then leaned back against the solid wood to help fortify her resolve.

Bent over, apathetically tossing clothing into a trunk, Ruark had not seen her enter, but after a few seconds he sensed her presence and turned his head, sucking in his breath at the sight of her. As he straightened up, his gaze slowly swept her up and down. Unnoticed, the shirt he held slipped through his fingers and dropped into the trunk.

"Do you need any help with your packing?" she asked in a throaty murmur.

A dark brow arched. "I'm going to need a lot of help with it, if you hang around too long in that gown."

"Would you like me to leave?" The sheer gown undulated in swirling folds around her legs and bare feet as she moved toward him.

"Lady, you're free to do whatever you wish to do."

Angeleen found his reply unnerving. Had she more confidence in herself, she would have recognized his remark as an invitation, not a rejection. But she had come too far to turn back now.

Wearing neither coat nor vest, his cravat dangling loosely around the opened collar of his shirt, Ruark waited for her response.

Angeleen reached up, pulled off the tie and drop-ped it on the floor. "I missed you tonight." She began to release the studs on his shirt. "I expected you to come back earlier."

"That's interesting. I missed you, too, and I *expected* to find you here when I got back."

Angeleen laughed lightly and slipped the shirt off his shoulders and arms. "What do you mean? I've been here all evening."

She trailed her mouth across his chest and stopped at a nipple. Her tongue lightly played with the nub, then the other one.

"Not here in my room—not here in my bed," he rasped hoarsely, unable to ignore the sensation she was creating. "I thought you might have made up your mind to leave me." He didn't tell her that he couldn't bear to open her bedroom door because he feared she was gone.

She felt the first measure of irritation. Lifting her head, she spread her arms out to her sides, her eyes flashed dangerously. "Do I look dressed to leave?"

His attitude proved more mortifying and exasperating than she could bear. Here she stood practically naked, offering herself before him, while he coolly argued the context of her words and idly mused on her departure.

"As a matter of fact, now that you mention it, leaving does sound like a good idea. I've stood here long enough freezing my bare buttocks off."

She spun around and headed toward the door.

Angeleen didn't take more than two steps when his arms locked around her waist and he pulled her back against him.

"You just said you weren't dressed to leave," he murmured in a husky whisper at her ear. The breath caught in her throat when his lips slid down the column of her neck.

His hands slid over her full breasts and up to her shoulders. She shuddered and relaxed against him. Closing her eyes, she tipped her head to the side to allow his lips more freedom.

He slipped off the straps of her gown and pressed warm kisses across her shoulders, then down the center of her back. Her legs trembled so much that she could barely stand, and he turned her in the circle of his arms. The gown fell to the floor in a heap at their feet.

"You're so beautiful, Angel. So beautiful," he rasped.

Her anger dissolved with the first touch of his lips. She rose on her toes and slipped her arms around his neck. He cupped her rear in his hands and lifted her as she wrapped her legs around his waist.

The taut nipples of her breasts were crushed against his bare chest as she kissed him, pressing deeper and deeper against him. He backed up until his legs struck the bed and he fell back with her still cleaved to him.

This new and exciting position exhilarated her. The smell of him heightened her passion, driving her to greater boldness.

She wanted to feel him in her.

She slithered down the length of him, her tongue and fingers trailing a path down his chest until her knees touched the floor. His trousers blocked her passage, so she opened them and slid them down his long legs that dangled over the edge of the bed.

His arousal strained at his drawers and she freed it, shoving the underpants and trousers off his ankles.

Clutching her shoulders, he sat up. "Angel," he groaned.

Unable to withstand her another moment, he swooped her up and threw her on the bed, covering her with the long, muscular hardness of his body as his mouth devoured her lips. His tongue probed and stroked like a heated poker that drove again and again into her mouth until she was breathless.

Her seduction had pushed passion to lust. His hands and mouth ravished her heaving breasts, the curves and hollows of her body, nibbling, suckling and stroking as she writhed and groaned beneath him.

In a final assault, his hands parted her thighs. His mouth and tongue explored and probed the core of her being and her body throbbed under wave upon wave of tremors.

Driven to mindless sensualism, she sobbed his name, pleading for mercy. Then she cried out in rapturous ecstasy when he raised himself up and entered her.

Linked together as one, they shared the final exquisite moment that hovered between madness and the sublime.

Chapter Eleven

From the moment they left St. Louis, the problems that had plagued Angeleen and Ruark were forgotten. Like honeymooners, they laughed and loved throughout the day and night. They played cards, backgammon, and chess. They read to one another, they bathed together, they explored each other's bodies—a modern Adam and Eve in a rolling Eden of iron and steel that was Paradise nonetheless to the enamored couple.

By the time the train tugging Ruark's private railroad car reached the city of New York, there was nothing they hadn't learned about pleasing each other.

Gawking in awe, Angeleen peered out of the carriage window at the crowded, bustling city and felt as if she had entered a different world.

With his hand on her elbow, Ruark guided her into the lobby of their opulent hotel as a porter followed with their luggage. Soon they were ensconced in a suite that offered not only a bedroom, but the added luxury of a sitting room and a private chamber with a privy and bathtub.

While Ruark attended business meetings having to do with his investments, Angeleen passed the time strolling the streets, peering into shop windows. She dared not window-shop with Ruark because whatever she admired, he would buy. Countless cartons and boxes from couturiers, furriers, and boutiques were already stacked in the suite.

She still couldn't get used to the sight of such abundant luxuries. After enduring a four-year involuntary "abstinence" while the Union blockade prevented the import of such necessities as food and medical supplies, Angeleen could not believe that the North was unscathed, continuing to enjoy great luxury, including the latest Parisian fashions.

She had, indeed, stepped into a new and different world.

And so the precious weeks were spent, exploring the shops, bistros, and landmarks of New York—and reveling in the arms of her passionate lover.

"How are we ever going to get all the purchases we made back to St. Louis?" Angeleen laughed gaily as she and Ruark left Macy's department store. They had spent the afternoon shopping for gifts for her father and the servants.

"I know Poppa will love the vest we bought him," she exclaimed. One month had passed since their arrival. The Christmas season was upon them, and they would soon be returning to Missouri.

Enjoying the day as much as she, Ruark grinned down at her. Angeleen's enthusiasm made everything they did together more pleasurable than he had ever known—from making love to the fundamental task of shopping, a chore he had loathed in the past.

A bonnet in the window of a milliner's caught her curiosity. When she stopped to admire the cumbersome red velvet hat bearing two white plumes, Ruark immediately voiced his opinion. "I hope you're not considering hiding your beautiful hair under that hideous thing."

"Well, it is improper for a lady to promenade in the daytime without a hat, Ruark," she replied.

"Who says so?" he asked with authority and then answered his own question. "Prune-faced old dowagers trying to distract attention from their wrinkles and sour looks." He raised a hand and lightly traced a finger along her chin and the curve of her cheek. "You've got nothing to hide, Angel."

As his voice and eyes caressed her, Angeleen felt herself responding to him, as she always did. "I want to make love to you," he said in a husky murmur.

"Ruark Stewart, that indecent look in your eyes could get you arrested," she teased, but her tone belied the depth of her response.

"Let's get back to the hotel. Now," he said urgently, and raised a hand to flag down a passing carriage.

Ruark undressed her as soon as the door of their suite closed behind them.

The next day as they ate breakfast, Ruark's attention remained fixed on the morning newspaper. Finally, shaking his head in disgust, he tossed the paper aside.

"It will be a blessing to get back to Missouri," he grumbled.

"I gather the news is all good this morning," Angeleen commented wryly as she popped a section of grapefruit into her mouth.

"Nothing out of the ordinary for New York." He leaned back in the chair, closed his eyes, and casually listed the latest events.

"President Johnson is still fighting the Civil War with the Republicans in Congress, even though the damn thing ended eight months ago. The police found another body of a young woman who had been raped and mutilated, the third in as many weeks. Four people died in a tenement fire, two of them infants. A five-year-old boy was trampled to death by a runaway horse and carriage, and the longshoremen are threatening to walk off the docks if they have to work side by side with Negroes."

"And the market, Mr. Stewart?"

"Is down," he grumbled as his eyes snapped open.

"That's probably what's bothering you the most," she challenged him, trying to tease him out of his black mood. She got up and walked over to him, leaned down, and kissed his cheek.

Ruark pulled her onto his lap for a long, lingering kiss. "That helped," he grinned when they broke apart.

Angeleen ran her hand along the stubble on his chin. "You need a shave," she complained. She sat up. "Do you want me to shave you this morning?"

He eyed her with speculation. "You wouldn't cut my throat this close to Christmas, would you?"

"Oh mercy no, me lord," she answered as she hopped off his lap, pleased that he had not denied her request.

"The water is still hot in the ewer." She hurried into the bedroom, happily contemplating her assignment, and poured a basin of water, then gathered up his razor, shaving mug, and several towels.

Angeleen shoved aside the breakfast dishes to make room for the shaving equipment. With a dramatic flourish, she shook out a towel and tucked it around his neck.

After soaking a washcloth in the hot water, she wrung the cloth out and covered his face. Then she poured a small measure of the water into the shaving mug and stirred it with the brush until foamy suds appeared. Removing the wash cloth, she painted his face with the soapy lather.

"So far, so good," Ruark said.

With light, deft strokes, Angeleen began to scrape his cheek with the sharp edge, dipping the razor repeatedly into the water to rinse off the soap.

"You're very skilled at shaving a man. You must have had a lot of experience," he commented as his initial pleasure suddenly turned to resentment. However, he did not recognize the deep feeling of jealousy he had for the other men she'd known; he felt only anger rising within him.

Unsuspecting, Angeleen continued at the task. "My brother once broke his arm and I had to shave him."

As much as he would have liked to believe her,

suspicion gnawed at his insides. What about her husband? What about this Robert she loved so deeply? "I thought all you Southern gals had house slaves to do such duties," he disputed.

"Ruark, we only had a few darkies at Scotcroft. They had too much to do to waste their time on that kind of task."

Ruark accepted the rebuke, but his mood remained sullen. "You rarely speak of your brother. Was he younger than you?"

"No, he was older. His name was—"

"Don't tell me, let me guess. Having met your father, it could only have been 'Laddie,'" he said mockingly.

His cynicism riled her to anger. Water splashed in all directions when she furiously tossed the razor into the water. "Shave your own damned face. And I hope you cut your throat in the process." She stormed into the bedroom, making a point of slamming the door behind her.

Ruark wiped the soap off his face as he bolted to his feet and followed her into the bedroom. Angeleen stood with her arms crossed on her chest, staring out of the window.

Ruark walked up behind her and pulled her back against him. "I'm sorry, Angel. I'm in a foul mood this morning. Must have gotten up on the wrong side of the bed."

Angeleen fought to quell her anger. "I should finish up my business in the next couple of days. We can shop for Nana's gift this afternoon and with any luck head for home the day after tomorrow. How does that sound to you?"

She turned in his arms, her anger abated. "I'd like that, Ruark."

His fingers tipped up her chin and he lightly kissed her. "And don't forget, we're going to a Christmas ball tonight."

Angeleen nodded, and Ruark kissed her again. This time the kiss was deeper and longer. Breathless, she looked at him adoringly when he released her.

While she dressed, he finished shaving. "I should be back in about four hours." He grinned engagingly. "I'm truly sorry, honey."

As soon as she was certain a safe amount of time had elapsed after his departure, Angeleen pulled on her cloak, picked up a muff, and left the hotel.

These few hours might be her last opportunity to buy him a Christmas gift. Although she had a few dollars, it was not enough to buy the gift she had decided upon. Since she wanted to surprise him and couldn't very well ask him for the money to buy the gift, Angeleen had decided to sell the pair of pearl earrings he had given her, hoping Ruark would not notice they were gone.

Once on the street, Angeleen sought the advice of a policeman. The lawman was quite surprised when she asked him for directions to the nearest pawnbroker.

The promise of snow hung heavily in the air as Angeleen hurried down the street, the chilling wind carrying a misty spray of cold seawater. She tightened her cloak around her and dug her hands deeper into the Persian lamb muff she carried, the earrings clutched securely in one hand.

Her steps led her to a shadier section of the city then she had seen before, and now thoroughly chilled, Angeleen regretted she had not taken a carriage.

She felt uneasy as she looked around at the dingy buildings. The cold weather had driven people inside and the street seemed deserted. As if to ward off her uneasiness, Angeleen pulled her cloak even tighter around her.

She was about to turn back when she spied the three golden balls in the front of the pawn shop. Relieved, she hurried into the tiny store.

The walls were lined with shelves holding dust-laden relics, once cherished items to the poor unfortunates forced to part from them. The old man who sat at a rickety desk eyed her with curiosity through glasses perched on the end of his nose. His crafty glance assessed the garment she wore. The long, gray paletot with deep scollops that hung to her knees was of the latest style and made of the finest wool.

Angeleen's appraisal of him was not as favorable. *I see all the carpetbaggers didn't go South*, she thought to herself as she observed the gleam in his shifty eyes.

Reluctantly, she pulled her hand out of the muff and laid the earrings on the counter before him. "I would like to sell these earrings, if you please."

The pawnbroker removed his spectacles, pulled out an eye glass from his vest pocket, and examined one of the earrings.

She waited impatiently as he did the same to the other. Then, after a surreptitious glance in her direction, the shopkeeper re-examined the jewelry.

"Twenty-five dollars," he said.

"Twenty-five dollars!" she exclaimed. "But they are real pearls. They're worth ten times as much." Indignant, she started to pick up the earrings.

"Fifty dollars. That's my top price."

Desperation led her to acquiesce. "All right." Angeleen returned the earrings to the counter top. "But you're practically stealing them."

He unlocked a drawer and counted out the currency. "Money is scarce. We just got over a war, you know," the pawnbroker said to excuse his thievery.

"And just how would you know?" she snorted. She snatched up the money and stomped out before the merchant could conjure a reply.

Near the hotel, she stopped at the jeweler's and bought Ruark the gold watch fob patterned in the shape of a horse that she had been admiring for weeks.

"You've made a fine purchase, madam," the jeweler said as he wrapped the gift.

Angeleen took the tiny package and returned to the hotel. The gift had been cleverly concealed by the time Ruark returned to their suite.

Ruark greeted her with a bear hug, lifted her off her feet, and swung her in a circle. "Sweetheart, I've got great news," he exclaimed after kissing her and putting her down. "T. J.'s in town."

"T. J.," she said, humoring him.

"T. J. Graham. My best friend," he declared in reply to her puzzled look. "Put on your best bib and tucker because I told him we would meet him at Delmonico's for lunch."

165

"Ruark, I'm sure you would rather have this reunion without me," she said considerately. "Why don't you go alone to meet your friend? The two of you can talk over old times."

Ruark shook his head. "Wouldn't think of it. Neither would T. J. He's anxious to meet you."

Angeleen couldn't imagine why this friend of Ruark's would want to meet her. "And just why is he so anxious?" she asked.

Ruark cleared his throat. "Well . . . ah, all through college T. J. and I had this . . . ah, rivalry. We always went after the other's girl. Once, he even wooed away the girl I was engaged to."

Angeleen was appalled. "Ruark, you *boys* are no longer in college. And I'm certainly not interested in becoming a pawn in your childish rivalries. So just go and meet your friend without me."

"Angel, that's not the only reason I want you to come. You've been alone all day. I can't expect you to spend your whole day cooped up in a hotel room."

Angeleen didn't dare mention her earlier errand, but she continued to resist. "Ruark, I'm a big girl. I've been alone before. If it will set your mind at rest, I'll go shopping for your grandmother's Christmas gift."

"No, we'll do that together, the way we planned." He took her hands in his. "Honey, I want you to come. We'll meet T. J., have a quick lunch, and then finish our shopping."

She eyed him coyly, if somewhat skeptically. "If this T. J. is as irresistible as you say, are you hoping that history will repeat itself?"

His face sobered and he cupped her face in his

hands. For an endless moment, his dark eyes probed the depth of her sapphire gaze. "No, Angel. I'm hoping that this time T. J. will meet his Waterloo."

T. J. Graham rose to his feet as soon as Angeleen entered Delmonico's on the arm of Ruark Stewart.

T. J. would have been brought to his feet whether Ruark Stewart accompanied Angeleen or not. He thought her to be the most beautiful women he had ever seen.

Angeleen blushed under the man's unwavering stare as Ruark made the introductions. Ruark had not exaggerated the man's effect on women. There was an aura of excitement about him, and she found herself hypnotized by the dark, coffee-colored eyes smiling into hers. He did not have Ruark's suave or manly handsomeness, but his dark looks had a roguish appeal that quickly engaged the female heart.

He stood as tall as Ruark, but whereas Ruark's body was lithe and muscular, T. J. Graham had a rugged, virile appearance. Were it not for the coat and trousers custom-fitted to his broad shoulders and tapering waist, he could easily be mistaken for a lumberjack or sailor.

Indeed, Angeleen was startled when Ruark introduced him as *Doctor* Graham.

"Doctor Graham," she acknowledged, swallowing her astonishment.

"It's a pleasure, Mrs. Hunter." T. J. brought her hand to his lips.

The moment he touched her, Angeleen knew, with a woman's intrinsic wisdom, that this man could never be more than just a friend to her. She lifted her head and offered him a dazzling smile.

"Have your friends always called you T. J., Doctor Graham?"

"Until now, Mrs. Hunter, when you addressed me as Doctor Graham."

His charm was infectious and she laughed lightly. "If you object to my formality, then I demand the same consideration from you. I insist that you call me, Angeleen. And if you prefer, I'll call you, T. J."

Ruark felt uneasy. He remembered that Angeleen had not welcomed such informality when they first met on the *Delta Queen*. *Is T. J.'s charm affecting her?* Ruark wondered, *or is she deliberately playing up to T. J. to make me jealous? Dammit, why did I even say anything to her about a rivalry? Now I'll never know for certain.*

He glared in disgust at the two. They seemed so engrossed in each other that he doubted either one would notice if he got up and left.

Angeleen began to sip from a glass of wine. "Just what do the initials T. J. stand for?" she asked, smiling at T. J. over the top of her glass.

"Thomas Jefferson," he replied.

Angeleen's sapphire eyes widened in surprise. "Thomas Jefferson! Why, Mr. Jefferson was a Virginian."

"And so am I, Angeleen."

She cast a look of displeasure at Ruark. "Ruark never told me his friend was a Virginian," Angeleen said. "Did you fight for the Confederacy?"

T. J. nodded. "Yes, ma'am."

That was probably all the little Rebel vixen needed

to hear, Ruark thought desolately. He took a deep swallow of wine.

"I'm sure there are many things he hasn't told you about our friendship, Angeleen. I would be glad to relate them all to you," he offered intimately.

"I'm sure you would," Ruark gritted through clenched teeth. He wondered why he had been so happy to see his old friend—the same bastard who had stolen the affections of his betrothed!

"I don't think I want to hear them." Angeleen's glance shifted to Ruark. "I have no ties to Ruark's past." She paused momentarily as their gazes locked. An unspoken message passed between them. "Or any hold on his future."

T. J. thought the remark unusual, to say the least, and wondered what mystery lay between the two. They obviously had a deep attraction for each other, yet both tried to disguise it. Ruark was visibly disturbed. T. J. had never seen his friend look this troubled, even over his broken engagement to Melanie Merryweather. *Good God!* T. J. thought. *Could it be this time Ole Ruark is really in love? If so, why didn't he say so?* They had a lot of catching up to do.

However, the waiter arrived to serve their food and the conversation shifted to a lighter vein. Nevertheless, throughout the meal, T. J.'s gaze continually returned to rest on Angeleen's face.

Chapter Twelve

By the time they left the restaurant, the earlier promise of snow had materialized. Under a steady traffic of people and carriages, the falling white flakes had been reduced to slush. T. J. gave Angeleen a quick kiss on the cheek, the two men shook hands, and Ruark hustled her into a carriage.

On the ride back to the hotel, Ruark brooded in silence and stared down at his feet. Angeleen stole several glances at him, but he might as well have been alone; her presence appeared to be forgotten.

She peered out the carriage window and tried to concentrate on the people scurrying along the sidewalk. But her thoughts continually returned to the silent figure staring pensively at the floor.

Ruark was in such a strange mood—had been all

day, she thought. Her body trembled with a feeling of insecurity. Was his mood because of her? Had he tired of her already? Had Ruark forced the meeting with T. J. hoping his friend would take her off his hands?

Angeleen closed her eyes to force back her tears. She told herself she wouldn't cry. After all, she'd known that one day Ruark would leave her. She just hadn't expected it would be so soon.

Or just how much it would hurt.

Ruark stopped the carriage at the jeweler's, and for a brief time the troubled thoughts of the pair were diffused as they put their heads together to pick out a gift for Sarah Stewart. After much deliberation, they decided upon a cameo to be carved out of white jade.

The jeweler agreed to have the pin ready by the following day and they left the store in slightly better spirits. Some of the earlier tension had eased, but neither could recapture the relaxed feeling of intimacy they had shared for the past few weeks.

The estrangement became even more evident when they arrived at the hotel. The once spacious suite suddenly became too small for the two of them.

They were overly polite to each other, avoided being in the same room together, and found themselves hugging the walls as they moved about, to avoid direct physical contact.

Each stayed scrupulously clear of the vicinity of the tub while the other bathed. But despite all these precautions, the young couple ultimately found themselves in the same bedroom, at the same time, dressing for the ball.

Much to Angeleen's dismay, her corset strings knotted and after several moments of useless struggling, she was forced to break her silence.

"Ruark, will you help me with these corset strings?"

In a stage of semi-dress himself, wearing black trousers with his shirt tails hanging loose, Ruark walked over in stocking feet to assist her.

"Why do you wear one of these gadgets?" he grumbled as he attempted to untangle the strings. "You don't need one."

"It would be improper not to," she replied. "Your friends have enough to say about me without adding more fuel to the fire."

"There you go again—*the scandalous Mrs. Hunter*," he mocked.

"Oh, Ruark, you know as well as I that all of the women are insulted by my presence. They don't want me at the ball."

"Well, I do," he declared, sounding like a petulant child demanding his own way. He gave the corset strings a final tug, causing her to gasp, and then he tied them firmly.

In the true nature of lovers, the suspicions and jealousies that the young couple were unable to voice now emerged as anger toward one another.

She turned to face him, unmindful of the assault her appearance made on his manhood.

Her black hair hung like a satin mantle to the middle of her back. Lace-trimmed drawers fell to just below the knees of her long, slim legs encased in white hose, and the short, silk corset that pinched her waist thrust up her breasts into a seductive cleavage.

Angeleen's sapphire eyes flashed like blue gems. Her tiny foot, shod in a black satin pump fetchingly adorned with a red tulle coquille, tapped an angry staccato on the bare floor.

"And Ruark Stewart always gets what he wants, no matter who doesn't like it," she accused him loudly.

"You're damned right!" he thundered back, returning her glare. But as the man-who-always-gets-what-he-wants snatched gold cuff links off a shelf and slammed the door of the armoire, he caught his hand in it. His fingers were smashed in the door.

Yelping with pain, he cupped the stinging fingers in his other hand. "Dammit, Angeleen, this is all your fault," he shouted as he blew on them to ease the ache.

Angeleen tried not to laugh, but his histrionics sorely tempted an outburst of giggles. "Let me see your hand."

"It's nothing," he said, long-sufferingly.

"Ruark, let me see your hand," Angeleen insisted. Reluctantly, Ruark thrust the injured fingers forward for her inspection.

"You're right, it's nothing," she declared after a cursory glance. "I've had hangnails worse than that." She negligently dropped his hand.

He inadvertently winced with pain. "You can be a real bi—nasty when you want to be," he muttered.

His accusation caused a pang of guilt and she reconsidered. "Well, let me see them again."

Angeleen held his hand in her own as she gently re-examined the injury. On closer inspection, she did observe a couple of slightly puffy and discolored fingers.

Relieved it was nothing more, she looked up. "I don't think any of them are broken."

As they gazed into each other's eyes, a riveting awareness suddenly quelled their previous anger. Angeleen pressed a light kiss on the tip of each of the injured fingers. "There. All better now."

Ruark reached out and ran a finger along the delicate line of her cheek. "Why are we arguing, Angel?" he asked huskily.

Her face curved with a soft smile as she shook her head. "I don't remember."

Ruark dipped his head to claim her lips. Slipping her arms around his neck, she molded her body to his and surrendered to the pleasure and excitement of the kiss.

He released the corset strings he had just tied. Within seconds her corset, chemise, and drawers lay in a heap on the floor along with his shirt and trousers.

The satin pumps dropped to the floor when Ruark swept her up into his arms, covering her lips in a bruising kiss.

Only the white silk hose remained when he laid her down on the bed.

Feeling as if she were all thumbs, Angeleen hurried to hook the crinoline hoop onto the end of her corset. Lighter and less cumbersome than the earlier models that encircled the body, the hoop now extended only at the back.

"I'm afraid we're going to be beyond fashionably late," she lamented as she slipped a white petticoat over the crinoline frame.

Ruark struggled painfully with his still tender fingers to put studs in the front of his shirt. "With the luck I'm having, we might not get there at all."

Completing the task for him, she returned to add the finishing touches to her dark tresses. After winding most of her long hair into a chignon at the back of her neck, she brushed a single thick curl to hang down past her shoulders. Then she tucked a tiny headpiece of ruched red tulle, dotted with the delicate ends of black peacock feathers, into the round bun at her nape.

Satisfied with the result, she stepped into a red silk-velvet gown. The decolleté bodice perfectly fitted her waist, and narrow cap sleeves exposed her creamy shoulders and slender arms.

Split at the waist in front, the velvet gown hung in panels on each hip over a red brocade skirt embroidered with gold thread. The back of the gown bunched into a bustle, flaring over the rear crinoline in a long gracious velvet train which swept the floor as she walked.

"You look beautiful, Angel," Ruark said proudly. "Your beauty puts every woman to shame." He studied her for a moment and smiled a devilish smile. "No doubt you'll raise quite a few eyebrows tonight."

He lowered his head and lightly traced his tongue across the inviting cleavage. "And after one look at this enticement, my love, you'll raise more than just eyebrows."

Shocked, Angeleen's bright blush matched the color of her gown. "Ruark Stewart, that remark was obscene," she scolded.

He chuckled warmly and slipped a white wool cape around her shoulders.

Angeleen's eyes sparkled with gaiety as Ruark waltzed her around the dance floor, and she beamed with delight as she gazed into his admiring glance.

"Oh, Ruark, after four long years of war, I'd almost forgotten how grand a ball can be."

"My pleasure, ma'am," he replied, amused and pleased by her enthusiasm.

A single look at the beauty of Angeleen Hunter took a man's breath away and stirred envy in the breast of many a woman in the room. Conveniently, her illicit relationship with Ruark Stewart furnished an excuse for the ladies to vent their jealousy under a guise of righteous indignation.

As the evening progressed, Angeleen couldn't help but notice their ostracism and she bore the slights nobly. After a while, she even began to make a game of the situation by responding to the snubs and haughty glares with innocent, sweet smiles.

A few of the more intrepid men, irresistibly drawn to her beauty or by their curiosity, dared to claim an occasional waltz. But for most of the evening her partners alternated between Ruark and T. J. Graham.

During a pause in the music, Angeleen voiced her thoughts to T. J. as they drank a cup of punch.

"I feel like a Rebel soldier standing alone with a whole hillside of Yankee cannon pointed right at me."

T. J. chuckled. "Take heart, Angeleen. You're not the only unpopular person in the room. There are many here who resent my presence as well."

Angeleen snorted cynically. "T. J., you know why these pious ladies resent me. And it's not because I'm from the South. I declare, some of them couldn't tell you who was fighting whom."

T. J. noticed the bitterness that had crept into her voice. Angeleen looked so hurt and vulnerable he wanted to take her in his arms to comfort her. "Hey, Angel Face, don't let them break you down," T. J. said tenderly.

Angeleen smiled sheepishly. "I guess my skin isn't as thick as I thought. Anyway, why should I expect them to act any differently?"

"Have you tried discussing this with Ruark?" he asked.

"What could he do to prevent it?" she scoffed.

"He could marry you, Angeleen."

She looked up, expecting to see his amused smile. Instead, his brown eyes gazed at her steadily. Shocked, Angeleen realized his remark was serious.

"T. J., Ruark isn't in love with me. Didn't he tell you he has no intention of marrying me?" She chided him with uncharacteristic flippancy. "I thought best friends always told each other their secrets."

"Yes, he told me," T. J. said, but he smiled, as if he were aware of something neither she nor Ruark realized.

177

Ruark, who had been in discussion with several gentlemen, glanced over and saw Angeleen and T. J. in deep conversation. He excused himself and walked over to the couple.

Slipping an arm possessively around her shoulders, he forced a casual smile. "So, what are you two planning? A foray on the armory?"

T. J. found Ruark's attitude insufferable. For a moment, anger glinted in T. J.'s eyes.

"We were speculating on when the night's entertainment would begin, dear ole friend." Then the tolerance turned to sarcasm. "Tell me this, *dear ole friend*, are Angeleen and I to be hanged or tossed to the lions?"

At Ruark's quizzical look, T. J.'s annoyance halted the game of words. "Why don't you let me get Angeleen out of here?"

Ruark connected with at least enough of T. J.'s statement to say, "Oh, come off it, T. J. The war's been over for months."

Any further effort to pursue the argument was thwarted when they were joined by two elderly men.

"Well, Stewart, don't you intend to introduce us to your lovely companion?" The speaker, a distinguished older man easily past seventy, smiled gallantly.

"Forgive me, Commodore," Ruark said cordially. "Gentlemen, Mrs. Hunter. Angeleen, it's my pleasure to introduce none other than the renowned tycoon, Cornelius Vanderbilt, and the honorable Thaddeus Stevens, Congressman from Pennsylvania."

"My pleasure, Mrs. Hunter," said Vanderbilt, whose eyes assessed her appreciatively.

His companion merely nodded. "Mrs. Hunter."

Angeleen smiled graciously. "My pleasure, gentlemen."

"I have to say, madam, you are unquestionably the loveliest woman in the room," Vanderbilt declared. His authoritative manner made the declaration sound unequivocal.

"You flatter me, Mr. Vanderbilt," Angeleen replied.

"Do call me Commodore. Most people do," Vanderbilt advised.

"And have you met Doctor Graham?" Ruark asked.

"Doctor Graham," Vanderbilt acknowledged as the two men shook hands.

Thaddeus Stevens nodded, but did not offer a hand. "Yes, I've met the gentleman from Virginia." The disdain in his tone bordered on rudeness.

"Virginia, you say?" Vanderbilt raised his eyebrows. "Stevens here is head of the Committee on Reconstruction. As a Virginian, I would think you might have some advice to offer."

"I'm aware of Mr. Stevens' position, sir," T. J. replied. The mutual dislike between T. J. and Stevens cracked like lightning between them.

Stevens shifted his cigar into the corner of his mouth. "I take my new responsibility seriously. Unlike President Johnson, I believe we have to take more time in allowing the Southern states to rejoin the Union. Johnson is trying to move too quickly."

"I think you Republicans just don't want to see all those Southern Democrats return to Congress," Vanderbilt chortled.

"And since when does your loyalty lie with the Democrats, Commodore?" Stevens challenged sharply, sending a cloud of blue cigar smoke into the air.

"My good fellow, I have found that the almighty dollar manages to transcend political lines and loyalties."

"I won't argue with that logic," Ruark agreed.

Stevens pursued his argument. "Johnson should never have given amnesty and paroles to political prisoners, nor lifted the blockade on Southern ports."

"For a man chairing a committee on reconstruction," T. J. challenged, "how do you expect the South to ever rebuild economically when all her ports are blockaded, Congressman?"

" 'Tis the price one pays for insurgency, Doctor Graham," Stevens declared righteously.

"Then you're in conflict with your late President Lincoln, as well, Mr. Stevens. Didn't he call for malice toward none, charity toward all?" T. J. asked.

"I should remind the gentleman from Virginia that the question of slavery was the only issue Lincoln and I agreed upon," Stevens said.

"Good God, Congressman, the South has been ravaged by the War. Isn't it time to put the bitterness behind us and work toward rebuilding?" Ruark said.

To everyone's relief, Vanderbilt turned to Ruark and changed the subject. "What are these rumors I hear that you're investing in railroads? Are we soon to become competitors, Stewart?"

A powerful force in the railroad industry, Cornelius Vanderbilt controlled the New York Central, one of the most extensive railroads in the country, and he eyed Ruark, his potential adversary, with regard. Yes, Ruark Stewart would be an impressive rival, indeed. Vanderbilt considered making an offer to join forces so as not to have to fight him.

"I can assure you the rumors are false, Commodore. I've swung some financial backing to a man in Michigan who is trying to develop a refrigerator car. If he succeeds, I think it will revolutionize the railroad industry."

Vanderbilt felt a sense of instant relief. His personal empire would remain unbroached.

"As you well know, Commodore," Ruark continued, "Chicago has become the primary railroad terminus in the country, and the largest stockyards, as well, are on the verge of opening there. If Sutherland succeeds in his attempt to develop a refrigerated car, railroads will be able to ship fresh meat, fruit, and vegetables. The city is already linked by rail to the east, and its proximity to the prairies makes it an ideal site to ship west as well. Those combined elements will make Chicago the railroad shipping center of the Union."

Vanderbilt nodded in agreement. "I'd say you've made a wise investment. Furthermore, if this refrigerator car is successful, all the railroads will profit."

"In a few months, the extension of the Chicago and Northwestern will be completed and that line will join with the Union Pacific," Ruark continued. "Then, once the Union Pacific links with the Big Four's Central Pacific rail coming from the West coast, this country will have a transcontinental railroad."

"And how long will that take?" Stevens scoffed. "Why, those two railroads have been laying track since sixty-one. They're nowhere near completion."

Vanderbilt shook his head. "You show as little foresight as I did, Stevens. I regret I didn't invest in that enterprise. The war may have slowed down the project, but now it's escalated. I've heard each railroad is laying over five miles of track a day. Won't be but a few more years before they meet, I'll wager."

The old man's eyes glowed with vision. "Yes, Thad, we'll see a transcontinental railroad in our lifetime."

The congressman remained skeptical. "Maybe you'll see it in yours, but I'll be long dead and buried."

"I certainly would like to be there to see the last piece of rail laid," T. J. said. "What a historic moment—the linking of East to West."

"Yes. I think I'd gladly give up half my fortune to witness such a moment, Doctor Graham," Vanderbilt sighed.

The musicians struck a chord and the old man smiled at Angeleen. "Well, young lady, there's something wrong with these men; haven't they any red blood in their veins? If I were five years younger, you'd be in my arms out there on the dance floor right this moment."

"An excellent suggestion, sir," T. J. replied. Anxious to escape the presence of the bellicose Pennsylvania congressman, T. J. had just been about to ask Angeleen to dance.

Ruark's eyes followed the couple as his friend took

her hand and led Angeleen to the dance floor.

"Angeleen, I intend to leave as soon as this waltz is over," T. J. said as they began to move to the strains of the music. "If you like, I will be glad to take you back to your hotel."

Angeleen glanced toward Ruark's tall figure across the room. She could see his gaze following their movements. Having no desire for a repetition of those earlier, unpleasant hours, she declined T. J.'s offer.

"I'll wait for Ruark. I'm sure he'll soon be ready to leave."

"As much as I like seeing you and Ruark, I can't take another moment of the opinionated, *dis*honorable congressman from Pennsylvania."

Her eyes lit with the merriment of mockery. "Oh, really! I would never have guessed. And he appears to be such a pleasant fellow, too. I just can't understand your attitude, Doctor Graham."

"Stevens is the worst possible choice to chair a committee to help the Confederacy recover. He'll surely be more of a hindrance than a help. The man's an uncompromising abolitionist who hates all Southerners."

When T. J. returned Angeleen to Ruark's side, several other men had joined the group and the conversation had shifted to a discussion of the Ku Klux Klan. T. J. excused himself and departed.

"I heard this Klan was formed by six Confederate soldiers in Tennessee," one of the men remarked.

"Six of the same rabble that our illustrious president was so quick to offer amnesty to," Stevens grumbled.

Vanderbilt shook his head. "I have it from a very good source that the Klan was started by General Forrest."

Angeleen's eyes widened in surprise. "I hope you're not referring to General Nathan Bedford Forrest? You do him a disservice, sir," she said indignantly. "Why, General Forrest is one of the Confederacy's most distinguished cavalry officers. My own brother had the privilege of serving under him."

"My apologies, Mrs. Hunter," Vanderbilt quickly replied. "I am only repeating a rumor." He smiled cordially. "Tell me, my dear, are you a member of the distinguished Hunter family of Virginia?"

"No, Commodore. My husband's family were simple Louisiana sharecroppers," she said defiantly, with a glance in the direction of Thaddeus Stevens.

His expression was smug. A waiter passed among them carrying a tray. Stevens reached for one of the glasses and quaffed the champagne as if it were water.

Angeleen knew she was being rude and dared not look at Ruark in fear of seeing his disapproval. T. J. had warned her to leave before these pretentious hypocrites attacked her. She realized she should have listened to him.

Stevens wasted no time in returning to his favorite subject—degrading the South and President Johnson. "Johnson is a fool to think that any Southerner will honor an oath of allegiance to the Union. Before you know, they'll all be joining this subversive Klan."

"Bosh, Stevens. The Army will crush the Ku Klux Klan before it can even get started," one of the men scoffed.

"And I disagree with you, Congressman," Ruark interjected. "I believe those Southerners who have taken an oath of allegiance are sincere. Lee is a good example."

Stevens laughed aloud. "He's the very kind I'm referring to. That insurgent took the oath just to keep his neck from getting stretched."

"I don't believe that," Ruark contradicted. "I believe he did it in a genuine effort to unite the Union. He set the example so others will follow suit."

Angeleen had heard all the callous remarks she could bear from the officious congressman. "I would like to remind you, Mr. Stevens, that General Lee was well thought of by both sides. After all, your President Lincoln had offered him the command of the Union Army."

"Which he injudiciously declined, little lady," Stevens snorted. The arrogant congressman was not in the habit of allowing his opinions to be challenged by a woman—especially a woman whom he considered a whore.

"And thank God for the Union's sake that he did," he snickered, shoving his elbow into the man next to him. As the two men enjoyed their laugh at Angeleen's expense, Stevens motioned to the nearby waiter to refill his glass again.

As a former military officer, Ruark had listened to the braying of the pompous ass as long as he could. "I wouldn't laugh too heartily, gentlemen.

Lee is an undisputed military genius. Not only he, but his other generals. Our military strategy didn't beat him. Lee was defeated because the North could afford a war; we had the industry—iron, steel, textile, munitions."

"Not to mention the banking capital of this country," Vanderbilt interjected.

Ruark nodded. "Seventy percent of the population gave us the advantage to man our armies as well as keep our farms active."

"And," Vanderbilt added proudly, "two thirds of the railroad mileage was here in the North to move and transport all those men, food, and medical supplies."

"And as you intimated earlier, Congressman," Ruark added, "the North had a navy that could blockade Southern ports and cut off the South's source of supplies. The Confederacy was doomed from the beginning. All we had to do was cut off their railroads and ports. We would have defeated the Confederacy much sooner, if Lee had accepted Lincoln's offer. Undisputedly, Lee's military genius, and that of his officers, was what prolonged the war."

"Well, even if he were the great general you claim him to be, the man's duty was to his country, not to the Confederacy," Stevens countered.

"I question the need to remind a Virginian where his duty lies, Mr. Stevens," Angeleen interjected. "Surely, such names as George Washington, Thomas Jefferson, James Madison, and James Monroe are familiar to you?"

Snickering, Stevens flicked his cigar ashes on the floor. "They sure are, little lady. But I'm surprised to hear you're familiar with them."

The steady flow of alcohol in his veins throughout the evening loosened Stevens' tongue beyond caution. "Well now," he said, exaggerating surprise, "didn't figure them Southern gentlemen allowed their women so much education. Thought they kept all you Southern belles occupied other ways."

The odious man had exceeded all limits of courtesy, and Ruark felt a mounting urge to smash the smirk off the bastard's face.

His anger was undisguised as his voice cut the tension like a knife. "Congressman, Mrs. Hunter is here as my guest. I insist that you apologize to her."

Stevens was convinced that Ruark could only be championing the woman as a ploy to guarantee himself a good roll in the hay later that night. Confident that the others were just as amused by the woman's statements as he was, the congressman decided to play along with Ruark.

Winking at Ruark, Stevens applied his most ingratiating campaign veneer. "I surely didn't mean to offend the little lady, Mr. Stewart."

Angeleen, too caught up in anger to give any heed to the man's insult, continued to defend her cause. "All those men were Virginians, Mr. Stevens; four of the first six presidents of this country. And four of the next six presidents were Southerners, as well, three among them Virginians. When hasn't this country looked to Virginia for leadership?"

"Well, I do thank you, little lady, for the history lesson." He grinned and poked the arm of the man

187

next to him. "Haven't noticed any *Virginians* in the White House in the last fifteen years, have you? Apparently we figured out how to run the country without them."

Angeleen thrust up her pert chin and nose. "Which is exactly why this country's in the mess it's in." She turned and stormed off.

Vanderbilt threw back his head in unrestrained laughter. "Well, Stevens, I'd say you've met your match in that young lady. You'd better hope that confounded—what do you call it?—Oh yes, suffrage movement is unsuccessful, or some day you could find yourself facing her in Congress."

All the men laughed at the preposterous notion. Even Ruark chuckled and then said quickly, "Gentlemen, excuse me. I believe Mrs. Hunter would like to leave."

"Don't forget our appointment, Stewart. Tomorrow, at my club for lunch," Vanderbilt called out as Ruark hurried away in pursuit of Angeleen.

For several moments Angeleen fanned herself furiously as she waited for Ruark to join her, unaware of the intense stare fixed upon her from a pair of eyes gleaming with hatred.

Suddenly, through the haze of her agitation, she sensed the hostility of an unseen presence and felt a sudden warning of danger. Her hand slipped to the nape of her neck to quell the shiver that raced up her spine.

She turned around, but saw no one paying any attention to her.

Angeleen stepped out into the corridor, hoping to escape the feeling, but the uneasiness continued even when Ruark joined her and slipped the cape around her shoulders.

As he took her arm and led her to the door, Angeleen glanced back for one final look.

The corridor was empty.

Chapter Thirteen

After a hasty breakfast the next morning, Ruark finished packing and prepared to leave for his luncheon appointment.

"Our train leaves at five. I'll be back as soon as I'm through with Vanderbilt. Finish your packing while I'm gone."

"That's easier said than done, Ruark Stewart," Angeleen grumbled, casting a disgruntled glance at the numerous garments, accessories, and boxes of jewelry he had bought her since their arrival in New York. "There just isn't luggage enough to hold everything."

Ruark hurriedly shoved some currency into her hands. "I'm late now, honey. I've got to get going. Ask the desk clerk to send someone to buy you another trunk." He kissed her and dashed off.

Preferring to tend to the task herself, Angeleen dressed and departed.

A low ceiling of dark clouds hung over the city, threatening another snowy day. With wind whipping at her hair and coat, Angeleen hurried along the street to Macy's department store.

Deciding upon a suitable trunk became a harder task than she had imagined, but after much deliberation, she finally made a selection. As she paid for the purchase, the eerie sensation she had experienced the night before returned—Angeleen felt a sinister presence watching her. She turned quickly, but saw nothing unusual among the other shoppers in the store.

The clerk assured her the trunk would be delivered to her hotel within the hour, and Angeleen hastily departed. Hurrying back toward the hotel, her uneasiness persisted; she felt she was being followed. Yet, when she looked back, the few people who had dared to brave the bitter wind appeared to be scurrying about their business, as anxious as she to get out of the cold.

Angeleen chastised herself for her faint-heartedness. Why was she feeling so skittish? What could happen to her in broad daylight on a busy street in the largest city of the Union? Still, she quickened her step, fretful of whatever might lurk in the menacing shadows of the alleys and narrow openings between the buildings.

As Angeleen passed the jewelry store, the proprietor, spying her through the window, opened the door and called to her. "The brooch Mr. Stewart ordered is ready, Mrs. Hunter." Angeleen could not refuse the chance to garner a few moments of welcome warmth.

The jeweler smiled with pride as he reached under the counter, extracted a tiny box, and presented a white jade cameo for her approval.

"Oh, it's lovely, Mr. Wilkins. I'm sure Mr. Stewart will be as pleased as I am."

Preening with satisfaction, the jeweler wrapped the package. "And I know Mr. Stewart will be pleased with the selection you made for him."

He handed her the gift. "Merry Christmas, Mrs. Hunter. I'm sure your holiday will be a happy one."

"Merry Christmas, Mr. Wilkins." Angeleen smiled as she uttered the familiar phrase for the first time that year. The holiday season had crept up on them, and Angeleen was suddenly struck by how different this Christmas would be from the dismal, heartbroken holidays of the past four years.

"Yes, I'm sure it will be," Angeleen responded cheerfully. Her face beamed as she thought of the approaching festive season. "Merry Christmas, indeed!"

Sinister thoughts forgotten, her spirits were light and her step quick as she walked the two remaining blocks to the hotel.

Stopping at the desk, Angeleen informed the clerk of her expected trunk delivery.

"I'm sorry, Mrs. Hunter, but you will have to use the back stairs," he cautioned. "One of the chandeliers collapsed over the stairway, and the main stairs can't be used until the fixture and broken glass are cleaned away."

Angeleen looked up at the row of mammoth crystal

chandeliers hanging from the ceiling. The thought of one of them crashing to the floor was terrifying.

"Oh, my, I hope no one got hurt."

"Fortunately, no one happened to be on the stairway when the fixture fell, but our two bellboys were cut by flying glass. That's why we're so shorthanded right now. We regret the inconvenience, but we'll have help as soon as a new shift arrives."

"That will be just fine," Angeleen said. "I'm certainly relieved to hear that nobody was seriously hurt."

She followed the long hallway to the rear of the building. As she started to climb the stairway, Angeleen heard the sound of footsteps. However, she didn't see anyone behind her. Uneasiness sent her dashing up the stairs. Unnerved to find the floor above deserted, she hurried down the hallway. Then she heard the sound again. This time, certainty erased all doubt in her mind—someone *was* stalking her.

She raced down the hallway to the door of her suite. Breathlessly, she fumbled with her key, rushed into the room, and bolted the door.

Angeleen pressed her ear against the door, trying to hear above the loud beat of her drumming heart. The hallway was quiet. After another minute that seemed like hours to her, Angeleen abandoned her post at the door.

Feeling chagrin over her skittishness, she removed her hat and coat, depositing them in the bedroom. With hands on hips, she surveyed the room and tackled the task of packing.

Not more than five minutes had passed when a

light rap sounded on the door. Her previous edginess leaped to her throat along with her heart. Trembling, she went to the door.

"Who . . . who is it?" she asked, fearfully.

"Macy's, ma'am," a male voice responded. "You ordered a trunk delivered?"

"Yes . . . yes, I did." Smiling with relief, she slipped the bolt, unlocking the door.

"Just put it in the other room," she said to the man toting the heavy chest on his shoulder.

"Yes, ma'am," he said cordially.

Angeleen took a coin from her purse, waiting at the door as he carried the trunk into the bedroom and set it on the floor. She thanked him upon his return and handed him the tip.

Before she could guess his intent or utter another sound, the man grabbed her outstretched hand, yanked her to him, and clamped his other hand over her mouth. His arm closed around her like a vise as he kicked the door shut behind him.

Angeleen struggled to free herself, but he forced her to the floor, his body and hand cutting off her breath while he shoved a gag into her mouth.

"That oughta shut yer damn mouth," he cursed as he tied a handkerchief around her mouth to secure the gag.

When he started to rise, Angeleen tried to squirm away. He slapped her face with such force that her head slammed against the floor, and for several seconds her head spun dizzily as he continued to hit her—all the while uttering an abusive stream of vile curses. When Angeleen whimpered under his blows, the brute unleashed a maniacal laugh.

Suddenly, he rolled off her, quickly got up, and turned to slip the bolt in the door. Writhing with pain, she scrambled to her feet and tried to pull away the gag to scream.

But the madman snatched her hair, yanked her back, and swung her around to face him. He brutally punched her in the stomach with a blow that doubled her over. She fell to the floor, strangling on the bile that rose in her throat.

"Can't let you choke on me, whore. You ain't gonna die till I'm done with ya." He rolled her over on her stomach and removed the gag.

Doubled up with pain, Angeleen retched on the floor.

When she finished, before she could utter a sound, he kicked her onto her back and shoved the gag into her mouth again.

The brute yanked her arms above her head and dragged Angeleen by the wrists across the floor into the bedroom. The pain in her stomach had glazed her eyes and she could no longer see the face of her attacker, but she felt his hands pulling off her shoes and hose and then the cold steel of a knife cutting away her clothing.

She recoiled in horror at the steady curses that spewed from his mouth like venom as he bound her hands and ankles to the bedposts with her own stockings and strips of her gown.

The attacker stared at the helpless woman spread-eagled before him, and with a lascivious gleam, he ran the point of his knife up her body from the junction of her legs to her navel without breaking her skin.

Angeleen prayed for oblivion as she felt his warm breath on her face. *God help me*, she prayed and turned her head away, closing her eyes.

But he jerked her head back, snarling threats of torture and death. The horror of his words increased her terror. The pain of his kick to her stomach had steadily built to a constricting inner pressure, and the gag muffled her scream of agony as the tautness erupted into a warm gush.

Just before she blacked out, Angeleen thought the madman must have carried out his threat; she felt blood.

Spying T. J. crossing the street, Ruark signaled the driver to stop the carriage. "Hey, T. J.," Ruark called, opening the door. "This is a bit of luck. I was just thinking about you. We haven't had much chance to talk and I'm returning to St. Louis tonight."

"Where's Angeleen?" T. J. asked. "I'd like to say good-bye to her before you leave."

"She's back at the hotel, packing. I had a luncheon appointment with Vanderbilt, but he was called away due to an unexpected problem at home. Climb in. We'll get Angeleen and all have lunch together."

Upon entering the hotel, they found startled confusion in the lobby caused by the distant echo of shrill screams. The two men hastily followed the desk clerk, who began racing down the hallway toward the source of the cries at the rear of the hotel.

Breathlessly, they halted at the open door of a storage room where they encountered a grisly sight—a body lying face down in a pool of blood. An hysterical chambermaid stared in horror and frantically struggled to speak.

"I—I opened the door and—and found him just like that," the frightened woman sobbed.

T. J. knelt down and took the man's pulse. He looked up at Ruark and shook his head. "He's dead," he said and turned the corpse over. "My God, his throat's been slit."

Shrieking in terror, the chambermaid fled down the hall.

Aghast, the desk clerk leaned down for a closer inspection and stammered in disbelief, "Why, it's Hank Burns, the delivery man from Macy's. He came in just a short while ago to deliver a trunk to your suite, Mr. Stewart."

"My suite?" Ruark said, shocked. Exchanging glances with T. J., both men reacted with the same fearful thought.

"Angeleen!" Ruark cried out and bolted up the stairway with T. J. in close pursuit.

Finding the door to the suite locked, Ruark pounded on the door and called out.

"Angeleen. It's Ruark. Open the door! Angeleen—"

"Don't you have a key?" T. J. snapped, impatiently.

"I gave it to her. Let's break down the door."

The wood splintered away from the hinges when the two men threw their shoulders against the door, and after another combined effort, the door shattered.

Angeleen's attacker was just about to climb on the helpless girl when he had heard Ruark call. In desperation, he frantically looked about, but finding no means of escape from the second-story room, he sped into the sitting room and ducked down behind the settee.

Stumbling through the broken door, Ruark and T. J. cast a cursory glance around the room as they ran to the bedroom.

"Oh, dear God," Ruark said when he saw Angeleen tied down in the bloodstained bed.

T. J. examined her quickly. "She's still alive."

Ruark had already removed the gag from her mouth and as he worked to release her hands, he caught sight of her attacker trying to sneak out the door.

"Hey, you—stop!" Ruark cried out heedlessly as he started to give chase. "T. J., take care of Angel," Ruark shouted as he bolted down the hallway after the man.

The desk clerk tried to stop the fugitive when he reached the clutter of people assembled at the bottom of the stairway, but the fleeing criminal shoved the older man into the crowd and escaped out the rear door.

"Call the police," Ruark cried as he raced past them in pursuit.

Once outside, the crazed killer struggled to climb over a fence which blocked his escape. Shrugging off his overcoat and frockcoat, Ruark scaled the fence easily and raced after the man.

The fugitive ran through an alley and across another street. With the chase now on level ground, the gap between them shrank rapidly.

Heads turned as the two men sped past. Then, when Ruark closed to within a few feet of the fiend, the man shoved a woman into Ruark's path and dashed into a narrow passageway between two buildings.

Both Ruark and the startled woman tumbled to the sidewalk. By the time Ruark regained his footing and reached the entrance to the alley, he saw no sign of the fugitive.

The narrow passageway led to a dead end, and Ruark realized his quarry must be lurking somewhere in the darkened shadows. He figured the man had no gun or he would have fired a shot by now.

He slowed his steps, spent a fruitless moment searching for anything that might be used as a weapon, and then cautiously entered the alley.

Finding the first door locked, he moved on to the next and discovered it was barred.

Suddenly, when a squealing cat darted from behind several barrels a short distance away, he spun around, then stood still in his tracks, alert for the slightest sound. For a moment he heard nothing. Then, from the distance, the high-pitched shrill of a whistle invaded the silence; following the chase, the police approached the scene.

His glance swept the area. Was Angeleen's attacker trapped in the alley, or had he slipped into one of the buildings?

His attention shifted to a heap of beer barrels stacked at the rear of a tavern. Approaching cautiously, he kicked aside several of the huge, empty casks. A rat, flushed from its haunt, scurried past him. Further investigation produced no sign of the scoundrel.

"Dammit!" he cursed and tried the door of the

saloon. Unexpectedly, the door opened.

Blue, hazy smoke floated in the air, and the odor of beer permeated the small room of the pub. Other than the bartender wiping the bar and a waiter stacking beer mugs at the far end, the pub was relatively empty. He saw two men standing at the bar, a man and woman sitting at a small table, and another man sitting alone in the corner.

Ruark received cursory glances from the patrons, but they soon returned to their own thoughts and conversations.

"What'll you have, sir, whiskey or beer?" the bartender asked.

"Neither," Ruark replied. "I'm looking for a man who might have just come in here."

Taking a swift side glance at Ruark, the bartender continued to wipe the surface of the battered bar. "You don't look like a policeman to me."

"Didn't say I was," Ruark answered, annoyed by the surly, noncommittal attitude of the barkeep. "And you didn't deny that someone just came in here."

His eyes swept the room and came to rest on the least likely suspect—the waiter, the only person in the bar who had totally ignored Ruark's entrance.

Ruark walked over to the waiter and spun the man around. His face looked vaguely familiar, and Ruark struggled to remember where he had seen him before. When recognition registered, Ruark knew he had found the assailant.

The culprit knew as well. He threw a tray of glasses at Ruark's head. Ruark ducked and the tray bounced off his shoulder, crashing to the floor.

The fugitive ran toward the front door, but Ruark tackled him. Broken glass crunched beneath their locked bodies as the two men rolled and thrashed on the floor, upending tables and chairs.

They broke apart. Blood dripped from a glass cut on Ruark's cheek as he climbed to his feet. The crazed killer drew a knife from his boot and lunged at Ruark.

The appearance of the knife created panic in the saloon, and in screaming pandemonium, the patrons spilled out onto the sidewalk.

Ruark knocked aside his opponent's knife hand and delivered a right punch to the madman's face. He felt the man's nose crunch beneath his fist.

Blood flowed profusely from the killer's broken nose as he jabbed again at Ruark, this time cutting a bloody swath on Ruark's arm. Ruark's fist connected with his opponent's chin to send him sprawling to the floor on his back.

Before the downed man could recover his footing, Ruark landed on him and twisted his wrist until the knife fell to the floor. He started to pummel Angeleen's attacker with both fists.

Attracted by the commotion, two uniformed policemen entered the bar and immediately rushed to pull Ruark off the man.

Ruark's explanation got him nowhere with the policemen, who were unaware of the events at the hotel. Cuffed along with the suspect, Ruark was hauled off to the station house in a horse-drawn paddy wagon.

Deeply worried about Angeleen's condition, Ruark spent a frustrating hour trying to explain his role in the situation. Finally, the policemen who were investigating the murder at the hotel checked into the station and all the details were pieced together. Another hour passed before Ruark could at last return to the hotel.

T. J. rose to his feet the instant Ruark, wrapped in a blanket to ward off the chill, stepped through the shattered door.

"Thank God, you're back! Where in hell have you been for the last two hours?"

"How is she?" Ruark asked, barely able to disguise the panic he felt. He moved swiftly toward the bedroom door, but T. J. intercepted him.

"She's resting and I want to talk to you first."

T. J. poured a glass of brandy and handed it to Ruark. "Sit down and drink this."

"Drink?" Ruark asked incredulously. "Tell me *now* what the bastard did to her," he bellowed out of fear.

"He beat her up," T. J. said grimly.

Ruark's dark eyes glinted with hatred. "Did he rape her?"

"No, but . . . *will* you sit down, Ruark?"

Ruark accepted the glass and sat down on the settee. "How badly did he cut her?"

T. J. shook his head. "He didn't cut her."

"Then where in hell did all the blood come from?" Ruark demanded.

"The beating she took caused a miscarriage."

"A miscarriage!" Flabbergasted, Ruark stared at T. J. Then he gulped down the astringent liquid in a single swallow. The liquor temporarily smothered his anguish and, after a moment, he collected his thoughts and confided to T. J.

"I didn't know Angeleen was pregnant. She never told me."

"She didn't even realize it herself. She wasn't more than four or five weeks along."

The liquor began to take its toll; Ruark felt numb, but his intense concern for Angeleen had not wavered. "How is she doing?"

"Well, the bastard scared her half to death, but I think she'll be all right. She refused to go to a hospital. Medically, nothing much can be done for her. It's too soon to tell if the lining of the uterus has been permanently damaged."

"And what would that mean?"

T. J. affixed a steady gaze on Ruark. "She might never be able to have a child."

The instant tic in Ruark's cheek was the only indication of his emotion. "So what do we do now?"

"We have to consider that the near-rape is the more terrifying incident just now. She'll need a lot of love and understanding, Ruark."

Ruark rose to his feet. "Can I see her now?"

T. J. nodded. "I gave her laudanum to ease her pain. Should help her sleep, too, but she's been fighting the medication. She didn't want to sleep until she knew you were okay. You did catch the bastard, didn't you?"

Ruark nodded. "Caught up with him a couple blocks from here."

"You look like hell. What happened to you? And where's your coat? I hope that blood on your shirt is his and not yours."

"Oh, just scratches. I cut my cheek on some broken glass, and the bastard sliced a lucky cut on my arm."

T. J. frowned. "For God's sake! Let me look at it."

"The police cleaned up the wounds after they arrested me."

"Arrested you?" T. J. exclaimed. "What in hell for?"

"Let me peek in on Angel, then I'll tell you the whole story."

Angeleen appeared to be sleeping. At the sight of the ugly bruises marring her face, Ruark gently traced his finger along the delicate line of her chin.

She raised her eyelids, and tears welled in her eyes when she saw him.

"Oh, Ruark, I was so frightened. I've never been so frightened before."

He gathered her in his arms and held her as she spent her tears. Finally, after several moments, she relaxed and he laid her back.

Angeleen tugged at his shirt sleeve. "You aren't leaving me, are you? Please don't leave me, Ruark."

"I won't, Angel." He sat down on the edge of the bed and clasped her hand, then leaned over and pressed a light kiss on her lips.

"He was so ghastly and evil. And he hated me so much. What did I ever do to him?"

"T. J., come on in here. You'll want to hear this, too," Ruark called out to T. J. who had discreetly remained in the sitting room so his two friends could have a private moment together.

T. J. came into the room. Before sitting down, he checked Angeleen's temperature and pulse.

His spirits considerably buoyed at finding Angeleen's condition less critical than he had feared,

Ruark noticed T. J.'s black bag and asked lightly, "And where did the medical supplies come from, Doctor Graham?"

T. J. cast an affectionate glance at Angeleen. "When my patient here refused to go to the hospital and insisted upon my treating her, I had no recourse but to send to my hotel for them."

Ruark stood up and extended his hand. "Thanks, ole friend. I'm glad you were here for her," Ruark said solemnly. "I owe you one." The two men shook hands.

"You owe me more than one favor, *ole friend*," T. J. gibed. "Besides, I didn't do it for you; I did it for her." Angeleen and T. J. exchanged a look of understanding.

Ruark felt an instant stab of jealousy as he realized that after the terror of her ordeal, she and T. J. shared more than a doctor-patient relationship. An inviolable bond had been formed between the two which Ruark knew he would never share.

Ruark cleared his throat and began to explain the background of the assailant. "His name is Jack Hawks. The police have been putting the puzzle together, and Hawks turned out to be the missing piece. He's the man responsible for the recent murders."

"You mean . . . ," Angeleen stammered, "I just fell into the hands of a mass murderer?"

"Not exactly, Angel. You were chosen by Hawks."

"But why me, Ruark? What did I do to him?"

Ruark patted her hand. "Just being born in the South made you a target, honey. According to Hawks' medical records, he was wounded and trapped behind enemy lines. It seems his hiding place was discovered by a woman, and she turned him over to some Confederate soldiers. Hawks was taken prisoner and sent to Andersonville, where he was badly mistreated. Apparently, his hatred pushed him over the brink and now he blames women for his suffering—Southern women, that is. The women he killed were all from the South."

T. J. shook his head. "God, how sick!"

"The police said Hawks' job in a pub enabled him to encounter two of his victims."

"But I was never in any pub, Ruark," Angeleen interjected.

"Ah, but remember the waiter last night who served drinks while you and Stevens were arguing?"

"Hawks," T. J. surmised.

Ruark nodded. "He often hired himself out as a part-time waiter to serve at parties. The police sergeant told me that's where he picked out another one of his victims. He targeted you after he overheard your argument with Stevens. Then, when Vanderbilt mentioned our luncheon engagement, Hawks picked the time and place. He confessed to following you to Macy's and waylaying the delivery man to get into your room."

"I knew I was being watched last night. I could feel danger . . . his hatred. The same thing today," Angeleen offered.

"Why didn't you tell me your suspicions last night, sweetheart?" Ruark asked.

"Ruark, last night everyone in that room hated me.

Hawks was no exception." She yawned and closed her eyes. "It still isn't over, is it?"

"Yes it is, love. Hawks is behind bars now. He'll never harm anyone again."

"I don't mean him. I mean the war. The last shot still hasn't been fired, has it, Ruark?" She began to slip into slumber.

T. J. nodded grimly. "She could be right." Ruark started to follow T. J. out of the room.

"Stay with me, Ruark," Angeleen managed to murmur before she finally succumbed to sleep.

Once out of the room, T. J. closed the bedroom door. "I felt Angeleen had been shaken up enough, so I wouldn't let the hotel move you to a different suite. But since you no longer have a door, much less a lock, why don't you crawl in with Angeleen tonight and I'll stretch out here on the couch."

"That's not necessary, T. J. I can hire a security guard for the night."

"I should remain here anyway, just in case she takes a turn for the worse. She could run a fever or start hemorrhaging."

Ruark frowned worriedly. "You mean she's still in danger."

"She's showing remarkable strength, Ruark, both physically and mentally. Let's hope she's not just putting on a brave front to cover up a lot of pain underneath. But I don't think so. Angeleen Hunter is a lady with a great deal of fortitude."

Ruark slapped him on the shoulder. "A true daughter of the Confederacy. Right?"

T. J. nodded. "That's right. A true daughter of the Confederacy."

*   *   *

Later that night, Ruark slipped into bed. As he gathered Angeleen to his side, she whimpered in her sleep. "He'll never hurt you again, Angel," he whispered and pressed a kiss to her forehead. "I won't let anyone hurt you again, ever."

Chapter Fourteen

Four days later, under the watchful eye of her doctor, Angeleen boarded Ruark's private railroad car. As he supervised the loading of their luggage, she said a sorrowful farewell to T. J. His steady presence had been a constant source of strength to her throughout the ordeal.

"Will we ever meet again?" she asked through the tears misting her eyes.

"Of course we will," he said lightly, concealing his own inner turmoil.

"T. J., I wish there was something I could do in return for all you've done for me."

He grinned and grasped her hand between his own. "I have a confession to make, my dear. I only went into medicine because I heard the patient always falls in love with her doctor." His brown eyes deepened. "But it has never worked for me."

"Then you must have some very misguided fools for patients, Doctor Graham."

He kissed her cheek and for a brief moment gazed deeply into her eyes. "Do me a favor, Angel Face. Don't give up on Ruark; he loves you. He just has a thick skull."

He kissed her again and hurried from the train.

Through the window of the car, Angeleen watched the two friends shake hands. Her gaze swung to the city's skyline in the distance and her mind drifted back to one of her mother's favorite adages, *the Lord never closes a door without opening a window*. The trip to New York had ended in a nightmare for her, but she now had something she never had before— a good friend. T. J. Graham would always be there when she needed him.

The snow that had only dusted New York piled high drifts in the passes of the Appalachians. As the train chugged through the snow-capped countryside of Pennsylvania and West Virginia, many of the passengers, Ruark among them, had to help shovel the deep snow off the track. After many such incidents and the need to make several switches in railroad lines, Angeleen and Ruark arrived in St. Louis on the day before Christmas.

At her first sight of the huge fir tree standing in the foyer, gaily decorated with candles, strings of popcorn, satin bows, and brightly painted pine cones, Angeleen became swept up into the spirit of the holiday.

Sarah greeted each of them with a hug and a kiss. A shocked gasp slipped past her lips when Ruark's bear hug lifted her off the floor.

"You put me down, you rapscallion," she scolded in a tone noticeably edged with pleasure, then seated herself in a nearby chair to restore her dignity.

"The two of you gave me an anxious moment," Sarah chastised, her blue eyes aglow. "I feared you were not going to make it back in time for Christmas."

"Nana, love, if I had to trudge through twelve-foot snow drifts toting Angeleen on my shoulders, I would not miss being here to spend Christmas with you."

She brushed aside his hyperbole with an indifferent wave of her fragile hand. "The important thing is that you're both home safe and sound."

Angeleen and Ruark exchanged a knowing glance. With her fading bruises concealed under face powder and his under a day's growth of beard, both hoped to avoid mentioning the incident with the killer.

However, neither had considered the far-reaching effect of the press. Harried and shaken, Henry rushed in waving a newspaper that vividly described the details of Angeleen's abduction and Ruark's pursuit of the killer.

Grim-faced, Sarah and Henry listened to Ruark's version of the incident. However, he carefully down played the tragic circumstances to avoid any further concern for the older pair.

When night fell, the candles on the tree were lit.

Soon after, the cook carried in a wassail bowl filled with hot spiced cider. Ruark passed out the gifts he and Angeleen had selected in New York to the servants and stablehands, as well as an envelope to each of them containing a sizable cash bonus. Then, after toasting the good health of all, everyone but Myra left to spend the evening with their own families.

Myra went happily about her duties, if somewhat absent-mindedly; she imagined herself being in church on the morrow wearing the latest Parisian bonnet brought "especially for her from New York."

Sarah lovingly fingered the cameo brooch pinned to her gown, and Henry proudly donned his new red vest. Then he put on the elegant, collapsible top hat given to him by Sarah and strutted around proud as a peacock, occasionally stealing an admiring glance at his profile in the mirror.

Angeleen adored the beautiful white opera gloves trimmed with tiny seed pearls given to her by Sarah, and the finely crocheted wool shawl lovingly made by Myra.

From the distance, the sound of the joyous Christmas message carried to their ears as a choir of roving carolers serenaded them outside the window. Ruark invited the carolers in, and soon the house rang with their songs and laughter. After a round of hot cider and savory rum cake, Angeleen added her piano skills and Ruark his baritone, much to the enjoyment of all.

The fragrant scent of cinnamon and cloves, pine, and burning wax permeated the air. With contented smiles, Sarah and Henry sat in the glow of the fireplace listening to the songs of Christmas accompanied by the crackling and popping of the logs on the hearth.

After the singers moved on with a raised chorus of well-wishes, Angeleen began to gather the soiled cups and plates.

"No you don't, young lady," Ruark ordered firmly, taking the pile of dishes from her. "You've had enough excitement and activity for one day." He sat her down at the table and then assisted Myra in cleaning away the cups and plates.

When the task was completed, Angeleen snatched two apples from a bowl on the table and went to the foyer. Ruark stopped her as she slipped on her cloak.

"Where are you going?" he asked

"I thought I would say hello to King." She put the apples into the pocket of her cloak.

"It's a long walk to the stable, Angel, and this has been an exhausting day for you."

"Ruark, I feel fine, and I really would like to see King," she emphatically replied.

"Well then, I'm coming with you."

As he proceeded to button her cloak, put a fur hat on her head, and hand her a warm muff, she shook her head with dismay and asked, "Ruark, what are you doing?"

"I just want to make certain you're dressed warmly."

"Indeed. Well, I'm all grown-up now. Ever since the incident in New York, you've been treating me like a child." Amused at his overprotectiveness, she snatched the muff out of his hands and departed.

Ruark grabbed his coat, the ends flapping loosely, and hurried after her.

Unnoticed by Ruark and Angeleen, a man turned into the driveway, his shoulders hunched down into an ill-fitting, threadbare suit coat that did little to ward off the chill of the night. His right hand held the front of the coat together, and a pinned-up coat sleeve dangled in place of his left arm.

The stranger had time for only a quick glimpse of the two figures before they entered the stable, but his glance swung immediately to Angeleen. A quick, warming rush of energy coursed through him and he moved toward the stable.

Bold King greeted Angeleen with a whinny and pushed his muzzle into her outstretched hand. Ruark stepped back into the shadows and sat down on a bale of hay, silently watching the reunion between Angeleen and her beloved pet.

After an initial series of hugs and kisses, whispered endearments, and affectionate petting, Angeleen produced the two apples. Bold King gobbled them down greedily.

"Didn't Poppa feed you while I was gone?" she cooed tenderly in the ear of the stallion.

Ruark felt a reasonable time had elapsed and she should return to the house. He was about to say so when the voice of a stranger interrupted his thought.

"Is it really you, Princess?"

Angeleen's arm appeared to freeze in midair. Startled, she turned her head to the source of the sound, certain her ears had deceived her.

Her eyes changed from shock, to incredulity, and

finally, unrestrained joy. Tears streamed down her cheeks.

"Robert," the name slipped past her lips in a whisper.

Suddenly, she sprang to motion. "Robert! Oh, Robert," she breathed ecstatically and ran to the man standing in the door.

The moment Ruark heard her call out the stranger's name, his stomach seemed to curl into a knot. He rose to his feet and watched jealously as Angeleen flung her arms around the man's neck, covering his face with kisses between her sobs.

"You're alive! They told me you were dead." Crying unabashedly, she buried her head against his chest.

"Don't cry, Angie," he murmured soothingly as he rested his cheek against her head and softly stroked her hair.

Watching the tender reunion, Ruark's hands clenched into fists. This must be her husband, Robert. He had intentionally avoided discussing the subject of her husband with Angeleen. Her ravings during her delirium had convinced Ruark that she still loved the man.

When Ruark stepped out of the shadows, Robert Scott became aware of his presence for the first time. He sensed Ruark's hostility and lifted his head. Their dark-eyed gazes locked in animosity. Robert released his grasp on Angeleen and stepped back.

At her brother's sudden withdrawal, Angeleen reached out to grasp his hands and drew back in shock. "Oh, no! Oh, dear God, Robert!" she sobbed. She clung to him.

Ruark, now aware of the man's infirmity, turned away feeling defeated. As he walked toward the stable door, Angeleen raised her head. "Don't go, Ruark."

Ruark's spine stiffened and he turned around. "I thought I'd go back to the house and leave you two alone."

The stranger remained silent, his dark gaze inspecting every detail of Ruark's appearance.

Demoralized by the unexpected turn of events, Ruark felt deep anger and frustration. He wanted to smash his rival's face—but, of course he could not. And Ruark realized, ironically, that the one-armed man actually had the unfair advantage; Angeleen's past love for her husband would be fortified by her sympathy and sense of loyalty.

He knew he should feel happy for her, but at the moment his only concern was that he was losing her.

"Ruark, this is Robert. My brother, Robert. We thought he was dead."

"This is your brother?" Ruark stared at the young man, taken aback to now see the resemblance between Angeleen and Robert. He was inundated with shame for his initial reaction—and he knew Robert Scott had sensed his hostility.

He extended his hand. "Ruark Stewart." The handshake was reserved—one man chagrined, the other wary.

Angeleen was not oblivious to the tension between Ruark and her brother, but her happiness would allow nothing to mar the joy of this moment. She bubbled over with questions.

"I can't wait to see Poppa's face when he sees you. Where have you been all this time? How did you find us?"

He chuckled warmly. "Hey, slow up, Angie. Where is Poppa?"

"He's back at the house," Ruark interjected. "And I think you should be returning there, Angeleen. The doctor warned you not to overexert yourself."

The man's steady gaze came to rest on Ruark again. Ruark knew he sounded stuffy and insensitive. He cursed silently and felt like a fool. Somehow, he had put himself on the defensive and was feeling guilty when he should be relieved.

"Have you been ill, Angeleen?" Robert asked worriedly.

In view of the circumstances, Angeleen felt it ridiculous that her own health would be cause for discussion. "Nothing serious, Robert. Ruark is just overly protective."

She cast a disgruntled glance at Ruark for even bringing up the subject and slipped her arm through Robert's. "Let's go and see Poppa."

Once in the foyer of the luxurious house, Robert Scott looked around, his interest piqued by more than ordinary curiosity; he didn't know what role his sister played in this household, but Ruark's possessiveness toward Angeleen fueled further suspicion in the young man.

Angeleen peeked into the drawing room. Myra must have taken Sarah to bed, and Henry still dozed before the fireplace. She put a finger to her lips and gestured for them to be quiet. "Let me wake him first," she whispered.

She tiptoed into the room and knelt beside her father's chair. Nudging him gently, she whispered softly, "Poppa. Poppa, wake up."

Henry opened his eyes and looked around perplexed. "I guess I dozed off for a moment. Where did everyone go?"

"It's late, Poppa," she said tenderly.

"Well, I'll be gettin' back to me room. 'Tis been a fine Christmas Eve, hasn't it, lass?"

Angeleen's eyes glowed with happiness as she picked up his hand and brought it to her lips. "If you could dream any dream you wanted, Poppa, what would make this night even happier for you?"

Henry patted her hand. "Ah, lass, I'd dream your mother and brother were here with us."

"I wish Momma was here too, Poppa," Robert said, stepping into the room.

Henry squinted through the dim light at the figure standing in the doorway. " 'Tis a cruel trick ye be playin' on an old man's eyes."

Robert stepped closer, into the light from the fireplace. " 'Tis no trick, Poppa. It's me. Robert."

Henry Scott rose to his feet. His glance took in the full sight of his son, including the pinned-up left sleeve. But neither sorrow nor sympathy flickered in the old man's eyes—instead, joy and pride radiated from his very soul. Then flowed unashamed tears of happiness.

"Son." Henry opened his arms and the young man walked into his father's embrace.

Ruark stood in the doorway, all but forgotten by the three Scotts. Looking at Angeleen, still on her knees as she gazed in awe at the miraculous reunion between her father and brother, he saw the supreme happiness that had transformed her face with a translucent beauty that stole his breath away.

He poured brandy into two glasses, and when Henry and Robert had parted, Ruark handed each a drink. "Here. I'm sure you're ready for this."

While they had waited in the foyer, Ruark took the opportunity to study Robert Scott. Angeleen's brother, a few inches shorter than he, had dark, tousled hair in sad need of a trim. A beard failed to conceal the gauntness of his hollow cheeks, and the stark look in his dark eyes, etched by war and suffering, reflected the horror they had witnessed.

Myra returned after bedding down his grandmother and, unobserved, Ruark asked her to prepare a tray of food for Robert. Then he quietly slipped out of the room.

They sat down before the fireplace as Robert gratefully consumed the hot bowl of soup and thick ham sandwich that Myra set before him.

"Now tell us where you've been. The war's been over for eight months," Angeleen pursued.

"I was wounded in Virginia. Grant launched an all-out drive to take Richmond. They called it the Wilderness Campaign."

Robert shook his head in torment. "Lord, it should have been called the Battle of Hell. Before it was over, the Yankees lost over fifty thousand men . . . and we lost the war."

He paused, his mind returning to the battlefield. "We fought for months. Lee vowed to protect Richmond just as Grant swore to take it. We ran out of food and supplies long before it ended. Most of us were sick or wounded. Many had begun to desert."

Angeleen's eyes filled with tears as she watched the shifting emotions on her brother's face. "A cannon-ball took off my arm and I woke up in a Yankee hospital in Pennsylvania. I was sick with fever and in and out of comas. I asked them to send word to my family."

"They never did," Angeleen said with dismay, sadly shaking her head. "Then one of the men from your outfit came back home and told me you were dead. That's all we ever heard."

"I was still feverish when the war ended, so the Yankees wouldn't release me. When I was well enough to get back on my feet, I went to Scotcroft."

Robert stopped his narrative to take a deep swallow of coffee. His sad eyes fell on Angeleen. "I saw Momma's grave before the Yankee carpetbagger ran me off the property. Big Charlie followed me and told me that the two of you had taken a riverboat to St. Louis. So I came North, asked a few questions, and here I am."

"We tried to save Scotcroft, Robert, but it was impossible. There was no money," Angeleen said woefully.

He smiled and squeezed her hand. "I understand, Angie."

Angeleen put an arm around each of them. "But we're together now, and nothing will ever separate us again," she said confidently.

Henry brushed a tear from his eye. "I'm thinkin' we should let the lad get some sleep," he cautioned

Angeleen. "Ye come wi' me, son. I hae a fine room over the stable. 'Tis plenty of space for the two of us."

"We'll talk in the morning, Princess," Robert said lovingly to his adored sister. He slipped his arm around her shoulders and the two followed their father to the door.

"Merry Christmas, Robert." Angeleen hugged him with all her strength.

"Merry Christmas, Angie," Robert said tenderly.

Thinking Ruark had already retired, Angeleen went to her own room. She foraged through an unpacked trunk and retrieved a nightgown and the velvet robe Ruark had given her. After undressing, she sat down before the fireplace to brush her hair and relive the memories of that miraculous night.

Deep in thought, a smile crossed her face. She put aside the brush, hugged her folded legs, and rested her chin on her knees.

Ruark found her that way.

He walked over and ruffled her hair. "A big night for you, Angel."

Smiling, she glanced up at him. "I don't think I can bear this much happiness, Ruark."

"I'm glad for you, Angel." He felt a stab of guilt remembering his initial moments of jealousy when Robert appeared. Ruark sensed that Robert Scott could still be an obstacle in their relationship, but he did not voice his suspicions to Angeleen.

Sitting down beside her, he handed her a brightly wrapped package, then lightly kissed her. "Merry Christmas, sweetheart."

"Oh, Ruark, with all the excitement tonight, I

almost forgot to give you your present."

She reached into the pocket of her robe where she had hidden her gift to him. "Merry Christmas." She handed him the small box.

"You open yours first," he insisted.

Angeleen cast him a girlish grin as she tore away the paper. Her eyes widened with astonishment when she lifted the cover of the jeweler's box and saw a necklace and earrings of sapphires and pearls.

"Ruark, it's exquisite. I've never seen anything so beautiful."

"Well, I have." He studied her face adoringly. "Put them on, so I can see how they look on you."

Angeleen shook her head. "I can't accept them, Ruark. Why, they must have cost a fortune." She closed the box and handed it back to him.

"Angel, I want you to have these." He opened the box and put the necklace around her neck. "The sapphires match your eyes. I knew they would," he said, pleased.

Angeleen fingered the precious gems. "Ruark, you've got to stop buying me these expensive gifts. They aren't necessary."

Ruark's hand closed over her mouth. "Hush, love. I enjoy giving you gifts. And remember, it's Christmas."

He held up her gift to him. Pressing his ear to the box, he listened as he shook it. "Now, what can this be?" Ruark pondered.

"Open it and find out," she suggested. "I'm afraid it's not precious stones, but it suits your style better. I hope you like it."

"Suits my style?" he asked with curiosity.

"It is very like you, altogether," she teased.

"Oh?" He raised an eyebrow. "And just how is that, me bonnie lass?"

"Well . . . just like you, you might say, it's a horse of a different color," she answered emphatically, her mouth set in a pout, but her eyes dancing with merriment.

As his long fingers tore away the paper, Angeleen noticed that a faint bruise still darkened the knuckles of his right hand, and she reached out, covering his hand with her own.

"Your knuckles are still bruised." Then she brought the injured hand to her lips. "There, all better."

The gesture brought back to both of them the memory of their spat in New York. He shifted his hand and gently stroked the discolored area of her cheek, then dipped his head and lightly brushed his lips across the bruise. "There, all better."

Held mesmerized by his dark eyes, she felt herself tremble. Finally, she shifted her gaze downward. "Well, open the gift."

She watched Ruark anxiously as he picked up the watch fob and dangled the gold horse in the air. "I love it," he said, genuinely moved by the thoughtful gesture.

Ruark gathered her into his arms. "Merry Christmas, sweetheart."

He carried her to the bed. After removing her robe and the necklace, Ruark tucked a warm quilt securely around her and sat down on the edge of the bed.

"Now you get some sleep," he ordered, brushing some errant strands of hair behind her ears. "Doctor's orders."

Angeleen slipped her arms around his neck. "I wish I were well enough for you to make love to me, Ruark."

He flashed the adoring grin she loved. "Not any more than I do, Angel."

He leaned down and pressed a kiss on her lips. He wanted to admit his earlier jealousy, but didn't know how to begin.

"Ruark, I . . ." She wanted to tell him how much she loved him, but feared the confession would only embarrass him. " . . . Merry Christmas."

"Merry Christmas, Angel."

Her gaze followed his broad shoulders as he walked to the door. Then with a smile of contentment, she closed her eyes and was asleep before he reached his room.

Early the following morning, Angeleen tapped lightly on Ruark's door and poked her head into the room. He had almost completed dressing.

"Merry Christmas." He pulled her into the room and kissed her soundly.

"Oh, this is going to be a glorious day, Ruark," she exclaimed. Seeing him struggle with his cravat, she shook her head. "Here, let me do that for you." As she knotted the tie, her cheeriness fled. "I wonder who will tie Robert's cravat for him?"

"He's alive, Angel. First things first," Ruark reminded her.

She smiled and finished the task. "You're right. Oh, Ruark, I'm so glad he's back."

He tweaked the tip of her nose. "I never would have guessed."

She sped to the window and peered out. Bright sunshine belied the sharp cut of winter. "And just look at this glorious day." She spun around in abandon. "Oh, how I wish I were well enough to climb on King and ride for hours."

Ruark eyed her with a raised brow; last night she had entertained a similar thought, only with him. He finished attaching the fob she had given him to his watch. "Angel, what did you do with my watch? I'd like to recover it, if I could."

Laughing lightly, she asked, "Your watch? You're holding your watch, Ruark."

"I mean the watch you took from me on the *Delta Queen*. It was a gift from . . ." The words faded as he looked up and saw her face. The glow had left her cheeks, and she stared at him as if he had just struck her.

"I didn't steal your watch, Ruark," she said solemnly.

Angeleen closed her eyes to press back the tears. Once again he had driven the knife of false suspicion into her heart.

Ruark regretted his words. He regretted having even harbored the thought. He walked over and put his hands on her shoulders. "I'm sorry, Angel. I was mistaken."

"I'll wait for you downstairs," she said woodenly and walked out of the room.

Ruark gritted his teeth and slammed his clenched fist on the armoire. "What in hell is wrong with me?" he cursed. "Last night—now this morning." At a time when she needed tenderness and understanding, he was driving her away with thoughtless, insensitive remarks. He hurriedly slipped the watch into his pocket and finished dressing.

As she walked down the stairway, Angeleen vowed to herself that she would not allow Ruark to spoil this day for her. His foolish mind had been set in one direction and she could not change it. Today was Christmas and last night she had been given a most blessed gift—Robert was alive.

In preparation for the Christmas breakfast Sarah Stewart hosted annually, the busy household buzzed like a beehive. The servants chatted happily as they rushed about filling the tables with tempting dishes that emitted savory aromas.

Spying Angeleen at the foot of the stairway, Sarah called out to her. "Angeleen, my dear, will you arrange these boughs? I seem to have lost my touch."

As Angeleen fussed with the centerpiece, she looked up just in time to see Ruark come down the stairway. He glanced hopefully in her direction for some sign of forgiveness, but she returned her attention to the task at hand.

Approaching her from across the foyer, Ruark turned toward the door when a rap sounded. Smiling to greet a guest, he opened the door only to be met by Henry's sad, crestfallen face. The old man stepped in alone.

"Where is Robert?" Angeleen asked.

"The lad's gone," Henry said sorrowfully. With downcast eyes, he walked away without further explanation.

Sarah and Ruark exchanged glances. Henry's reticent response said more than words could convey.

Dazed, Angeleen moved to the door and opened it, as if she expected Robert to appear. Ruark walked over to her and softly closed the door.

"Come on, honey, and eat some breakfast," he said gently.

Angeleen looked at him as if he were a stranger. Then she shrugged aside his hand and raced up the stairway. When Ruark began to follow, Sarah stopped him. "Give her this moment alone, Ruark. She needs it."

Grim-faced, Ruark strode over to Henry who stared desolately into the fire. "Where did he go, Henry?"

"The lad always had a short temper. He said he'd nae come to a house where his own sister was sellin' her body to keep a roof over her head. He went back to Rafferty's roomin' house in St. Louis."

"Rafferty's?" Ruark thought for a moment. "I know the place . . . it's near the wharf." With a purposeful stride, he returned to the foyer and put on his cloak.

"Where are you going?" Sarah asked.

"I'll be back, Nana."

Within minutes he was thundering down the road on his gelding.

Robert Scott jumped to his feet when Ruark pounded on the door and burst into the room. "Get out of here, Stewart. *My* money's paying for this room."

"I intend to, and you're coming with me. I don't care if I have to drag you back. You're not going to spoil Angeleen's Christmas."

227

Robert ignored the threat. "You heard me, Stewart, I said get out, or I'll have you thrown out. When I see my sister again, it won't be under the roof of a bastard like you."

"Maybe I am a bastard, Scott, but Angeleen doesn't need two of us in her life right now."

Some of the anger drained from Robert's dark eyes. He asked warily, "What are you talking about?"

Ruark propped a foot on a nearby chair and leaned his elbow on his knee. "There is something you haven't been told. Your sister was brutalized and almost murdered by a fiend in New York."

Having turned away, Robert spun around in astonishment. "What did you say?"

"I promised Angeleen I wouldn't tell anyone the full story, but I think it's necessary that you do know." For the next several moments, Ruark described the grisly details of Angeleen's brush with death, including the miscarriage.

"The doctor said she could be suppressing all this behind a brave front. I think your appearance has pushed all the horror out of her mind, but I doubt if she can handle your rejection of her. Apparently, you're some kind of a hero to her," Ruark added with disdain.

"I didn't know any of this." Robert slumped down on the edge of the bed.

Ruark waited silently as the man struggled with this disturbing information. After a few moments, Robert got to his feet and pulled on his coat.

"I'm coming with you, Stewart, but only for Angeleen's sake. I haven't changed my thinking. Someday, I have a score to settle with you."

Unperturbed, Ruark straightened up and walked to the door. "I'll be waiting."

He opened the door and glanced back at the angry man. "Can you handle a mount? We can rent one at the livery, or ride double on my gelding."

Robert scoffed his contempt. "One arm or two, Stewart, I've forgotten more about handling horses than you'll ever know."

"Oh, let me guess," Ruark groaned. "Next I'll have to hear how you rode with Jeb Stuart."

"Up to and including the day he died, Yankee," Robert countered contemptuously, following Ruark out of the room.

By the time Angeleen rejoined the others, Ruark and Robert had arrived back on the scene. At the sight of her brother, Angeleen's joy exploded, her happiness rebounded. She even forgot her displeasure with Ruark, unmindful of the role he had played in her brother's return to the festivities.

Chapter Fifteen

Angeleen's happiness was short-lived. Every time Ruark put his arm around Angeleen, Robert seethed with anger and bitterness. Once the day's activities had ended, he left with a cool good-bye. The bridges had not been mended.

When Robert did not appear all the following week, on New Year's Day Angeleen took the matter to her father.

"Have you heard from Robert, Poppa?"

Henry glanced up from the tack he was mending. "Aye, lass. Your brother's stayin' in St. Louis. He's got hi'self a job dealin' cards in a gambling house." Henry quickly returned his attention to the leather straps in his hand.

"Well, why doesn't he come to see us?" she asked, confused.

"The lad's stubborn. He says he hae nae to say to ye until ye come to your senses."

Angeleen sighed deeply, finally understanding the reason for Robert's absence. First her father, now her brother. Why were men so convinced a woman didn't know her own mind, her own heart?

Desolately, she fed Bold King an apple. "Well, at least he's staying in St. Louis."

After patting the stallion's neck, she turned with tears misting her eyes. "And he's alive, Poppa. And we're all . . . together." Her chin began to quiver.

Henry put his arms around her. "Now, now, lass," he soothed. "The lad will come around. Just gie him time to chew on the taste of it."

After leaving the barn, crestfallen, she walked back to the house and met Ruark, just on the verge of departing. He stopped when he saw her despondency. "Aren't you feeling well, Angel?"

"I'm fine. I was just talking to Poppa."

Knowing Angeleen would eventually voice her thoughts, Ruark waited patiently. He suspected that her brother's departure and attitude were the crux of her problem.

"Poppa said Robert has a job in St. Louis."

"I know. He's a dealer at one of the local . . . gaming houses."

"You knew?" she exclaimed. "Why didn't you tell me?"

"I just assumed you already knew, Angel. Matter of fact, I'm playing cards there tonight." Ruark kissed her quickly and climbed into the waiting carriage.

Angeleen watched the carriage rumble down the

driveway. As she returned to her room her mind began to toy with an idea.

After dinner as Ruark dressed to go out, Angeleen approached him. "May I accompany you tonight?"

He appeared surprised. "Angel, I'm going to play poker. You would be bored."

"If I am, Ruark, I could always come back in a carriage."

A note of irritation crept into his voice. "I prefer you to stay home."

"Ruark, I've been cooped up in this house for a week. I would like to get out for a while."

"I prefer you *stay home*, Angeleen," he repeated, this time emphatically.

"Very well." She spun on her heel and left. *Stubborn bullhead*, she said to herself and promptly decided she would go unescorted.

As soon as he left, Angeleen dressed in one of her new gowns and waited at the window for Ruark's carriage to return, then she intercepted the driver.

"Daniel, Mr. Stewart expects me to join him. I'm ready to leave."

The driver looked somewhat perplexed. "Are you sure, ma'am? Mr. Stewart said nothing about this to me."

"Well, I'm sure it was just an oversight on his part," Angeleen declared as she climbed into the carriage. Shaking his head, Daniel hopped up on the driver's seat.

Nearing the waterfront, Daniel turned off the road and followed a long driveway to the white-columned entrance of a converted mansion, ablaze with light.

The driver looked dubious as he assisted her from

the carriage. "Do you wish for me to remain, Mrs. Hunter? Mr. Stewart told me not to return until midnight."

Angeleen glanced at the many parked carriages lined up in a row. "Oh, would you, Daniel? I don't expect to remain long." She intended to leave as soon as she talked to Robert.

"Whenever you're ready, ma'am."

In answer to her knock, a black man opened the door. He appeared surprised, and his eyes looked to either side of her. "Your escort, madam?"

Fearing the establishment was a private club and she would be turned away, Angeleen declared boldly, "I'm here as the guest of Mr. Stewart."

He stepped aside and permitted her to enter. As Angeleen handed him her cloak, he nodded toward a double set of closed doors. "I think you will find Mr. Stewart in the gaming room."

Angeleen glanced about with interest as she entered the room opulently decorated with crystal chandeliers and red settees. Half a dozen round tables were placed around the room, most of them occupied by five or six men. A wide staircase with black mahogany banisters and red carpeting led to the floor above.

As her gaze swept the room, Angeleen was relieved to see other women present, but she saw no sign of her brother.

However, she did see Ruark Stewart approach, his eyes black with the fury of a raging bull.

"Why did you follow me here?" he demanded in a low whisper through gritted teeth. "I told you to remain at home."

Her temper flared to match his anger. "Ruark, do not issue orders to me. I am not a servant in your household."

"Dammit, Angel, you know that's not what I mean. I asked you not to come because this is just no place for you. I'll take you home now."

"I came here to speak to my brother. I didn't come to spoil your evening. So, please, Ruark, return to your card game."

Angeleen faced him defiantly. For a long moment, Ruark stared at her, tempted to take her by the arm and bodily remove her, but when he saw her determination, he thought better of it.

"Very well, Angeleen. I guess you've made up your mind."

His surrender brought a smile of relief to her lips. She didn't want to quarrel with him. "Thank you, Ruark. I'm sorry for being such a problem, but I do want to speak to Robert."

A dimple danced in each of her cheeks and Ruark was helpless to resist the sight. "Now please go back to your game."

He smiled grudgingly. "Very well, Angel, but stay close." He kissed her cheek and returned to the poker table he had hurriedly abandoned.

Angeleen strolled aimlessly around the room, hoping that Robert would soon make an appearance. Soon impatient, she decided it would just be her luck for him not to show up that night. She finally sat down on a couch near the stairway to await her brother's arrival.

Until then, Angeleen's thoughts had been occupied. Now as she sat idly staring around her, she took the opportunity to observe the other women in the room.

They were all young, too young for the ages of the men present. With a sudden start, it dawned on Angeleen why gentlemen did not bring their wives to such an establishment; the house offered more than just gambling, she concluded as she noticed several couples climb the stairway and disappear into rooms above.

No wonder Ruark had been angry.

Mortified, Angeleen wandered through an archway into an adjacent sitting room. The fresher air brought relief from the pungent odor of cigar smoke that hung in layers throughout the game room. Drawing deep breaths of air, she tried to escape the oppressive atmosphere. She felt cheap and soiled. Why hadn't Ruark simply told her the truth about the place? He was so adamant about other things. Swept by warmth, Angeleen raised a hand to her heated brow.

"Are you feeling ill, *mademoiselle?*"

Startled, Angeleen glanced up to discover a young woman standing a short distance away. "No, it's just that the smoke and heat are so stifling."

"Yes, I agree." The young woman began to fan herself.

For a moment, Angeleen closely studied the speaker, a tiny girl who couldn't have been a day over seventeen. A red satin gown, with black lace peeking out from the low neckline, clung to her curves.

The young woman's face was heavily coated with powder and rouge, her eyes darkly lined with kohl. A black plume had been tucked into the mass of honey-blond curls piled on top of her head, and several love curls dangled from her temple.

She looked like a painted porcelain doll.

"Are you from this area?" Angeleen asked in an attempt at conversation.

"*Oui*. My parents lived right here in the French Quarter. But they've been gone these past two years. The doctor called it influenza."

"Oh, I'm sorry," Angeleen said. "Have you no other family?"

"None. My brother was killed in the war."

Angeleen felt an instant empathy for the young woman. Another uncounted casualty of the hideous and senseless war.

An awkward silence developed between them until the young woman smiled and nodded. "It has been a pleasure, *Mademoiselle*. Good luck." She went back inside.

Angeleen lingered for several minutes, reflecting on the woman's unusual parting remark. Then she returned to the game room, intending to leave the wretched establishment.

Upon entering, Angeleen was pleased to see that Robert had just arrived. He saw her at once and his expression shifted into an angry scowl. Hurrying to her side, Robert took her arm and forced Angeleen back into the sitting room.

She felt his painful grasp, amazed by the strength in his hand. "Robert, please unhand me. You're hurting me."

He released his hold on her. "What are you doing here?"

She stepped back, shocked by his obvious anger.

His black scowl looked almost murderous. "I wanted to talk to you."

"Stewart brought you here!" he exclaimed through gritted teeth. "This is no place for a lady. The man treats you like a common whore."

Angeleen reached out and clasped his hand, bringing it to her lips. "No, he doesn't, Robert. But I am his mistress. Why can't you accept it? Poppa does." She smiled softly and pressed his hand to her cheek.

Robert snatched away his hand. "Never. As long as I draw a breath, I'll never accept it," he fumed. "You are my sister, Angeleen." Outraged, he stormed away.

Fearing Robert would force a confrontation with Ruark, Angeleen hurried after him. Much to her relief, he sat down at a table on the opposite end of the room from Ruark.

The young woman Angeleen had spoken to earlier stood behind the chair of a player at Robert's table. Angeleen glanced curiously at the man, then noted with uneasiness the abject cruelty she saw in his thin, angular face and narrow eyes.

At the moment he had just lost the pot to an obese man seated opposite him. Snarling in disgust, the loser threw down his cards.

The white flabby jowls of the heavy-set man shook with laughter as he swept up the pot. Then, with pudgy, truncated fingers that appeared to have no knuckles, he stacked his winnings into a pile.

An aura of malevolence about both men caused Angeleen to turn away with a shudder of revulsion. She strayed over to a nearby red velvet settee, sat down, and decided to wait another quarter of an hour before trying to speak to Robert again. However, her brother's mood seemed so black, she doubted she would have any success. Now she was afraid to leave Robert and Ruark together. Angeleen considered feigning illness, certain Ruark would depart with her.

Casting a fretful glance at Robert, she saw him pick up the deck to deal. She watched, as fascinated as the others, while Robert's long fingers adroitly shuffled the deck with only his right hand.

"Well, we can't accuse the man of slipping an ace up his sleeve," the thin man said tactlessly.

Robert ignored the remark and quickly peeled off the cards. His function was merely to deal, not to participate in the hand. The betting eventually narrowed down until only the same two men remained in the game.

"I have no more money. Perhaps you will accept my marker?" the girl's companion asked after several raises.

Lord! Don't men ever set a limit on how much they're willing to lose? Angeleen thought in disgust.

"No offense, my friend, but I am not interested in your marker. Have you nothing more of value?" the fat man asked.

The girl's companion reminded Angeleen of the river scum she had seen in Natchez Under The Hill. However, his accent was not that of a Southerner. Unwilling to relinquish the pot, he looked about in desperation. Then his narrow eyes gleamed in triumph as he turned to the woman behind him.

"Give me your ring, Celeste."

She drew back in alarm. "No, Sam. It was my mother's. The ring has no value to anyone except me," she said softly.

"Don't argue, slut. Do as I say," Sam snarled. He grabbed her wrist and twisted the ring off her finger.

Angeleen was appalled. She jumped to her feet, shocked by the man's brutishness, and her eyes swung toward Robert. Her brother sat silently with the rest, but the grim set of his clenched jaw and a twitching nerve in his cheek revealed the anger of a man fighting to keep control.

The fat man picked up the ring and examined the narrow gold band. For the moment, his squinting eyelids obliterated the round, piggish eyes that looked pink against the pale flab of his face.

"The young woman is your wife, my friend?" he asked, lifting his head to gape lasciviously at Celeste's breasts.

"Hell, no!" Sam snarled. "Do you agree to the ring?"

"The girl is right, my friend. The ring is of little value. But perhaps we can work out . . . an arrangement."

Sam frowned. "Arrangement? What kind of arrangement?"

"The young lady, perhaps." Smirking lewdly, the fat man motioned with a slight nod of his head toward the stairway.

Grasping his meaning, Sam's mouth curled into a smirk. "Agreed."

Celeste's eyes widened in shock. "No, Sam. What are you saying? I won't go with him."

The fat man licked his lips, his pig eyes gleaming salaciously. "The young lady appears unwilling, my friend. If she prefers your company"—his brow rose suggestively—"perhaps we should consider a threesome?"

"That's worth another fifty-dollar raise in the pot," Sam snickered.

The fat man nodded. "I call your raise, my friend."

Sam turned over four queens. The fat man's eyes gleamed like pink diamonds as he turned over his hand and spread out four kings.

Laughter rumbled from the core of his huge stomach. "The queens are dead; long live the kings." The man stood up and reached out a hand to Celeste. "Come, my dear."

Sobbing, Celeste backed away. "No—please. Please, Sam, I don't want to do this."

Sam grabbed her hand and began tugging the reluctant girl toward the stairway.

"No," Celeste whimpered. "Please, I don't want to."

He shoved her ahead of him. "Ah, quit that spewling. You'll enjoy it the same as us."

Each man took her in hand, forcing Celeste to climb the stairs. Angeleen stood transfixed, watching the scene unfold as if she were having a nightmare. She couldn't believe no one would come to the aid of the defenseless girl.

Angeleen looked for help toward Ruark, but he was absorbed in a card game at the other end of the room, unaware of the situation.

The sound of her brother's voice broke the spell. "The lady said she does not wish to join you gentlemen." His chair made a piercing screech on the wooden floor as he shoved it back and rose to his feet.

The two men on the stairs looked back over their shoulders. Robert's words had galvanized the other men at the table to action; they knocked over chairs in their haste to scamper out of the way.

Sam's face curved in contempt at the sight of Robert standing alone, and he turned to confront Robert as Celeste slumped to her knees on the stairs. The fat man released her hand, but Sam maintained his grasp on her.

"What business is it of yours?" Sam growled.

Robert Scott had nursed his black mood throughout the bully's base treatment of the girl. In the throes of anger, Robert visualized his sister eventually being debased in this heinous manner at the hands of Ruark Stewart. His imagination raged out of control, and his consequent fury spurred him to bold action. He wanted to kill the man.

"Where I come from, sir, we treat our women with considerably more respect." His icy tone revealed his malice. "I repeat, the lady does not wish to join you. I insist you release her at once."

The tense scene had stopped every other movement in the large room. Not even a murmur could be heard as all eyes were fixed on the two men.

Horrified, Angeleen stood with a balled fist raised to her mouth. She did not notice that Ruark had moved to her side.

"You talk brave for a one-armed cripple. You expectin' I'm gonna tie an arm behind my back to fight you?" Sam snickered.

"You may choose the weapon, you Yankee scum," Robert said calmly.

The fat man saw murder in Robert's eyes and recognized that the quarrel went beyond championing the whore. He mopped at his brow with a lace-trimmed handkerchief. "Aw, she's not worth fighting over. Let's forget the whole thing." He hurried down the stairs and out of the door as quickly as his short, trembling legs could carry him, abandoning his winnings on the table.

A lethal threat raged beneath Robert's controlled demeanor. Sam realized that Robert had no intention of backing down, and he recognized that the situation was more serious than he'd thought. He stepped down to the foot of the stairway.

"I killed enough of you stinkin' Rebs during the war, all nice and legal-like. But I ain't gonna hang for killin' one now. 'Specially a damn one-armed cripple."

He glanced back at Celeste, who was slumped on the stairway. "You comin' with me?" When the young girl shook her head, his mouth curled in contempt. "Well then stay, you worthless trollop. You belong here with these other whores. You ain't no good in bed anyway."

He stopped in front of Angeleen and she backed away in revulsion. Having noticed her before, Sam's mouth curled in a salacious smirk as he swept her with a scorching perusal. "Now you, honey, you look like a man could have a real fine time humpin' ya. Wanta come along with me?"

A powerful hand grabbed Sam's shirt front and slammed him against the wall. "Get out of here while you're still able to walk," Ruark intoned and promptly flung him away.

Sam hit the floor sprawled out on his back. Scrambling to his feet, and mewling a final curse, he stumbled through the door.

Sam's departure triggered the room to action. The sound and motion of men at their gaming tables resumed as if nothing had happened.

Ruark took Angeleen's arm. "Come on, Angel, let's get out of here."

"Oh, Ruark, look at her," Angel said sadly. She nodded toward Celeste, who was still sitting on the stairway. "The poor girl doesn't know what to do. We just can't leave her here."

"Honey, she's not a stray cat you take home with you. I'll give her some money to tide her over until she takes up with another Sam. Her kind know how to take care of themselves."

Shrugging off his hand, Angeleen glared up at him. "Her kind? And is she any different than I am, Ruark?"

She walked over to the table. Smiling grimly at Angeleen, Robert nodded toward Celeste. "Well, sister dear, *there but for the grace of God . . .* "

"No lectures, Robert," Angeleen snapped in anger. Snatching Celeste's ring from the table, she hurried over to the girl and sat down.

"Are you feeling all right, Celeste?" she asked gently.

Celeste smiled and nodded. "Yes . . . I feel much better now. And good riddance to that hateful man."

"Do you have somewhere to stay tonight?" Angeleen said.

"Oh, yes. I have a room nearby."

Celeste glanced at Ruark, who stood waiting with Angeleen's wrap in his hand. "I think your gentlemen friend is becoming impatient, *mademoiselle*. And I must thank the man who intervened in my behalf."

"That was my brother, Robert. Robert Scott," Angeleen said.

Celeste had not let Robert out of her sight. Just then, she saw him putting on his cloak to depart and jumped to her feet. "Oh, he is leaving. I must go." She hurried away without even saying good-bye to Angeleen.

Grinning broadly, Ruark approached her. "Well, are you ready to leave now?" he asked, extending a hand to help her get up.

Deep in thought, Angeleen took his hand absentmindedly, feeling somewhat rebuked by the woman's indifference to her offer of help.

After putting her wrap around her shoulders, Ruark walked around Angeleen in a circle, his eyes scanning the floor in an apparent search.

His movements interrupted her distraction. "Whatever are you looking for?"

"Well, I don't see any stray dogs or cats clinging to your skirts, so I guess we can leave now. But perhaps we'll encounter one or two on the way home."

His roguish eyes caught hers and she smiled at herself. As much as she hated to admit it, Ruark had been right. Celeste appeared to be able to take care of herself.

When Celeste caught up to Robert, she found him

engaged in a low-keyed conversation with the owner of the establishment.

"I'm sorry to have to discharge you, Mr. Scott, but my establishment has a reputation to maintain. Discretion and confidentiality are the tools of my success," Celeste heard the middle-aged woman say. "I cannot have any confrontation between one of my dealers and a client." She shoved several bills into his pocket. "Good luck, Reb."

For a moment before departing, Robert's gaze shifted across the room to Ruark and Angeleen, and he saw them laughing together. Then he left without another word.

Celeste followed him outside. "*Monsieur* Scott, please wait."

Robert stopped to wait for her. Celeste went on, "I'm so sorry you lost your position because of me. I'm grateful for what you did for me tonight. If it weren't for you, I would be—" She blushed, unable to continue.

Robert felt the fool. He didn't know what to say to the girl. His anger had cooled, and he knew he had not acted out of chivalry on behalf of this girl, but because of his anger and frustration with Ruark Stewart.

Nodding in embarrassment, he started to walk away, but she rejoined him. Once again Robert halted his step. "Goodnight, Miss—"

"Dupree." She smiled up at him. "Celeste Dupree."

Robert studied her more closely and for the first time noticed her beautiful green eyes, which sparkled like emeralds in the dim light of the lamppost.

"Goodnight, Miss Dupree."

Just then Angeleen and Ruark came out of the building. She called to her brother as their carriage appeared. "Robert, can we drive you home?"

"Good Lord, Angel. The man hates the sight of me," Ruark grumbled at her ear.

"He's my brother, Ruark," she snapped in reprimand.

However, their exchange was for naught. "I prefer to walk. It's just a short distance," Robert called out and waved good-bye.

As Ruark assisted Angeleen into the carriage, he glanced at the couple walking down the driveway. His mouth curved into a satisfied smile as he reflected on what a superb judge of character he was. "I told you the little stray cat would find a new home," he boasted.

Angeleen popped her head out of the open door of the carriage. "You mean . . . Robert?" She grinned with surprise, and then pleasure, comforted, even delighted, to hear her brother would not spend the night alone.

"My, my, Miss Angeleen. That's a wicked smile," Ruark teased. He shoved her head back into the carriage and was about to climb in himself when he saw a figure step out of the shadows behind Robert. Glimpsing a flash of metal in the man's hand, Ruark shouted, "Robert, look out behind you."

Years of war had taught him survival, and Robert acted instinctively as he shoved Celeste to the ground. Dropping down beside her, he withdrew a derringer from his boot just as the assailant fired. Robert returned the fire, and his bullet found its mark. The man fell to the ground.

Ruark sprinted down the street as Angeleen bolted out of the carriage and raced behind him. Reaching Robert and Celeste, the four cautiously approached the fallen man and found that he was dead.

"Why, it's Sam!" Celeste exclaimed.

The shots had attracted attention. By the time a policeman arrived, a crowd of curious spectators had surrounded the corpse.

As a witness to the shooting, Ruark explained what he had seen, and the officer assumed that Sam had been killed attempting to rob the couple. None of the four contradicted the policeman's theory.

"The bastard tried to bushwhack you," Ruark said to Robert after Sam's body had been hauled away.

"He wasn't the first Yankee who thought he could get away with it," Robert replied. He frowned grimly. "Guess I should thank you for the warning."

"I guess you should," Angeleen said, relieved. "Ruark just saved your life."

She turned to Ruark. "Robert's not the only grateful one. I should thank you, too."

Devilishness gleamed in his eyes. "And I know just how you can," Ruark said.

Angeleen saw Robert's cheek begin to twitch. Before another fight could break out, she kissed her brother and said a quick good-bye. Then, taking Ruark's hand, she practically ran back to the carriage.

"Hurry, Daniel," she called out, slammed the door, and shoved Ruark back into the seat.

Ruark pulled her onto his lap. "My God, woman, your eagerness is downright gratifying."

His mouth traced a moist trail down the column

of her neck as his hand slid inside her wrap to cup a breast.

"You know I was only trying to avoid an argument between you and Robert," she protested.

Ruark succeeded in slipping the gown off her shoulders, baring her breasts. He dipped his head and ran his tongue across each of the pert tips.

At the soft sound of her quick intake of breath, his teeth closed around one of the nipples and he tugged at it. This time a gasp slipped past her lips.

"Ruark, Daniel—"

"Cannot see or hear a thing unless you are unable to contain yourself and cry out in ecstasy."

"You arrogant oaf," she chided. Her admonishment stopped abruptly as his mouth closed over one breast and he began to suckle. An erotic shiver raced the length of her spine.

She closed her eyes to shut out everything except the exquisite sensation he was creating. Her fingertips tingled as she wove her fingers through the thick texture of his dark hair, pressing him ever tighter against her heaving breasts.

He slipped his hand under her gown, seeking the throbbing core of her. His strong, long fingers parted her and found the sensitive nub.

The rhythm of his toying intensified. "Damn you, Ruark. Oh, damn you," she moaned, driven to that divine moment of madness. Her body erupted with tremor upon tremor.

Ruark raised his head to look at her. Her incredible sapphire eyes were so deep with passion, they looked black. He loved to watch her at her moment of climax—the moment after she waged a losing battle, not against him, but against her own sensualism.

When her spasms ceased, her head slumped against his chest.

"I'll get even with you for this," she threatened in breathless gasps.

"Oh, I hope so, Angel. I hope so," he whispered as his mouth closed over hers.

Chapter Sixteen

Robert waited until the carriage bearing Angeleen and Ruark had rolled away. Once again he allowed his anger to cool. How could his beloved Angeleen claim to love that arrogant bastard?

He spun around hurriedly, determined to get home quickly and put the events of this damned night behind him. The quick movement caused a dizziness and he staggered, clutching his head.

"*Monsieur*, what is wrong?" Celeste asked, still beside him. "Lean on me." Her arm encircled his waist in an effort to support him.

When Robert lowered his arm, his hand felt wet and sticky. Looking at it, he discovered blood on his palm.

"*Mon Dieu!* You are bleeding!"

Annoyed by her alarm, he wiped his hand on his

coat and shrugged off her concern. "It's nothing but a scrape."

"But, *monsieur*—"

"For God's sake, my name is Robert," he snapped, then realized shamefully that he had unleashed his temper on Celeste when she only meant to be helpful.

However, Robert's dizziness persisted, and he allowed her to assist him. Somehow, the tiny girl managed to get the wounded man up the flight of stairs to his room, where Robert collapsed on the bed and fell instantly asleep.

Celeste examined his injury. Relieved to see that Sam's bullet had only nicked Robert's scalp, she sponged away the blood and cleansed the wound. Then she put her ear to his chest. The rhythm of his breathing seemed steady and strong.

Satisfied that it was not necessary to summon a doctor, Celeste tried to make Robert as comfortable as possible. She removed his cloak, then his boots and stockings. Her movements slowed when she got to the coat with the left sleeve folded and pinned to the upper half.

After slipping the coat and shirt off his shoulders, her glance moved to the left arm. The limb had been amputated to just above the elbow. Shaking her head sadly, she turned her attention to removing his trousers.

Celeste allowed her glance to travel the length of him. Robert's chest was muscular and his shoulders broad and sloping. A thick matting of dark hair trailed down to his underwear. He had long, muscular legs and the solid bulge in the underpants indicated that the rest of his body was perfectly formed.

This pleased her.

Although exhausted from the struggle of undressing him, she did not relax until she had him tucked securely beneath the bedding. Then Celeste slumped down in the room's only chair, which was small, wooden, and very uncomfortable.

For what seemed like hours, Celeste watched the still man on the bed. Feeling chilled, she wrapped his cloak about her. She did not want to leave until he regained consciousness and she could be certain he would be able to fend for himself.

A smile softened the young woman's face as she studied Robert Scott. His eyes, set wide apart, were fringed with thick, dark lashes. Although the nose seemed a bit too broad, and the chin too square for him to be considered handsome, nonetheless his face was not unpleasant to gaze upon.

His features were softened by sleep; but awake, she knew, the troubled dark eyes gave him a perpetually wary expression. Celeste wondered whether the man ever laughed, or if he was always in anger. Then her gaze shifted to where the blanket lay flat on his armless left side.

"Perhaps you have good reason not to smile, Robert Scott," she said softly.

In the last two years, ever since she had been orphaned, she had known the company of many men. None had been as cruel as Sam Brazer, yet no man had ever defended her the way this stranger had tonight. Why had he acted so courageously, to the point of risking his life for her sake? Her chest

and heart felt heavy at the thought of how easily
Sam might have killed Robert.

When she could no longer keep her eyes open,
Celeste pulled off her gown, kicked off her shoes,
and crawled beneath the covers beside him. She had
barely closed her eyes before she slept.

Upon arriving home, Angeleen prepared herself
for bed. As she sat brushing her hair in her favorite
spot before the fireplace, Ruark entered the room
carrying a tray.

"M-m-m-m-m, that smells good," she said.

Ruark sat down on the floor beside her. "I made
you a cup of hot chocolate."

Her face beamed with pleasure. "You spoil me,
Ruark. I'm not used to being waited on. But I have
to admit, I enjoy it." After a few sips of the hot brew,
she flashed a dimpled smile. "It's delicious."

Ruark leaned over and lightly kissed her. "So are
you."

"I shouldn't drink this. It keeps me awake."

"Well, then I'll just have to stay awake with you."
His brow arched in devilishness. "I'm sure we'll think
of something to do."

Angeleen's smile faded as she cast a sheepish
glance at him. "Ruark, I should have listened to
you tonight and never left the house."

"It's over and done with, Angel. Accept what you
can't change and don't dwell on it."

"I wish my brother had that attitude. Do you think
he'll ever forgive me?"

Ruark grinned. "Maybe you, Angel, but certainly
not me."

He took the cup out of her hand and put it aside. Gathering her into his arms, he traced a trail of kisses down the column of her neck. Angeleen sighed and lay back in his arms.

"Now that you're all warm and mellow, I've got something to tell you."

Her eyes were clear and trusting as she waited for him to continue. "I'm leaving for England next week. I have several horses entered in races in Europe."

Her heart sank to her stomach at the thought of being separated from him. "How long will you be gone?"

"Through the whole racing season, Angel. At least nine or ten months."

He might as well have said nine or ten years; it sounded like an eternity to her.

"Will you come with me, Angel? I know I have no right to ask you—"

Her joy burst forth, unrestrained. "Oh, yes, Ruark. Yes, yes, yes."

"Hey, slow down, Angel, and think about it," he said, pleased. "We'll be gone for almost a year. Are you certain you want to leave your father and brother that long?"

She slipped her arms around his neck. "I don't have to think about it, Ruark. I want to go with you."

He hugged her and then kissed her deeply. As his passion increased, he raised his head and smiled down into the exquisite glory of her upturned face.

"This is New Year's Day, the beginning of a new year. Happy New Year, Angel."

"Happy New Year, Ruark," she whispered in the

second before his mouth covered hers.

That night, for the first time since the incident in New York, Angeleen lay in Ruark's arms as he made love to her.

Ruark had exercised excessive control after their return to Missouri. Even though she had recovered physically, he feared that an aggressive move on his part would cause her to withdraw.

He had deliberately aroused her sexuality in the carriage, hoping to bring her to a climax while she was fully clothed and feeling less vulnerable. Her response had been more than he had expected.

Now, as he filled her, she slipped her arms around his neck, and her sigh sounded as melodic as a symphony to his ears.

When Robert Scott opened his eyes, he saw Celeste lying beside him, her blond curls tumbled on the pillow in delightful disarray. This startling, but fetching, discovery caused an instant swelling in his loins.

He lifted the blanket and saw that she was partially dressed, whereas he had been stripped down to his drawers. His passion quelled as quickly as it had been aroused. Mortified, Robert turned his head away from the sleeping girl.

Robert Scott was a proud man—perhaps too proud for his own peace of mind. From the moment he had awakened in a Pennsylvania hospital and discovered the loss of his arm, he had not sought female companionship, not even the paid services of a prostitute. The cannon ball that severed his arm had stripped his self-esteem as well.

Ignoring the throbbing pain in his head, Robert quickly rose to his feet and pulled on his shirt. Having concealed the gross infirmity, a sight surely repugnant to her eyes, Robert finished dressing.

He picked up the red satin gown Celeste had hastily cast aside and placed the dress at the foot of the bed. Then he slipped out of the room, quietly closing the door.

When Celeste awoke a short time later, she was disappointed to discover Robert gone. "The foolish man should have stayed in bed," she scolded aloud.

She arose and, with typical feminine curiosity, examined the room. A thread-worn oval rug covered the middle of the floor. The bed, the chair, and a broken-down armoire were the only furniture.

Celeste inspected the armoire. Robert's few clothes were neatly stacked in piles. Unable to find a robe, she picked up her gown but she could not smooth out the wrinkles.

"There must be water somewhere," she lamented and grabbed the ewer from the top shelf of the armoire. Poking her head out of the door, she saw no one in the hallway and trotted down to the end of the corridor to the bathroom which had a pump, tub, and several towels. After filling the ewer, she grabbed a towel and returned to Robert's room.

Celeste washed her face and hands, then picked up Robert's hair brush and tried to create order out of disorder.

When she finished, Celeste put on her shoes, slung her wrap around her shoulders, and left the room.

Seated in the cafe across the street, Robert lowered the newspaper he had been reading when he saw Celeste come out of the building. Through a window streaked with grime and yellowed with stale smoke, he saw the girl pause momentarily in the doorway, then walk up the street. His pensive gaze followed the swing of her hips until she turned the corner and disappeared from sight.

He left the cafe and returned to his room.

As soon as she reached her lodging, Celeste removed her gown and hung it on one of the many empty pegs that lined the wall. She would press the dress later. Rummaging through a rumpled pile of clothes, she found a frothy black pelisse ornately trimmed with feathers.

Celeste looked around in dismay at the room she had shared with the late Sam Brazer; clothes and discarded newspapers lay everywhere. The room was a disaster compared to Robert's tidy chamber.

The time had come to clean up the room and rid herself of everything belonging to Sam. Since he had nothing of value she could sell, she began by haphazardly throwing his clothes, personal items, and litter into a carton he had stashed in the corner of the room.

Then, wanting every trace of Sam gone, and most particularly his scent, she immediately changed the linens on the bed.

"Good riddance," she mumbled to herself. Life with Sam Brazer had been difficult, and she felt relieved to be done with him.

She had picked up the broom and begun sweeping the floor when a rap at the door interrupted her labor. On opening the door, she was taken aback by the sight of her landlord, Mr. Haley, a short, skinny man, bald except for a fringe of stringy hair that hung to his shoulders.

He stuck his head into the room, the gaze in his narrow eyes shifting like a ferret's. Seeing no sign of Sam, a lecherous idea brought a smirk to his gap-toothed mouth.

"Mornin', Miz Dupree."

"Good morning, Mr. Haley." Her voice remained cordial but she despised the man. He was the last person she wanted to see at any time, but especially at this moment.

"Came to collect the rent."

"I don't have the money now, Mr. Haley, but I'll give it to you tomorrow."

"Can't ya git it from that boyfriend of yours?" he asked, still sniffing about for a chance opportunity.

"Sam's gone." Celeste turned away and put the broom in the corner.

Haley stepped in and closed the door. "Whad he do, run out on ya?"

"No, he's dead. Got shot trying to kill a man."

"Well now, I'm real sorry to hear that," Haley said, with as much sympathy as a snake coiled to spring. "So whata ya gonna do now? I ain't runnin' no charity house, you know."

Celeste sighed desolately. "I'll have you the money by tomorrow, Mr. Haley."

"Now, Miz Dupree, how many times have I told ya to call me Chester?" He put a hand on her arm. "The way I see it, there's no use in you gettin' all upset about nothin', girlie. Just maybe we can work us out a little . . . trade."

Celeste tried not to shudder with revulsion at the sight of grime-caked nails on the bony fingers encircling her wrist.

Pulling her arm away, she avoided responding to his proposition by nodding at the box in the corner. "Why don't you take that box of Sam's clothes, Mr.—ah, Chester. I've got no need for them."

"It's for sure Sam don't neither." He snickered and shuffled over to pick up the box of clothes. "I'll be back tomorrow, first thing in the morning, girlie." He grinned, the gaping smile coming into play.

Celeste almost shoved him out the door, then leaned back against it in relief. Somehow, she would have to get enough money to pay for her lodging. She couldn't bear the thought of that man touching her. *Men!* She shook her head at the thought.

In truth, men had never dealt with her kindly.

Her parents had succumbed to influenza during the War. When the fifteen-year-old girl was also stricken with the dreaded disease, the kindly old doctor who had treated her parents took her into his home to tend her.

But when the crisis passed, and she was well on the road to recovery, she awoke one night to find the doctor mounted on top of her. Frightened and having no place to go, she remained with him. Only the housekeeper knew how the doctor used the orphaned girl as a plaything.

When the old man died, the housekeeper wasted

no time informing the family of the relationship; they immediately dispensed with Celeste.

She found a position as a maid in the home of the sheriff, which lasted until the night his two teenaged sons overpowered and raped her.

The sheriff and his wife threatened that if she told anyone of the incident, they would swear she had seduced their innocent sons, and she would be sent to prison.

Once again Celeste found herself on the street. She easily fell into the role of living off men. The war ended, and the city took in the returning Union troops. She caught the eye of a Yankee captain and became his mistress. That kept a roof over her head and food in her stomach—until his duty ended and he returned to his wife in Massachusetts.

She then moved on to Lieutenant Brady, another officer who paid the rent in return for her services.

Sam Brazer had been selling contraband liquor to the Union Army, and his primary dealings were with Brady. When the Army left St. Louis, Sam lost the market for his illegal sales, and Celeste lost the source of her meal ticket.

Seeing an easy mark, Sam wanted Celeste. She had never cared for the man, but since she could find no other gainful employment, Celeste consented and bore the man's frequent brutality for the sake of a place to live.

Now he too was gone.

Celeste glanced desolately into the mirror. Once again, the need had arisen for her to find yet another provider.

* * *

Robert ignored the steady rapping at the door—it was probably only Celeste again. He had purposely avoided her in the week since Sam Brazer had tried to kill him—a week since Celeste Dupree had awakened feelings he had hoped were buried forever.

Even liquor wasn't helping his misery. His hand shook as he poured more whiskey into the glass before him. He rarely sought the bottom of a liquor bottle for solace, but today he made an exception. One more drink, Robert figured, and he would pass out cold.

The door opened and, in his typical fashion, Ruark Stewart strode in as if he owned the place. After a disgruntled glance at the intruder, Robert downed the liquor in one gulp and poured himself another drink.

Ruark spoke first. "I understand you lost your job."

"Job?" Robert snarled. "Big loss! Dealing cards in a whorehouse to perverts and rich bastards cheating on their wives." Casting a smirk of contempt at Ruark, he added, "You sure were in the right company, Stewart."

The liquor began to take its final toll; Robert felt numb, and for the first time in months his missing arm quit aching. He poured another drink and gulped it down.

"Before you drink yourself into oblivion, I have a proposition for you."

"Save your breath, Stewart. I'm not interested in any of your propositions . . . you're talking to the wrong Scott."

Ruark tried to control his temper, but the man had to be one of the most irritating people he'd ever met. "Dammit! Will you listen to what I came here to say?"

Robert lashed out in fury. "No. You listen to me, Stewart. Get the hell out of my room. Now."

"With pleasure," Ruark declared, "as soon as you listen to what I came here to say."

"If you came here for my sister's sake, I don't want to hear it. I listened to you once—not again."

Changing his approach, Ruark said calmly, "It has nothing to do with Angeleen. This concerns my grandmother."

The conversation was ludicrous to Robert. He turned away with a cynical snort, but Ruark ignored the rebuff. "Grandmother owns the mercantile store in town. She needs a replacement for the manager, who died last week."

"You must take me for a fool, Stewart."

"On the contrary, Scott. I think my grandmother is the fool for even considering you. I personally advised her against the idea. And I assure you, neither Angeleen nor I had anything to do with the offer. I'm merely the messenger."

Robert raised his glass, toasting the air. "Kill the messenger." He chuckled in appreciation of his own humor, but Ruark ignored the gibe.

Robert pushed up from the table. "Well, Mr. Messenger, thanks, but no thanks. Relate that to your grandmother for me and close the door on your way out."

Picking up the bottle, Robert kicked away the chair and staggered over to the bed where he plopped down on his back with his head on the pillow and the hand holding the bottle dangling limply over the side.

"You'll have to tell her that yourself. Grandmother expects you tomorrow for lunch to discuss this further." Ruark opened the door but before departing, he turned back and his eyes took a final, derisive sweep of the outstretched man.

"And clean yourself up before coming, Scott. You look and stink like hell."

"Bastard!" Robert bellowed as he sat up and pitched the bottle at the door. The liquor splashed against the wall and ran down the door as the bottle smashed into pieces.

Robert fell back and passed out.

Chapter Seventeen

As she had done hopefully every day for the past week, Celeste Dupree rapped on Robert's door. But once again, he did not respond. She was about to turn away when her pert nose twitched in distaste at the smell of whiskey. Glancing down, she saw that the pungent liquid had streamed under the door of Robert's room into a small puddle at her feet.

Distressed, Celeste turned the handle and the door opened.

Upon entering the room, she drew back in surprise. Newspapers were strewn about the once-tidy room, which now reeked from the odor of stale whiskey. Celeste quickly examined Robert and found that he was only sleeping, so she removed her cloak and set to work.

Despite the cold, she opened the small window.

As the fresh air began to obliterate the offensive odor, Celeste picked up the broken pieces of the liquor bottle, then sopped up the spilled whiskey with newspaper.

The job was soon finished, and she returned her attention to Robert Scott. Clearly, he had passed out from alcohol. Her lips curved into a determined pout; she was obligated to this man and would not allow Robert to destroy himself.

With steadfast resolve, she stripped him of his clothing, including his drawers, and quickly covered him with the bed quilt. Robert's suit was badly soiled and wrinkled, but she hung it up for her future attention.

Aware that the temperature of the already chilly room must have dropped at least another ten degrees, she hurried over and slammed down the window.

Armed with a firmness of purpose, she strode out the door and down the stairway, and pounded on the proprietor's door. After a lengthy argument, Celeste extracted a promise of several buckets of hot water from the disgruntled landlord. Returning to the floor above, she dragged the heavy wooden bathtub down the hallway into Robert's room. While awaiting the arrival of the hot water, Celeste made several trips back and forth to the bathroom for buckets of cold water to dump into the tub.

"You gonna give him a bath?" the landlord grumbled as he came in followed by his young son, each toting two heavy buckets of hot water.

"If I must," Celeste said. "Will you help me get him into the tub?"

"The wife and I run a decent boarding house. I'll not let my son be a part of such shenanigans," the man declared righteously.

"*Monsieur*, I only wish to give him a bath. You can't deny that he needs one," she declared.

After a lingering look at Robert's condition, the man grimaced and relented. "Well . . . get yourself out of here while my boy and I get him into the tub."

Celeste smiled, relieved that she wouldn't have to argue further. "As you wish, *Monsieur*. I'll wait in the hall."

She paced the floor impatiently until the proprietor and his son joined her. "Lady, you sure got your work cut out for you. He was cussin' us up and down aplenty," the man complained as he and his son hurried down the stairs.

The landlord's warning put a dent into her armor of determination. Cautiously, Celeste stuck her head in the door. Robert sat in the tub looking about in confusion.

Through the liquor-induced haze, he recognized Celeste. "What the hell are you doing here?" Instinctively, he covered the end of his crippled arm with his right hand.

"I only came to make certain you were well, Robert."

He felt betrayed. "You . . . you what? Was this your damn idea?"

"I thought you needed a bath."

His head snapped up. "If I wanted a bath, I would have taken one." His eyes glared accusingly. "You *said* you were grateful to me. How could you let them see me like this?"

"I had to, Robert. I needed their help to get you into the tub."

Despite his anger, the combined effect of the lingering alcohol and the hot water began to lull him into languor. "You strip a man of his dignity, Miss Dupree."

"I'm usually accused of just stripping him of his clothes," she retorted.

Seeing his eyes droop, Celeste quickly moved into action. She scooped up a basin of water from the tub and poured it over his head. Robert yelped with displeasure, but she ignored his outcry and lathered his hair.

"You have good hair, Robert," she commented as she kneaded and massaged his scalp. "Now close your eyes so I can rinse it."

She poured several basins of water over his head, then, satisfied that all the suds were out of his hair, she tossed the bar of soap back into the tub. "Now wash yourself. I'll be right back."

Donning her cloak, Celeste took the door key so that Robert could not lock her out of the room. She crossed the street and entered the cafe. After a careful count of her few remaining coins, Celeste ordered a pitcher of coffee and two freshly baked raisin muffins.

When she returned to the room, Celeste found Robert had completed his bath and had just managed to pull on a clean pair of drawers.

"Robert, put on a shirt or you'll catch a chill in this cold room," she chided in a protective tone. Celeste hastily wrapped her cloak around his shoulders.

"What are you doing?" Robert grumbled, shrugging off the evidence of her mothering. The movement jarred his throbbing temple, and he buried his aching head in his hand. "Just leave me alone."

"You need something to eat."

"I'm not hungry." Celeste ignored him and poured coffee into the whiskey glass. His dark eyes blazed with anger as she handed it to him. "You must eat to keep up your strength."

Robert knocked the glass out of her hand. "Stop mothering me! I don't need a mother. I had a mother. Do you understand? Just leave me alone." With each declaration, his voice had grown louder. He jumped to his feet, but the pain in his head was so severe that he fell back with a groan.

Celeste retrieved the glass and poured him some more coffee. "Drink this," she ordered. When he looked up at her through pain-racked eyes, her voice softened. "Please, Robert?"

Too exhausted to resist, Robert grudgingly accepted the glass and drank a few sips of the hot coffee. It tasted good and warmed him. "Thank you."

For a brief second their gazes locked, then he lowered his head and drank some more of the coffee. "I'm sorry, Miss Dupree. I realize my actions appear boorish to you, but I prefer my privacy."

"No, *Monsieur*, you prefer to sit alone and feel sorry for yourself." She began to gather up his dirty clothing.

"I'm not interested in lectures, Miss Dupree." Robert wanted her gone. First an unwelcome visit from the overbearing Ruark Stewart, and now unwanted attention from this maternalistic prostitute. He couldn't understand why people just didn't leave him be.

When he saw Celeste throw his soiled clothing into the tub of water, Robert erupted. "What the hell are you doing now?"

"I'm soaking your dirty laundry."

Rising, he strode to the table and, without thinking, poured himself another glass of coffee. However, the move did not go unobserved by Celeste. She smiled and began to scrub a pair of his socks.

"What is the reason for that self-congratulatory smile on your face?" Robert challenged.

"I don't know what you mean, Robert."

"You know damn well what I mean," he snapped. He picked up one of the muffins and began to chomp on it.

Her smile widened. "I mean, I'm not certain what is meant by 'self . . . congratulatory smile.' "

"Doesn't matter," he grumbled, "but that's what's on your face." Robert took a big bite out of the other muffin. "I hate raisins."

Celeste kept her head lowered and her eyes on the wet clothing. "Do you have any clothesline?"

"If I did, I probably would have hung myself by now," he growled.

She plopped the wet clothes down on the table, and her hands flew to her hips. "Your foolish talk and actions drive me to anger. You speak so freely of other people's faults, Robert Scott. Well, I have never known a man with so much self-pity," she raged. "Others have suffered too, you know."

Celeste snatched her cloak from the bed. "You are right, *monsieur*, I have no business being here."

Ashamed to admit the truth of her words, Robert stared speechlessly at the tiny woman. As she passed him, he reached out and grabbed her arm. Celeste stood stiffly, but did not turn around to look at him.

"Forgive me, Miss Dupree. You have been most kind and generous. I apologize for my bad manners." To his further surprise, Robert realized, even though he spoke the words by rote, he meant every word he said.

Turning, Celeste looked him in the eye. "I wish you good luck, *monsieur*." She opened the door to depart.

"Celeste."

She turned to him again. "Will you stay for just a few minutes?" Robert asked hesitantly. He felt embarrassed asking her the question after just ordering her out of his room.

"I seem to disturb you, *monsieur*."

"No. It's not your fault. It's mine. Lately I've fallen into the habit of being short-tempered and quick to condemn."

Celeste hesitated, uncertain whether she should leave or not. "If you are sure you want me to." At his sheepish expression, she slipped off her cloak.

He hung her wrap on a peg, and then Robert did something he hadn't done in weeks. He smiled.

"Would you like some coffee, Miss Dupree?"

She shook her head. "You called me Celeste, before, *monsieur*," she reminded him.

"And you called me Robert."

They stared in awkward silence at one another until Robert turned away and began to bail the water

270

out of the tub. Celeste busied herself by cleaning up the coffee he had tossed on the floor.

After returning the tub to the bathroom, Robert came back carrying a length of clothesline. Without a word, he tied one end of the line to a hook and the other end to a hook on the opposite wall.

Celeste silently draped the wet clothes over the line and when the task was finished, she looked about in satisfaction.

"Well, I guess there isn't much more for me to do here. I suppose I should leave."

"I'll walk you back to your flat, Celeste."

After several deep breaths of the brisk and invigorating outside air, Robert's head felt considerably better. The couple strolled along the waterfront in a companionable silence until they stopped to listen to the calliope of a docking riverboat.

"How I loved that sound when I was growing up," Robert said.

At the note of poignancy in his voice, Celeste glanced up and saw that, although he wasn't smiling, Robert's face was no longer blemished by harshness or anger.

Like fragrant flowers, the sights and sounds of that bygone day bloomed afresh in the garden of his memory. "When Angie and I were youngsters, every time we heard the calliope, we would race down to the dock. She'd get so excited, she'd jump up and down clapping her hands and dancing to the music."

Celeste remained silent, not wanting to disturb this moment of intimacy. "Momma always promised that someday all of us would make a trip to St. Louis on the biggest boat on the river." Then his

271

look of pleasure shifted to pain and his expression hardened. "But . . . it never came to be."

He turned and walked away. Celeste hastened her steps to follow.

The decolletage of an ivory satin gown showcased the beauty of Angeleen's bare shoulders and rounded breasts.

"Oh, miss, you look lovely," Myra exclaimed as she stepped back after putting the finishing touches to Angeleen's hair.

With a critical eye, Angeleen studied her image in the mirror. The sapphire jewels Ruark had given her for Christmas glittered elegantly at her neck and ears.

"I don't think my appearance much matters, Myra," Angeleen remarked. The hostile reception she'd received at the ball in New York was still a painful memory.

"I know Mr. Ruark will be so proud of you." The maid's eyes glowed with pleasure.

Angeleen wished she shared the woman's confidence, but that was impossible when she knew the lions of St. Louis society were gathered downstairs waiting to devour her.

When the strains of a waltz floated up from below, Myra hurried over and opened the bedroom door. "Oh, the music's started. You'd best hurry, miss."

Angeleen sighed deeply, squared her shoulders, and picked up a pearl-encrusted fan.

Below, Ruark greeted the arrival of Mason Denning and his family. He glanced up and saw Angeleen descending the stairway. Pride gleamed in his dark eyes. Quickly excusing himself, he hastened over to the foot of the staircase. "You look lovely, Angel." He gave her hand an affectionate squeeze, then drew her over to the Dennings.

"Angeleen, I don't believe you've met Mason Denning, his wife Cynthia, and their daughter Penelope."

Denning nodded slightly, Cynthia cast a haughty glance, and Penelope offered a timid smile.

"How do you do." Angeleen smiled graciously.

"If you'll excuse us, Mrs. Hunter has promised me this waltz." Ruark took her arm and led her away.

"Why that's the woman he met on the riverboat," Cynthia snorted with an indignant *humph*.

"Yes, the one who rode off on Stewart's stallion," Mason replied.

Cynthia Denning was outraged. "I'm sure she did it intentionally, just to attract his attention."

"Oh, I'm certain she had already succeeded in doing that, my dear," Mason commented as his gaze followed the fetching figure on the arm of Ruark Stewart.

"I think she's very pretty," Penelope Denning mumbled in a nasal tone.

"Be thankful you are not she, Penelope," her mother voiced righteously.

"Why?" the girl asked with a wistful gaze at Ruark smiling down into Angeleen's eyes as he waltzed her around the floor.

"How dare that tramp openly flaunt her illicit affair with him," Cynthia fumed. "Why, it's an insult to decent people."

"Now, Cynthia," Mason cautioned, "you hold that

273

tongue of yours. Ruark Stewart is one of the bank's largest depositors. I'll not have you jeopardize an important business relationship over an unsubstantiated rumor."

"Unsubstantiated, indeed!" Cynthia huffed. "I have it on the best authority. Our cook told me that the mother of the lady friend of one of the Stewart grooms said the Hunter woman's father was working in the Stewart stable."

"And what is that supposed to indicate?" Mason asked with a husbandly sufferance born of twenty-two years of marriage.

"Why, that the woman is Ruark's mistress, of course," she said smugly. Cynthia took her daughter's arm. "Come, Penelope." Cynthia led her daughter away leaving her poor husband looking bewildered.

Mason Denning had suspected that Angeleen Hunter was more than just Ruark's houseguest, especially after discovering that she had accompanied Ruark on a recent visit to New York. What perplexed the banker was how his wife's confusing line of deduction had led her to the same conclusion.

Cynthia Denning wasn't the only mother among the invited who eyed Angeleen with interest. Ruark Stewart had long been a favorite among St. Louis society. The handsome and wealthy bachelor was sought after by hopeful mothers and wishful daughters alike.

Aware of the attention focused on them, Angeleen laughed up at Ruark as he improvised a succession of fast turns. "Please, Ruark, I'd hate to miss a step with all these sets of eyes trained on us."

He grinned in reply. "I thought, as long as we appear to be the main attraction, we should entertain them with a dazzling terpsichorean display." To further his intent, he proceeded to spin her around in another flourish of turns.

Breathless, Angeleen scolded, "Ruark, will you behave yourself. You're making a spectacle of us."

"They're all just envious, my love."

"Envious? I doubt that," she scoffed.

"The women are envious because you're the loveliest woman in the room; the men are envious because you're not in their arms."

"So that's the reason you keep me, Ruark—for the satisfaction of showing me off to your associates and friends."

"I won't deny I keep you for my satisfaction, Angel, as you well know." He pulled her closer into his arms and succeeded in raising several eyebrows even higher among the spectators. "But that certainly has nothing to do with my associates and friends. Now stop worrying about their petty spite and just enjoy the music."

He shrugged aside her misgivings, executed some additional intricate twists, and continued to waltz her around the dance floor.

Just as cognizant of the young dancing couple as those around her, Sarah Stewart sat watching Ruark and Angeleen. Sarah's blue-eyed gaze rested on her grandson, her thoughts concealed behind the faintest of smiles.

Why doesn't the young fool marry the girl? she thought. *In two days they'll be leaving for Europe and I won't see them for almost a year—if I live that long. It's high time that boy realizes that I'm not getting any younger waiting for him to take a wife so I can stop worrying about him and die in peace.*

Sarah's thoughts were suddenly invaded by the voice of the woman who sat next to her.

"My, your grandson and Mrs. Hunter make a handsome couple," Cynthia Denning commented to the older woman. The gossip raised her fan to her mouth and leaned over to whisper, "Should we expect to hear wedding bells soon?"

Sarah's eyes gleamed with perception. "My grandson and I have a reciprocal agreement, Cynthia. I don't question him about his romances, and he doesn't question me about mine."

The dowager's smile broadened as Cynthia Denning sat back and rapidly began to fan herself.

Despite the unsuccessful attempts of a few, the party progressed smoothly. Those loyal to Ruark were cordial to Angeleen, while others, such as Cynthia Denning, prickled under the evidence of Ruark's infatuation and Sarah Stewart's undeniable acceptance of Angeleen.

The day after the ball, Angeleen sat on Ruark's bed nervously twisting a handkerchief as she watched Ruark pack his trunk. Unable to ignore her any longer, Ruark glanced over his shoulder.

"Okay, what's bothering you, Angel? You haven't said a word in the past fifteen minutes, and if you don't stop fidgeting, you're going to chew off your lip and reduce that handkerchief to shreds."

"I have something to tell you," she said hesitantly.

His spine stiffened as he steeled himself for what she had to say. Ruark had been aware of her anxiety, and his suspicions had been running rampant for the past quarter-hour.

"You've changed your mind about going to Europe with me." That thought had been foremost in his mind. So much depended upon her answer; he braced himself for the worse.

When he had begun the affair with Angeleen, he had not expected to become emotionally involved. But she was unlike any woman he had ever known, and he couldn't imagine a day's passing without her being a part of it.

"Well, it does have something to do with going to Europe," she replied.

Closing the lid of the trunk, he sat down on top of it and waited for her to continue.

"I'm scared, Ruark."

"Scared? Of what, Angel?" He shifted to sit beside her on the bed.

"I've never taken an ocean voyage before." She gave him a sheepish side glance. "I can't swim, Ruark."

"Is that all!" After the doubts that had plagued him, Ruark felt ecstatic. He expelled a sigh of relief. "Honey, what does it matter that you can't swim?"

"Well . . . the ocean is so big, Ruark. What if the ship sinks? Or, at least, springs a leak?"

His laughter erupted spontaneously. "Angel, there are no snags or obstacles in the middle of the ocean. You're safer on the Atlantic than you are on the Mississippi."

His words of assurance gave her little comfort. She eyed him skeptically.

Ruark threw an arm around her shoulders, hugging her to his side. "Honey, I promise, I won't let anything happen to you."

"Well, I guess the Almighty would never try to beard that declaration," she teased.

Ruark sensed her acceptance. "Now, let's get you packed. Or . . ." He leaned her back on the bed. " . . . We could forget the packing for now," he mumbled between nibbles and quick kisses to her lips and face.

Angeleen shoved him away and sat up. "If you expect me to be ready to leave in the morning, I have to finish my packing."

When she tried to rise, Ruark grabbed her hand and pulled her down beside him. "I'll help you pack later," he said, pressing a trail of kisses along the column of her neck. "Much later," he murmured in a provocative whisper at her ear.

A shiver raced down her spine and Angeleen closed her eyes. Ruark opened her dressing gown and under the arousing sensation of his touch she felt her breast swell to fill his hand.

With a blissful sigh, she slipped her arms around his neck and parted her lips as his mouth closed over hers.

Saying good-bye to Sarah Stewart the following morning was not easy for Angeleen. Ruark's grandmother had been a beacon of strength to her from the moment she had come to Missouri.

After hugging and kissing Sarah, Angeleen

moaned, "I'm going to miss you, Nana Sarah."

"I hope so, child, because I shall certainly be missing you." Sarah tried to maintain a stern image. "I don't understand why the two of you have to run off to Merry Old England, anyway," Sarah protested, hiding her heartache under the complaint.

"Now, Nana, don't try to change her mind. I had a hard enough time convincing Angeleen to go as it was," Ruark chided lightly, drawing Angeleen out of Sarah's arms.

Sarah obscured her sniffle in a lacy handkerchief. "Don't pay me any mind, child. I'm just sorry I can't go with you. Be off with you, if you must, before I make a blubbering fool of myself."

She opened her arms to Ruark. "Now come here and give your grandmother a kiss."

As Ruark embraced his grandmother, Angeleen stepped quietly out of the room and walked down to the stable to say a farewell to her father.

She lingered at King's stall, saying good-bye to the beloved stallion while Henry watched silently. Finally, unable to put off the moment any longer, Angeleen turned to her father.

"I'll miss you and King, Poppa. I wish you both were coming with us."

Henry swiped at his nose and tried to look stouthearted. " 'Twill do ye good to see more of the world, lass. Have the lad take ye to Scotland. 'Tis a sight ye'll nae forget to yer dyin' day."

"I'll ask Ruark, Poppa," she said.

" 'Twould be a pity, indeed, to miss me homeland when ye be sa near," he rambled on, trying to put off the final words of parting.

Finally, unable to fight the urge any longer, Henry hugged her tightly. "Aye, I'll miss ye, lass."

Tears trickled down Angeleen's cheeks as he kissed her. "I just wish Robert were here too."

"I told yer brother ye'd be leavin' this day." He shook his head sadly. "The lad's blind with bitterness these days."

"Tell him I love him, Poppa."

"And he loves ye, too, lass. Ye know that."

"Yes, I know, Poppa. Try to make him understand how much I love Ruark."

Henry gave her another quick hug and stepped back. Tears glistened in the old man's eyes as he tried to smile. "Ye best be hurryin' now. I'll take ye to the carriage."

Hand-in-hand they walked up the path to where Ruark waited at the open door of the coach.

Sarah Stewart stood with a wrap around her shoulders, braving the chill of the brisk wind. Myra and the cook had a steadying hand on each of Sarah's arms.

"Have a pleasant time, miss," Sarah said. The cook nodded in agreement. Both of the servants mopped at their tears with white handkerchiefs.

Angeleen hugged each of them. "I'm so grateful to all of you. You've been so good to me."

"Now, child, you're not leaving forever," Sarah declared. "You'll be back before you know it." Angeleen nodded and kissed her.

"Good Lord, ladies! I've never seen such a display of tears," Ruark grumbled. "None of you ever carried on like this when I went to Europe before."

"We did when you were younger—before you

developed such a smart mouth," Myra declared.

Chuckling, Ruark kissed the two servants. "Take good care of Nana for me and I'll bring each of you one of those romantic French painters from Montmartre."

"Oh, be off with you, you rapscallion," Myra scolded. She threw her arms around him and kissed his cheek.

Angeleen gave her father a final kiss and hug, then allowed Ruark to assist her into the carriage.

"You're in complete charge of the stable, Henry," Ruark said to the saddened man. "Take good care of my horses."

Henry nodded. "I'll nae fail ye. And ye take good care of my daughter," he said solemnly.

"You have my promise," Ruark said as the two men shook hands.

He took his grandmother into his arms. "Now Nana, don't you get any ideas about going anywhere while I'm gone."

The old woman looked up with a twinkle in her blue eyes. "Not much chance of that. The Lord doesn't want me and the Devil's afraid of me. Guess you're stuck with me for a while."

He kissed her and for a moment held her in his arms. "Now get back in the house before you catch a cold." He climbed into the carriage and sat down beside Angeleen.

Daniel flicked the reins and as the coach began to roll away, Henry called out, "And when ye return, Bold King's get will be here to greet ye."

Angeleen leaned out the window for a final wave. Three white handkerchiefs fluttered in response.

By the time the carriage reached the depot, the train had already gathered up a full head of steam while awaiting the last passengers to board.

As Daniel and the porter loaded the luggage, a figure stepped out of the shadows and called out to Angeleen. Turning, she saw her brother standing nearby.

"Oh, Robert," she cried joyously. Ruark released her arm and she ran to her brother and hugged him.

"I couldn't see you go without saying good-bye, Angie."

Angeleen smiled into his dark eyes. "I love you, Robert."

"I love you, too, Princess."

The whistle of the train sounded several sharp toots. Angeleen glanced nervously over her shoulder to where Ruark waited on the platform of his private car.

"I wish we could have more time together. Ten months sounds like a lifetime to be away."

"It will pass faster than you think," Robert said.

"Keep an eye on Poppa, Robert. He's going to be very lonely."

"I will," he promised.

The train whistle sounded again. "Good-bye, Princess, and have a good time in Europe. We'll be thinking of you."

Robert kissed her cheek and stepped away.

She climbed onto the platform and reached out to him. Robert took her hand in his and they held on to each other. Then the train began to move and their hands slipped apart.

Oblivious to the piercing wind that stung her cheeks and whipped her long hair into streamers, Angeleen stood on the platform of the car waving to Robert until he was out of sight.

Chapter Eighteen

Driven by a strong northwest wind, a winter rain that mercifully had not developed into snow fell steadily throughout the day. Sodden, cold, and hungry, Celeste returned to her boarding house, wanting nothing more now than to get out of her wet clothes and under a warm quilt.

For two weeks she had sought employment of a respectable nature, but to no avail. Now, delinquent in her rent, she had no other option except to resume her previous occupation as a prostitute. Celeste preferred the life of a "kept woman," for she had long ago discovered the advantages of tolerating the demands of only one man rather than the lechery of any man who paid the price, but she no longer had any choice.

Appalled, she saw a padlock on the door of her room. "You bastard, Haley!" Celeste cursed. Infuriated, she pounded down the stairs and hammered on his door. "Mr. Haley, are you in there?"

Bleary-eyed, the landlord opened the door. "Whatta ya makin' so much noise for this time of night?"

Water dripped down Celeste's cheeks from her sodden hair. "Mr. Haley, why did you put that padlock on my door? I told you I'd have your rent in a few days."

"You've been telling me that for two weeks, lady. Told ya before, I ain't running no charity house. Pay up or get out."

"Well, can I stay another night at least? I've got no place to go, I'm soaking wet, and all my clothes are locked up in my room."

"You're not gettin' nothin' 'till I get my rent," he snarled.

Driven to desperation, she cried angrily, "You're just getting even because I won't go to bed with you."

The man's face curled into a vicious snarl. "Well, I hope you like sleeping in the rain *better*. Now, get out of here, whore, you're gettin' the floor wet." He slammed the door.

"Well, at least it's a lot cleaner than you are," Celeste shouted. She kicked the door and immediately gasped with pain. Then, annoyed with herself, she had to hop out of the rooming house.

For several moments, she stood huddled against the shelter of the building as she tried to decide what to do. Finally, she limped away.

Near midnight, fearing she would wake his land-lord, Celeste tapped lightly on Robert's door. When there was no response, she tried the door handle, and to her relief the door swung open.

She entered the room cautiously and waited for a moment. Not hearing a sound, Celeste lit the lamp and discovered the room empty. Hurriedly, she peeled off her cloak and hung it on a peg. Gooseflesh lined her arms and she scurried down the hallway to the bathroom, returning with a towel.

Stripping off her wet clothing, she briskly dried her hair and body. The friction soon reddened her skin, warming her.

When she started to become chilled again, she pulled the blanket off the bed and draped it around her while she searched about for something to wear. She found a shirt.

Celeste replaced the blanket on the bed, then, wondering how to warm her frozen feet which by this time felt like two blocks of ice, she climbed into the bed and crept under the covers.

Celeste knew Robert would not turn her out in the rain. Perhaps she could make a pallet on the floor, and he would allow her to stay with him until she could afford to pay Mr. Haley.

Yes, that was what she would do, she told herself. As soon as she felt warmer, she would get up and make a place to sleep on the floor.

Celeste drifted off to sleep before she could decide what she could use to make the pallet.

Robert saw the dim glow of light coming from beneath the door of his room. He stopped for a moment and then slowly opened the door. Glancing at the bed, he saw the sleeping girl and quietly entered the room. Putting aside the bottle he carried, he shrugged off his cloak and tossed it on a chair, then walked over and for several seconds stared down at Celeste asleep in his bed. The girl had been in his thoughts often. His passion flared and the ache in his loins intensified as he felt himself swelling.

Half-stumbling, he hurried down the hallway to the bathroom. Once behind the privacy of the closed door, tears glistened in his eyes as he stood with his cheek pressed against the rough wood of the door and wrestled to control his aroused passion.

When Robert returned to the room, Celeste was still asleep, so he sat down at the table and opened the bottle of whiskey. For over an hour, he sat in brooding silence, drinking the whiskey and reflecting on the girl in his bed.

Since his injury, no woman had stirred his passion as Celeste did. From the time of his first meeting with Celeste, he had wanted her.

Finally feeling the blissful effects of the whiskey, he knew he now would be able to sleep. Staggering to the bed, he collapsed on top of it next to his unexpected visitor.

Robert was awakened by bright sunlight shining in his eyes. He sat up to discover that he had slept in his only suit. Disgusted, he swung his legs over the bed, and then clutched his throbbing head at the sight of Celeste sitting at his table looking well-rested and refreshed.

"Good morning, Robert."

He lifted his head, which felt as heavy as an anvil. Her smile was as bright as the sunshine, and he couldn't decide which annoyed him more at this hour of the morning—the smile or the sun in his eyes. In the mood for neither, he resumed holding his head.

"What are you doing here, Celeste?"

"I didn't hear you come in last night," Celeste said in a cheery voice. Too cheery, for a man with a hangover. "You must have been very late."

"What difference does it make to you?" he grumbled. "Why did you come here?"

"I couldn't pay my rent, so I've been locked out of my room."

Appalled, Robert raised his head. "So you came here?"

"I knew you would understand," she said.

"Celeste, you can't stay here."

Robert stood up and Celeste hurried over to put the bed in order. "I can do your housecleaning and your laundry."

He grabbed her arm. "For God's sake, stop that."

The aggressive move startled her. For a brief moment they stared into each other's eyes. Then her bravado collapsed, and the desperation she felt surfaced as tears misted her eyes. "Please, Robert, I have nowhere else to go."

"Celeste, I have no room for you here. You can see that for yourself."

"I won't get in your way. I'll make a pallet on the floor for a bed. Just for a few days," she pleaded.

He could not withstand her pleas. Reluctantly, he agreed. "But only until Saturday. No longer," he declared as a firm rap sounded on the door.

Anticipating that the caller could only be his landlord, Robert swung the door open. "What do you want? I don't—" But surprise stopped his comment as he stared at the woman before him; Sarah Stewart was the last person he'd expected to see.

She regarded the stunned look on the disheveled young man's face and smiled with amusement. "May I come in, Mr. Scott?"

"Yes, of course, Mrs. Stewart." He stepped back and opened the door wider for the dowager to enter. Robert saw that she was not alone.

"Oh, I'm sorry if I've disturbed you," Sarah apologized upon seeing Celeste. "I can return at a later time."

Celeste knew that whatever the woman had to say to Robert would not be for her ears. "That's not necessary, *madame*. I was just leaving." Grabbing her cloak, she bobbed her head politely and hurried off.

"What a lovely young woman," Sarah remarked kindly after Celeste's hasty departure. She turned to her companion, who stood patiently beside her gently holding her arm. "I won't be long, Daniel."

Hesitating, the driver gave Robert a wary glance. "Are you sure you don't want me to stay, ma'am?"

"I will be fine, Daniel. Just wait with the carriage." Sarah patted his hand and he reluctantly let go of her.

"As you wish." He cast a final warning glance at Robert and took his leave.

"I'm sorry, Mrs. Stewart, this is the only seat I have to offer," Robert said as he assisted Sarah to the wooden chair.

"It will do fine, Robert."

Robert hastily snatched the bottle of whiskey off the table and put it on the window ledge. "I can't offer you tea or coffee, ma'am. A glass of water, perhaps?"

"Water would be delicious after all those stairs," Sarah remarked.

He picked up the soiled glass and frantically scanned the room for something to clean it with. Unsuccessful, Robert turned to her and smiled with embarrassment.

"Excuse me, ma'am." He grabbed the ewer on the way out and hurried down the hallway to the bathroom.

Within minutes, Robert returned, carrying the glass, now sparkling, and a fresh pitcher of water. Sarah sat with her hands resting on the handle of her cane and regarded Robert through clear blue eyes as he poured the drink.

"Ma'am." He handed her the glass.

"Thank you, son. You're a gentleman, Robert. I can tell it comes naturally."

Sarah rapped her cane on the floor. "Lord, as much as I loved that Yankee sea captain of mine, men from the North just haven't got the chivalry of you Southern gentlemen. They're too preoccupied with making money and playing the stock market."

And seducing innocent girls, Robert thought bitterly.

Sarah gestured toward the bed. "Do sit down, Robert. I don't expect you to stand." After he seated himself stiffly on the edge of the bed, she added, "Your mother must have been very proud of you."

She had touched a sensitive nerve, and his expression changed. "I think she'd have second thoughts now, ma'am." His eyes deepened with sorrow. "I'm not the same man she said good-bye to when I went off to war." His shifting mood showed in the bitter lines of his face. "Maybe it's better she's not around to see what I've become."

"I think you're being much too hard on yourself, Robert," she said kindly.

Perhaps it was Sarah's age, her dignity, or the compassion in the old woman's eyes, but for some inexplicable reason, Robert found himself confessing to Sarah Stewart his deep and haunting anxiety.

"Most of the time I feel as if I'm stumbling around . . . as if I were in a nightmare. Everything seems obscure, confused. Scotcroft. Angie. Momma."

He suddenly turned to Sarah, his eyes filled with pain. "I can't stop looking for . . . Momma." The word was wrenched from the depth of his soul. "She was here when I left. My mind won't accept that she's gone."

Sarah's heart ached for him as Robert shook his head in hopelessness. "I keep expecting to see her come through the door."

His tone intensified with conviction. "*I know* I'll wake up at Scotcroft, and we'll all be together. I won't be missing an—I'll be whole again."

Suddenly, embarrassed by exposing so much of his dark inner thoughts to her, Robert jumped to his feet. "Forgive me, ma'am. I'm sure you didn't come here to hear my problems."

"No, I've come so you could hear mine," Sarah declared. She spoke confidently even though she had been deeply moved by the pain of his confession.

Trusting her own counsel, she was now certain she wanted Robert. "I am in need of an honest man. I think you are that man."

"I think not, ma'am."

"I understand my grandson explained to you my need for a manager to run my mercantile store."

"Yes, he did, ma'am."

She eyed him reproachfully. "As a matter of fact, young man, since I'm not in the habit of making business calls, I held up lunch for several hours one day waiting for you."

Passing over her comment, he spoke his mind. "And I'm not interested in charity ma'am—especially Stewart charity."

"Charity? Is that what you think I'm offering?" She rapped her cane again on the floor to emphasize her point. "Lord, no! Anyone who works for me *earns* the salary I pay him."

Robert's dark eyes deepened with suspicion. "Why would you trust me over any local resident, Mrs. Stewart? You barely know me."

Sarah smiled. "I never had much formal education, Robert, so I had to develop an inner and greater knowledge to succeed—an instinct about people. My Charles always counseled me to keep the right man on the deck and trust the Lord to put the wind in the sails. I think you're that man, Robert."

He walked over and stared pensively out of the window. "I won't deny the offer is tempting, ma'am. Were it not for your grandson—"

She cut him off before he could finish. "My grandson has nothing to do with or say about my business enterprises."

Sarah waved her hand dismissively. "Oh, I'm aware of the bad blood between you and Ruark. But when you get to be as old as I am, Robert, you will long since have learned the truth of the saying that time heals all wounds."

Leaning heavily on her cane, Sarah raised herself to her feet, indicating that the conversation was at an end. "What do you say to twenty-five dollars a week?"

Robert gave a rare grin. "I'd say I'd be overpaid."

"Then we have a business agreement. May I expect you for lunch tomorrow to go over the details?"

"Why not? Wouldn't make sense not to hear you out. May I see you to your carriage, ma'am?"

Daniel's face expressed his relief at Sarah's appearance. He opened the door and helped her into the carriage. A moment later, her face appeared in the window.

"I can expect you tomorrow, Robert?" More question than request, her tone was a reminder of the last time he had ignored her invitation.

"As you wish, ma'am. But it's not necessary to go to any trouble just for me."

"Nonsense. You eat lunch the same as I, don't you?" Then her blue eyes sparkled flirtatiously.

"Besides, it's not often I get to have lunch with a good-looking young man. Even if I am the one extending the invitation."

"Perhaps I'll have the pleasure of returning the pleasure, ma'am," Robert said gallantly.

"I knew there was a good head on those shoulders the first time I saw you," she said. She tapped her cane on the ceiling of the carriage. "Home, Daniel."

Robert stood grinning as the carriage rolled away.

"You are smiling, Robert," Celeste said, moving to his side after Sarah's departure. "The news has been good for you?"

"Looks like I may have a steady job, Celeste." He started to walk briskly down the street.

Celeste followed on his heels. "What kind of a job?"

"As manager of the mercantile store in town." He stopped to allow her to catch up with him.

Celeste's eyes brightened with enthusiasm. "Manager! Why, Robert, that is a *position*, not just a job."

They walked to the dock and Robert collected the few dollars he had coming from his relief job as a ticket seller for the boat line. Stopping at the market, they bought a loaf of bread, a hunk of cheese, and several apples, then returned to the room.

As they ate their sparse meal, Robert's mind dwelled on the sleeping arrangements. "What can I use to make you a pallet?"

"Too bad we don't have some straw," she lamented.

"Of course, I should have thought of it sooner."

Celeste grabbed an apple and gave chase when Robert hurried out the door.

Angel Hunter

Henry Hunter broke into a broad grin at the sight of his son. Although Angeleen had been gone for only a week, Henry thought of her often and of how long it would be before he would see her again. He hugged his son affectionately and glanced curiously at Celeste, who had discreetly walked over to watch the horses in the corral.

From the girl's heavily rouged cheeks and lips, Henry could tell his son had been reduced to taking a prostitute for companionship. The question of his daughter's virtue was still a sensitive issue with Henry. As for his son, that was a different matter—after all, a man had needs to be served.

"Poppa, I need some straw," Robert said.

"We've plenty of that, lad. How much will ye be needin'?"

"As much as I can carry," Robert replied.

" 'Twill nae be missed. But I could hitch up a wagon and be drivin' ye back if ye need more than an armload, lad."

"No, this will do," Robert said as the two men tied up a big bundle of the dried hay.

"And just how will ye be puttin' this to use, lad?"

Robert hesitated to answer the question. So he stretched the truth. "A softer mattress for sleeping."

Shaking his head in remorse, Henry lamented, "It grieves me to be thinkin' of ye alone in a cold room. Why canna ye stay here? There's always a hot meal and a warm bed at the day's end."

"Poppa, we've discussed this before. I'll not live in any house of Ruark Stewart's."

"Yer a stubborn mon, Robert Scott."

Robert slapped his father on the back. "Comes naturally, Poppa. But not as stubborn as you think. I'm coming back tomorrow to have lunch with Mrs. Stewart. I might be going to work for her."

Henry gulped back his delight lest his joy ruin good fortune. "She's a fine lady, lad."

"I figured that out for myself, Poppa." Robert picked up the bundle of hay and slung it over his shoulder.

With a heavy heart, Henry watched his son walk down the road with Celeste at his side. Since returning from the war, Robert had appeared sullen and withdrawn—a far cry from the boy who had idealistically ridden off to battle. Henry wondered sadly if they would ever return to the companionship he and Robert had once shared.

"Aye, lad, yer a stubborn mon," Henry muttered softly.

For an additional twenty-five cents a week on the rent, the landlord gave them another blanket and pillow. Then, returning to his room, Robert set himself to making Celeste a pallet using newspapers, straw, and two towels.

Celeste was delighted with the result. That night, as she took off her dress to retire, Robert turned away, but not before glimpsing the appealing sight of her bare arms and shoulders. He lay awake for many long hours before he was finally able to sleep.

The following morning, Robert was quiet and reserved. Celeste attributed his mood to nervousness about his new job. When he returned from his meeting with Sarah Stewart, his spirits appeared lighter, but within hours his mood deteriorated again into sullenness.

As they prepared to go to the market, Robert growled, "Wash your face, Celeste. Must you advertise you're a whore?"

Celeste would have willingly done anything he asked, but the gruff demand hurt her. Tears mingled with the soap and water as she scrubbed the makeup off her eyes and face.

That night Robert did not touch his food, choosing instead the bottle he had ignored the previous day. Then he retired to bed without a glance in her direction.

After preparing herself for bed, Celeste lay down on the pallet. "Goodnight, Robert," she said softly.

Robert did not reply.

Later, his cry woke her. Startled, Celeste sat up, and in the faint ray of moonlight streaming through the window, she saw him thrashing restlessly. Hurrying to the bedside, she leaned over him, trying to decipher his tormented mumbling.

Alarmed by the sheen of perspiration on his brow, Celeste placed a hand on his forehead. She sighed, relieved to find he was not feverish.

Robert sat up startled, instantly awake. "You were calling out in your sleep, Robert." She continued to stroke his head as she would a child.

"I'm sorry if I woke you," he said contritely. "I must have been dreaming."

Recalling his torment, her compassion swelled. "It was no dream, *mon cher*. You had a nightmare."

"I've had it before . . . many times." The words sounded choppy.

"Wouldn't you feel better if you talked about it?" She crawled on the bed and grasped his hand.

Surprisingly, he did not try to withdraw from her, but lay back docilely. Celeste knelt on the bed beside him, holding his hand between her own.

In a voice hoarse with emotion, Robert began to describe his dream to her. "I'm always alone. At Scotcroft . . . our home in Louisiana."

He paused, slowly recalling the scene. "I'm walking from room to room, but everything is changed. I keep looking for something, but I don't know what I'm looking for. Then I go to the front door and I see Momma walking toward the river. I call to her and she stops and looks back, then continues to walk away."

He did not seem able to go on. Celeste squeezed his hand, encouraging him to continue. "What happens then, Robert?"

His voice rose in anguish. " 'Momma, wait,' I call out and begin to run toward her." He looked at Celeste, and she saw the tortured anguish in his eyes. "But no matter how fast I run, I never get any nearer to her. She goes farther and farther away into the distance. I keep yelling, 'Momma, stop. Wait for me.' " His eyes misted and his voice trailed to a whisper, "But she never does."

Celeste's heart ached for him. She kissed his hand and pressed it against her cheek. She wanted to hold him, cradle him in her arms.

Not knowing the words of comfort to offer, Celeste began to stroke him and press kisses on his face.

Suddenly he snatched her hand away and rapped out sharply, "Don't do that."

Celeste drew back in surprise at his tone. The words were spoken in fright, not anger. She looked into his eyes and saw that she hadn't been mistaken. Robert was afraid—afraid of her.

With a woman's intuition, she gradually began to understand what was behind his fear.

Slowly, she pulled her petticoat over her head.

His gaze shifted to her naked breasts. Celeste smiled seductively when he attempted to moisten his parched lips with his tongue. She leaned across him, the peaks of her breasts pressing into his bare chest as she traced her tongue around the circle of his mouth.

Trailing her fingers across the plane of his chest and stomach, she boldly slid his drawers down his long, muscular legs, now taut with tension. He made no attempt to stop her.

He sucked in his breath as she lightly ran her nails up the insides of his thighs to his throbbing, erect organ. Lowering her head, she curled her tongue around the pulsating warmth.

To his mortification, he erupted as quickly as a schoolboy, and she tasted his release.

Her confidence in the power she had over him inflamed her own passion. While oral stimulation had often been a repulsive demand from other men, he had asked for nothing—yet, to taste even more of him now became her only desire.

She felt his pounding heart beneath her mouth as she lowered her head and slid her tongue across his chest. When she stopped and tugged at a hardened nipple, his body responded with another erection.

She smiled with satisfaction. Then, driven by the urgency of her own arousal, she straddled his hips and mounted him.

Driven to near-madness by the force of his long-denied masculinity, Robert went wild. With a ferocious growl, his mouth found her thrusting breasts. Ravenous, he suckled at the taut peaks.

In the throes of ecstasy, she threw back her head, her hands knotting in his thick hair as she pressed his head even tighter to her breast.

He suddenly stopped and reared up his head. No, his own passion and manhood had been too long denied; he would not let her ride him. He would be the one to finish what she had begun.

He rolled over, trapping her beneath him. His mouth captured hers, and she whimpered under the intense pleasure of his thrusting tongue.

He covered her face and mouth with kisses, then traced a trail to her swollen breasts. Cupping a breast, he held the quivering mound to his mouth.

Moaning under the exquisite torture of erotic sensation, she writhed beneath him, her whimpers turning to ragged gasps when he slipped his hand between her legs and his long fingers probed the core of her womanhood.

"Please, Robert, please," she pleaded as the fire swirling within her inflamed her blood. Her body convulsed under wave upon wave of inundating spasms.

He drove into her, his groan a mixture of triumph and carnal pleasure when he felt her tighten and encase him. The tempo of his thrusts intensified and he raised his head to crush her mouth beneath his own.

She wrapped her arms around his neck and clung to him as their bodies convulsed rhythmically.

Robert collapsed on her, and for several moments both lay exhausted, the rasp of their breathing the only sound in the room.

He lifted his head, his dark eyes gazing down into her round green eyes now suffused with disbelief.

"Did I hurt you?" She shook her head.

He rolled off her and lay back. "I'm sorry, Celeste."

Her chest still ached from the intense pounding of her heart, but she answered softly, "I am as much to blame."

Instead of giving him the emotional release he so desperately needed, his unprincipled actions only tended to further convince Robert of his own inadequacies as a man.

"You're not to blame. I had no right to take you the way I did. I had to prove something to myself . . . and I did."

This was an unusual confession to Celeste. Men had always taken and used her in whatever manner they chose. She raised herself up and leaned over him, the long strands of her hair grazing his bare chest like a brush with silken bristles.

"Robert, I understand the passions of men. It was my fault for exciting you."

Good God, she's patronizing me, he thought scornfully. His eyes flashed angrily. "Why do you blame yourself? I acted like an animal. I didn't make love to you; I rutted with you."

"No man has ever made love to me, Robert. Not in the manner you mean," she said gently.

For a breathless moment, he stared up into her steady gaze. *So young, yet so old*, he thought sadly. His own self-absorption, which had dominated his mind for months, was temporarily forgotten, and his anger abated. "How old are you, Celeste?"

Her eyes brightened. "Eighteen in two months."

Robert thought about how long she had lived at the mercy of men like Sam Brazer and himself. "And how many men have you known, Celeste?"

"Many, *mon cher*," she said candidly.

"Well, now you can add a one-armed wretch to the list." His face shifted grimly. "Go back to sleep, Celeste."

She started to get up, but he stopped her. "You might as well stay here. No sense now in sleeping on the floor."

Celeste lay back and Robert slung his arm around her shoulders, drawing her to his side. "We're some pair, aren't we?" he said sarcastically.

Ignoring his sarcasm, Celeste smiled and snuggled closer. She felt warm and contented.

Chapter Nineteen

One month from the time Angeleen and Ruark left St. Louis, they arrived at the seaport of Liverpool, England. Despite a record crossing of fourteen days, Angeleen had been ill during the entire cold, choppy trip across the Atlantic.

Now, gaunt and peaked, she thankfully left the ship. However, dread of the return voyage hovered in her mind. The thought somewhat marred the relief she felt at once again planting her feet on solid ground.

She sat in the carriage and waited as Ruark directed the loading of their luggage. Soon her nausea passed, and by the time Ruark joined her, she managed to offer him a smile.

After looking at nothing but ocean for two weeks,

Ana Leigh

she found the ride through the countryside a welcome change, and Angeleen was pleasantly surprised when the carriage stopped at the small, elegant manor owned by Ruark.

In the weeks that followed, the freedom to walk the sweeping lawns, a merciful respite from the confined, rolling deck of a ship, pushed distressful thoughts of the return voyage out of her mind. She began to feel her own self again, an improvement which did not go unnoticed by Ruark.

One day as they strolled together through the gardens, Ruark suggested a diversion while they awaited the day of the big race.

"Angel, what do you say we each pack one bag and take a short trip?"

"A trip? Wherever to?"

"Well, now what wud ye proud father be sayin' at knowin' his bonnie lass hae been settin' her wee foot on the blessed ground of her forefathers?"

"Scotland?" Angeleen exclaimed. "Oh, Ruark! He'd love it. I mean, I'd love it—I mean what about the race?"

"We have plenty of time—that is, if we don't spend too much time packing," he added with a glint of amusement in his eyes.

Angeleen hugged him for all she was worth, rained kisses on his astonished face, and started to run toward the house.

"Hold up there, Angel. Where are you going?"

"To pack one bag, of course," she called out as she sped on her way.

Ruark smiled, once again delighted by her enthusiasm. In their short life together, notwithstanding their earlier differences he had found her easy to please and appreciative. He marveled at her faithful willingness to follow his desires. He shook his head and wondered, *How did this angel ever come to be mine?*

And so they traveled into Scotland, visiting scenic and historic sights with the eager eyes and rapt fascination of *bona fide* tourists.

On the return trip, Angeleen talked excitedly about all they had seen. Each sight and sound had been etched on her mind, and on the very afternoon they returned to the manor, she sat down at a desk and took pen in hand; her father would be the first to know of her love for the beauty and the people of his homeland.

After Ruark had checked with the servants and the stable hands, he joined her, amazed that she had already written several pages.

"What are you doing, Angel, writing a book?"

Surprised, she looked up. Not minding the break in her concentration, she took his hand and bubbled happily, "Oh, Ruark, thank you. Thank you for taking me there. I think I could live in Scotland forever."

He smiled thoughtfully. While he too had been taken by the beauty of the country, the businessman Stewart could not think of Scotland as a place to live forever.

But gazing into her adoring face, a feeling of comfort and harmony came over him. *He could easily imagine living with his angel forever.*

On the day of the Grand National, Angeleen went to the track with Ruark rather than join him there later. At the early dawn hour, a heavy fog still hung in the air, adding to the chill, and she hunched her shoulders deeper into her cloak as she waited for Ruark and the jockey, Jems Dennehy. The two men were walking the course one final time to review the angles of the turns and the distances between the fences.

Jems had ridden many steeplechases in Ireland, but he had never ridden the Grand National; the four-mile triangular course of Aintree, with its thirty fences, offered the greatest challenge to the endurance and courage of horse and jockey alike.

Despite the early hour, the artisans of the track had begun their daily rituals: gardeners raked the walking paths, sweepers canvassed the grounds for scraps and cigar butts, turf-accountants checked the morning workouts of the horses to set the odds.

In an attempt to stay warm, Angeleen walked back to the shed row where Ruark's red chestnut, Gallant Red, was stabled. The small horse, standing well below sixteen hands, possessed a strong, well-muscled stride. The spunky little stallion had a classic sculptured head and intelligent, gentle eyes with a disposition to match.

As she patted the animal, the pungent smell of sweat, soap, and manure unexpectedly assailed her nostrils. Leaning back against a post, she fought nausea and light-headedness until the dizziness waned.

To escape the odors, she quickly returned to the grandstand and sat down to await Ruark. By the time he came back, the spell had passed.

After an observant glance at the huddled figure,

Ruark said tenderly, "Bet you'd enjoy a cup of hot tea right about now."

"Well, I won't deny it would surely help," she responded with a smile.

He hugged her to his side. "You're a good sport, Angel."

Angeleen cuddled into his warmth. The strength of his arm around her always erased all her woes, and she began to feel warmer already.

"The Earl of Sanforth has invited us to a pre-post breakfast. Are you game for it, Angel?"

She looked up at him with an adorable pout. "If there's a chance for a cup of hot tea, Mr. Stewart, I'm game."

"Oh, I'm sure you'll find a lot more than tea. Knowing Chelsey, he'll have a spread grand enough for Queen Victoria."

Angeleen soon discovered that Ruark had not exaggerated. No expense had been spared to transform the bright yellow tent erected next to the clubhouse into a lavish dining hall. Lounges, chairs, and tables were set about the improvised room for the convenience of the guests. Chefs had been on duty since dawn preparing a multitude of succulent dishes from Crepes Suzette to Yorkshire pudding. As they entered, she saw uniformed waiters carrying silver trays pass among the guests offering glasses of champagne.

Ruark seated her at a table and after she declined breakfast, he ordered her a pot of tea and a freshly baked scone. He chose a plate of thick slices of ham and scrambled eggs.

By noon the tent was filled by a high-spirited

crowd awaiting the big race. Preferring to avoid the press of people, Angeleen sat quietly while Ruark circulated among his many friends and acquaintances. Seeing her sitting alone in the corner, the host approached her.

Tall and slender, the sixty-year-old Seventh Earl of Sanforth possessed penetrating eyes and a great bushy moustache. A pleasant man, Sanforth possessed the grace, *savoir faire*, and self-assurance which come from generations of wealth.

"Are we boring you, my dear?" he asked kindly, drawing up a chair to sit down beside her.

"Not at all, Lord Sanforth. I find all of this very fascinating . . . but bewildering. It's difficult for me to believe that less than a year ago, I had to struggle just to stay alive."

At his alarmed look, she added for his clarification, "The Civil War, my lord. My home was in the South."

Sanforth nodded his full head of white hair. "Of course." He leaned forward to share a secret. "Confidentially, my dear, we British were quite sympathetic toward the Confederacy. Matter of fact, I personally found the exploits of your General Stuart most engrossing. The young daredevil reminded me of myself when I commanded my own light horse regiment in India."

"I'm glad to see you were more fortunate than he, my Lord. General Stuart's death was a serious loss to the South."

"Why isn't that poor man allowed to rest in peace?" Ruark declared. Angeleen looked up, surprised to discover he had moved to her side. "It's almost post time, Reb. Do you want to come with me to the saddling enclosure?"

"Of course," Angeleen replied. "I wouldn't miss it." She put her hand in his, and he drew Angeleen to her feet.

"I should be leaving now, too. Good luck, Stewart," Sanforth said, shaking Ruark's hand. Then he picked up a glass of champagne and raised it in the air. "Attention, my friends."

The crowd quieted down to hear the earl's announcement. "I offer a toast. To the 'chasers, the noblest warhorses of them all."

"Here! Here!" a chorus of voices responded.

When the guests with entries in the race departed for the stable, the rest of the jovial crowd, with glasses in hand, moved outside onto the chairs set up in front of the tent.

As Ruark led her through the crowd, Angeleen was amazed to see the transformation that had taken place outside; the race track now teemed with thousands of people as the air reverberated with the shouts of turf accountants calling out their odds and vendors hawking everything from chocolate to pencils.

Horses and jockeys eager for the big race waited in the saddling enclosure. Bobbing his head haughtily, Gallant Red looked like the true champion he was, with his mane now braided in a neat row and his coat brushed to a sheen.

Jems, wearing the Stewart red-and-black racing colors, appeared dashing and handsome.

While Ruark exchanged a few final words with the jockey and trainer, Angeleen offered her well-wishes to Gallant Red. "Good luck, love," she said with an affectionate pat. "Run a good race."

"Jockeys up," an official called out.

With a final flick of his whip toward Ruark, Jems nudged Gallant Red forward to join the parade to the post, which was led by Vindicator, the odds-on favorite owned by Sanforth. Gallant Red proudly pranced before the grandstand to the tune of creaking leather and jingling of stirrups.

After several moments, the horses were finally lined up as evenly as possible, and the race administrator dropped the starting flag.

Gallant Red dashed forward in the midst of the field of fifteen horses and Jems let the Red find his stride as they raced toward the first fence. The horse leaped the first barrier smoothly and continued to run, moving up from the middle toward the front.

He hurdled the succeeding barriers, but the dreaded Becher's Brook with its deep ditch and treacherous angle turn loomed ahead.

Jems shortened the reins a fraction to keep the horse under complete control and Gallant Red took off in a perfect leap. As he rose, the horse ahead of him went down, and Gallant Red swerved instinctively to avoid the obstacle in his path. However, two other horses were not as successful, and they too went down.

Having gained more valuable ground, Gallant Red executed the next jumps easily, and by the time they passed the stands after the first turn of the course, he was among the six horses in front, with Vindicator leading the field.

With the final fences ahead, Jems urged Gallant

Red closer to the leaders. Suddenly, the rider in front of him misjudged the jump and his horse crashed into the barrier, shattering part of the post as horse and jockey went down.

Unable to check the jump, Jems leaped the barrier and the jagged point of the broken post scraped Gallant Red, gouging a deep gash in his stomach. The plucky little horse continued on with a stream of blood flowing from the cut.

Unaware of the horse's injury, Jems saw a hole in the pack, made a daring move, and Gallant Red claimed the lead. However, with every barrier he leapt, Gallant Red painted a stripe of blood on the shrubbery.

Blood mingled with the clods of dirt that splattered the faces and goggles of the jockeys following him as Gallant Red cleared the last barrier, lengthened his stride and stretched out for the final surge to the finish line.

Suddenly, weakened from the loss of blood as he neared the winning post, the stout-hearted little Red keeled over on the track.

Jems rolled clear, and Vindicator leaped over Gallant Red, followed by the remaining horses, which were forced to swerve or hurdle the fallen animal.

Horrified, Angeleen waited for the horse to rise, but Gallant Red lay motionless. "Wait here, Angel," Ruark ordered.

Angeleen, having no intention of remaining behind, hurriedly joined several other breeders who followed Ruark and his trainer through the gate onto the track.

His face distorted by agony, Jems kneeled over

the downed animal. Tears streaked his cheeks as he looked up helplessly at Ruark. "I dinna know the lad was bleedin', sir. He never slowed his stride."

"I understand. It's not your fault, son," Ruark said solemnly as he knelt beside his horse.

Sanforth patted Ruark's shoulder. "He ran a hell of a race, old man."

As Angeleen reached the spot where Gallant Red lay in a pool of his own blood, the plucky little stallion tried to raise his head, his kind eyes already glazed.

Then, the once proud head fell back in death.

Ruark rose slowly to his feet as the grim sight of the horse ambulance arrived on the scene. Unable to move, Angeleen stared transfixed at the pool of blood draining from the lifeless body. Her senses were swept by a wave of blackness and she collapsed in a faint.

She awoke on a couch in Sanforth's tent. Finding herself the center of attention, she sat up in embarrassment. "What happened?"

"You fainted, Angel," Ruark said gently. "How do you feel now?"

"I'm fine, Ruark. I'm sorry to be so much trouble to you."

Sanforth handed her a glass of iced water. "Here, my dear, drink this."

After a few sips, she returned the glass. "Thank you. But I think I would enjoy a cup of tea."

Sanforth smiled and patted her hand. "A true Britisher at heart! I'll join you, my dear." He left them to order the tea.

"Will you be all right, Angel, while I leave for a

few minutes?" Ruark asked.

They exchanged glances. Angeleen knew of the unpleasant task that still lay ahead for him. She gazed compassionately into his anguished eyes. "I'm so sorry, Ruark. I know how you're feeling." She grasped his hands. "I wish there were something I could do."

"Your just being here helps, Angel." He kissed her cheek and hastily departed.

Later, the grief-stricken pair shared a silent ride as they returned to the house. Angeleen could guess the pain Ruark suffered. She herself could not erase the memory of the proud little horse prancing out for what would be his final race.

Suddenly overwhelmed with the desire to be surrounded by the familiar sights and sounds of home and those she loved, she felt desolate. Just plain homesick.

"Poor Jems. He looked so broken-hearted when we left him."

Ruark nodded. "He blames himself. The vet said Gallant Red would have bled to death regardless. I told Jems I expect him to ride the Grand Prix in Paris."

Shocked by this startling announcement, Angeleen said, "You're continuing?"

"Of course. Why would you think otherwise?"

"Well, I thought with Gallant Red . . . gone, we'd be going back to America."

Ruark looked incredulous. "Angel, I'm a horseman; that's my business. As much as I loved Gallant Red, I have to look at his death as simply a business loss."

She stared at him, appalled. "But he was more than just . . . just an investment, Ruark. Gallant Red was a living, breathing, creature. He felt love and pain the same as you or I."

"I'm sure he did, Angel. And he died a champion. What more could he—or anyone—ask for?" He patted her hand. "Honey, you can afford to be sentimental; I have to be practical."

She eyed him warily. This was Ruark Stewart, the driven businessman talking; this was the same Ruark Stewart who had confronted her the first night she arrived in Missouri. In the flush of love, she had allowed herself to forget that such a Ruark Stewart existed.

She remained quiet the rest of the trip, pondering a suspicion that had plagued her for days.

Chapter Twenty

Two weeks later when they crossed the English Channel to France, Angeleen felt certain she knew the reason behind her siege of illness—she must be carrying Ruark's child. She even attributed her sea sickness to the probability of her impending motherhood. Her anxiety diminished the pleasure she would have taken in touring the most exciting city in the world—Paris.

Even the prospect of visiting the salon of Charles Frederick Worth, the most renowned couturier in the world and the favorite dressmaker of Empress Eugenie herself held very little appeal to Angeleen.

"I don't need any more clothes," she declared when Ruark instructed the carriage driver to take them to Worth & Bobergh.

"Angel, no one comes to Paris without purchasing a Worth gown."

She arched a brow. "Then I could have the distinction of being the first."

"Honey, this will be an experience you'll never forget."

Irritated, she eyed him narrowly. "So you've been there before."

Ruark lifted her hand and clasped it between his own. "My dear Angeleen, we both know our lives did not begin the day we met. There have been others; a husband in your past, for instance."

Taken back by this unexpected reference to Will Hunter, Angeleen stared at him. "I'm surprised you have not asked me about my husband before this, Ruark."

"I'm not asking now, Angel. Your marriage is none of my business. I admit, at one time I did think that Robert was your husband."

"Robert?" She laughed lightly. "Good heavens! Why, they were worlds apart. Will Hunter was an unmitigated bastard."

"I'm sure you have your reasons for the way you feel about your husband. Was he killed during the war?" Ruark asked.

"Oh, he was killed during the war, all right, but not in the line of duty. Will shot himself in the foot to avoid *going* to war. Then his mistress stabbed him to death."

The shocking revelation drew a long, low whistle from Ruark. "Now I understand why you never mentioned him. Did you ever love him, Angel?"

Unflinchingly, she looked him in the eye. "Nev-

er. I hated the bastard from the day I met him."
She punctuated her irritation by adding, "And furthermore, I don't want to know anything about the
women in your past, Ruark."

She turned away and stared out of the window.

What Ruark had hoped would be a pleasant outing had just turned quite sour.

Silence prevailed for the remainder of the carriage
ride. However, as they entered the famous establishment at 7 Rue de la Paix, Angeleen's ire began to
fade; she couldn't help but be amused by the several
young men who greeted them as they entered the
opulent fashion salon.

Dressed identically in black, glossy suits made of
broadcloth, the men wore their hair curled in rather
peculiar styles. They also used ostentatious hand
gestures while speaking in dramatically clipped
British accents. Along with fluttering arm movements, their stiff-bodied way of walking confirmed
a manner of outrageous affectation. Altogether, the
fawning young men reminded Angeleen of a gaggle
of chirping, fin-flapping penguins.

"Ah, madam, sir," warbled the head penguin, who
then proceeded to besiege them with a great flurry
of words. "Without qualified reserve, we are indeed
gratified to extend felicitations and bid you welcome. It behooves me to express my distinct pleasure in introducing you, madam, to our grand establishment, verily to the pinnacle, yeah the very apex,
of *haute couture*."

He paused to press his fingertips together and
then, haughtily raising his brows, he closed his eyes.
"Yes, indeed, to the House of Fashion where only the

noblest of nobility and the genteelest of gentry convene to acquire the ultimate vogue and unparalleled elegance uniquely created by Worth and Bobergh."

The obsequious man opened his eyes, casting an eager glance at the gentry standing before him, only to discover his latest potential fashion-plate trying to conceal a yawn.

"Ah, yes. I see Madam is anxious to behold our finery. And so you shall. But, to recapitulate, as I say, we are most delighted at your visit and we are confident that Mr. Stewart and madam will experience the utmost satisfaction upon viewing the extraordinary collection artistically created by Mr. Charles Frederick Worth himself, fashioned from the finest silks of Europe and Asia and, in addition, the exquisite—"

"Yes, yes," Ruark interrupted. "Before the fashions go out of style, get on with it, Reeves, if you please."

And even if you don't please, Angeleen thought, amused at Ruark's comment.

"As you wish, Mr. Stewart." Annoyed to have his speech cut short, Reeves clapped his hands and then waved impatiently at another black-suited gentleman as though the hapless subordinate had caused the delay.

"Come, come, Reginald. Time is of the essence. Do escort our honored guests to the upper rooms immediately."

As Reginald led them to the stairway, Angeleen looked around with curiosity at the ornate furnishings, crystal chandeliers, and large colorful portraits which were hung against flower-embossed, gold-leaf wallpaper. They passed two life-sized marble statues proudly affirming the attributes of the female form.

To tease Angeleen, Ruark paused before them to have a better look. "Come, come, Reginald. Time is of the essence," she whispered, tugging Ruark's sleeve. "And anyway, my dear, the merchandise is upstairs."

The stairway proved to be a showcase in itself. Angeleen marveled at the sweeping grandeur of the broad curving structure richly carpeted in deep crimson. Banking each side of the stairway stood vases filled with hundreds of fresh-cut flowers.

After climbing the massive stairway, they finally arrived at the door of Charles Frederick Worth, the renowned Englishman whose bold designs had revolutionized the fashion capital of the world.

Upon entering the salon, Angeleen had to force herself to keep from laughing when she first laid eyes on the great man himself.

A large cigar poked out from beneath an enormous moustache, the ends of which trailed down into the thick folds of his several chins. Dressed in a costly red velvet jacket, white silk pants that buckled at the knee over white stockings, and red velvet slippers, Worth lay reclining on a sofa.

"Ah, Mr. Stewart, what a pleasure to see you again." Dramatically undraping his rotund body from the couch, Worth slowly managed to rise to his feet.

He shook Ruark's hand, then turned a discerning eye on Angeleen. "Mrs. Hunter." Bowing slightly, he kissed her hand.

"You are right, Mr. Stewart, a rich sapphire velvet

to complement her vibrant coloring will produce a dazzling effect. I look forward to creating the design for such a beautiful lady."

Angeleen glanced in astonishment at Ruark, surprised to hear that he had already communicated with the dressmaker. Ruark merely winked at her.

"Excuse me for a moment, my friends. To be creative, the artist must be appropriately attired." Worth started to walk away and then turned around. "It puts me in the proper mood, you see." With that, he shuffled his bulky body across the room and disappeared behind a fragile Japanese silk screen.

Somewhat annoyed that the two men had already made a choice for her, Angeleen whispered to Ruark. "And what if I don't want sapphire velvet?"

"You have to take it anyway." He squeezed her hand and added, "Sapphire puts me in the proper mood, you see." Her eyes smiled at him, in spite of herself. But before she could answer, she was distracted by the reappearance of Worth. Having donned a smock and beret, the man had recreated himself, by dress and by stance, into the very vision of Rembrandt.

The only thing missing is his easel, Angeleen reflected, now in doubt whether he intended to clothe her or paint her.

"Shall we proceed?" the dressmaker intoned, motioning them to follow. In his new mood, he became surprisingly light of foot as he led them into a room entirely decorated in black and white, which contained only black or white bolts of various silks.

In a sudden flurry of movement, he pulled all the pins out of her hair and it tumbled to her shoulders. With a dramatic flair, Worth draped a bolt of white silk over her shoulder. "Do you see the striking contrast against her dark tresses, Mr. Stewart?"

When Ruark nodded, Worth quickly snatched a bolt of black and draped the material across her other shoulder. "Aha, now see how the black accents her coloring to bring out the rich tones of her hair? We must create a black-and-white design for this lovely lady."

"I trust your judgment, Mr. Worth," Ruark replied. Once again, Angeleen had been given no choice in the matter.

"Now, come along," Worth said with a pleased smile and led them into another room elaborately furnished with comfortable chairs and couches. One of the black-suited young men immediately lit a cigar for each of the men, poured them a glass of brandy, and offered Angeleen a glass of white wine.

As Worth and Ruark discussed the races, Angeleen felt ignored. When she tried to interject a comment, Worth looked at her with the tolerance reserved for the slightly addled.

"Ah yes, madam," he humored, "but fret not thy sweet little head concerning matters of the chase. After all, the complexity inherent in the sport of kings is best understood, and therefore properly discoursed, only by gentlemen of the turf."

She didn't care whether he dressed every Empress in Europe, Asia, and all the ships at sea. The pompous buffoon had already decided she had no taste and now obviously assumed she was devoid of a brain as well. As their voices droned on, she drifted off into rhyme for her own amusement.

> *Alas, pity this poor Rembrandt's ghost,*
> *Stuffed with buttons, bobbins, and boast.*
> *For despite all his sashing,*
> *methinks this icon of fashion*
> *Couldn't raise his wee . . .*
> *thimble for passion!*

Her eyes flashed with a mischievous gleam at the bawdy thought. Then imagining the same Mr. Charles Frederick Worth in the nude, adorned with nary a stitch, except for one small gold leaf, Angeleen suddenly giggled out loud.

Ruark glanced at her, and as if reading her mind, he nodded and winked.

Observing their secretive exchange, Worth rose to his feet. "Shall we move along to the Rainbow Salon?" Angeleen was delighted to find the room contained bolts of silks and rich brocades in a myriad of colors. Admiringly, she picked up a bolt of soft yellow silk.

"Ah yes, a wise choice, madam. Perhaps, worn with a white dotted net?"

"I think I'd like that," Angeleen agreed, amazed to find her personal choice would be considered.

"Lovely. Lovely," Worth exclaimed.

Moving on to the next room, they found the salon crowded with wooden forms on which many of Worth's designs were elaborately displayed. As Angeleen walked among them, admiring the exquisite fashions and luxurious fabrics, she grudgingly gave credit where credit was due; Charles Frederick Worth appeared to have no peer—he was a brilliant designer.

"Feel free to browse, madam. And if, perchance, a particular design should catch your eye, I would be willing to duplicate the garment providing the style will suit your figure."

"Since Mrs. Hunter is one of a kind, Mr. Worth, what she wears should also be," Ruark interjected firmly.

Worth nodded in understanding. "As you wish, Mr. Stewart."

When Angeleen had completed her inspection, Worth picked up a tiny bell. "Now, madam, if you would be kind enough to accompany one of my dressers."

In response to the soft tinkle, a woman appeared in the doorway. "Monique, prepare Mrs. Hunter for the Salon de Lumiere," he ordered.

"The blue satin, monsieur?" she inquired.

Deep in reflection, Worth tapped one of his several chins. "No, I think the red mousselaine de soie would be more appropriate."

In an ornate dressing room, Angeleen was quickly stripped and a red nightgown of sheer, gauzy silk pulled over her head. Pencil thin straps glided onto her shoulders, and the high Princess waistline of the filmy gown hugged her breasts and dropped to the floor in shimmering folds.

Angeleen thought the gown appeared more daring than the one Ruark had purchased for her in St. Louis. "I hope your employer does not think I'm going to parade before him in this," she declared indignantly.

323

"Oh, Monsieur Worth will not be there, *madame*," Monique assured her as the young woman brushed Angeleen's hair to a satiny mantle on her shoulders. Then, with a lively twinkle in her eyes, Monique added, "Just Monsieur Stewart."

She opened the door and Angeleen stepped into a darkened room. The mirrors lining the walls and ceiling reflected the gaslight from the few burning lamps, but the room glowed with an aura of nighttime intimacy.

Ruark, who was seated on a plush couch, sucked in his breath and rose to his feet to stare, awestruck. "You're the most desirable woman I've ever known."

He started to move toward her. "No, don't come any nearer, Ruark. Don't touch me. I'm sure there are a dozen pairs of eyes watching us from behind all these mirrors. I think this place is not what it appears to be."

He grinned. "The House of Worth is a reputable fashion house, love. Nevertheless, if you expect me to keep my hands off you, I'd suggest you get out of here—now."

She turned to leave, but he stopped her. Running his hand slowly up her bare arm, he asked hoarsely, "Do you like the gown, Angel?"

Angeleen gazed up into the dangerous gleam in his dark eyes. "I think the point is whether *you* like it, Ruark." His hand had stopped at her shoulder, and she placed her hand over his. "I can see it passed the test."

"Sweetheart, you'd excite me wrapped in a burlap bag from head to toe and tied at the neck."

Her mouth curved in a seductive smile. "Someday, I may remind you of that," she warned as she slipped through the door into the dressing room.

After being measured, then remeasured, Angeleen finally rejoined Ruark and Worth in his salon.

"It will be my pleasure to design fashions for someone as lovely as you, Mrs. Hunter."

"We will remain in Paris for another month before returning to England," Ruark informed him.

"I can assure you, I will have the gowns completed by then," Worth said.

He kissed her hand, shook Ruark's, then removed his smock and beret. By the time they left the room, Charles Frederick Worth had returned to his reclining position on the couch.

When they entered their hotel suite, Angeleen went into the bedroom and hung up her cloak. She turned to discover Ruark leaning against the doorway with his arm behind his back. A sly grin played on his face.

"What is it?" she asked, perplexed.

He raised the arm he had been concealing. The red nightgown dangled from his finger. "Will you model this for me, Angel?"

The promise of deviltry in his eyes excited her. "Don't you have to get to the race track?" she asked breathlessly.

"I've got an hour."

He shifted his tall frame and approached her. "No mirrors, Angel. Nobody here except you and me."

"But the gown is meant for a darkened room and dim lights," she purred in a weak line of defense.

Not to be deterred, he walked over to the window and closed the heavy drapes, casting the room into shadows. "What's your excuse now, Angel?"

He came and stood before her, then began to remove the pins from her hair. She felt her excitement rising and her breath quicken. She knew by the time he finished undressing her, her passion would be out of control—such was the profound impact his amorous touch always had on her.

She closed her eyes and felt him release the buttons of her bodice. Then her skirt slipped off her hips. A shock of cool air stroked her bare breasts as, piece by piece, he removed the rest of her clothing.

She opened her eyes when she felt the silken gown slide over her head and cling to her body. He was watching her. Waiting. The hunger in his gaze ignited every nerve end in her body, and the need for his touch burned deep beneath her flesh.

She reached out slim arms and her fingers opened his cravat, then his shirt, sliding it off his shoulders and down his arms. Kneeling, she removed his shoes and released the belt of his trousers. She slid trousers and drawers down his legs, lifting each foot until the clothing was free of his body.

Still on her knees, she lifted her head and looked up into his dark gaze. He grasped her under the arms and slowly drew her up the length of him until he held her suspended from the floor.

As she slipped her arms around his neck, they kissed—a long demanding kiss that soon erupted into repeated kisses as each began savoring the taste of the other.

She cleaved to him and threw her head back as she felt the exquisite sensation of his mouth closing around her breast. Curving into him more, she pressed her body against the hardened plane of his.

He carried her to the bed and tossed aside the spread and quilt. She reluctantly released her hold on him as he laid her down against the white sheet.

Her dark hair was fanned out over the pillow, and the red gown shimmered like a crimson blaze.

He lowered himself and gathered her into his arms. Rolling onto his back, he tangled his hands in her hair and drew her to him, making her lips tingle with the intensity of his kiss.

Now entwined, they rolled back and he straddled her hips. For a moment they gazed into one another's eyes and she guessed his intent even before his hands clutched the neck of the gown.

Her smile told him she understood, and deliberately, he slowly ripped the gown down the front. Smiling, she reached up, encircled his neck, and drew him down, feeling the strength of him pressed against her own heated flesh.

She writhed beneath him, pleading for mercy as his mouth and hands ravaged her nakedness, the seductive gown a torn and discarded symbol on the floor.

When he entered her, she gasped with rapture as he filled her and she tightened around him. The tempo of his thrusts increased and she matched her rhythm to his until they soared together in a sublime moment of ecstasy.

Angeleen put off seeing a doctor for several more weeks to avoid confirming her suspicion. Finally, she knew she could no longer delay the visit.

The death of Gallant Red had left her with little

desire to witness another steeplechase, so one morning after Ruark left for the track, Angeleen went to the office of a local physician. He confirmed that she was four months pregnant.

That night, after Ruark made love to her, she still couldn't bring herself to tell him. She knew what his reaction would be, for the sting of his words, uttered long ago, still burned in her memory. *I don't want the mother of my children to be a whore.*

A whore. For a moment, Angeleen reflected on the idea and acknowledged that, if she hadn't been a fallen woman *then*, she surely was one now.

She slept fitfully that night, wondering how to broach the subject of her pregnancy to Ruark on the following morning, the day of the Grand Prix de Paris.

At breakfast he offered her an opening. "I got a note from Worth and he said your gowns would be delivered today."

"You shouldn't have spent so much on them, Ruark. You have to conserve your wealth for the future, when you have children."

Her expression saddened as she realized that she and her child would never be a part of that future.

Seeing her sudden mood shift, Ruark recalled T. J.'s earlier warning that Angeleen might not be able to bear children. He wondered if she was suffering at the thought of not being able to give him a child. He never knew for certain what thoughts lay in the depths of those incredible sapphire eyes. But that aura of mystery continued to be one of the qualities that made her so intriguing.

For a moment, he studied the dejected face of his beloved and thought how wrong he had been at the time of their first meeting. Since then, he had learned that Angeleen was all the woman he would ever need. She was not only beautiful, but intelligent, witty, compassionate, a delightful companion, loyal to what she believed, and a wonderful lover—so motherhood be damned. Children could always be adopted, he reasoned. But there would never be another woman like his Angel—never could there be another woman for him. As soon as they returned to America, he hoped she would consent to be his wife.

In an effort to force aside her fears, he said reassuringly, "You mustn't worry your head about how much I spend on you, Angel. Besides, I have no thoughts of children now."

Angeleen felt he couldn't have expressed himself more clearly, and the statement he made when Gallant Red died echoed in her ears. *"You can afford to be sentimental . . . I have to be practical."*

The ever pragmatic Ruark Stewart, she thought bitterly. *Yes, Ruark, it would not be practical to have thoughts about children now. Not when you're enjoying life with a mistress. Plenty of time in the future for children . . . born of a suitable wife, of course.*

She had always known that leaving him was inevitable. She had faced this dreaded hour, replayed it in her mind every day from the moment she had agreed to become his mistress.

Why even tell him her news and subject both of them to an embarrassing good-bye when he asked her to leave? So she made the decision; she wouldn't tell him she was carrying his child.

Angeleen raised her head. "You're right, Ruark," she agreed impassively as the thought of never seeing him again tore her heartstrings to shreds.

As soon as he left, Angeleen packed a single bag, leaving behind the lavish gowns and expensive jewels he had given her. She was certain that if he tried to follow, he would think she had returned to England, so studying the shipping manifest, she discovered a ship due to sail for America from LeHarve on the morning tide.

Her final task was to leave a note. She merely thanked him for everything and told him she had wearied of the way they had been living. Tucking the note into an envelope, she propped it on the nightstand beside the bed.

Then, drawing upon the fortitude intrinsic to her nature, Angeleen picked up her bag and for a moment paused for a final look. Then she closed the door and departed.

Later in the day, Ruark paused outside the door and examined the sapphire and diamond ring he intended to give Angeleen that evening when he asked her to marry him. Always able to sense her absence as well as her presence, Ruark knew when he entered the suite that she was not there.

With a sense of foreboding, he walked into the bedroom.

Chapter Twenty-One

Angeleen had plenty of time to think on the lonely return trip. She kept her own company as much as possible to avoid drawing any attention to herself. The morning sickness which had plagued her previous crossing of the Atlantic had been replaced by the heartache of missing Ruark.

Upon docking in New York, she immediately posted a letter to Robert to assure him that she was well and would contact him later. She knew he was the only one she could trust to keep her confidence. Once Ruark returned from Europe, St. Louis would be the first place he would look for her.

Angeleen had come to several conclusions. She could not remain in New York, nor would she return to St. Louis. And she would certainly not go back to Louisiana.

But being almost five months pregnant and possessing only limited funds, Angeleen knew she would soon have to get herself securely settled to await the birth of her baby.

Throughout the whole voyage, one person came again and again to her mind—the single person who could offer her both the stability and the medical assistance she required. Thomas Jefferson Graham.

She would go to Virginia.

Wistful longing for Ruark and happy memories of their life together continued to dominate her thoughts as Angeleen gazed out of the train window. Even the *clickety-clack* from the rails reverberated his name.

Angeleen did not fear the desperate straits that lay ahead; she had known the dregs of poverty before and had survived. Impending motherhood held no dread, for she would have Ruark's child as a living legacy of her love for him.

Her fear lay in the battle she now waged with her own memories. Continuously, her thoughts drifted to wondering what Ruark might be doing at this very moment. In her mind's eye, she saw him cheering home his winner at the race track, seated across from her at a breakfast table, buttoning his shirt. She could hear his warm chuckle, smell his masculine scent. And above all—the most treasured memory, yet the cruelest torment—she could feel his lips and the touch of his hands on her body.

She leaned her head back against the seat and closed her eyes. But every mile of railroad track

echoed the haunting refrain—*Ruark . . . Ruark . . .
Ruark.*

The next day, after finishing his examination of
Angeleen, T. J. shook his head in disbelief as he
washed his hands.

"So you've left Ruark and he doesn't know you're
carrying his baby."

"And you've got to swear to me that you won't
tell him, T. J.," Angeleen insisted as she buttoned
her gown.

Frustrated, T. J. threw down the towel he was
holding. "Dammit, Angel, you're carrying this too
far. Ruark is my best friend. And friendship or not,
a man has a right to know he'll soon be a father."

"I thought you were my friend too, T. J. I swear
that if you don't promise to keep this confidence,
I'll leave now and never return."

"Just how do you expect to support a child?" he
challenged, seeing the wisdom of getting off that
particular issue.

"I have enough money to get started until I can
find some type of employment."

"And who in hell is going to hire a woman who is
five months pregnant?" he argued, slamming himself down in the chair behind his desk. "At least
Ruark would support you and the baby." He shook
his head, realizing he had just returned to the only
logical conclusion.

She came over and sat down. "T. J., I'm not going
to argue with you. Do I have your word that you
won't tell Ruark?"

His shoulders slumped in defeat. "All right, Angel.

As your doctor, I will keep your confidence."

She smiled with relief. "Thank you, T. J. I knew I could count on you, and I would want none but you to deliver my baby."

He came around the desk. Grasping her shoulders, he drew her to her feet and smiled into her trusting eyes. "Now tell me, where do you intend to live, Angel Face?"

"I hope I can find a furnished room in town."

T. J. thought for a moment and then suddenly one of his patients came to mind. "I might have a better solution. I have a patient who lost her husband a few weeks ago. She's planning on returning to Wisconsin and has a small farmhouse here, a few miles out of town. I know she'd be willing to sell it cheap."

Angeleen's eyes brightened with hope. "How cheap is 'cheap,' T. J.?"

"We'll go and find out. And then I'm going to see to it that you eat a good, hot meal."

Later that day, true to his word, T. J. eyed her sternly. "I want to see every crumb disappear from that plate," he ordered.

"T. J., I can't eat another bite. I haven't eaten this much in months," Angeleen pleaded.

He shook his head. "And it shows. Look at you. You're nothing more than skin and bones. No wonder Ruark never suspected you were pregnant."

"Well, I was very nauseated in the beginning. I couldn't eat at all." She put aside her napkin and smiled. "How can I ever thank you, T. J.? The house is perfect for my needs. And the vegetable garden and chickens will keep food on the table. Come next spring, I'll be able to plant the garden myself."

"I just hope you know what you're letting yourself in for," he warned.

"During the war I kept Scotcroft going to keep from starving. I'll certainly be able to tend a small garden and a few chickens," she snorted.

"And raise a baby," he added with the kind skepticism of a Dutch uncle.

"You just watch me and see for yourself," she said confidently.

Reaching across the table, he clasped her hand. "I believe you can, Angel. You've got the spunk and fortitude to face whatever comes. I knew that the first time I met you."

He shook his head sadly, "But, honey, you've got no common sense when it comes to men."

The following week, Angeleen fell into another stroke of luck when T. J. introduced her to Virginia Harris. The petite redhead owned "The Right Touch," a shop in town known for fine fabrics and handcrafted accessories.

She hired Angeleen to do the finishing touches, which involved adding embroidery to scarfs and gloves, tatting to handkerchiefs, and tulle to parasols. Since all the stitchery could be done at home, Miss Harris felt Angeleen's delicate condition need not be a consideration for employment.

As they left the shop, Angeleen chatted happily about her good fortune. But with her curiosity piqued by a wink T. J. had given the lovely proprietor, Angeleen couldn't resist teasing her benefactor.

"Did I detect that the red hair of the charming

Miss Harris has caught your eye, Doctor Graham?"

T. J. offered an outrageous grin. "Well . . . let's just say, Ginny is one of the more colorful blossoms in the garden."

Chapter Twenty-Two

Robert heard the tread of determined footsteps against the wooden floor the moment the front door slammed. He didn't even look up when Ruark Stewart burst through his office door.

"Where is she, Scott?" Ruark demanded.

"I have no idea," Robert said calmly. He thought it senseless to mince words.

"Henry said he doesn't know where she is, and I believe him. That means *you do*. Angeleen wouldn't disappear without contacting someone to put all your minds at ease."

Unperturbed, Robert looked up at him. "Stewart, if I knew my sister's whereabouts, I'd go to her. Especially now that a bastard like you has thrown her to the wolves."

"Is that what she told you?" Ruark shouted

incredulously. "She left me. Dammit, Scott, I love your sister. I want to marry her."

"Too bad. It appears she doesn't want to marry you."

Robert derived a great deal of pleasure from watching Ruark squirm. Truthfully, he didn't know his sister's present whereabouts. Her letter to him had been posted the day her ship docked, and she had implied she would be leaving New York immediately and would contact him later.

What pleased Robert was the fact that Ruark Stewart *believed* he knew where Angeleen could be found, which gave Robert the upper hand with the arrogant bastard.

Ruark leaned across the desk and shook his balled fist at Robert. "I warn you, Scott, if I find you know more than you're telling me concerning Angeleen's whereabouts, St. Louis will be too small to hold the two of us."

Robert leaned back in his chair and smiled confidently. "Your threats have never frightened me, Stewart. Frankly, you got just what you deserve. You had no right to treat my sister like a whore."

As soon as the words left Robert's mouth, Ruark fired back immediately. "You mean the way you treat Celeste Dupree? Where's the difference between us, Scott?"

Robert's eyes flashed angrily and he jumped to his feet. "The difference is that Angeleen is my sister."

"No, you stinking hypocrite," Ruark thundered. "The difference is that I'm willing to marry the woman I slept with."

For a long moment the two men glared across the

desk at one another. Finally Robert sat down and picked up several papers lying on the desk. "Get the hell out of my office, Stewart. I've got a business to run."

Ruark's exit was as stormy as his arrival.

Long after Ruark's departure, Robert sat staring at the door. Ruark Stewart was right about one thing: Robert had never looked at his relationship with Celeste in the same light as he had Ruark's with Angeleen.

But his sister loved Ruark. At least she once had. Celeste shared his bed only to keep a roof over her head; no woman would stay with a one-armed freak because she loved him.

But, as Ruark claimed, the issue here was the man's motive, not the woman's. He'd never intended to marry Celeste, only use her. He was the hypocrite Ruark accused him of being.

Throughout the day and on his way home that evening, Robert's thoughts continued to dwell on Ruark's words.

Celeste greeted him with her usual warm smile when he returned to the small house they now shared, and as they ate their evening meal, he studied her intently.

Her appearance was now far different from the woman he had first met. She no longer painted her face and eyes, her soft curls were always brushed neatly, and the flashy clothing had been abandoned for the plain skirts and bodices he bought for her at the Emporium.

She cooked his meals, kept his house tidy and his clothing clean and darned—and she shared his bed.

Stewart was right about that, he conceded.

In truth, she had all the burdens of a wife without any of the respect reserved for the role.

Furthermore, Robert's nightmares had become less frequent since Celeste entered his life. In her subtle manner, she had restored his confidence in his own manhood.

"You are quiet tonight, Robert," she said as they lingered over coffee at the dinner table. "Your business did not go well with you today?"

That, too, had been missing in his life until she appeared, he realized. Someone who listened.

"Ruark Stewart has returned to St. Louis. He thinks I know the whereabouts of my sister."

"Did you show him her letter?"

"No," Robert said. "I didn't want to give him the satisfaction. If Angeleen left Stewart, she must no longer love him."

Celeste lowered her eyes and drank her coffee. Robert sensed her displeasure. "You don't approve?"

She looked up at him. "I think you do not understand women, Robert. You cannot be certain that she left him because she no longer loves him. Men do not comprehend that women have many reasons for what they do."

"And what are your reasons for staying with me, Celeste?"

Her smile carried the wisdom of the ages. "As I just said, women have reasons that men do not understand." She got up and began to clean and scrape the dishes.

Robert carried his cup to the sink. "Tell me what your reason is for staying with me."

Celeste blushed, unable to look at him. "Well, you're ill-tempered, but you do not beat me," she said.

"Go on. I want to hear all your reasons," he said, convinced that her main reason for staying with him was for the sake of convenience.

"You are clean in body and mind. I have known men who were not."

"And go on," he insisted.

Robert could see her struggle with the answers, but he wanted it all in the open once and for all. Once he heard her admit that she stayed with him, despite his unsightly infirmity, because she wanted a roof over her head, his suspicions would be confirmed.

"You are a gentleman, and I have known men who were not."

"Go on," he said impatiently.

"You are a good lover, Robert, and a considerate one. That, too, is important to a woman. Most men are not."

"Dammit, Celeste, stop telling me about the men you've known. I want to hear your real reason for remaining with me," he shouted.

She flinched under his raised tone and when she looked up, tears glistened in her eyes but she did not shed them.

"I remain with you because I love you."

Dare a beggar look at a king? She waited for his laughter.

Stunned, Robert stared at her. She had said the one thing he'd never expected to hear. He reached out and tipped her chin to meet his dark gaze.

"Will you marry me, Celeste?"

"No, Robert." Celeste returned to busying herself with the dishes.

Her refusal aroused his earlier suspicion. "I thought as much," he said.

She shoved the dishes aside and turned away from him. Robert stared at the back of her tiny shoulders squared so bravely, her spine held so stiffly.

"You are an educated gentleman, Robert. In time you will be able to afford the kind of wife you deserve. While I'm . . . I'm nothing but a whore."

He turned her to face him and cupped her cheek in his hand, his thumb brushing aside a tear sliding down her cheek. "I want you to be my wife," Robert said gently.

He kissed her long and tenderly. When he drew away, she smiled up at him through her tears. "It is as I said, Robert. You know nothing about women." Her face broke into a wide, radiant smile that carried to her eyes. "But yes! Yes, I'll marry you."

Robert pulled her against him to once again claim her lips. As the kiss intensified, so did their passion. She closed her eyes as he trailed kisses down the slim column of her neck. Releasing her bodice, he shoved it off her shoulders and closed his mouth around her breast.

Tremors raced the length of her spine when his tongue created exquisite sensations in one breast and then the other. Throwing back her head with a rapturous sigh, Celeste laced her fingers through his hair and whispered breathlessly, "Perhaps, I was wrong, *mon cher*. There is much you do know about women."

Chapter Twenty-Three

Angeleen finished gluing the final pink pearl to the last of the eight fans for the forthcoming nuptials of Andrea Louise Adams. The future bride's mother had ordered each of the bridal attendants' fans to be encrusted with pearls that matched their gowns.

Angeleen sat up and rubbed her lower back. For the past several hours, the nagging ache had persisted, and she sighed, relieved that the grueling, back-bending task was finished.

As she stretched her aching muscles, she suddenly lurched forward, gripped by a stabbing pain. Angeleen's eyes widened in shock when a few moments later, the pain repeated itself.

She glanced worriedly at the clock. T. J. wouldn't arrive for at least another hour. Living alone, with her delivery time so close, T. J.'s daily habit of stopping after his office hours to check on her had brought a welcome sense of security. Now she wasn't certain whether to wait for him or to start walking into town.

Forcing herself to remain calm, Angeleen set about preparing for the birth of her baby. She pumped several pots of water and put them on the hearth to boil. Then she brushed out her hair and divided it into two loose pigtails. Removing her clothing, Angeleen thoroughly bathed herself before putting on a white nightgown.

When T. J. arrived a short time later, Angeleen was all prepared to have her baby.

However, the baby had other intentions. After twelve hours of labor, the baby still had not made an appearance.

T. J. sponged her forehead and tried to make Angeleen as comfortable as possible, but there was little he could do except hold her hand when the spasms became excruciating.

After the long labor, her early confidence had been dulled by pain, and she began to express her fright and doubts. "I wish Ruark were here," she said as she gazed at T. J. through pain-racked eyes.

"He would be, honey, if he knew," T. J. assured her.

"T. J., if anything happens to me, I want Ruark to have the baby." She gasped in the clutch of a contraction.

"Nothing's going to happen to you. You're doing fine. The baby probably just has a stubborn streak, like its father."

"And mother," she managed to gasp when the pain momentarily ceased.

Instantly, she clutched his hand as the next seizure gripped her. "Tell Ruark I never stopped loving him."

"I think you should tell him that yourself after this is over," he urged with a reassuring grin. "Maybe if you had told him sooner, he *would* be here now. I know this is no time for lectures, honey, but you are the two biggest fools I've ever met. How can you keep on hurting each other like this?"

"I thought you were a kindly, sympathetic doctor," she murmured, clamping down on her lip to keep herself from screaming as her body contracted.

T. J. stroked her forehead. "Everything looks fine, Angel. Just keep pushing. It shouldn't be too much longer."

But several more hours passed before T. J. laid her newborn son in her arms.

Angeleen slept through most of the morning. When she awoke, T. J. gave her an envelope that had been sent to him to give to her. Her eyes misted with tears as she read the message.

My Dearest Angeleen,

I am writing this letter with a heavy heart. The ways of the young are often confusing to me, but I trust you and my grandson have your reasons for what you do. It is not for an old woman to question them.

Robert tells me you are soon to give birth to Ruark's child. How I wish you were here in the

*cradle of our arms, but I know T. J. will take
good care of you.*

*I beg you to honor this one request; do not
deny the child its rightful name of Stewart, for
it is my intent to make the child my heir.*

*My dear Angeleen, our prayers and thoughts
will be with you through the days ahead and I
hope you have enough love in your heart to one
day bring the child here for us to meet.*

*With deepest love, I shall always remain,
Your Nana Sarah*

Angeleen folded the letter and returned it to the
pale blue envelope just as a light tap sounded on
the door.

T. J. poked his head into the room. "Hey, I've
got someone here who is real anxious to see his
mother."

Angeleen brushed aside her tears and opened
her arms. "Then give him to me, Doctor Graham,
because there's a mother here who is real anxious
to see her son." Smiling lovingly, she gazed down at
the little bundle he placed in her arms.

"It's time to get down to business here. I have to
fill out a Certificate of Birth. What are you naming
the little guy?"

"I thought I'd name him Thomas"—she glanced
up shyly at T. J.—"after his godfather."

"My honor, ma'am," T. J. said dramatically, ex-
ecuting a thespian bow.

"And Henry, after his grandfather." Angeleen
paused and glanced at the tiny blue envelope lying

on the table. "And . . . Stewart . . . after his father."

T. J. squeezed her hand. "Good for you, Angel."

He put aside the certificate. "I can fill in the rest of the details later."

He leaned over and spoke to the little pink face with the heavy thatch of dark hair on its head. "Well, Thomas Henry Stewart, what is your opinion of your new name?"

Dimples danced in her cheeks when Angeleen giggled as the baby cooed in contentment, closed his eyes, and promptly fell asleep.

T. J. grinned and winked at her. "I think he likes it."

Chapter Twenty-Four

The moment he walked into the den, the tidy little box sitting in the center of his desk drew Ruark's attention like a magnet. He opened the package and stared in shock at his missing gold watch.

"Myra!" he shouted at the top of his voice. The poor woman came hurrying into the room. "Myra, where did this package come from?"

"A Captain Redman of the *Delta Queen* came here and left it. He said the watch apparently had slipped between a table and the wall. They found it dangling from a nail when they ripped out the table while doing some remodeling in your cabin on the boat."

"Oh, I see. Thank you, Myra." *For a foolish moment he had hoped it was a sign from Angel.*

Myra shook her head sadly as she watched Ruark walk desolately up the stairway. He started to go to his room, then changed his direction and went to the room Angeleen had used.

Nothing had changed. Her clothes were still intact, as if awaiting her return. Even the ones he had brought back with him from Europe were now hung up or folded and put away in drawers. As he wandered aimlessly around the room, he could smell the faint scent of her perfume that lingered in the air.

Twelve months. A whole year since he'd returned from Europe and still no trace of her.

Wherever you are, I'll find you, Angel. Even if it takes the rest of my life.

He looked down and realized that he still clutched the watch in his balled fist. Spreading his fingers apart, he stared numbly at the timepiece. It seemed to burn his palm, a painful reminder of the stinging accusation he had once flung at Angeleen. The memory seared his conscience.

Ruark opened one of the drawers and saw that it contained Angeleen's lingerie. He lifted out a white chemise and ran the smooth satin along his cheek.

With a shuddering whisper, he pleaded, "Oh, God, Angel. Where are you?"

"Mr. Ruark," Myra said softly, suddenly breaking into his reverie.

"What is it, Myra?" he asked without turning to face her.

"There's a gentlemen from the Pinkerton Agency waiting for you in the den."

"Tell him I'll be right down."

Tears glimmered in the eyes of the hardened businessman as he returned the garment to the drawer. Ruark wiped away the tears, slammed the drawer, and left the room.

When Ruark entered the den, the portly man sitting on the sofa stood up. "Good evening, Mr. Stewart."

"Parker," Ruark acknowledged briskly. After a brief handshake, Ruark sat down at his desk.

"These look familiar, Mr. Stewart?" The Pinkerton detective dropped a pair of pearl earrings on the desk.

Ruark recognized them at once. He picked up the earrings and glanced up excitedly at Parker. "Where did you get these?"

"She pawned them in New York, but the pawnbroker had a recent fire that destroyed his records, so he couldn't remember when she pawned them. But he recognized her picture fast enough when I showed it to him."

Ruark felt the flow of adrenalin through his body. This was the first breakthrough they had had in a year.

"So I figured she stayed in the East and never came back to Missouri," Parker continued. "I started checking out all the courthouses in the surrounding states."

Clarence Parker was a methodical investigator and enjoyed relating to his clients the skill and perseverance involved in being a detective.

"Well, get on with it, Parker," Ruark said impatiently.

"Finally tracked her down in Virginia."

Ruark jumped to his feet. "You've found her! Why in Hell didn't you say so sooner? Where is she?"

Parker wrote down the address and Ruark snatched the paper out of his hands. "Thanks. You did a good job. Send me your bill." He rushed from the room.

"Wait, there's more—" Parker found himself talking to himself. Ruark had already dashed up the stairway.

The detective wanted to tell him how he had come by the information and tracked her down after discovering a document in the Fairfax County Courthouse—a registration filed by a Dr. T. J. Graham for the birth of a male infant, Thomas Henry Stewart, October 19, 1866. Mother: Angeleen Elizabeth Hunter, nee Scott; Father: Ruark Charles Stewart.

"Oh, let him find out about the kid for himself," Parker grumbled. "If she knew she was carrying his kid, she must have had a good reason to be running away from all the Stewart dollars."

Sighing in relief that Tommy had finally gone to sleep, Angeleen laid her son in his crib and tiptoed over to the vanity. In thirty minutes T. J. would arrive for dinner and she still had to make the rolls.

As Angeleen brushed her hair, she thought of how much she would miss T. J. in the next two months while he was away. In the past year, since she had come to Virginia, T. J. had been a tower of strength to her, the best friend she had ever had. She tucked the long ends of her hair into a snood, then softly closed the door behind her and hurried to the kitchen.

She had just finished preparing croissants when a knock sounded on the door. Wiping her floured hands on her apron, she hurried to answer.

"You're early," she said gaily with a broad smile as she opened the door. The smile froze, then dissolved to a stricken stare.

"Hello, Angel. May I come in?" Ruark asked. His tall frame seemed to dwarf the doorway.

Shocked, she groped helplessly for a response. "Ah . . . yes . . . yes, of course. Please come in." She stepped back and allowed him to enter.

For a hushed moment, his dark gaze devoured her, until he finally spoke. "You're looking as lovely as ever."

"Thank you." Her throat felt so dry, the effort to say the simple words was painful.

"How have you been?"

"Fine." Her fingers itched to brush back the hair that had tumbled over his forehead. Nervously, she turned away, and for want of something to do with her hands, removed her apron. His glance quickly swept the homemade tarlatan gown she wore.

"You're looking well, too, Ruark."

"Life goes on," he said with an intended flippancy that didn't quite succeed.

Ruark cleared his throat and glanced around the small, but tidy, drawing room. "You seem to have made a nice home for yourself. Are you comfortable here?"

"Very." Angeleen cast a worried glance at the bedroom, fretful that Tommy would choose this moment to wake up crying.

"You're a difficult person to track down, Angel. It took a long time to find you."

She couldn't continue to just stand staring at him. The male essence of him was too disturbing. It was unbelievable—after all this time, one moment alone with him and all she could think of was how much she wanted to be in his arms.

"I'm in the middle of preparing dinner, Ruark. Why did you come here?"

"I hoped by now you would have come to your senses and be ready to come back," he said in a clipped tone. There was so much to say, but the words did not come easily.

Her head shot up defensively and her eyes clashed with his. This was familiar footing to her. All the doubts, the regrets, the yearnings she had struggled with in the past year were stripped away in the single, overbearing assertion.

For a brief moment, her foolish heart had hoped. Apparently, he expected she would admit the error of her ways and come crawling back to him. Just an "I love you" from him would have brought her to her knees—that's how much of a fool she might have been.

But Ruark would never change. How could she have thought otherwise?

She didn't need him; she had his son.

"Good-bye, Ruark. I think the last word's been said between us."

Angeleen turned away to return to the kitchen, but before she took two steps he grabbed her by the shoulder and spun her around to face him.

His fingers spanned her throat, tipping her chin

up to look at him. "There will never be a last word between us, Angel."

His mouth plummeted down in a bruising kiss, his hand on her throat preventing an escape. Whimpering beneath the kiss, she fought to resist the demand of his lips.

He covered her face and eyes with quick, urgent kisses, then claimed her mouth again, parting her lips and driving his tongue into her mouth.

Despite her struggles, she could feel her passion rising and began to battle herself as well as him.

He pulled the snood off her head and her hair tumbled to her shoulders as he laced his fingers through the long thickness. "Lord, baby, I missed you," he mumbled hoarsely.

"Ruark, stop," she pleaded when he slid his lips down the column of her neck.

"Don't say that, Angel. You want me as much as I want you."

His hands moved to her breast and she felt his heated touch through the cotton gown.

"Don't," she cried when he started to open her gown. She backed away, only to be stopped by the wall behind her.

His body trapped her, and he slipped the dress off her shoulders and cupped her breast through the thin fabric of her chemise.

"Stop it. Stop!" she cried.

Her rising passion began to obliterate her sanity, but she continued her struggle to resist him. The evidence of his own arousal ground against her hips, pressing her tighter against the wall as she tried weakly to shove him away.

"No. No, don't," she sobbed when he began to raise her skirt.

"Let her go, Ruark."

Ruark spun his head toward the speaker. T. J. stood in the doorway.

"Get the hell out of here, T. J.," Ruark snarled, sounding like the animal he had become.

"Under other circumstances, I might, ole friend. But I heard the lady say no." T. J. weighed his next words carefully. "I presume . . . you didn't."

Ruark's passion was quelled as quickly as it had risen. Shifting his glance to Angeleen, he saw her recoil with shame and humiliation.

Appalled by his actions, he now faced the full impact of how close he had come to debasing the woman he loved and the memory of what they once shared.

He took a shuddering breath and straightened up. "I'm sorry, Angel."

Ruark started to move to the door, then stopped and withdrew the earrings from his pocket. He tossed them on the table. "I believe these are yours."

With a guilty gasp, Angeleen recognized the pearl earrings still vibrating on the nearby table.

As T. J. stepped aside for Ruark to pass, Ruark said to him, "What are you doing here, T. J.?"

"I was invited," he said succinctly.

Pride leapt to the fore as Ruark mistakenly presumed the reason for T. J.'s presence. "Oh, forgive me. I appear to have intruded on your little domestic scene." Ruark smiled without amusement. "Come to think of it, T. J., you always did have an affinity for my used . . . effects."

"Spoken like a real officer and a gentlemen, Captain Stewart," T. J. said bitterly.

Ruark did not respond. He simply walked away.

Chapter Twenty-Five

Over a year and a half had passed since Ruark left Virginia and he had once again gone to Europe. He had not returned to America in all that time, deliberately keeping an ocean between himself and Angeleen.

The bond of brotherhood between Ruark and T. J. had weathered another crisis. They were able to put aside their grievances, as they had so often in the past, when Ruark, upon returning to America, sought out his old friend.

"Heart and lungs sound good, Ruark. You pass with flying colors," T. J. said, pulling the stethoscope out of his ears.

"Well, I just don't seem to have too much energy these days," Ruark complained as he buttoned his shirt.

T. J. put aside the stethoscope. "I'm going to give you some doctor's advice, ole friend. It's time you went back to St. Louis. You've been away from home too long. Forget Europe for a while."

"I'm ahead of you there, T. J. This was my last crossing. I sold my house in England and my racing stable over there. That's what detained me so long. I've come back to stay."

"That's good news," T. J. said. "Now go back home and surround yourself with the people who love you."

"I guess you're right. I did half-promise Nana to come home this year for my birthday. But after that, I'm coming back East." He paused, before adding decisively, "I still have some unfinished business here."

Having touched on the foremost question in his mind, he asked, "Has she married?"

Without glancing up, T. J. casually began to scribble on the file before him. "No."

"How is she doing?"

Suppressing a smile, T. J. kept his attention averted from Ruark. "Fine as far as I know. Haven't seen too much of her in the past year. I've been out West. Had a good offer from the Union Pacific, and I've been thinking of closing up my practice here."

T. J. shut the file and rose to his feet. "Well, come on. I'll buy you a birthday drink."

As they walked out, he punched Ruark in the shoulder. "I swear I see some gray hair at your temples. Didn't want to mention this before, buddy, but you are beginning to show your age."

"Wouldn't you like to think so," Ruark joshed.

Later that day, after seeing Ruark off at the train station, T. J. hurried to the telegraph office.

A few hours later, Sarah Stewart opened the wire just delivered to her and read the message from T. J.: *He's on his way.*

Her clear blue eyes gleamed with cunning. Smiling slyly, Sarah tore the wire into shreds.

Ruark entered the house quietly so as not to disturb anyone at such a late hour. For a moment he stood and looked about with contentment at the familiar surroundings. It felt good to be home.

T. J. was right. He had been away too long.

After lighting the lamp in the den, he poured a drink and sat down at his desk. He rifled through several stacks of mail, but was too tired to consider opening any of it. So he shoved back his chair, picked up his drink, and walked over to the couch.

Bone-tired, Ruark sat down to finish his drink. He took a deep swallow of the brandy and emptied the glass. Before he knew it, the sleep which had eluded him so successfully earlier suddenly overpowered him. The glass fell to the rug as he slipped into slumber.

Streaming through the east window, bright sunlight teased Ruark awake. He opened his eyes to the last thing he had expected to see. Blinking several times to clear his vision, he realized that he had not been mistaken.

Frowning angrily, a dark-haired young boy stood beside the couch staring down at him, his little chin jutting out pugnaciously.

"Well, hello," Ruark said as he sat up.

"Shoes off!" the boy demanded. The youngster moved to the foot of the couch and tried to remove one of Ruark's shoes. "Shoes off. Mommie says."

Ruark stopped him. "No, you don't have to do that."

"Do, too." His little chin set firmly. "No shoes." Then his round blue eyes widened in certainty. "Mommie says. Shoes no sleep."

Puzzled, Ruark raised a questioning brow, but preferring to take the line of least resistance, he conceded, "Your mommie is right, son." Then he suddenly grasped the boy's meaning, and feeling as if he had just achieved a brilliant business coup, Ruark grinned broadly. "You *meant* to say I shouldn't sleep with my shoes on."

The boy's annoyed look conveyed the impression he *had* said it. He continued to tug at Ruark's shoes.

"Well, what I meant is that you don't have to take off my shoes. I'm all through sleeping now."

To Ruark's immense relief, the youngster abandoned his mission.

Ruark wanted to get up but knew he would have to physically move the boy aside if he did. Yawning, he settled back.

"Cover mouth." The youngster's frown reappeared as he shook his finger at Ruark. "Mommie says."

Ruark regarded the boy through bleary eyes. "Mommie is right again. It's not polite to yawn without covering my mouth." Reflexively, he yawned again, only to be reprimanded immediately.

"Cover mouth."

"Oh, sorry," Ruark apologized. "We must listen

to Mommie." Just where in hell was "Mommie"? Ruark wondered, disgruntled. What kind of mother would let a child run loose in someone else's house? The youngster couldn't be more than two years old, Ruark reasoned. Left unattended, the boy could seriously injure himself.

Slapping his hands on his knees, Ruark tried to relax. "So, what's your name, young man?" he asked pleasantly.

"Tommy." Youthful curiosity gleamed in the youngster's inquisitive, dark-blue eyes.

"Well, how do you do, Tommy. My name is Ruark. And how old are you, Tommy?"

"Two." The lad held up two fingers.

"Well, you're certainly a big boy for being just two years old," Ruark said.

Having exhausted his repertoire of child-conversation, Ruark began to fidget under the boy's unwavering stare. Pulling out his watch, Ruark pushed the case lever. "Why, it's only seven o'clock," he said as he looked into the lad's large, uncomprehending eyes. "What are you doing here so early in the morning, Tommy?"

"Nana here. And Grampie." The youngster stared in fascination at the watch. Seeing the child's interest, Ruark snapped it closed and held up the watch and fob for the boy's closer inspection.

Tommy giggled with delight as he saw the gold horse dangle in the air. "Horsie." His head bobbed excitedly. "King horsie, too."

Ruark nodded. "Yes, this is a horse just like Bold King."

Another mistake. The precise mind of the two-year-old immediately challenged him. "Uh-uh," the boy said as he adamantly shook his head. "King *black* horsie," Tommy corrected with an engaging pout, and then reached for the timepiece.

Ruark let the boy hold the watch and lifted the youngster onto his lap. He smiled, watching the boy's delight as he played with the fob.

"Tommy, where are you?"

Ruark froze at the sound of the voice—a voice that had ceaselessly flitted into his mind and heart for the past two years. Still clutching the watch, the youngster slipped off his lap and ran out of the room.

"Mommie, look."

"What have you got there, honey?" Angeleen knelt down and he ran into her arms.

"Horsie." He held up the watch.

She recognized Ruark's watch fob immediately. Frowning, Angeleen reprimanded her son. "Tommy, you have been told not to go into the den. Did you take this watch out of a desk drawer?"

"No, he didn't. I gave it to him."

Startled, Angeleen's head snapped up at the sound of the deep voice. Ruark stood in the doorway of the den. For a lengthy moment, they stared at each other in stunned silence. Finally, she stood up.

"What are you doing here, Ruark?"

"I live here. I might ask the same question of you."

"But you aren't supposed to return for another week," she stammered.

"Perhaps someone should have informed me of that fact," he replied caustically.

Their eyes remained locked until Angeleen became aware of Tommy yanking at her hand. "Run along upstairs, honey. It's time for your bath."

"Mommie come." He tugged again at her hand.

"Mommie will be up shortly, honey." She kissed his cheek. "Now run along. Myra's waiting for you."

The youngster attempted to hop across the floor on one foot, gave up the effort and ran to Ruark. "Horsie."

Ruark grinned and patted his head. "Thank you, Tommy."

When Tommy failed a second time at a series of one-footed hops, he abandoned the endeavor, choosing instead to be a horse. Neighing, he swatted himself on the hip and galloped to the stairway.

"Use the railing, Tommy," Angeleen cautioned. When the lad reached the top step safely, she turned to Ruark.

His dark eyes were still trained on her face.

Nervously, she started to follow her son, but got no farther than the second step when Ruark's hand on her arm halted her climb.

"I want some answers, Angeleen."

She took a deep breath and turned to face him— which was a mistake. They now stood eye-to-eye, their lips only inches apart. He clasped her shoulders, and she found herself held firmly in his grasp.

"What are you doing here?"

"Visiting my father and your grandmother. I plan my visits to be here when you're away."

"I'm sure you do," he said sarcastically. "So this isn't your first trip?"

"No."

His disturbing nearness flustered her. Unaware of the gesture, she slipped her tongue out of her mouth to wet lips that suddenly felt dry.

His gaze shifted to her mouth. Momentarily shaken, Ruark focused his mind on a single thought. In a broken cadence, he asked hoarsely, "And the boy?"

"Is my son." Angeleen met the full impact of his dark eyes.

"And who is the lucky father, Mrs. Hunter? It is still *Mrs. Hunter*, isn't it?" he asked bitterly. His fingers pressed deeper into her flesh.

"Ruark, you're hurting me. Please release me."

"I'm sorry." His grip loosened and he dropped his hands to his sides. If she thought the subject had been dropped as well, she quickly discovered how wrong she was.

"Angeleen, who is the boy's father?" The question was direct and determined. He had no intention of letting her leave until she answered him.

But a voice from above interrupted them. "Why, any fool can tell by just looking at the youngster. He's the spitting image of his father at age two."

Their glances swung toward the speaker. Leaning on the silver handle of her cane, Sarah Stewart looked down from the top of the stairway.

"Nana Sarah, you told me Ruark wouldn't return for another week." A note of desperation surfaced in Angeleen's accusation.

"Did I, child? Now how could I ever have made such a mistake? I'm afraid old age has reduced me to senility," Sarah said innocently.

The old woman tapped a finger on her chin in deep reflection. "Oh, of course! I remember now.

Ruark told me he would be home for his birthday."
She smiled sweetly. "That's today, isn't it? Happy
birthday, Ruark. We shall have to celebrate later."
She turned and disappeared down the hallway.

Sarah's performance had not fooled either of
them. "What in hell is going on around here?"
Ruark grumbled. He grabbed Angeleen's arm and,
ignoring her protests, led her into the den, slamming
the door behind him.

Towering above her, he demanded gruffly, "Now,
the truth. Is Tommy my son?"

Ogre or not, Angeleen refused to cower. She had
gone through too much in the last two years to let
him intimidate her. "No," she denied emphatically.
"He is *my* son. I am his mother—the kind of mother
you consider unfit to raise any child of yours."

"What the hell kind of a riddle is that?" he snapped.
"I want a direct answer now, Angeleen."

"I'll give you the only answer you're going to get
from me—my son and I will be out of here as soon
as I pack."

She tried to get past him, but he grabbed her
shoulder and jerked her around to face him. "You're
not going anywhere until you tell me the truth. Is
Tommy my son?"

His anger building toward rage, he began to shake
her. "Damn it, Angeleen, tell me the truth. Is Tommy
my son?"

"Yes!" she cried. "Yes, he's your son." Her eyes
flared in defiance.

His hands slipped from her shoulders. Having
heard her confirm his suspicion, he now could not
comprehend the truth.

"Why didn't you tell me, Angeleen? Is this some kind of sick revenge? Do you hate me so much?"

His misconception of her motives unnerved her. As she struggled with her conscience, her anger abated. "I don't hate you, Ruark. You were honest from the start. You made your position clear, and I was just trying to stay out of your way."

"Riddles again, Angeleen?" He felt his rising anger.

She could understand his initial shock, but not the reason for his wrath. "Why are you so angry with me? I'm not asking you for anything, Ruark. Or making any demands. I'll leave at once."

"Of course. You're free to go anytime you wish, Angeleen. You told me what I wanted to know."

Angeleen glanced at him quizzically. In the blink of an eye, his whole manner had changed; now he was calm and unperturbed, his voice impassive, his eyes enigmatic.

"I'm sorry about everything, Ruark. Truly, I am. It was never my intention to make you angry." She walked hesitantly toward the door.

Ruark, however, had not yet delivered the final word. "But my son stays here."

The stony declaration caught her unexpectedly. Spinning around, disbelief flared in her eyes. "You can't be serious? Surely you don't think I'd leave here without taking Tommy with me. You have no legal right to him."

"Is that so?" His eyes looked cold as ice and a nerve twitched in his jaw. "What name, may I ask, is on the youngster's birth certificate?"

"Thomas Henry . . ." Angeleen stopped as the word

froze in her throat. He had trapped her.

"Go on, *Mrs. Hunter*," he goaded. "Thomas Henry . . . ? Could it be Stewart, by chance?"

She suddenly realized how damaging that fact would appear to a court of law. "I only gave him the name of Stewart because Nana Sarah insisted," she rallied defensively.

"I rest my case," Ruark said smugly and sat down behind the desk."

"I'll change his surname as soon as I can." In her anxiety, she did not hear the desperation that had crept into her voice.

"Now, why would you do that, *Mrs. Hunter*, when I have no intention of denying my son his rightful name or inheritance?"

"I won't let you get away with this, Ruark. I'll fight you if it takes every dollar I can raise."

"Please do, Angeleen. For every lawyer you hire, I can afford to hire ten. Every dollar you raise, I'll raise a thousand. I'll break you, Angeleen. I'll make certain you won't have a penny by the time this is all over. And the end result will be the same—Tommy will be mine."

"Tommy is mine," Angeleen fired back. But Ruark had laid his cards on the table and Angeleen knew she was in a battle for her son. She buried her head in her hands to choke back her tears.

"Please, Ruark. Please, don't do this to me. I'll beg if that's what you want. I'm begging you now. He's the only thing that matters in my life. Tommy's mine. He's mine," she repeated in a dazed litany.

"He's mine, too, Angeleen. You never considered that when you denied me the knowledge that I had a son, did you? I guess that's what makes me so angry."

"You never wanted him," she accused.

"You never gave me any choice. Because of your inconsiderateness, I'll never know the thrill of holding my first-born child in my arms, see him take his first step, or hear his first word."

He rose to his feet, consumed by the injustice of her actions. "You didn't consider any of that, did you, when you formed this conspiracy behind my back? Everyone in this household knew but me. Well, I can't turn out my own grandmother, but I can dismiss all the hired help who were a part of it."

Horrified, she stared aghast. "You wouldn't? Oh, God, Ruark, blame me, if you must, but not them. Most of them have served your family from the time you were a child."

"More reason why they should know where their loyalties lie."

What had her bad judgment wrought? Angeleen thought hopelessly. Not only Tommy, but other innocent people would suffer from her actions.

She sank down on the couch in defeat.

"What do you want from me, Ruark?"

"Well, now, that is a matter for thought."

Angeleen watched desolately. Ruark walked over and stared out of the window. As she waited, she could feel her mounting hysteria. Just as she was on the verge of screaming, he suddenly turned to her. Her frantic gaze met the triumphant gleam in his dark eyes.

"Come over here to the window."

Angeleen walked over, and Ruark held back the drape to give her a better view. "Beautiful, aren't they?"

She could see Bold King's two foals, Prince Consort and Bold Prince, frisking in a corral.

"Which one is your favorite, Angeleen?"

"Bold Prince has always been my favorite," she said, confused.

Grinning wryly, he said, "Prince Consort's my favorite. The colts are scheduled to run against each other in an exhibition race at the end of next week."

At the sight of her puzzlement, he continued. "I expect you to remain here until the race is over. As little time as that is, it will give me a chance to get acquainted with my son. We'll marry immediately."

"Marry?"

"Of course. That's a foregone conclusion. We must marry for Tommy's sake."

We must marry. How ludicrous, she thought bitterly. Would he have said as much two years ago?

Marriage to Ruark would be the fulfillment of her fantasies. But married because *we must marry* could never be.

"What is behind this crazed scheme, Ruark?"

His mouth twisted in a sardonic smile. "Isn't it obvious to you, Angel? Of course I intend to legitimize our son. Now that I've discovered I've a son, I intend to enjoy the pleasure of his company. But I also want you here. I can't chain you to keep you in Missouri, but I doubt you'd bolt and leave our son behind."

He eyed her grimly. "But if you don't give me

369

your promise to remain, I'm afraid, I'm left with no choice, Angeleen. I might be forced to break you. If you're penniless, you'll have no place to run to."

"If that's your intent, what are you waiting for, Ruark? I, more than anyone, am aware how swiftly you move to get what you want."

"Yes, I could break you now; I have the money and the connections. But I don't want to if I don't have to. I'm trying to be fair. Certainly a damn sight fairer than you were with me."

"Fair!" She slapped away his hands and glared at him. "I've worked my fingers to the bone to make a home for Tommy. Now Mr. Almighty Rich-And-Powerful Ruark Stewart tells me I have to dance to his tune or he'll pull a few of his political strings and strip away everything I've built in the last two years. Is that what you call fair?"

"Oh, don't sound so victimized, Angeleen. Had you informed me that I had a son, I would have gladly provided a home for him."

His anger rose with every word. "As Tommy's father, I had every obligation to do so, every right to see to the needs of my son."

"How dare you speak of your rights—you, who told me I was unfit to be a mother of any child of yours."

"Dammit, Angel, I don't even remember saying that."

"You have a convenient memory. Don't try to deny it now just to suit your purpose." She laughed scornfully. "How well I remember it, Ruark. You drove a knife through my heart that morning—the morning after you made love to me for the first time. Strange that you can't remember your own pompous mandate!" she cried. "Every day we were together, your scornful words echoed in my mind."

Their gazes clashed: cold black marble, meeting hard blue sapphire.

"So revenge *was* your motive," he said reflectively.

"No, that's not true. Revenge never entered my mind."

"Yet you deliberately condemned a man for a lifetime because of a few senseless words spoken in ignorance."

"Senseless? Oh, they made plenty of sense at the time, Ruark. You thought I was nothing but a lying, cheating whore. Unfit to be the mother of any child of yours."

Ruark closed his eyes and fought for composure. When he reopened them, the black marble was gone, his eyes now softened to the pitiful expression of a wounded deer.

"How could you doubt my love? Lie to me? Leave me knowing you were carrying my child? Didn't you think you just might be driving a knife through my heart, too?"

He moved away and once again sat down behind his desk. The inner pain he had exposed became quickly reburied under the mask of the calm, uncompromising businessman.

"I've stated my terms."

"And if I remain here as your wife, am I also expected to share your bed?"

"As attractive as the thought may be, I will not make that a condition. I will not force you to share my bed, Angeleen."

"And should I disagree?"

His brow arched in amusement. "I'm more benevolent than you, my dear. As your husband, I would relent and permit you free access to my bed at any time."

Angeleen considered the moment too grave for his distasteful humor. Her look of outrage told him as much.

"And if I refuse your challenge?" she repeated.

He glanced up with a ruthless smile. "Then I cease fighting fair, Angeleen."

Her hands balled into fists at her sides. "You're a bastard, Ruark."

"As is our son, Angeleen, through no fault of his own."

"You'd think a woman wouldn't have to marry two bastards in her lifetime, would you?" If she remained with him another moment, she knew she would claw that damnable smirk off his face. Angeleen moved to the door.

"Agreed, Angeleen?"

She paused, her hand on the doorknob. With Tommy's future at stake, there were no other options open to her. She would have to wed Ruark and agree to his conditions or he would surely carry out his threat and demand his paternal rights. As an unwed mother, she would never be able to convince the court to let her keep her son, and she could lose Tommy forever. However, married to him, she might still have a chance; certainly more than she had at the moment.

One other issue remained unresolved. "And what of your threat toward the servants?" she asked.

"They can remain," Ruark said indifferently. In truth, he never had intended dismissing them, but he would hardly admit as much to her.

Drawing a shuddering breath, the words slipped past her lips. "Agreed. But only until after the race." She sped from the room and rushed up the stairs.

After her departure, Ruark remained seated. Two weeks. He had two weeks. A smile of cunning crept across his face as he formulated his next move.

Myra hurried back to the parlor to Sarah Stewart and Henry Hunter, who anxiously awaited her return.

"What did they say to each other?" Sarah asked excitedly.

"Oh, don't go getting yourself all worked into a lather," Myra warned. "You'll bring on a heart attack."

"Will you get on wi' it, woman," Henry sputtered, as anxious as Sarah to hear what had been said.

"It's a pity a woman of my age is reduced to listening at closed doors and peeping through keyholes," Myra grumbled. "I haven't done that since I first came here over thirty years ago."

"Hush your complaining prattle and tell us what happened," Sarah said impatiently.

The three people gathered in a circle as Myra began to relate the conversation between Ruark and Angeleen.

Henry cast his eyes heavenward. "Glory be to God," he murmured when Myra reported the news of the impending marriage. Then he lowered his head so as not to miss a word Myra said.

"I love it!" Sarah exclaimed when Myra finished repeating the whole conversation. "I knew that grandson of mine would insist they wed."

"Aye, but what if the lass refuses to remain?" Henry remarked. "Me daughter has her grandmother's stubborn nature, I'm fearin'."

"We're playing for high stakes here, Henry—Tommy's future. At the very least, we've succeeded in getting the young fools to agree to marry. Now we've got to get them to settle down right here and give our youngster a normal home. You don't want Tommy way off in Virginia, do you?"

"Of course not," he agreed.

Convinced their cause was rightful, the dowager's hand fluttered to her cheek. "Oh, I do hope Angeleen will forgive us for deceiving her."

Myra was more of a realist. She put her hand on her hip and grimaced in disgust. "I'm thinking we'd be wiser to be worrying if Mr. Ruark will forgive us. I don't think we've heard the last word from him on the matter."

"Oh, my," Sarah opined. "We're not much better off than we were before. We still are as entangled in the web as ever."

The three conspirators nodded their heads in accord.

Chapter Twenty-Six

"I don't understand why Tommy isn't here," Ruark said later that evening as they were seated at the dinner table. Robert and Celeste, as well as Henry, had joined them for the meal.

"Tommy goes to bed at seven o'clock, Ruark. A consistent routine is very important in the life of a growing child," Angeleen said calmly, determined not to let this Johnny-Come-Lately father dictate how to raise her child.

"Under the circumstances, Angeleen, the boy should have been allowed to join us for dinner tonight."

Not bothering to hide her indifference, Angeleen continued to eat. "What circumstances are you referring to?"

"My birthday, of course. A father wants his son

present to help celebrate the occasion."

"Did it ever occur to you, Ruark, that some people might not consider the occasion of your birthday worth celebrating?" Smiling graciously, Angeleen turned her head to the woman beside her. "Please pass the salt, Celeste."

At the far end of the table, Sarah Stewart suppressed a smile, her thoughts concealed behind her lowered eyes. What spunk the girl had, and what a magnificent match for her grandson! Tommy was only the first of many offspring this splendid union would produce, Sarah decided triumphantly.

She knew many wounds had yet to heal, but at least they no longer festered beneath the surface. Now exposed, time and fresh air would take care of them.

As her glance swept those gathered around the table, Sarah marveled at how much Angeleen had enriched their lives. The incredible girl had not only brought them Tommy, but her father and brother as well; Henry and Robert had truly become part of their family. The once near-empty house now echoed daily with the sound of voices and laughter.

Of course, an occasional argument did erupt, she thought tolerantly as her gaze shifted to Robert Scott. He and Ruark were like spatting brothers. She wondered if Robert resented Ruark as much as it appeared, or if the two men had just fallen into a pattern.

Her judgment of Robert Scott had not been wrong. Since taking over the management of the Emporium, he had made a rousing success of it. Through clever marketing, timely sales, and rotating of stock, the store was headed for another record year with the biggest shopping season yet to come—Christmas.

Sarah was even considering Robert's suggestion of opening another store in the state capital in Jefferson City.

Let us pray that time will heal your wounds, too, Robert, Sarah thought sadly, for she was fond of this young man whose scars were still so evident.

Throughout the dinner, Ruark sat silently scowling at the others, all of whom, much to his annoyance, seemed to be enjoying themselves. By the time Myra carried in a birthday cake, Ruark was out of the party mood.

"Don't leave yet, Myra," he ordered in a brusque tone after the cake had been cut. "What I have to say involves you as much as the others." Myra looked at Sarah with raised brows, as if to say, "Here it comes."

"Yes. Well, what I have to say, my *dear* family and servants alike, is . . . all of you could easily be counted as my worst enemies."

"Amen, brother. I'm standing up to be counted, right here and now," Robert gibed.

Ignoring him, Ruark continued. Shaking his head as though admonishing a child, he turned to Myra. "I have been betrayed by the faithful family retainer who raised me from childhood."

Myra, flustered and inwardly annoyed, avoided his dark gaze by staring at the floor. Ruark waited long enough to make sure his words had the desired effect, and then started on Henry.

"Next, there is the man to whom I entrusted the

377

care and welfare of my racing stable, the man who is the grandfather of my son. He, too, has betrayed me."

Henry fidgeted with his hands as he hung his head in shame; being a father himself, he could well understand Ruark's frustration.

Though Ruark spoke in a deadly serious tone, Sarah was somewhat embarrassed by his dramatics. To relieve the tension, and to conceal a smile, she daintily put her handkerchief to her mouth and cleared her throat. The gesture diverted Ruark's attention from Henry to her.

"And you, madam! To think I was deceived by the grandmother I have loved and trusted my whole life."

Fortunately, Sarah's struggle to appear contrite succeeded, for had she given free rein to her thoughts, she would have giggled.

"But now we come to the worst offender—the mother of my son."

Neither amused nor embarrassed, must less flustered or shamed, Angeleen gave a look of sheer boredom and total disdain to the Father-Come-Lately. As her eyes met his, Ruark did not chance any additional comment to Angeleen. Rather, he attacked the entire captive and disarmed audience.

"All have betrayed me. Not just once, in an isolated incident, but time and time again for the past two years."

Sarah lost her struggle. "Not quite two years, Ruark. Tommy won't be two until the end of next month."

Ruark paused, shaking his head at his duplicitous

grandmother. "Don't any of you care how much I've missed of my son's infancy?"

"Of course we do, Ruark," Sarah said compassionately. Ruark had a right to be angry, and his grandmother knew it. "Do you think we enjoyed this? Our consciences truly bothered all of us."

"I assure you, Stewart, mine didn't," Robert declared.

Henry came to, breaking his uncustomary silence. "Son, will ye hush yer mouth. Isn't there enough shame here tonight?" He cast a look of censure at his son.

"Had you not rushed off to Europe as fast as you did, we would have resolved this sooner," Sarah reminded him. "No one intended for this complicity to last as long as it did."

The confession brought a quick response from Angeleen. "Then you had no intention of keeping my confidence." Her accusing glance swept the people at the table. "Ruark isn't the only one who's been hurt by your deceit. I trusted all of you, and you betrayed me as well."

"Why, of course, my dear. We love both of you. We would never consider deceiving just one of you, and not the other. Why, that would be taking sides!" Sarah reasoned.

"You might regard that logic as a rather warped version of honor among thieves, Angie," Robert remarked, immensely amused at the conspirators and Ruark, now all enmeshed in the same net of confusion.

Henry felt that enough had been said, and before any tempers flared, he expressed the thought that was foremost in his mind. "Yer son wasna gettin' any younger, lass. 'Tis time the two of ye resolve yer differences and do what's right for the lad."

Even though Myra had reported the impending nuptials, Henry wanted the assurance of hearing it for himself.

"Angeleen and I intend to," Ruark said. "Judge Sweet will be here tomorrow evening to marry us. We hope that all of you will attend."

Every eye swung to Robert Scott. "Why are you all looking at me?" he asked defensively. "I want what's best for Tommy. I love him too, you know."

Pouring a glass of wine for Myra, Ruark invited the maid to join them. Then he rose to his feet.

"Every one of us has said and done things we've regretted. We all must shoulder some guilt. But, Henry is right. The time has come to put these grievances aside, to forgive and forget, and to do what is right for Tommy. To these ends, I propose a toast." His wary glance shifted to Angeleen. "And I hope the rest of you will join me."

He raised his glass in the air. "To Tommy."

Praise to God for Tommy, Sarah thought fondly as they lifted their glasses to echo the sentiment.

Ruark's fixed look settled on Angeleen as she repeated the pledge. Their gazes locked as she slowly brought the glass to her lips.

Ruark glanced up and put aside the morning paper he had been reading when Tommy wandered into the den.

"Good morning, Tommy."

The youngster stood silently, staring at Ruark curiously. "What is it, son?"

"Ruark Dada?" he asked.

"Oh, so that's it." Ruark patted his knee. "Come on over here, Tommy."

The youngster scampered over and Ruark lifted him on his lap. "Did Mommie tell you I'm your daddy?"

Tommy nodded. "And did she tell you that you and Mommie are going to stay here with me?"

"And Nana. And Grampie."

"That's right," Ruark agreed.

"Unkie Roba. Auntie 'Es."

"Yes, them too," Ruark acknowledged. "Will you like that?"

Ruark waited for the answer, but the youngster's attention had already strayed to the watch fob hanging out of Ruark's vest pocket. "Horsie, Dada." Tommy reached for the watch.

Tommy's giggle pealed as pleasantly as wind chimes in a summer breeze when Ruark tapped the dangling horse with his finger so that it swung back and forth.

Clapping his hands enthusiastically, Tommy cried, "Horsie run, Dada." He reached out and grabbed the watch, accidently pressing the catch on the cover. The boy stared with astonishment when the watch popped open.

His round eyes widened with pleasure as he examined this new discovery. "Mommie!" he shouted gleefully, pressing his lips to the picture of Angeleen tucked into the inside of the cover.

"Love Mommie," the youngster announced. "Dada love Mommie?"

"Yes, Daddy loves Mommie," Ruark confided. He put a finger to his mouth motioning Tommy to silence. "Sh-h-h-h, this has to be our secret, Tommy," he whispered. "We won't tell Mommie."

Tommy mimicked Ruark and put a finger to his pouted lips. "Sh-h-h-h."

Hearing the sound of his mother's voice in the hallway, the youngster jumped down and ran to the door. Grinning broadly, he stopped and looked back at his father, cocked his little head, and put a finger to his mouth. "Sh-h-h-h."

Ruark's heart seemed to spring to his throat. *Sweet Lord, he has his mother's dimples.*

Tommy waited until Ruark repeated the warning gesture. "Our secret," Ruark reminded him.

The youngster nodded and scampered off in pursuit of his mother.

After a day of successfully avoiding Ruark, Angeleen smiled smugly as she stepped back and viewed the effect of her carefully premeditated efforts in the mirror.

She had made a special trip into St. Louis that afternoon to acquire the gown. It had long sleeves and a high collar that buttoned at the neck, and it had been fashioned, with nary a shred of design, out of cheap black wool.

"Are you sure this is what you want to do?" Celeste asked, astonished, her youthful face distorted by a grimace. "You look so—so—"

"Matronly," Angeleen offered. "Yes, that's just the way I want to look."

Her long black hair had been parted straight down

the middle, pulled back tightly against her head and braided into two plaits, then twisted into a thick bun at the back of her neck—a severe and unattractive coiffure altogether.

"Your beautiful hair looks like a prison warden's," Celeste declared.

Angeleen took Celeste's hand. There was so much of her sister-in-law's life that still remained a mystery. "Have you ever been in prison, Celeste?" she asked compassionately.

"Well, no."

Relieved, Angeleen smiled and squeezed her hand. "Then how do you know how a prison warden would look?"

"Well, you look how I imagine one would look," Celeste qualified. "I once saw some female prisoners being transferred in a wagon and I can say you do look like one of them, for sure."

"I'm just hoping Ruark won't miss the point," Angeleen said, looking as pleased as a cat licking its paws.

As she swept down the stairway, her appearance drew astonished gasps. Robert read her message and grinned. He lifted his glass in tribute to her.

Looking handsomer than ever in a light gray suit expertly tailored to his wide shoulders, Ruark walked over to the bottom stair where Henry had just joined his daughter.

"Yer hair, lass. And that dress," Henry said, appalled. "What are ye doin', daughter? 'Tis over ninety degrees outside." He shook his head in disbelief. "And I'm thinkin' 'tis nae a proper gown fer a bride to be wearin' on her weddin' day."

"I think she is sending me a message, Henry," Ruark commented with aplomb. "I see you found a burlap bag. But even in your prison uniform, you still look beautiful to me, Angel. You make a lovely bride."

Henry walked away shaking his head. He would never understand the workings of the female mind.

Delighted that Ruark understood her charade, Angeleen simpered with satisfaction. "How astute of you, Ruark. It's so rewarding when one's efforts do not go for naught."

"Lordy, ma'am, if I wasn't aware of all that luscious flesh under that shroud, I could be plum nervous wondering. Come to think of it, I am plum nervous at the thought of all that luscious flesh."

Her eyes flashed angrily. "Whatever lascivious behavior you choose to conduct outside this house is of little concern to me; but you would be wise to put those disgusting thoughts out of your mind where I am concerned."

"Not an easy task, Angel, I've tried. But *the mind unlearns with difficulty what it has long learned*—or so I've heard tell."

He held up a long-stemmed white rose which he had been concealing behind his back. "Your wedding bouquet. I didn't think you would want anything too ostentatious."

She snatched the rose from him and took the time to breath deeply of its fragrance as she composed herself. "Thank you for that one consideration, at least."

"Speaking of consideration, regardless of your seven o'clock curfew, you might have relented for one night and let Tommy stay up to attend our wedding."

"Perhaps I'm being old-fashioned, Ruark, but I find there is definitely something unhealthy about a two-year-old attending the wedding of his parents."

Chuckling, Ruark hooked her arm through his. "I may concede that point to you. Shall we get on with this as quickly as possible? I'm afraid, in that wool dress, you're apt to wilt sooner than the rose."

He led her to a distinguished gentleman seated in a chair next to Sarah. "Judge Sweet, my intended, Angeleen Hunter."

The judge rose to his feet. "My pleasure, madam. Shall we proceed? Ladies and gentlemen," he announced, quieting the room, "if you will join us, the ceremony can begin."

"Let the games begin," Robert muttered in the far corner.

"Dammit! Is your brother going to make a drunken scene?" Ruark grumbled for her ears only.

"I'm sure Robert is not drunk. He was trying to be humorous," she defended.

"Someone should tell him he failed," Ruark remarked.

Someone intended to. Celeste hurried over to Robert, her angry eyes sparkling like green jewels as she scolded him.

"Robert, do not embarrass your sister. She feels bad enough as it is. Why do you continue this petty squabbling with Ruark? He only wants to do right by her. I would think you'd be grateful to him for that."

"Don't tell me he's got you fooled too," Robert

snorted. "All praise and magnify Mr. Ruark Stewart. Amen, Brethren!"

"Your bitterness is destroying you, Robert. Soon there will be nothing left of you." Disgusted, she walked away.

The wedding ceremony was over as quickly as it began. Within minutes, the marriage certificate had been duly signed and witnessed.

Ruark immediately took Angeleen's arm. "Will you join me for a private drink, Angeleen?"

"I think not." As she started to leave, he gently restrained her with a hand on her arm.

"Please, just a moment. We have to talk."

"We did our talking yesterday, Ruark." She glanced at the wedding certificate he held. "Your threats and coercion got you what you wanted."

"This paper only binds us legally. I want you to agree to become my wife, Angel." He was almost pleading with her, a far cry from his position the previous day.

Angeleen remained impassive. "I am your wife, Ruark."

"You know what I mean. I want a real wife. We had it once, Angel. We can recapture that magic again."

"Magic is a false conception—an illusion, Ruark. We're ignoring our guests." She walked stiffly away from him.

By the time they sat down to dinner, Angeleen's attempt at humor had backfired; she began to feel the debilitating effects of the hot dress.

The doors stood open and the windows were raised in the hope of catching an evening breeze.

But not a limb swayed nor a leaf rustled to stir the humid air.

The men had long since removed their coats and vests and sat around the table in rolled-up shirt sleeves. Angeleen dabbed at the perspiration dotting her brow. She hadn't eaten any breakfast or lunch, and now; feeling light-headed and nauseated, she only pecked at her food.

When her discomfort became too severe to ignore, she laid aside her napkin. "If you'll excuse me, I'm not feeling well."

She rose too swiftly to her feet. Inundated by a wave of dizziness, she grabbed for the table as her knees buckled.

Ruark had been watching her throughout the meal and guessed what was bothering her. Attuned to her every movement, he shoved back his chair and caught her before she fell to the floor.

Angeleen's faint set everyone into a twitter. Celeste and Myra moved to follow when Ruark lifted Angeleen into his arms.

"It's the heat. Finish your dinner. I'll take care of her."

By the time he reached her room, Angeleen had begun to come out of her faint. Kicking the door shut behind him, Ruark laid her on the bed.

His course of action was clear to him. Without hesitating, he unbuttoned the dress and pulled it off her, encountering a stiff white petticoat which had added to her discomfort. Ruark gave the garment the same treatment that he had given the dress. He then dispensed with her shoes and stockings. Only her chemise and drawers remained.

Still groggy, she asked weakly, "Wha . . . what happened?"

"You've had an attack of heatstroke, Angel. What were you thinking of—a wool dress in this weather?" he said gently.

She was too ill to realize what had happened to her. A clearer impression began to take shape when he placed a cool, wet cloth on her brow.

She opened her eyes and almost screamed aloud when she discovered she was lying practically naked in bed with Ruark bending over her.

"What are you doing?"

"Just lie quietly, Angel." He wrung out another cloth and wrapped the wet compress around the back of her neck. "Does that feel better?"

"Yes, much better. Thank you."

Ruark went over to the armoire, and after rooting through the drawers and tossing clothes in all directions, he returned with a white cambric nightgown.

"Let's get you into this. I want to get your drawers off."

Swept by another wave of dizziness, Angeleen was too weak to argue. "Go ahead, I never could stop you once you made up your mind . . ." Her voice trailed away to almost a whisper . . . "to take off my drawers." The last words barely passed her lips before she slipped away.

Despite the seriousness of the situation, Ruark grinned as he raised her head and shoulders. Supporting her with one arm, he pulled the chemise over her head and tossed the piece of lingerie aside.

It was impossible to remain impersonal. Sucking in his breath, he stared at her firm, rounded breasts—lovelier than he remembered. Motherhood had only enhanced her beautiful body. His hands trembled as he quickly dressed her in the nightgown and laid her back.

Ruark pulled off her underdrawers. The thin, transparent gown barely concealed the lovely body that lay exposed to his hungry perusal. For a moment, he closed his eyes, remembering the feel of her beneath him.

Disgusted with himself, Ruark threw aside the summer quilt and pulled up the sheet to protect her from a chill—and the depravity of his own desires, as well. He sat down on the edge of the bed and put another cool compress to her head.

The wet cloth revived her once again. She opened her eyes, and he took her hand. "How are you feeling now, Angel?"

"Much better." She returned his smile.

"What are you doing?" she asked when he began to pull hairpins out of her hair.

"I'm removing this helmet you're wrapped in."

He released the coiled plaits and unwound each long braid. After combing his fingers through her hair, he fanned out the ends of the long locks on the pillow. Satisfied with the result, he sat down again and smiled at her.

"There, that's perfect," he said, pleased to see her hair freed from restraint. Then he leaned over and tucked a few errant strands behind her ear.

"I didn't intend to be so much trouble." She glanced up sheepishly. "It was a stupid thing to do. Damn you, Ruark, why do you always end up with the last laugh?"

"Have I laughed, or even said anything?" he asked innocently.

"No, but I know what you're thinking."

"Oh no you don't, lady, or you wouldn't lie there looking so calm."

An awkwardness suddenly developed between them as they each wrestled with the thought. The smile left his face, and Ruark rose to his feet.

"Is there anything else you need?"

"I think I'd like to try to eat something, or at least have something to drink. Some milk toast would be fine."

"I'll have Myra bring you up a tray." He squeezed her hand. "Goodnight, Angel."

Her confused gaze followed Ruark as he walked to the door.

What have we done to each other, Ruark? she asked herself as he departed.

Angeleen slowly awoke to the feel of lips pressed to hers; her eyes were rewarded with the wide smile of her son.

"Tommy wake."

Angeleen slipped her arms around his neck and kissed him. "So, Tommy's awake, huh? Well, good morning. How's my little snuggle bunny this morning?"

He settled down against her, and she hugged him to her side. "What do you think we should do today?"

"Horsie. Ride horsie," he shouted.

"Again? All you ever want to do is go to the stables

and see the horses. You're sure no fun." She tickled him, and Tommy began to squirm and laugh uproariously.

A light tap sounded and Ruark popped his head into the room. "Hey, who's making all this noise in here?"

"Mommie." Tommy giggled and snuggled closer to his mother.

Ruark closed the door and walked over to the bed. "So, Mommie must be feeling much better this morning?"

"Yes, I'm fine. Thank you," she said curtly.

After Ruark's departure last night, she had realized how close she had come to falling under the spell of his charm—the charm he had always used so successfully with her.

His desire to forgive and forget had sounded sincere. He could afford such benevolence. And in truth, Ruark had gotten his way. But she had no choice; had she fought him, he wouldn't have hesitated to take Tommy from her.

She would remind herself of that fact, if ever again she was foolish enough to allow her feelings for him to creep into her thinking.

"Come, Dada." Tommy patted the bed for Ruark to lie down beside him.

"Don't you dare," she hissed through clenched teeth.

Her command was a challenge he couldn't resist. Ruark quickly climbed in beside them.

Indignant, Angeleen snapped angrily, "I don't believe this is happening!"

She started to rise, but at the sight of her transparent gown, fell back hurriedly and covered herself with the sheet.

"Doesn't your word mean anything? You agreed I wouldn't be forced to share a bed with you," she accused.

"I agreed you wouldn't have to share *my* bed. Nothing was ever said about yours," he said complacently.

"Oh, don't split hairs," she muttered. "You're nothing but a lowdown, scheming—"

"Watch your language, Mommie. Remember, our son is listening."

Ruark picked Tommy up and sat him astride on his stomach. "Did I hear someone say something about a horsie ride?"

He began bucking his hips and every bounce brought a squeal of pleasure from Tommy.

Despite her irritation, her son's childish laughter was too infectious for Angeleen to resist. She smiled and surrendered to the delight of watching his enjoyment.

However, the steady bouncing on the bed shifted her closer and closer to Ruark. Before she realized it, she was pressed firmly against him. When he finally stopped rocking, Tommy fell across his chest giggling.

Flushed with pleasure, his little hands clutched Ruark's cheeks. "Kiss, Dada."

"What do you think I came in here for?" Ruark replied. He gave the boy a sound hug and kiss.

Seeing the smile of contentment on his mother's face, Tommy pursed his lips. "Kiss Mommie." Angeleen raised her head and shoulders, leaned over

Ruark's chest and kissed her son.

Ruark grasped her shoulder. Shocked, she realized that her breasts were pressed against him, and she met his startled gaze. The arousing affect was clear in his eyes.

"Mommie, Dada kiss." Tommy waited expectantly, his innocent little face glowing with pleasure.

Angeleen was horrified. "Oh, no, honey. Not Daddy and Mommie." She tried to draw back, but Ruark would not release his hold on her.

The mind of a two-year old is rarely diverted by a command. Tommy's brows lowered in a frown. "Mommie, Dada kiss," he repeated.

"Yes, Mommie, we can't disappoint our son."

Ruark's hand slipped to the back of her neck and he slowly drew her head to his.

As if by design, their mouths fit together from the first touch and her lips parted beneath his. For a few threatening seconds, each lost awareness of everything except the well-remembered thrill of a shared kiss.

And as the kiss deepened, his hand on her neck pressed her ever tighter against the hard wall of his chest. The nipples of her breasts hardened and grew taut as her passion rose.

Breathlessness forced them apart. Stunned and shaken, they stared into each other's eyes. Like an awakened giant, a latent force had been aroused. Tommy's presence prevented Ruark from taking her now—but were it not so, both knew she would have done nothing to stop him.

"You must never do that again," she implored in a part-whisper, part-plea.

Ruark stared down into her frightened eyes. "I can't promise you that, Angel. I *won't* promise you that."

Tommy did not like being so long ignored. Plopping down between them, he separated their bodies just as a rap sounded on the door. Any further discussion was halted when Myra came into the room.

The maid drew up abruptly at the sight of the three of them together in bed. "That's a sight I thought I'd never see," she said candidly.

"Myra, I am literally a prisoner in this bed. Will you please bring me a robe so I can get out of here?"

"It's time I got dressed anyway," Ruark said, climbing out of the bed.

Ruark knew he had a tiger by the tail. His desire for Angeleen had been held in rein for two years, but now unleashed, it could no longer be quelled. He left without another word.

Myra did not say anything as she handed Angeleen a robe, but her body language conveyed her sentiment.

"Before you rush out of here to report this to Nana, will you take Tommy with you? I'd like to get dressed myself."

"Yes, ma'am," Myra replied, unruffled.

Smiling, she lifted Tommy into her arms. "Your momma wants to get dressed, sweetheart. You come with Myra. We'll go and visit Nana."

Chapter Twenty-Seven

Angeleen leaned back, rested her head on the rim of the tub, and raised her left hand to study her wedding ring. Yesterday, she had not given Ruark the satisfaction of even glancing at the ring he had slipped on her finger during the wedding ceremony; but this morning she gazed fondly at it as the bright sunlight glittered on the diamonds flanking an exquisite marquise-cut sapphire. A brilliant diffraction of colors danced before her eyes.

Smiling with pleasure she closed her eyes and enjoyed the luxury of lazing in the water—no meals to cook, no dishes to wash, no floors to scrub.

But more important than the absence of chores was the new and significant dimension that had been added to her life; she felt alive—really alive.

Oh, there had been much self-satisfaction in proving her independence, but how that feeling paled compared to the thrill of seeing Ruark walk through a door and the stimulation of their daily challenges of each other.

Angeleen appreciated the difference between living life and merely enduring it.

After dressing, she turned back to the mirror for a final inspection. "Just look at you," she scolded. "Your cheeks are flushed, your eyes are glowing. When was the last time you felt this good? Over two years, that's for sure. And all because of *him*. Just being around him does this to you. Damn you anyway, Ruark Stewart!"

Looking more like a schoolgirl than a matron, Angeleen skipped down the stairs, her dark curls bouncing on her shoulders. She halted on seeing Myra alone in the drawing room.

"Where's Tommy?" she asked with a bright smile.

"With Mr. Ruark," Myra replied.

Angeleen's smile dissolved into a look of distress. "With Ruark!" she exclaimed. "Where did they go?"

"Last I saw, they were hand-in-hand, headed toward the stable."

Angeleen dashed out of the door and strode down the path to confront the latest challenge. How dare he take *her* son anywhere without first asking her!

At the sight of his daughter storming into the stable, Henry knew trouble would surely follow. He braced his shoulders, lowered his head, and prepared for the worst. "Poppa, where is Ruark?"

"He took the lad ridin'." Henry started to walk away. Angeleen had the disposition of her grandmother, and he wasn't going to bear the brunt of her nasty tongue.

After glancing at the empty stall usually occupied by Ruark's gray gelding, Angeleen's eyes rounded in indignation, and she hurried after her father. "You mean he took Tommy out on that gelding?" she shouted.

She charged out of the stable just as Ruark came trotting up on Silver Dollar with Tommy perched on the front of the saddle.

"Give him to me at once," she ordered.

Ruark was taken back by her show of anger. "Thank you for the offer, but I'm sure the groom will be glad to take my mount." His controlled tone contained an edge which she ignored.

"I'm talking about Tommy," she snapped.

Angeleen snatched the youngster out of his grasp when Ruark handed him down to her. "Don't ever take my son again without asking me," she snapped again.

Climbing down, Ruark asked, appalled, "Without *asking* you?"

She hugged the startled youngster to her breast as if he were a babe in arms. "Well . . . without telling me where you're going with him."

Frightened that his behavior had caused his mother's anger, Tommy started to cry. When Angeleen spun on her heel and stormed up the path, Ruark tossed the horse's reins to a nearby groom and followed her. Tommy's bellowing intensified with every step Angeleen took.

"Let me take him," Ruark offered.

Her clutch tightened around her son. "No, it's your fault he's crying."

Ruark grasped her shoulders and brought her to an abrupt halt. "No, Angeleen, it's your fault. You've frightened the boy."

He continued without raising his voice. "Furthermore, I don't intend to ask your permission to take *our* son anywhere. In the future, I expect you to refrain from creating scenes in public. Any problem between us can be aired in private."

Ruark lifted Tommy out of her arms. "Come on, Sport, we'll go have that glass of chocolate I promised you."

Immediately, Tommy's tears ceased to flow. Frustrated, Angeleen stood with her hands on her hips as Ruark swung the boy to his shoulders and started to walk away. Then he stopped and looked back. "Aren't you going to join us, Mommie?"

Shaking her head at the outrageous audacity of the man, Angeleen hastened to catch up.

When she awoke the next morning, Angeleen hurried to Tommy's room only to discover his bed was empty. Ruark had been there ahead of her. She dressed and sped toward the stable.

The two sat on the top rung of the fence intently watching Prince Consort gallop around the track. Ruark had a firm grasp around Tommy's waist, and the youngster's arm lay curled around his father's neck.

"Five seconds faster than yesterday," Henry shouted when the colt thundered past the finish pole.

"How can there be such a difference?" Ruark questioned.

" 'Tis strange, indeed. I've noticed the two lads match their speed to each other when they run together," Henry remarked.

"But Prince Consort is the fastest," Ruark exclaimed with a satisfied smile.

Henry took off his hat and scratched his head. "Aye. I'd be guessin' eight or nine tenths of a second."

"Well, what do you know," Ruark remarked, looking as pleased as a fat cat licking the milk off its whiskers. "That's my boy."

Ruark spied Angeleen out of the corner of his eye and jumped down from his perch. "Okay, Sport, let's have a cheer for our horse," he said as he swung Tommy into his arms.

"Hooway for 'Rince Com Sort," Tommy yelled.

Smirking at his wife, Ruark patted his son on the head. "And that's my boy, too."

Once again she looked bemused as he started to stride off. Ruark stopped and turned around. "We're going for a horsie ride, Mommie. Want to join us?"

Gritting her teeth to refrain from screaming, Angeleen followed.

The days passed swiftly with Tommy the object of a tug-of-war between his parents. Angeleen took into account that to Tommy, Ruark was a new "playmate," and she tried to remain objective. In her heart, she was happy that he enjoyed the companionship of his father so long denied him. Watching the two of them playing hide-and-seek or wrestling together on the floor, tugged at her heartstrings.

And Ruark was a good father, she admitted grudgingly. The love Ruark felt for his son was evident, and Tommy responded uninhibitedly.

Yet, she could not deny feeling jealous of Tommy's affection for his new "Dada"; playing second fiddle in her son's life was a difficult role for Angeleen.

These thoughts crossed her mind one morning as she lay in bed listening to the occasional high pitch of Tommy's laughter and Ruark's warm chuckle drift through the open window of her room.

Curiosity got the better of her. Sighing, Angeleen got up and walked over to gaze out the window. It was going to be another humid day, and heat hung on the air in heavy, undulating waves. Even the stream that flowed past the house had narrowed to a shallow brook.

She saw Ruark and Tommy sitting Indian style under the shade of the tree just outside her window. Angeleen's heart leapt to her throat at the sight of the two dark heads bent together as they intently scrutinized the tiny caterpillar Ruark had put in Tommy's hand.

When the wooly insect began to squirm up his arm, Tommy's infectious giggle brought a warm glow to Ruark's eyes—and to Angeleen's heart.

She rested her head against the casement, smiling as Ruark rose and lifted Tommy up so the boy could return the caterpillar to a leaf on the tree.

She watched with a sentimental gaze as the two walked hand-in-hand to the stable. Suddenly, realizing that she would be left behind, Angeleen bolted into action and began to dress. She arrived at the stable just as Ruark was about to ride off with Tommy.

"Wait for me. I'm coming too," she called. Ruark didn't respond, but his eyes glowed with satisfaction. Within minutes, mounted on Bold King, Angeleen joined them.

They followed the course of the same stream that flowed past the house, until Ruark reined up in a copse of trees at the pool that was the source of the clear, running water.

Dismounting, Angeleen walked over and sat down on the bank. Ruark followed and plopped down beside her. "It's too damn hot for comfort." Seized by a sudden thought, he sat up. "Let's go for a swim."

"Now?" she asked aghast.

"Why not?" he answered, pulling off his boots and socks.

"We have no bathing costumes," she reminded him primly.

Ruark's brow arched wolfishly. "Who needs a bathing costume?"

"Goody," Tommy squealed. Following his father's example, he pulled off his shoes and stockings.

"Come here and let me undress you," Angeleen said.

"You talking to me?" Ruark asked with a wicked smile.

"Of course not." She threw him a prim look and to her consternation discovered that Ruark was already naked. He winked and waded into the water.

Angeleen's hot blush added to her discomfort. She

suddenly became all thumbs as she fumbled with the remainder of Tommy's clothing.

"Mommie, hurry," Tommy cried impatiently. Then, like an animal freed from a cage, he darted into the water after his father.

"Ruark, hold on to him. That water looks deep near the middle," she cautioned needlessly; Ruark had already scooped Tommy up and was holding him in his arms.

Removing her own boots and stockings, Angeleen sat down and dangled her feet in the stream. "Mommie come play," Tommy called out from midstream.

"Yea, Mommie. Come play," Ruark invited.

"Don't be silly," she replied with an envious look in their direction.

After several more moments of watching them splashing and enjoying themselves, Angeleen could no longer resist the temptation. She cautiously glanced around. Satisfied they were alone, off came her bodice and riding skirt. Wearing only a thin camisole and drawers, she waded into the pool.

"Oh, this feels glorious," she sighed, lowering her shoulders beneath the cool spring water.

After several more moments of splashing, Ruark carried Tommy back to shore, quickly helped him into shirt and pants, then returned to the water. Curling up contentedly, Tommy watched his father and mother swim.

After cavorting with Angeleen for several moments, Ruark finally waded out of the stream, pulled on his trousers, and sat down beside Tommy. The youngster had dozed off, and rather than disturb the sleeping child, Ruark sat quietly watching Angeleen as the hot air dried his skin.

As much as she hated to leave the cool water, Angeleen finally returned to shore. Ruark nodded toward Tommy and put a finger to his mouth cautioning her to silence.

"Let him sleep," he said quietly, shifting over to sit beside her. "We should have brought along a lunch basket and a blanket. I bet Tommy would have enjoyed a picnic."

Angeleen smiled fondly at her sleeping son. "Tommy enjoys just about anything."

"He's a great little guy, Angel. You've done a wonderful job raising him alone."

"And I see you're very good with children, Ruark. Tommy adores you."

"Well, I still have a lot of catching up to do."

When an awkward silence developed between them, Ruark leaned back on his elbows, his glance sweeping the area. "You know I haven't been to this place in years. When I was younger, this spot was my favorite swimming hole. Seems strange to be coming here now with my son. I don't know where the years have gone."

"Oh, I venture to guess you probably idled the time away in things like college and a war." Dimples flashed in her cheeks. "But I know what you mean. It seems impossible that Tommy will soon be two. These past two years have just flown by."

His jaw hardened grimly. "Funny, they passed like centuries to me."

Seeing his sober face, Angeleen reached out instinctively. "I'm sorry, Ruark. I wish I could change the past. Had I known your true feelings, I never would have kept Tommy's birth a secret from you."

Unconsciously, his fingers curled warmly around her hand, then both became aware of the contact. Simultaneously, the pair glanced down at their entwined hands. Their startled gazes met and locked for an interminable moment.

Angeleen withdrew her hand and nervously reached for her clothing. "Don't you think you should put the rest of your clothes on?" she snapped, much too aware of his nearness.

"Why?"

"You just can't sit there practically naked. Someone might come along."

His hand on her arm stopped her from rising. "Is that the only reason my nakedness bothers you, Angel?"

She couldn't look at him—dared not lest he read the answer in her troubled eyes.

"Look at me, Angel," he said softly.

She turned her head and her reluctant glance met the full impact of his dark eyes. Desire arced between them like a lightning charge.

"Don't do this to me, Ruark," she pleaded as she felt her increased heartbeat.

"We're doing it to each other, Angel. I feel it, too," he whispered.

As he lowered his head to hers, Tommy stirred nearby and opened his eyes. "Tommy thirsty, Mommie."

She turned away from Ruark and hurriedly finished dressing.

Angeleen made no further attempt to intrude on

Ruark's mornings with Tommy. In fact, she avoided Ruark whenever possible. She had a decision to make—and she couldn't think rationally around him.

On the final day before the exhibition race, Angeleen strolled down to the stable. Ruark and Tommy were off on one of their nature studies, Henry had gone into town, and the two colts were grazing in the corral.

After an affectionate greeting, Prince Consort galloped away, but Bold Prince lingered as he always did, the recipient of several more loving pats.

This colt was Angeleen's favorite; he looked so much like his sire that she had fallen in love with Bold Prince the first time she saw him. Hugging the colt, she cooed in his ear, "I know you're going to win that race tomorrow, my love."

"Nope. Prince Consort will beat him by a nose."

She swung around to discover Ruark standing behind her. He hooked a boot in the rung of the fence and whistled lightly. Prince Consort came trotting across the field. "This one, on the other hand, is my boy." He patted the horse affectionately.

"I did notice a certain arrogance about him."

"Bold Prince belongs to you, you know. I signed his papers over to you."

"What are you talking about?" she asked and returned to fondling the horse.

"He foaled first. I always intended for King's first foal to be a Christmas gift for you . . . but I never had the opportunity to present him to you, did I?"

"And you still don't. Once and for all, Ruark, I don't want any more of your damn gifts. You can take your papers and sign them right back to yourself." She turned to leave.

His temper flared. She had used him as a whipping board for the last time!

He grabbed her arm and swung her to face him. "I've stood all that I intend to. I've had enough of your looking at me as if I just crawled out from under a rock and cringing away from me as if I'm some kind of untouchable. What in hell did I ever do to you to deserve this treatment?"

His eyes now blazed with fury as his anger intensified. "You were wrong, lady, but you're trying to shift the guilt to me. Examine your own goddamned conscience before you point any fingers of guilt. We'll settle this once and for all."

"Settle what?" she asked, trying to display a show of verve in the face of his anger.

"This issue between us."

Angeleen responded with sarcasm. "What do you prefer, Ruark, swords or pistols?"

"Something much more painless—but apropos." He glanced at the two colts. Their ears were pricked up alertly as if both horses understood what was being said.

"We'll settle it with the race tomorrow," he said impetuously.

"The horse race?"

"Winner take all."

The more Ruark thought about the idea, the more excited he became with the prospect. "The matter of Bold King has always been a thorn in your a—ah, side. Rather poetic justice, wouldn't you say, that a son of his will now determine our future together?"

Angeleen still failed to grasp what he had in mind. "I don't understand what you mean."

"It's clear enough to me. Since you refuse to accept Bold Prince as a gift, I'll make a bet with you. If he wins tomorrow, all three of the horses are yours—Bold King, Prince Consort and Bold Prince. Three thoroughbreds. You'll be one damn rich lady, Mrs. Stewart," he snickered.

She eyed him with suspicion. "And if Prince Consort should win?"

"Winner take all. If my colt wins, no more talk of leaving. No more separate bedrooms."

"Good Lord, you are insane! Do you really think I would barter my body on the outcome of a horse race?"

"We've made love too often, Angel. You know what we're like together. You liked it as much as I did. I'm giving you the chance to climb back into my bed without having to swallow your pride."

"You're crazier than I thought, Ruark." She laughed nervously and started to walk away.

"And if there's no bet—well, then you don't have any guarantee I'll let you take Tommy when you go," he added ominously.

The remark brought her an abrupt halt. She turned around. "And if I agree to the bet, Tommy goes with me?"

He hesitated, realizing that he had rashly backed himself into a corner as well. He met her glance squarely. "I'll be honest with you, Angel. Bet or not, I'll never completely surrender my son."

"No, I don't expect you to, Ruark. I would bring him back twice a year, at the least."

Ruark nodded. "I guess I couldn't ask for more than that. Then we've got a bet, Mrs. Stewart. Shall we shake on it?"

Each smiled confidently as they shook hands.

Later that day, a late business appointment kept Ruark in town, so he was not among the glum group who sat around that evening speaking with a forced cheerfulness; the possible outcome of the precipitous bet gave them all cause for concern.

Strolling aimlessly around the room, Angeleen trailed her fingers lightly across the piano keyboard. "Will ye play a tune, lass?" Henry asked.

"If you wish, Poppa." Angeleen sat down and began the familiar notes of Henry's favorite song, "The Blue Bells Of Scotland."

Upon the last note, Henry dabbed at his eyes. "Aye, I remember how yer mother played that same tune, lass." He kissed her cheek. "I'll be sayin' a goodnight to ye now."

Henry shuffled out of the room mumbling softly to himself and nodding his head in response.

"I too will say goodnight, my dear." Sarah patted Angeleen on the shoulder. "Tomorrow is a big day for all of us."

"Goodnight, Nana Sarah."

Angeleen remained at the piano, moving into the melancholy strains of the "Londonderry Air." Deep in thought, she was unaware that Ruark had returned and now stood silently in the veiled shadows of the darkened room.

In the dim glow of a gaslight, her yellow silk gown

shimmered in iridescent shades of orange and gold against the stark magnificence of her long, black hair which flowed to the middle of her back. His hungry gaze roved the line of her slender neck and shoulders, bare except for a single rope of opalescent pearls.

Quietly listening to the music, Ruark lit a cigar and continued to watch her. He shifted his gaze to the ring on her hand as her slim fingers moved across the keyboard.

Angeleen began a haunting rendition of "Dixie." In a low tone, she slowly sang the plaintive words, and her heart swelled with sadness.

. . . Look away, look away, look away, Dixie Land.
For I wish I was in Dixie . . .

Feeling the rise of tears, she stopped and pressed her forehead against the piano top.

"Homesick, Angel?" Ruark asked gently.

Startled, she looked up as he stepped out of the shadows. "Ruark. I didn't realize you had returned."

"Or you would have escaped to your room."

Angeleen started to rise. "It *is* late. I will say goodnight."

"Please don't stop playing, Angel. I enjoy listening to you."

She relented and sat down. As she struck the chords of a familiar spiritual, Ruark leaned his elbows on the piano and stood drawing on his cigar as he listened contentedly.

"Big Charlie and I used to sing this song as we worked the fields back home," she said.

"I'll get it back for you, if that's what you want," Ruark said.

She glanced up perplexed. "Get what back?"

"Scotcroft. Your home. If that's what you want, I'll get it back for you."

"Of course. Those long Ruark Stewart pursestrings are capable of spanning oceans and continents if necessary." Her hands pounded down on the keys in a shattering crescendo. Shoving back the piano stool, she rose to her feet.

He grabbed her arm before she could move away. "What's the point of having money if you don't use it? If you hesitate to use the dollars you have, then you're just as poor as the pauper who has none. Money buys what you want in life."

She stood rigidly, and for an instant her cold gaze looked unflinchingly into his. "Does it, Ruark?" Then she shifted her eyes to the hand restraining her.

Ruark released her and she walked away. Tossing his cigar in the fireplace, he followed her.

"Angel, please don't run away this time."

His hand gripped her waist and he turned her to face him. Unexpectedly, he reached out and touched the pearl earring that dangled from her ear. "I didn't think when I gave you these, what a vital role they would come to play in our lives. Did you know that's how I traced you to Virginia?"

"I'd like to forget that day, Ruark." She walked over to the window just to escape the nearness of him.

"And I'd like to forget the day I walked into a Paris hotel room and read your note. *Thanks for everything . . . I've wearied of our life together.*"

He grasped her shoulders and spun her around to face him again. "Dammmit, Angel, didn't I deserve a better explanation than that?"

She looked into his angry eyes. "I've already explained my reason for leaving; I only tried to make it easier for you."

"How could you think an ambiguous message like that would make it easier for me?"

Her temper flared. "What should I have said, Ruark? I'm leaving you for another man? Would that explanation have satisfied you?"

"Why not? I thought as much at the time."

Her eyes widened in shock, stunned by his unexpected remark. "You actually believed I left you for another man?"

"Among other things." He released her and strode angrily to the fireplace. "A dozen reasons went through my head. Everything but the real one."

"How stupid of me. Naturally, you would think a whore like me would always be looking for greener pastures."

Anguished, he turned to face her. "That's not true. How many times and ways can a man say he's sorry?"

She shook her head helplessly. "Ruark, all we're doing is rehashing the same argument. Neither of us can change the past."

He stared wistfully into her eyes. "I guess I should have asked you this before." He took a deep breath and forced out a question that had plagued him. "Is there someone waiting for you in Virginia?"

"No."

"Then why?" he asked perplexed. "Why go back

there when everyone you know and love is right here?"

"I wish I understood the reason myself. I don't know if it's pride or hurt or anger. Maybe a combination of all three. For whatever reasons, we've hurt each other deeply, Ruark, and sometimes, with that much pain, bridges are burned and there's simply no way of crossing back." Tears began to mist her eyes.

He cupped her cheeks in his hands. "I know what I said, and what I agreed to. Even if you win that race tomorrow, I can't make any promises. I don't know if I can give you and Tommy up, Angel."

He took her in his arms and held her. He felt no force of aroused passion, only a need to hold the woman he loved in his arms.

Neither did Angeleen feel passion, merely a need to feel his arms around her. Tomorrow might be too late. The undeniable need existed now.

Ruark released her, dipped his head, and their lips met in a sweet, gentle kiss.

"Goodnight, Ruark," she said softly, when they separated.

"Goodnight, Angel," he responded sadly.

Ruark remained at the foot of the stairway. Only the rustle of her silk gown broke the silence. Angeleen paused at the top of the stairway and looked back. For a brief moment, their gazes met.

Aware that their every gesture, every waking thought expressed their love—still their stubborn pride left the simple phrase unspoken.

Chapter Twenty-Eight

The day of the race dawned warm and sunny, and by noon, when Robert and Celeste arrived at the house for an early lunch, a clear blue sky without a sign of a drifting cloud promised another long, hot day.

Angeleen had given Celeste some clothes from the wardrobe Ruark had brought back from Paris. Now, dressed in a fetching gown of pale green foulard with a pert green casquette perched on her mass of gold curls, Celeste's green eyes glowed with excitement from under the protection of the white parasol she twirled in her hands.

Angeleen had chosen to wear an ankle-length gown of white dotted net. Worn over the soft silk of a yellow petticoat, the sloping sides of the Princess-style skirt were joined at the back of the waist and tied with a yellow silk sash.

Unlike many women of the day, Angeleen had no need for the scalpettes and frizzettes used to give the hair a fuller look; her thick, dark locks were pulled up into an enormous chignon of curls. Trimmed with yellow tulle, a tiny white pillbox casquette sat at a captivating angle on her forehead.

When Angeleen stepped outside to join them, Sarah and Celeste were already seated in the carriage, with Robert waiting beside the open door.

Just as a carriage turned into the driveway, Angeleen opened a yellow silk parasol to ward off the effects of the blazing sun. Her face brightened with a welcoming smile when a tall, handsome figure in a gray top hat, frock coat, and pin-striped trousers stepped out of the coach.

"T. J.!" she exclaimed with pleasure. "Why didn't you tell us you were coming?"

Grasping her hands, T. J. kissed Angeleen's cheek and then stepped back to admire her. "Mrs. Stewart, you look as lovely as a spring muse." As he hugged her affectionately, he eyed Robert.

"How do you do? I'm T. J. Graham." He reached out to shake Robert's hand. "You must be Angeleen's brother. You two bear a striking resemblance to each other."

"Robert Scott. Pleasure meeting you, sir."

Grinning, T. J. slipped an arm around Angeleen's shoulders. "And how has married life been treating you, Mrs. Stewart?"

"How did you know Ruark and I married?"

He winked at Robert. "News of such magnitude travels swiftly."

She eyed him suspiciously. "Thomas Jefferson

Graham, did you have anything to do with this double-cross?"

Hedging the question, T. J. looked about curiously. "Where's the lucky groom?"

"Oh, he and Poppa took the two colts to the track hours ago." She hugged him again. "Oh, T. J., I'm so glad you came."

"This is one race I wouldn't miss," he replied.

"We met in Virginia during the war, Captain Graham, but I doubt that you would remember," Robert said.

At T. J.'s look of puzzlement, Robert continued. "A young man in my company had been badly wounded in the stomach. You were in charge of the field hospital and operated on him. Corporal Donovan would have died without your help."

"Was that a Corporal James Donovan?" T. J. inquired. Robert nodded and T. J. said, "I remember the young man very well."

He regarded Robert with renewed interest. "Scott . . . Lieutenant Scott. Of course, now I remember you. That's why you look so familiar. I thought it was your resemblance to Angeleen. Corporal Donovan told me you had carried him for ten miles through enemy lines."

"It was worth it, sir. You saved his life. He would have died in the field."

"No, Lieutenant, *you* saved his life. He would have died in the field if you hadn't carried him out of there."

Avidly listening to the conversation, Angeleen glanced with pride at her brother. Other than on the first night of his return, Robert had not spoken of his experiences during the war.

Suddenly, an acerbic voice questioned, "Are you all going to stand out there talking the afternoon away while Celeste and I bake inside this carriage?"

The sudden reproach by a familiar voice brought an instant grin to T. J. "Nana Sarah!"

He hurried over to the carriage and climbed in. Grabbing Sarah, he hugged her tightly, then gave her a solid kiss on the lips. "Nana, I adore you. And this is my final offer—will you marry me?"

Sarah shoved him away and dourly grumbled, "Get away with you, you young hellion. After being married to Charlie Stewart, a real man if there ever was one, I'd never settle for a young scalawag the likes of you, Thomas Jefferson Graham."

Her eyes danced with merriment. "Besides, why hasn't some sweet, unsuspecting young girl caught you in her net by this time? I swear all you young people today are addle-brained."

"How could I wed anyone but you, my love?" T. J.'s warm eyes rested on her aged face. Lifting her hand, he brought it to his lips. "How have you been, sweetheart?"

Sarah tried to disguise her pleasure. "What are you doing, taking my pulse?" she muttered when he didn't release her hand.

T. J. settled back in the seat and for the first time observed the beauty in green seated opposite him. He leaned forward and tipped his hat. "Thomas Graham, ma'am. And you are—"

"My wife, Celeste," Robert declared, having followed him to the door of the carriage. Robert's possessive tone conveyed a slightly jealous reaction.

"Mrs. Scott," T. J. said with a respectful smile.

"I've heard a great deal about you, Dr. Graham," Celeste acknowledged with a fetching smile.

"If we don't get underway, we're going to miss the race," Sarah advised.

T. J. stepped out of the carriage and grabbed Angeleen's hand. "Ride with me, Angel. I want to hear how my ole friend convinced you to marry him."

"Coercion," Angeleen replied. Then she glanced deliberately at Sarah. "With the assistance of Mistress Perfidy Stewart and her entourage." Glancing askance at T. J., Angeleen added, "Of which, I'm now convinced, you are a member."

The roads leading to the track carried various models of conveyance, from the tallyhos of the elite drawn by matched sets of hackneys to the springboard wagons of the farmers hauled by sway-backed mares.

Word of the unusual exhibition race had reached the ears of the surrounding community. There would be no legal betting, since the event was neither a stakes nor a claiming race. Although side bets were made, the prospect of wagering was not the attraction; both horses would be wearing Stewart colors and the curious were eager to see the competition between the two horses who were not only stable companions, but sired by the same stallion.

A few among the old-time trackmen present remembered Bold King's promising but brief career that had been cut off abruptly by the outbreak of the war.

While a string orchestra played a lilting Strauss waltz, Sarah Stewart sat in a rocking chair on the shaded veranda of the clubhouse holding audience with the many well-wishers who trooped past to greet her. Looking as regal as an empress, she wore a gray gown of tussah silk and a large-brimmed bonnet adorned with white ostrich feathers. It was hard to believe that in only a few months, this grande dame would celebrate her eighty-third birthday.

Shortly before the scheduled exhibition, Angeleen and T. J. went back to the saddling enclosure to join Ruark.

"Well, Doctor Brutus," he greeted T. J., "I do wish to thank you for keeping my son a secret from me."

"Had to honor my patient's confidentiality, ole friend." T. J. grinned. "Of course, your son's birth *was* a matter of public record." T. J. extended his hand and Ruark grudgingly shook it.

The innuendo was not missed by Ruark. He had long acknowledged to himself that his departure from Virginia had been too hasty. Had he not gone to Europe, he would have discovered the truth about Tommy long ago.

The reunion with T. J. was interrupted by a freckle-faced young man carrying a camera case and tripod. "Mr. Stewart, remember me? Ben Ryan from *The Examiner*. May I get a photograph of you and Mrs. Stewart for the Sunday edition?"

Ruark had suffered through a recent interview with the young man, but agreed reluctantly. "You'd better hurry. The race is scheduled to begin in ten minutes."

"I would like to get a photograph of each of the colts if you and Mrs. Stewart wouldn't mind. This race has attracted a lot of local attention."

"Well, let's get on with it then," Ruark said impatiently. He took Angeleen's arm and led her over to his horse, Prince Consort.

Ryan shaded his eyes and studied the angle of the sun. After much posturing, he finally had his tripod positioned to his satisfaction directly in front of Prince Consort.

"Mrs. Stewart, if you don't mind." He moved Angeleen to the side of the colt. "Hold his rein in your left hand. And you, sir, if you would be kind enough to do the same with your right hand on the other side."

Hurrying back to the box camera, he disappeared under the black drape. "Superb!" he called out. "This will make a wonderful picture for the society page. Now smile, and don't either of you move."

He snapped the picture. At the sudden pop and flash of gunpowder, Prince Consort reared up, pulling free from Angeleen. Ruark struggled to maintain his grasp on the reins as the panicky animal tried to bolt. Henry and several of the grooms rushed to Ruark's assistance just as Ryan set off another explosion, hoping to capture a picture of the action.

Prince Consort became frenzied. It took several more harried moments before the men were able to get the colt under control.

"Get that damn camera out of here," Ruark lashed out angrily, his eyes blazing with fury.

"I was hoping for a picture of the other colt, Mr. Stewart," the witless photographer replied.

"I'll kill him," Ruark growled and lunged at Ryan.

Angeleen grabbed Ruark's arm before he could inflict any bodily injury. "Calm down, Ruark. Didn't you warn me against public scenes?" she cautioned.

"Calm down! I've got my whole future riding on this race and that damn fool just spooked my horse."

T. J. had already folded up the tripod and shoved Ryan's equipment into the man's arms. "I'd advise you to disappear while you've still got a camera."

Ruark's head shot up in alarm as the call to the post sounded. With a knot in the pit of his stomach, he watched the two jockeys climb on the backs of the colts for the parade to the post.

Jems Dennehy was atop Prince Consort, and Ruark stopped him as he passed. "I think he's too spooked for a good run, Jems, but give him the best ride you can."

"Dinna worry, sir. The colt must still hae some run in him." He winked at Ruark and trotted off.

Swinging their heads from right to left, the two colts pranced to the starting line.

Angeleen stole a glance at Ruark standing beside her at the fence. He appeared to be tense and solemn. In the numerous races she had attended with him, she couldn't remember a time when he looked so grim while waiting for a race to begin.

The starter raised the red flag. The hush that gripped the crowd exploded in a roar when he dropped his arm.

Both horses broke with an early burst of speed and charged down the backstretch. Matching stride for stride, they passed the half-mile pole and, as they rounded the far turn, Prince Consort swung a little wide. The other jockey immediately tucked Bold Prince into the rail and shot into the lead.

In spite of a determined effort by his stable companion, Prince Consort closed up the gap between them and the two horses rounded the final turn together.

The crowd was on its feet, waving their hats and jumping up and down as the gallant pair pounded down the homestretch. As they neared the finish line, the two beautiful black colts raced as one—nose-to-nose, stride-on-stride, heads thrust forward, ears pricked high.

Suddenly, a white hat flew out of a spectator's hand and skimmed across the track. Still unnerved from his recent experience, the distraction was enough to make Prince Consort break his stride.

Bold Prince dashed across the finish line ahead of him.

Angeleen felt more numb than elated. She glanced furtively at Ruark. "Congratulations, Angel," he said.

"I . . . I don't know what to say, Ruark," Angeleen stammered helplessly.

"To the victor falls the spoils," he quoted, forcing a smile. Then his jaw hardened into a grim line. "I believe you're expected in the winner's circle, Mrs. Stewart."

Angeleen watched helplessly as he disappeared into the crowd.

Chapter Twenty-Nine

Arriving home, Ruark went immediately to his den. He sat down, propped his arms on the desk, and rested his head in his hands. *That damn-fool bet!* He had made the biggest gamble of his life—and lost. Ruark cursed himself for his own stupidity; how could he have acted so rashly? He had given Angeleen the very out she hoped for!

He looked the picture of despair when Myra and Tommy came downstairs. Hearing Tommy skip across the floor, Ruark raised his head and grinned. That was all the invitation Tommy needed. He crawled onto Ruark's lap and greeted his father with a hug and kiss.

After one look at the black scowl on Ruark's face, Myra didn't have to be told the outcome of the race.

She shook her head and departed without saying a word.

Ruark walked to the window when a carriage rumbled up the driveway. Glancing out at the arrivals, Ruark knew the time had come to face the issue; he would talk to Angeleen immediately.

He carried Tommy outside, his troubled gaze clouding with envy as he watched T. J. assist Angeleen out of the carriage. At the sight of his mother, Tommy slipped away from Ruark and ran into her outstretched arms.

Trying to appear casual, Ruark strolled over to the carriage. "Angeleen, I'd like to talk to you." With a pointed glare at T. J., he added, "Privately."

"I think the two of you could use a mediator," T. J. remarked.

"What makes you think I need the advice of an arrogant, self-satisfied . . . jackass?" Frustrated because of the stupid bargain, and irrationally jealous at seeing Angeleen on T. J.'s arm, Ruark exploded in a preposterous rage. "I hope you don't think you can get away with this, Doctor Brutus?"

"Get away with what?" T. J. exchanged a perplexed look with Angeleen.

"Foisting your lechery on my wife!"

"Lechery?" T. J.'s teeth flashed in a grin. "Well, I guess that proves it, ole friend. Your brain always was between your legs."

Resigned to the inevitable, T. J. took off his hat and laid it aside. "You've had this coming for a long time." Then he removed his jacket and cravat, laying them in a neat pile next to the hat.

Ruark returned a sardonic grin as he rolled up

his shirt sleeves. "Yea, I should have beaten the hell out of you the night you slept with Melanie Merryweather. What kind of man sleeps with his best friend's fiancée?"

"Fiancée?" T. J. snorted. "Your *fiancée* was bedding every guy in the dormitory. I kept you from making a fool of yourself, buddy. I never could stand the little—"

Remembering Angeleen's presence, T. J. cut off his words. Rolling up his shirt sleeves, he clenched his fists. "Any time you feel lucky, ole friend, muscle up your best punch. You're only going to get *one*."

Horrified, Angeleen gasped in dismay, "Good God! You two aren't going to fight, are you?"

Her exclamation became a moot point. Ruark delivered a solid blow to T. J.'s jaw, sending him slamming into the carriage horse.

The startled animal whinnied and reared up, catching the driver off-guard; horse and carriage careened down the driveway, with the driver struggling frantically to bring the animal under control.

T. J. returned the punch and sent Ruark sprawling.

Snatching up Tommy, Angeleen ran toward the house. "Help! Somebody stop them!" When Myra and the cook came hurrying out of the door, Angeleen shoved the youngster into the maid's arms. "Take Tommy. I don't want him to see this."

Myra gladly accepted the lad, but she had no intention of missing the fireworks.

Rushing to where Ruark and T. J. now thrashed together on the ground, Angeleen tried to separate them. "Stop this! Both of you stop this at once." She anded on her backside for her practical advice.

"Dammit, now look what you've done," Ruark houted to T. J.

Both stopped their struggling while each man ook an arm and helped Angeleen to her feet. Then Ruark delivered a wallop that sent T. J. reeling backwards.

Arriving in time to see T. J. land on his backside, Robert jumped out of Sarah Stewart's carriage to nvestigate. Angeleen immediately rushed up to him and tugged at his arm.

"Robert, you've got to stop them. They're going to kill each other."

He ran over to the two men on the ground, Ruark straddling T. J. as he pummeled him for yet another past grievance. "And this is for the time you left me stranded on Cape Charles with those man-hungry Schuster twins. Remember that, *ole friend*? By the ime you came back two days later, I was lucky I could walk."

T. J. wrestled free, and separating, they climbed to their feet. Blood streamed from T. J.'s nostrils, but his quick uppercut to the jaw knocked Ruark down.

"Well, that was for Cynthia Chandler. She was mine 'til you bamboozled her with your money." T. J. spat blood from a cut lip.

"Money? Hell! Boredom with you drove her right into my arms," Ruark snorted, wiping the blood off his face with his shirtsleeve.

Straining his neck not to miss one blow of the ruckus, Daniel jumped down from his perch, helped Sarah out of the carriage, then deserted his mistress to join the spectators. "Who's winning?" he asked gardener leaning on a pitchfork.

" 'Bout even," the man said noncommittally.

"What is going on here?" Sarah demanded a she joined them, her hand tucked into the arm o Celeste, who had thoughtfully waited to assist th older woman.

"Nana Sarah, you must stop them," Angelee pleaded. "They won't listen to me."

"Well then, let the two young fools battle it ou child. This fight's been spoiling for a long time."

Having just returned from the track and attracte by the commotion, Henry and the grooms cam racing up the path to join the gaping crowd.

T. J. swung a right punch, but Ruark blocked wit his left and sent T. J. sprawling with a punch to th jaw. Standing above him with clenched fists, Ruar jeered, "Come on, *ole friend*, get on your feet."

"Get up, Captain Graham," Robert urged as h hurried to help T. J. get up. T. J. weaved unsteadily shaking his head to clear away the fuzziness.

"Mr. Stewart's got him now," one of the groom said confidently.

"I've got a dollar that says the Doc will take hin yet," Henry replied.

"That's a bet," the groom said.

"Put my dollar on Mr. Stewart too," Danie declared, pulling a folded bill out of the top o his boot.

Appalled, Angeleen glared at the men. "I can' believe this. You should be trying to stop this figh instead of making bets on two men pounding eacl other senseless."

The scuffle moved across the lawn, and the crowd pressed forward in pursuit.

"This is for that bastard, Sherman," T. J. growled, levying a firm blow on Ruark's jaw. Crashing into the middle rung of the fence, Ruark rolled end over end into the corral and lay sprawled flat on the ground. The grazing colts whinnied in panic and galloped away from the sudden intrusion as Robert and the grooms eagerly straddled the fence to watch.

Ruark picked himself up and blearily waited as T. J. crawled through the rungs of the fence. Mustering everything he had left, Ruark smashed a right jab into his face. "And that's for Bull Run." He quickly followed with a left stab. "And the Second Battle of Bull Run."

Withstanding the one-two punch, T. J. swung his right fist, making direct contact with Ruark's chin. "It's called Manassas Junction, you stupid Yankee. We won those battles, we oughta know what to call 'em."

"Oh, Good God!" Angeleen wailed. "The fools are re-fighting the Civil War."

"I'll put five dollars on Captain Graham," Robert shouted as the two campaigners climbed out of the corral still primed for battle.

"Well, I'll cover that bet, young man," Sarah declared adamantly when Ruark ducked T. J.'s punch.

Angeleen's mouth gaped in astonishment. "Nana Sarah!" Sarah's eyes twinkled with mirth as she offered the shocked girl a culpable smile.

In a huddled group, the spectators followed the

combatants, who were now rolling across the lawn as they pummeled each other.

"Give it to him, Captain!" Robert called out, then gave a Rebel yell.

Ruark hadn't heard the mesmerizing war cry of the Rebs for years, and he turned in surprise just as T. J.'s fist connected with his jaw, sending Ruark flopping into the stream.

Thinking it was all a game, Tommy clapped his hands and squealed with delight. "Dada watar."

Barely able to stay on his feet, T. J. stumbled into the stream and stood over his downed opponent.

"And *that* was for Cemetery Ridge."

Picking Ruark up by the shirt front, T. J. delivered another blow and then another. "And for Shiloh and Vicksburg."

"Spotsylvania, Captain. Don't forget Spotsylvania." Robert shouted. "Or Jeb Stuart."

Celeste stormed over to him. "You stay out of this, Robert Scott!" She pushed Robert off his perch on the fence.

"What did I do?" Robert asked innocently as he lay on his backside.

Too exhausted to continue, T. J. dropped Ruark and fell to his knees fighting for breath. The two grooms leaped down and rushed to Ruark's side. They sat him up and began to splash water on his head and face.

"You've got him on the ropes, sir. You can't stop now. Don't you see he's tiring?"

"Yeah, get up, sir. You can do it. Just remember what those stinking Johnny Rebs did to us at Fredricksburg," the other said passionately.

Groggily, Ruark staggered to his feet. T. J. rose and tottered before him. Bloodied and exhausted, both men weaved back and forth, near collapsing.

"Dammit, stand still and fight like a man," Ruark cursed.

"And this one's gonna be for General Stonewall Jackson." Dredging up his remaining strength, T. J. clenched his fist to deliver the final blow, but stumbled into Ruark instead. Knocked off balance, the two bloodied combatants fell into the water.

Ruark lay back, too exhausted to move. "Stonewall Jackson? I thought he was accidentally shot by a Reb picket?"

T. J. lay beside him in the shallow stream, enjoying the soothing feel of the cool water on his aches and pains. "Well, anyway, if it weren't for you damn Yankees, he never would have been there in the first place."

Any ill-will Angeleen might have harbored toward Ruark shattered under the first blow he suffered. Seeing the man she loved being beaten before her eyes soon became more than she could bear. Breaking free from the crowd, she rushed to the stream, flung herself down, and cradled Ruark's head in her lap. "Darling. Oh, my darling," she sobbed. As tears streaked her cheeks, she picked up a section of her wet skirt and sponged the blood off his face.

Glancing at T. J. stretched out prostrate, her eyes blazed in anger. "You ought to be ashamed of yourself, Thomas Jefferson Graham. Just look what you've done to him. I'll never forgive you for this. Never. How dare you call yourself a doctor!"

Perplexed by her emotional defense of Ruark

and the uncharacteristic attack leveled at T. J., the two combatants exchanged sidelong glances. Then Ruark saw the doctor who had delivered Tommy grin at him, and the two men erupted into uproarious laughter.

Suddenly a stab of pain shot to his head from a swollen eye.

Angeleen glanced down in time to see him wince with pain, and her heart swelled with compassion. Cradling his head against her bosom, she cooed softly, "Tell me where you hurt, darling."

Ruark had no intention of telling her; *showing* her fit more into his scheme of things.

Daniel hurried over to help Ruark to his feet, but Angeleen waved aside the man's offer of assistance. "I'll take care of him myself.

"Just put your arm around my shoulders, Ruark," she said softly, putting a firm arm around his waist to support him.

Whatever her reason for the sudden change of heart, Ruark had no intention of arguing with providence; he intended to milk the opportunity for all it was worth.

"Anything you say, sweetheart," he replied, draping an arm over her shoulder.

Since a clear winner had not emerged from the fracas, all bets were cancelled. Grumbling, the spectators slowly disbanded.

However, there was no question in Robert's mind as to which man had won the scrimmage. He walked over to T. J., who struggled to garner enough strength to get to his feet.

"We sure whipped him, Captain Graham." Robert

hadn't felt this good in years. T. J. had done what he himself was physically unable to do—punch the smirk off the face of Ruark Stewart.

Robert now felt vindicated, a weight lifted from his shoulders. Reaching out a helping hand, he pulled T. J. to his feet.

"Robert, how long do you intend to carry on this ridiculous feud with your brother-in-law?" T. J. asked. "Take a look at them," he advised, pointing to Angeleen and Ruark walking up the path.

Halfway up the driveway, Ruark had surprisingly undergone a miraculous recovery, and his arm around Angeleen had slipped from a clutch into an embrace as he hugged her to his side.

"Can't you see it's a lost cause?" His gaze rested perceptively on Robert. "And so is the South's, Robert."

For a moment the two men stood silently and stared with understanding into each other's eyes. Finally, the battle-scarred veteran raised his head with pride. "I know. I guess I wanted to believe it wasn't true."

Robert glanced over to where Celeste stood alone, watching them. "I've been a fool about a lot of things, Captain Graham."

"It's Doctor Graham, Robert. I haven't been in the army for over two years. But I really prefer you call me T. J."

"My pleasure, T. J." Robert grinned and squared his shoulders. "But we sure did whomp him good, Captain."

"Yep, Lieutenant Scott, we sure did." T. J. flexed his aching jaw, fearing it had been dislocated.

Grinning painfully, he slapped Robert on the shoulder. "And it felt good doing it."

The two men walked up the path to Celeste. Robert reached out and clasped her hand.

Chapter Thirty

Alone in the privacy of Ruark's room, Angeleen sat him down on the edge of the bed and knelt at his feet to remove his boots. "And I'll get that bloody shirt off you, too," she said.

Ruark made no effort to resist. He definitely approved of her present course of action.

Concentrating intently on his injuries, Angeleen was unaware of the lewd thoughts racing through his mind. As she bent over him, her fingers releasing the buttons of his shirt, the perfumed fragrance of her hair began to tease his nostrils, sending a surge of passion to his loins.

Lord, how I love her, he thought. *How I ache for her.* She was so close, he could have reached out and pulled her into his arms. Yet he dared not—lest he had mistaken her compassion for a change of heart.

She slipped the shirt off his shoulders, and Ruark closed his eyes as he felt the satin slide of her fingers on his naked flesh. He knew of nothing that compared to the feel of her touch.

Myra's entrance carrying a basin immediately ended his erotic reflection. For several seconds she stood over him, shaking her head and clucking her disapproval like an agitated hen.

In a move to silence her, Angeleen took the basin out of the maid's hands. "Thank you, Myra. How is Doctor Graham?"

"Looks just as bad as Mr. Ruark here."

"Well, you'd better get back to him then. I can take care of this myself."

Myra left, still shaking her head in disgust.

Dipping a cloth into the liquid in the basin, Angeleen dabbed at the corner of Ruark's mouth. "What's in that water? It smells like hell," he grumbled.

"Just a little vinegar. It will take away all the soreness."

Ruark knew that no amount of vinegar would ever ease the real source of his ache, but he wasn't going to discourage her from administering to him.

After a close examination of his face, she sighed deeply. "You're going to have a black eye, you know. I just can't believe you and T. J. would do this to each other. I thought you were best friends."

"We are—now more than ever."

Angeleen continued to pat the vinegar on his wounds. "And men claim the female mind is complicated! Why, if two women did this, they'd never speak to each other again."

"Oh, but it's okay to bloody each other with your catty tongues," he said in defense of manhood.

"And you men don't? I noticed that between blows, neither one of you hesitated to use your nasty tongues." She shoved him away and carried the basin to a nearby table.

Ruark followed her and quickly locked the door. Hearing the click of the key in the lock, Angeleen turned in surprise.

"We have to talk and I don't want any interruptions," he explained in response to her wary look.

"Ruark, get back on that bed and rest," she said. "We can talk later."

"Now," he insisted, taking her hand. "And you come with me."

Angeleen allowed him to lead her back to the bed. He lay back, and she sat down on the edge of the bed, docilely crossing her hands in her lap. "What is it you want, Ruark?"

"I want *you*, and you damn well know it," he said emphatically, but then softened his tone. "How can you sit there looking so serene when you know I want you so bad I'm hurting?"

Her eyes calmly met his and he continued, "Why all this dumb-show of avoiding me? You've put me through sheer hell the past two weeks, and I think you never had any intention of returning to Virginia. Did you?" His stern voice demanded, but his hopeful heart was not so certain.

"Whatever makes you think that?" She nervously offered the waning shreds of her resistance. "After all, I have a house in Virginia. Now that I won the race, I—"

"Angel," he interrupted her stream of words, "look at me."

When she looked into his eyes, she could no longer continue the charade. The foolish pride that had boxed her into a corner so long ago disintegrated. He, too, saw that the masquerade was over.

"No more games, Angel. No more misconceptions, no more lies. Once and for all, are you going to stay here with me?"

The look in her eyes deepened. "Do you want me to?"

Ruark slipped a hand under the thick scarf of her long locks and cupped the back of her neck. "What do you think?"

His fingers gently massaged the stiff muscles of her neck. Relaxing in response to his touch, she sighed. "I think I like being independently wealthy. Now I can make my own decisions. No more mandates. No more . . . bets. Isn't that right, Ruark?" Rising a questioning brow, she smiled at him.

"That's a sure bet," he agreed laughingly.

Then Ruark drew her head down to his and lightly kissed her. "Besides, you've always been independently wealthy. You have intelligence. Courage and fortitude. Beauty. I don't think you have any idea how wealthy you are."

"Well, I know I'm three thoroughbreds wealthier today than I was yesterday. So just remember, Ruark Stewart, the next time you get too sure of yourself, I can always pack up my son and ride off on my ponies," she teased.

"Or who knows, I just might race my thoroughbreds against the Stewart stable."

Ruark chuckled warmly. "Angel, you *are* the Stewart stable. At least for the time being. I just lost three of my best prospects."

Ruark pulled her down into his arms. "But don't joke about leaving, Angel; don't even think it. Promise me you'll never leave me again?" he pleaded.

For a long moment he lay gazing with torment into her eyes. "Two years. We've wasted two years from our lives that we can never regain. How can one man be such a fool? I should have married you the moment I met you. No wonder T. J. tried to beat some sense into me."

Angeleen smiled and gently stroked an ugly-looking bruise on his cheek. "Oh, I think a couple of those punches were meant for me, too," she said tenderly. "T. J.'s just too much of a gentleman to strike a lady."

He kissed her, and her lips parted to accept the warm and exciting pressure. Swept by a tantalizing, suffusing heat, she closed her eyes and allowed the delicious cravings of her body to prevail.

They both knew nothing would ever part them again, and he tenderly said, "I love you, Angel."

She opened her eyes and smiled into his, which glowed with the warmth of his love. "I love you too, Ruark." Then her face curved into an impish grin. "Even if you do look like Quasimodo at the moment."

Ruark broke into laughter. "Ouch!" He grabbed his jaw.

Leaning over, she lightly brushed his lips with her own. "There, all better," she said.

He tried to release the buttons on her gown, but

pulled back in pain. "Damn that T. J." He held up his aching hand. "Will you kiss it and make it stop hurting, honey?"

She tenderly took his hand in the palms of her own and pressed kisses on each of the bruised knuckles. "There, all better."

Her sapphire eyes narrowed as she released the buckle of his pants. "I'm going to kiss away all your aches, my love."

He groaned with rapturous gratitude a short time later when she did.

At six o'clock, Ruark and Angeleen finally came down for dinner to find everyone assembled in the drawing room. For a few anxious moments, Ruark and T. J. regarded one another's battered faces.

"God! I thought *I* looked bad," Ruark exclaimed.

The two men broke into laughter as they reached out and shook hands. With the camaraderie of a vintage friendship, both knew the fight had settled the friendly feud once and for all.

At dinner, Angeleen's announcement that she would remain with Ruark came as a relief to everyone, although a surprise to none. However, when she also informed them that she and Ruark were taking Tommy to Virginia as a chance for the three of them to be alone together, that announcement met an outcry of protests.

But despite vociferous objections from a great-grandmother, a grandfather, an uncle, and an aunt, Ruark and Angeleen stood firm in the decision. Tommy was coming with them.

When they finished dinner, Angeleen slipped

upstairs to check on Tommy while the men moved to the library to savor a cigar and a glass of brandy. Declining the invitation to join the men, Henry gathered the women together for the evening card game.

"Will ye join us, lass?" he asked when Angeleen returned.

"Not tonight, Poppa."

"Then let the game begin, ladies. As me dear sainted mother always said," Henry expounded as he dealt the cards, " 'Tis nae the winnin' of the game's the pleasure, 'tis the doin' of it.' "

Even Grandmother Scott's been vindicated, Angeleen thought affectionately as she listened to him croon like a shepherd to a flock of lambs.

"So, me little darlin's, name yer pleasure."

"Let's play that game where the squinty jacks are wild," Sarah suggested.

"You mean One-Eyed Jacks, darlin'," Henry corrected. "One-Eyed Jacks 'twill be," he announced. "And ye, Miss Myra, hae the first chance to open."

For a lengthy moment that seemed to stretch into hours, Myra reflected on her hand. "Oh, get on with it, woman. Are you opening the hand or aren't you?" Sarah blurted impatiently.

Myra regarded her through a jaundiced eye, then pushed her bet into the pot. "I open for one," she said with a crafty smile.

Celeste picked up two of the kidney-shaped dry beans from the pile in front of her. "I'll see that bet, and raise it one."

Henry beamed with pleasure. "Aye, that's the way of it, lass." His face split in a wide, Celtic grin.

"Now, 'tis up to ye, Miss Sarah. What will ye be doin', foldin' or bettin'?"

Poppa and his sporting ways, Angeleen thought tenderly. She couldn't ever recall a time when she had seen him so much at peace.

Smiling with loving indulgence, Angeleen moved away and strolled over to the open French doors. Crossing her arms across her chest, she leaned back against the frame, breathing deeply of the garden perfumed by the spicy fragrance of phlox, primrose, and the sweet aroma of lavender.

Bright moonlight cast a silvery glow on the spacious lawn and leafy boughs. Only the synchronized chirp of crickets and the gentle neigh of a mare to her colt disturbed the stillness of the night.

A sudden outburst of laughter from Ruark and T. J. caused her to swing her glance toward the circle of men. They were laughing uproariously at a war anecdote Robert had just related.

As Ruark threw back his head in laughter, his glance met hers. Momentarily captivated, their eyes transmitted a silent message of love. Angeleen smiled at him, then stepped outside.

"Are you still angry with me, pretty lady?"

Startled, she turned and discovered that T. J. had followed her. Angeleen reached for his hand. "Of course not. Forgive me, T. J., I'm so sorry for those nasty things I said to you."

She kissed his palm and cupped it to her cheek. "You're the best friend I've ever had, and I love you dearly."

"I'm happy for you, Angel. And for Ruark. The two of you are the only family I have."

"Then why are you leaving us to run off to—Utah, did you say?"

"The offer to be a doctor with the Union Pacific is an opportunity of a lifetime, Angel."

"But won't it be dangerous, T. J.? All those Indians and outlaws?"

"Honey, that's why they need a doctor. But the joining of the railroad linking east to west will be a monumental moment, and I'll be there to witness it."

Angeleen's eyes misted with tears as she gazed into his warm brown eyes. "If that's what you want, then I'm happy for you, T. J. But we'll miss you."

He pulled her into his arms and kissed her cheek. Then, his arm slipped around her shoulder, they walked back into the house.

A week later, a small crowd gathered at the Union Station depot to say good-bye to Ruark and Angeleen as they prepared to depart for the East. Henry, Robert and Celeste, T. J., and even Sarah on the arm of Myra, had come to see them off.

Tommy trembled with excitement in the arms of his father as Ruark carried the youngster from one to another for a last hug and kiss.

Then, after Angeleen had boarded, Ruark handed her their son and turned back for a painful good-bye to T. J.

"Still don't know why you're going West, but don't forget to duck all those Sioux arrows," Ruark said as the two men shook hands.

"Made up my mind that night in New York with Vanderbilt. It'll be the beginning of a whole new chapter in this country's history, buddy, and I'm going to be there when they drive in that last spike."

"Well, just don't lose your trousers—or your scalp, ole friend."

After the train left the depot, the small crowd remained until only puffs of gray smoke in the distant sky marked the engine's passage.

Sarah was the first to break the silence. "At last, finally a *fait accompli*. So why are we all looking so glum?"

"Aye, 'tis a job well done," Henry seconded. "And wud hae been long over and done, had na one interfered." Five people turned accusing glances on Robert Scott.

The young man shrugged his broad shoulders. "How was I to know Ruark's intentions were honorable?" he protested in his own defense. "Angie told me she wanted to leave him."

"And you believed her," Myra snorted. "Had you asked, any one of us could have told you differently. We all figured it out fast enough."

"See, *mon cher*, is it not as I said?" Celeste chided, her blond head bobbing charmingly. "You do not understand women."

"But I never tire of your trying to teach me, my love." He tousled her hair, then put his arm around her waist. Celeste laid her head on his shoulder and they strolled away.

Henry nudged Myra with his hip, doffed his top hat—the latest style, which flattened when not worn—and crooked an arm in invitation. "Wud ye be carin' to join me in a bit of a nip at the nearest pub, Miss Myra?"

Flustered, Myra broke into a broad smile, straightened her bonnet—a genuine Parisian facsimile—and fluttered her eyelashes coyly.

"Don't mind if I do, Mr. Scott."

She linked her arm through Henry's and the two followed behind the younger couple.

T. J. watched them leave, a smile of pleasure on his handsome face. Glancing at Sarah, T. J. got an idea.

"And how about you, Miss Sarah? May I interest you in the prospect of a cool lemonade at the nearest confectionery?"

Sarah Stewart's clear blue eyes danced with the lingering deviltry of a once youthful beauty. She had a better idea. "I would be delighted, Doctor Graham," she murmured. "But confidentially, young man, I have an excellent bottle of French brandy back at the house."

T. J. erupted into laughter. "That's an offer too inviting to resist."

He doffed his hat, bowed slightly, and tucked her arm through his. "Don't mind if I do, Miss Sarah. Don't mind if I do."

Carried to their ears on the gentle wings of a summer breeze, the tuneful melody of a calliope sounded a gay farewell as a huge sternwheeler chugged into the river, caught the swift current, and began her journey south on the Mighty Mississippi.

Dear Reader:

Don't you think Thomas Jefferson Graham deserves a better fate than to be left standing at a train depot, particularly after having waved good-bye to friends who had already found love?

I hope so, considering that he's going to encounter more than just excitement leading to that climactic event on May 10, 1869, at Promotory, Utah, when Leland Stanford tapped the golden spike into the final rail linking the Union Pacific and Central Pacific railroads.

I hope you'll be there with him—a redheaded spitfire named Rory Callahan will. Be sure to watch for

THE GOLDEN SPIKE
by
Ana Leigh
Coming in 1993

Why don't you drop me a line and let me know what you think of the idea:

Ana Leigh
P.O. Box 612
Thiensville, WI 53092

WOMEN OF COURAGE...
WOMEN OF PASSION...
WOMEN WEST

This sweeping saga of the American frontier, and the indomitable men and women who pushed ever westward in search of their dreams, follows the lives and destinies of the fiery Branigan family from 1865 to 1875.

PROMISED SUNRISE by Robin Lee Hatcher. Together, Maggie Harris and Tucker Branigan faced the hardships of the Westward journey with a raw courage and passion for living that makes their unforgettable story a tribute to the human will and the power of love.

___3015-2 $4.50 US/$5.50 CAN

BEYOND THE HORIZON by Connie Mason. The bronzed arms and searing kisses of half-breed scout Swift Blade were forbidden to her, yet Shannon Branigan sensed that this untamed land that awaited her would give her the freedom to love the one man who could fulfill her wild desire.

___3029-2 $4.50 US/$5.50 CAN

LEISURE BOOKS
ATTN: Order Department
276 5th Avenue, New York, NY 10001

Please add $1.50 for shipping and handling for the first book and $.35 for each book thereafter. N.Y.S. and N.Y.C. residents, please add appropriate sales tax. No cash, stamps, or C.O.D.s. All orders shipped within 6 weeks via postal service book rate. Canadian orders require $2.00 extra postage. It must also be paid in U.S. dollars through a U.S. banking facility.

Name _____

Address _____

City _____ State _____ Zip _____

I have enclosed $_____in payment for the checked book(s).

Payment <u>must</u> accompany all orders.☐ Please send a free catalog.

Winner of 6 *Romantic Times* Awards!

Cassandra Clayton could run her father's freighting empire without the help of any man, but without one she could never produce a male child who would inherit it all. When Cass saved Steve Loring from a hangman's noose, he seemed to be just what she needed—a stud who would perform on command. But from the first, Steve made it clear that he wanted Cass's heart and soul in the bargain. Although his sarcastic taunts made her dread the nights she must give him her body, his exquisite lovemaking made her long to give him all that he asked—and more!

_3345-3 $4.99 US/$5.99 CAN